# JAMIE'S WAR

*A little boy's passage through
a world war*

## JIM MARSHALL

ISBN: 978-1-917778-54-1

# CONTENTS

*This book is dedicated to my brother Norman*
*Without whose care and love*
*None of this would have been possible.*

# JAMIE ALFRED SMALL

January and February had been cold, very cold indeed. The year 1939 had started with bitingly cold winds, deep frosts and, not the least of worries, the threat of war hanging over everyone's heads; none felt as threatened as heavily pregnant Margaret Small.

She and her husband John lived in Brooke Hill, a small town to the south of what was later to become the sprawl of Greater London. At that time, it still remained in the county of Surrey and was a moderately prosperous dormitory, sending most of its working inhabitants on a daily commute to Victoria or London Bridge – courtesy of The Southern Railway Company. These commuters were, in the main, the middle echelons of insurance, banking or the Civil Service. The most senior commuted from points further west and south. Brooke Hill was a civilised little town with pretensions.

March the first came in like a lion – bitingly cold wind and threatening snow. St. David shivered in misery. Margaret shivered as well, despite the central heating provided by her unborn infant. This infant, sex as yet indeterminate, wriggled and kicked about and made Margaret even more miserable. She was getting close to her thirtieth birthday, and this would be her first-born. John had brought to the marriage three years earlier a small son by the name of Desmond. John's first wife had died tragically when Desmond was a mere 10 months old. Now a serious little chap of eight and a half, Desmond attended the local junior school and was thus spared the sight of his stepmother's physical misery. He was currently staying with Margaret's mother and father, a short walk away, as Margaret was not sure when she would have to be whisked away for the delivery.

By Thursday the second of March, the midwife was certain that 'things' were imminent and took Margaret and a small bag of necessaries to the local hospital. A few ragged snowflakes accompanied this short journey which was conducted in silence – Margaret in some discomfort and the midwife desperate not to skid on the treacherous road surface.

On the third of March, nineteen thirty-nine, six months to the day before Britain declared war on Germany, Jamie Alfred Small made his noisy entrance into the world; Lusty of lung, puce of countenance, he yelled his first act of defiance to the midwife who was attending, what at that time was called, the end of the confinement.

Weighing in at a hefty nine pounds and one ounce, he was cleaned up, wrapped in a soft towel and handed to his mother who was lying back on her pillows, understandably exhausted. The three were the only ones in the delivery room, situated just off the small five-bed maternity ward of the cottage hospital.

"Noisy one you've got here, ducks!" observed the midwife, a large, maternal woman in her fifties. Margaret was not too exhausted to bridle at the term 'ducks' – she would have preferred 'Mrs Small' – or, even better, 'Madam'. However, swallowing her distaste at the vulgar salutation, she looked down at the still bellowing face of her first-born. Jamie was fighting the wrapped towel, furious at the restrictions of it and his mother's arms. Was this, Margaret wondered, an omen of things to come? She desperately hoped not. And, she wondered, where in the hell was John?


John Small, Jamie's father, was a policeman whose devotion to 'duty' was known throughout the length and breadth of the Surrey Constabulary. No doubt he would have the most compelling of reasons why he had been unable to attend the birth – not that he would have been allowed into the delivery room; those days were still another thirty or so years away. Jamie had managed to get his two little podgy arms free of the towel; fists tightly clenched, he continued to shout his defiance at the world in general and the towel in particular. The tiny face was screwed up into a tight blob of anger, mouth open, colour a deep red. Margaret, in a rare show of understanding for the plight of others, unwrapped the towel, loosened her grip on her baby. Arms and legs free to thrash about, Jamie deigned to lower the decibel level a little; now, he was managing with the more usual cry of the newborn. It was an inauspicious start to what was to turn out to be a strange little life.

Desmond seemed delighted with the addition of a small and highly vocal brother and took it upon himself to change nappies, warm bottles, push the pram and make endless cups of tea for his stepmother. Margaret was not a typical housewife and had been used to a maid when living with her own parents. She still seemed to think that cups of tea, slices of cake and so on appeared from the kitchen at set intervals by the hands of other people. Desmond, in other words, was indispensable but was quite content with his role in life and never complained.

Jamie was baptised on the first Sunday in April. The local vicar had been pressed into Army Chaplain duties and his place was taken by an elderly and, supposedly, retired old chap who had officiated as rector of a nearby parish for the previous forty years. He viewed the infant who was to star in the show with some misgiving.

"Is he always this *vociferous?*" he enquired as Jamie raised his protests to double fortissimo.

"Unfortunately, yes", said Margaret, handing her charge to an old school friend who had very reluctantly agreed to stand as godmother. This formidable lady was named Evelyn and had the physique and vocal delivery of a prop forward.

"Shush!" she commanded, setting the altar bells jangling in the distance.

Jamie switched his near-sighted gaze to the craggy features that loomed over him – features barely relieved with the faintest smear of pale lipstick. Such a command was apparently not to be tolerated. Double increased to triple fortissimo.

The vicar, Margaret, Evelyn (with howling bundle), Desmond (grinning), two acolytes nursing bruised eardrums, all proceeded to the font where a blessedly abbreviated ceremony was conducted. Very surprisingly, Jamie quite liked the water on his forehead and tried to lick it off the tip of his nose.

Evelyn, despite her impressive lung power, proved no match whatsoever for her godson and escaped with a huge sigh of relief once the party had moved out to the porch.

One acolyte looked at his companion as they gratefully retreated to the vestry. "Bloody 'ell! he whispered. "Fancy being woken up at three in the morning to that noise".

The old vicar, visibly shaken by the encounter, retreated to the rectory for a lie down and a restorative draught of single malt.

Such was the entry of one small boy into Brooke Hill society.


By the time Jamie was six months old, war had been declared. Darkness was the most noticeable change – blackout curtains draped inside windows; sticky tape criss-crossed the glass panes to minimise flying shards when the inevitable bombs were dropped. Streetlights had been extinguished; signposts had been removed; even the weather forecasts, that most typical of British guessing-games, had been discontinued for the duration. Ration books were issued, gas masks distributed; in the Small's house a Morrison Shelter now stood where the dining table had previously been. Margaret was horrified to receive a 'gas mask' for her baby, a large bag into which the baby had to be placed if and when a gas attack was predicted. Of course, after such frenzied preparations, nothing at all happened for months. Britain entered the period of the 'phoney war'.

In the early months of nineteen forty, it was deemed preferable that children from London and its suburbs should be evacuated to the countryside. Desmond, Jamie's brother, older by more than eight years, was sent off to a farm in Dorset. With tiny suitcase in hand and a label attached to his overcoat buttonhole, he waved a tearful goodbye to his father as the train, packed to capacity with bewildered children, pulled slowly out of Brooke Hill railway station. It would be two years before the reduced family saw him again.

Jamie, by this time getting on for his first birthday, had continued much as he had started; he was loud and boisterous. His hair had sprouted into tight ginger curls; his face and arms were sprinkled liberally with freckles. He was already managing to stand with the aid of the legs of furniture, had tried unsuccessfully, to take a tottering step unaided. Failure brought forth howls of pent-up fury. He was not the most loveable child. Margaret had got to the point of giving up with him. He insisted on feeding himself with a small spoon; the resultant mess brought shrugs of despair from his mother and chuckles from Nancy, the daily help whose job it seemed to be to clear up the wreckage. This roly-poly woman spent most of her life wobbling with laughter between bursts of Irish dialect that left Margaret and anyone else completely at a loss. However, she loved little Jamie and never scolded him for his messes. Jamie, sensing from the very first this acceptance and feeling, was completely at ease with her. He was also at ease with his grandmother, a normally strict and correct Victorian lady, who lavished him with cuddles and little presents.

Unfortunately, Jamie was not at ease with his father or mother. Margaret, a self-centred young woman, was prone to leave him in the care of others – not that Jamie minded that in the slightest. When, on rare occasions, he was with his mother, he was the recipient of scolding, plus repeated demands that he 'cease that infernal din'. He was not at ease with his father for the very good reason that he seldom clapped eyes on him. John was absent from the home for most of the time, his police duties in wartime had doubled or trebled. Whenever John was at home he seemed utterly perplexed by his son; there was no understanding whatsoever between child and parents; unfortunately, there was little between the father and mother either!

By the autumn of nineteen forty, the 'blitz' was well under way; nightly, bombers would arrive over London and other major centres. Unfortunately, Brooke Hill was situated very close to three important fighter airfields; it received more than its fair share of devastation. Quite a fair bit of Jamie's young life was spent in the Morrison Shelter; this, of course, did not suit him at all; in it, he felt restricted, and restriction was not something that he would tolerate at any time. He had started to speak quite early; one of the first words that he spoke, and spoke with a deal of vociferation, was 'No!' This would be shouted in defiance at any attempt to cajole him into an action that did not meet with his instant approval. Following on from this was, 'Me do!' This was again shouted at anyone who attempted to attend to him, change him, feed him – whatever. By the age of two he had developed into a highly individualistic little boy, confident to the point of recklessness, rude and extremely loud. However, a change came over him when he was allowed out into the back garden on his own. His parents deemed that the rather forward and precocious boy was safe in the hedge and fence-surrounded garden; there were no ponds – nothing more dangerous than the odd stinging nettle, and he would soon learn to avoid those, wouldn't he?

His world was suddenly magnified many times; space abounded; room to manoeuvre; new things to examine. He took to plants and wildlife with a devouring passion. He would spend hours rooting through the flower beds in search of worms and insects. Not that he wanted to harm them in any way; he examined them minutely, observing how they moved, where they went. His special love was the variety of hedgerow birds that nested in the bushes that bordered the garden. In the thick privet he found a robin's nest that, at that time of the year, was devoid of nestlings. However, he marvelled at the intricacies of its construction, the softness of the little cup; it never for an instant occurred to him to harm it in any way. This was in direct contradistinction to his treatment of the few toys that a wartime economy had provided. These were in various stages of destruction, Jamie being curious as to how they worked. His deep interest in the flora and fauna brought about a sea-change in his behaviour. Although he still travelled from point to point at breakneck speed, his general demeanour at other times became quiet and thoughtful. Margaret was delighted at this; not only was he out of sight for hours at a time, he was actually quiet when he was in the house.


In the spring of nineteen forty-two, Jamie's world was enriched beyond measure – Desmond came home again. Nobody seemed to know exactly why he had returned to the fold; he appeared suddenly one afternoon, little case in hand, same label still attached to his coat. He was now nearly twelve years old; a quiet, studious boy, forever with his head in a book about engineering or mechanics. Jamie was startled when Desmond made himself known to the little brother. He had, of course, no recollection of this stranger. Desmond, on the other hand, had every recollection of the loud and demanding baby that he had left behind. He was pleasantly surprised at the change in Jamie who was now, for most of the time, quiet and deeply interested in the wild world around him. It was just what Jamie needed; at last, he had someone who seemed to take an interest in him. Desmond made Jamie his first little cart to pull around the garden; he read him stories at night, made his meals for him, taught him how to tie his shoelaces properly. Desmond became surrogate mother and father to the little boy. But, and to Jamie it was a *big* but, Desmond went to school five and a half days every week. At first, he was at a loss how to fill the day when big 'buvver' was away. Desmond quickly twigged this and commenced to set Jamie tasks to do during his absence; Jamie would have to find six different insects or twelve different leaves from trees and bushes. Desmond made a point of giving Jamie his first half-hour in the evening, going over with him the finds of the day – explaining whenever he could, looking them up when he could not. Then it was the inevitable hours of homework before he would read his brother to sleep.

Summer and autumn of that year were times of great contentment in the Small household; John was deeply immersed in his police work; Margaret had the freedom to pursue her main interests – magazine reading and music concerts on the wireless; Desmond's knowledge of the world of engineering expanded; Jamie roamed his wonderful 'garding', finding new things to marvel at. Only on the odd occasion did he leave the confines of house and grounds – and then mainly at Desmond's instigation; he would take his brother for walks when he thought it was safe to do so. His beloved Nana and Granddad would sometimes call for him to take him back for an hour or so to their huge bungalow. Only once that year did his mother think it necessary to take him anywhere – and then it was into the town to buy him a few new clothes. Not that the clothing coupons went very far!

Jamie knew exactly what to do at the sound of the air-raid siren. That horrible contraption would start low down in the audible frequencies then rise to a monotonous wailing. He would immediately leave whatever he was doing, scamper into the house and dive into the Morrison Shelter where he would find his mother already crouching. Most often the sound of aircraft and exploding bombs would be from afar; however, when the 'Brrrrr-Brrrrrr' of the German bombers was quite close, Jamie would cower into a corner, curled up in a little ball with his arms clasped over his ginger head. Bombs exploding in the near vicinity would have him shaking with fright; but he would *never* cry. Of course, what he was in need of was a cuddle from his mother. It neither occurred to him to seek it nor Margaret to offer it. The most charitable description of Margaret's attitude to her son was one of semi-toleration; sometimes amused by his antics, more often exasperated at his constant noise. Thank the Good Lord, she often muttered, that he spent so much time out of doors.


The late winter of nineteen forty-three saw yet another momentous change in Jamie's young life. His mother had, in his eyes, been getting quite fat over the preceding winter, not that he had made any mention of the fact. Suddenly, Nana was there every day until, one evening, mother was taken away in a large white van. His Nana took him home with her for a week, where Jamie was 'spoiled rotten' in the words of his highly amused Granddad. Then he was taken home again to find mother back home with a curious, noisy thing in a cot by her bed. Jamie had a little brother. This rather odd bundle was introduced to him as Robert – Robert Frederick Small, to be precise.

Where Jamie had been loud, angry and combative, Robert was quiet, acquiescent and still. He was, to quote old Nancy the 'daily', just a 'perfick wee thing'. Jamie simply carried on as normal; his little brother was no fun at all! However, Margaret did *not* go back to her previous ways. Robert, being the absolute antithesis of her raucous older child, brought out her caring, maternal side – so much so in fact that she could hardly bear to be parted from the baby. It appeared to her that, at long last, she had a little person who relied on her, seemed grateful for her ministrations. For almost the first time in her life Margaret was content – or as near as she was ever likely to get to that utopian state.

Jamie's next milestone was September, nineteen forty-three – he went to school for the first time. His Nana had managed to get him a place in a small, private infants' establishment that was owned and run by an old acquaintance. It was just under a mile from Jamie's home, up a steep hill. His Nana took him the first morning; thereafter, he came and went entirely on his own. He saw absolutely nothing odd about this, although he was aware that nearly all the other children were accompanied to and from the school. He seemed to 'fit in' quite well, albeit a little withdrawn from his fellow students. His gaze was always fixed on the grounds beyond the classroom windows, his thoughts far away among the hedgerows. He appeared to the staff to be just a little aloof, to prefer his own company. Given his home life since the age of a few months, this was hardly surprising.

When little Robert was a few months old Jamie had taken to wheeling him down the road in his pushchair. Margaret, devoted as she was to her youngest, could not quite bring herself to venture far away from the house. She was more than a little agoraphobic – a charge that she would have vehemently denied had anyone had the temerity to voice it. Desmond also took Robert for 'walkies' when his studies allowed him the luxury of a spare half-hour.

The year slowly passed into winter – quite a hard winter with snow and ice blanketing most of the country. Jamie's rather odd young life carried on exactly as before. The formative years from one to four had been, to say the least, odd! He was still the loud, scampering little boy; sometimes full of himself, boastful and intolerant of others; sometimes withdrawn and 'far away'. He was certainly an 'individual'; whether or not this individualism would be to his benefit or to his detriment, none could say. Devoid of paternal attention by force of circumstances, of maternal attention by, seemingly, deliberate choice, he was only at ease with his brother Desmond, his Nana and Grandfather. With them he felt wanted – sometimes!

# JOHN ALBERT SMALL

John Albert Small was born in eighteen ninety-nine, two years after the Diamond Jubilee of Queen Victoria, the third and last child of Gus and Connie Small. Willie Small was already eighteen months old, Charlie Small was four years old, when John was placed into his exhausted mother's arms by the local 'deliverer', who had attended the sickly mother during the ten-hour labour. "There you are, dear; another boy for you"; the kindly, but grossly overworked woman with no qualifications whatsoever, had hurried off to a house in the next street. Gus Small had wanted to be available for Connie at the labour; as had happened first with Charlie, then again with Willie, he had succumbed to the call of the pub and seven pints of porter. Connie lay back on the rough pillow and cradled the new infant in her arms. Little Charlie was sent running to the neighbour to tell her the news; Connie desperately hoped that this kindly soul would return with her son to give her some help. Willie, in a makeshift cot by the side of the bed, jumped up and down with excitement, grasping the metal bars with his little fists. "Babba, babba, Mamma!" he shouted repeatedly until Connie's head was throbbing. She put her hand through the bars to fondle the little blonde curls. "Hush, hush-a-bye, little angel", she pleaded.

The neighbour, herself the mother of three young daughters and two teenage sons, came bustling up the narrow uncarpeted stairs, Charlie galloping after her. She saw the exhausted face, thin from years of under-nourishment; the condition was familiar, all too familiar. She wondered if the poor girl would survive this time. Gently, she took the strangely quiet new arrival from the thin arms, went down to the scullery to wash the still baby, wrapped it tightly into the cleanest piece of towelling that she could find, took the bundle back up the stairs. Connie received her new son and placed its tiny mouth at her breast, relieved to find that the cheeks immediately started to work as John began to feed. The neighbour made tea and some toast for Connie and left the enlarged family to settle down for the night. Gus came home at three the next morning; he was never a roaring drunk, simply morose and very quiet. With barely a glance at the new baby, he fell asleep on the old bed, snoring loudly until being woken at six by the 'knocker-up'. This old company retainer, retired from physical work, went the rounds every morning 'knocking-up' the workers who had to report to the dock gates at six-thirty sharp six mornings a week. He carried a long pole, one end of which had a small rubber ball attached; it was this he used to 'knock' at the appropriate bedroom windows. Gus, groaning with the agony in his head, stumbled down the stairs, found boots and coat, immersed his unshaven face in a bucket of water and staggered off down the street for his mile walk to the dock gates; he had worked at Tilbury Docks since reaching his fourteenth birthday. Now, at aged thirty-two, he gazed forlornly at a future of another thirty-three years of this drudgery; the working day was eleven hours long with but a half-hour for lunch. The work was unrelenting and physically draining. He was but one of thousands.

Connie died of tuberculosis when John was three years old. The whole street lined the pavements as her cheap coffin wound its way to the churchyard for a 'parish' funeral. Gus was absent, fast asleep in an alley between the pub and the bakery. Charlie, in his 'spare' time cooked the meals, cleaned the house.

John's early life in the streets of Tilbury was unremarkable. He attended the small school at the end of the street and learned his reading, writing and arithmetic – sufficient to equip him for the post of some minor clerk, should such a position ever be found. It was his days with the irrepressible Willie that kept him sane; the brothers would 'cadge' a lift on any old boat that crossed the river to the south side. For hours on end, they would roam the Surrey countryside, venturing as far as the Crystal Palace, Streatham Hill and Dulwich Village. Gradually, during their early years, the sprawl of tenement houses 'joined up' these villages, smothering the grasslands and hedgerows with brick and mortar. The brothers eventually grew tired of this depressing onwards sprawl, mourned the loss of the birds and flowers, started instead to creep into the Electric Palace to watch endless hours of silent films.

Charlie joined the Royal Navy in nineteen eleven; at sixteen, he had already spent nearly two years with his father in the docks, had seen an opportunity to travel the world. Willie and John were then in their last year of childhood comradeship, for later that year, Willie, now fourteen, took Charlie's place six days a week unloading bales and boxes. Gus, his liver irreparably damaged, collapsed one evening at the pub, was buried beside his wife. Willie and John were 'fostered' by the neighbour.


In the autumn of nineteen fourteen, Willie was nearly seventeen years old, John fifteen and a half. Posters of Lord Kitchener pointed accusingly from every hoarding, demanding service to King and Country. Willie, in the fever prevalent throughout the working population of the country, managed to join the London Fusileers by adding just a few months to his age. John never saw his beloved brother again as Willie was killed a mere three months later in the Flanders mud. Charlie sent the odd letter home from his various postings; His ship, a Dreadnought, was sunk at the battle of Jutland. He survived and earned a DSM by saving many shipmates, his captain included, trapped behind a buckled bulkhead. John, desperate for some life other than the sameness of the docks, also forged his age in nineteen sixteen. He went to France and was gassed on the Somme battlefields along with thousands of others. Recovery in a Norfolk hospital saw him posted back to France as A1. He was still fighting from one miserable trench to another when the Armistice was signed in November of nineteen eighteen. He was nineteen years old, his spirit deadened from months of artillery barrage, flares, terror of enfilading machine-guns, gas, stench, misery. He returned some months later to be discharged with a suit of clothes, a pair of shoes, a poor mackintosh and a hat. A grateful country, promising 'homes fit for heroes' offered no work, merely poverty and more misery. Seeing an advertisement in a newspaper, he applied for a position with the British Police Force for India. He arrived in Calcutta three months later to find himself a target for the Independence Movement, instead of German snipers. He stuck this for a mere two years before his initial engagement was completed, allowing him to return, fare paid, to England. The situation in the 'Old Country' was by now even worse. He managed to 'grub along' for some months with the occasional labouring job but was again enticed into the police service, answering another advertisement for trainee constables in the Surrey Police Force. He passed the training with flying colours, his military and police service standing him in excellent stead. He was 'passed out' in early nineteen twenty-three and sent to the police station in Wandleford, a part of the Wandle Division.

Charlie, now a petty officer aboard a cruiser, wrote him letters which arrived at the rate of one a week at the police house where he was quartered with ten other colleagues. A year later, John met and married Doris Sweet, a pretty and shy girl, daughter of the proprietor of the tobacconist three doors down from the police station.

The newlyweds managed to obtain a small flat nearby; one bedroom, a box room, a sitting-cum-dining room, a tiny bathroom and a kitchen. They were blissfully happy. John thought that, at last, his life was coming into some happy order. In nineteen twenty-six, little Valerie arrived; two years later came Peter and, last of all, Desmond in nineteen thirty. The little apartment was full to overflowing, but it was a happy home, full of laughter and funny stories at night to get the two older children to sleep. John was offered the post of junior sergeant, accepted with alacrity; this enabled the family to move into a two-bedroom flat, Doris able to augment the family income by part-time work in her father's shop. With Desmond only a month over one year old, Doris became ill. A diagnosis proved hard to obtain until, like with his own mother, John was told that TB was present. The once pretty girl shrunk as the weeks went by. John was in despair, seeing his dreams come to nothing yet again. Their friends, the Kings in the next flat, were childless. Olive King managed the Small household and helped to nurse the rapidly failing Doris. John buried his young wife when the frosts of December nineteen thirty-one were at their hardest. He returned 'home' to console his children, they deemed too young to attend the service. Valerie and Peter were informally 'adopted' by the Kings after Christmas, John being unable to care for them as he would have wished. He moved away from the flat and took up residence yet again in the police quarters. Little Desmond was placed, temporarily, in the local orphanage as he needed the care of trained professionals. Contact with Desmond's brother and sister was stopped as the staff thought that it would be too upsetting for him to see them, having again to be parted when it was time to leave. Gradually, any memory of his siblings faded completely from the tiny mind. He saw his father every weekend, when John was careful to avoid mention of Valerie and Peter, ever mindful of the warnings of the staff.

The building next to the Wandleside police station was split into three floors of offices. The top floor was rented by a firm of architects, busy with the design of 'superior' homes to the south of the large town. The head of the firm had a secretary who often sunned herself on a balcony during her lunch break. John saw her one day, lazing in a deck chair. She was stunningly beautiful, dark chestnut hair falling in waves around a perfectly oval face. She exchanged polite smiles with John whom she had observed regarding her from a second floor window in the station. The exchanges became almost a routine as the summer progressed until, greatly daring one day, John opened the window to bid the girl a tremulous 'good afternoon, miss'. He, as the weeks and months went by, became more and more entranced with this goddess-like person; she became more intrigued with the polite and rather shy young police sergeant. One day, late in September, they actually met; John was emerging from the front doors as the girl came down the steps of the office block. They spoke, face to face, for the first time.

# MARGARET CLEMENTS

Margaret Emily Clements was born in nineteen-o-nine, the only child of Alfred and Gertrude Clements. Alfred himself was one of four children. His father, and Margaret's paternal grandfather, was Jonathan Clements. The oldest of the four children was Edward; then came Alfred, Amelia and Frederick. Jonathan Clements, Margaret's grandfather, had a brother, Fiennes; Gertrude was his daughter. Alfred and Gertrude had been brought up almost as brother and sister until, with Alfred at twenty-three and Gertrude at twenty-two, the pair realised that their relationship meant considerably more to them than being near siblings. They had been deeply in love with one another for years. Despite all warnings to the contrary, these first cousins had married in nineteen o-five. Margaret had been born four years later.

Alfred had studied architecture at university, was determined to have his own practice in as short a time as possible. He was lucky in that he was exceptionally gifted, managing to put together plans and styles that made him in constant demand by the 'new money' of the suburbs. He and Gertrude lived three miles south of the Wandleford office, in the pleasant little town of Brooke Hill. He had designed a large bungalow which he had seen erected on an extensive plot that he had managed to buy. He, Gertrude, Margaret and the live-in maid Daisy, lived in relative luxury.

From her earliest days, Margaret had been a problem. She did not feed well, was truculent and nearly always tearful. When she had learned to walk and talk, she was demanding; she was either deeply morose or wildly excited, never managing to be merely contented. The rest of the large Clements family had warned repeatedly that any issue of first cousins was likely to have 'problems'. Now they saw for themselves what their union had produced. Not that they did not love and cherish the little girl; far from it. Margaret was lavished with every present and comfort that she increasingly demanded. However, more worrying, were the times that she seemed to disappear into another world. In that world, she imagined all manner of improbable friends, all rich, important or impossibly perfect. Most children, they knew, had times of fantasy; Margaret's would last for weeks on end. She would speak of these people as if she truly believed in their existence; they assumed an importance far beyond the imaginings of a healthy child.

When it was time for her to attend school, they found a private establishment nearby that catered for the daughters of 'gentlefolk', as the publicity proudly proclaimed. Margaret became the fifteenth child at the school but was soon a cause of problems for the proprietor and her assistant. With great reluctance, the proprietor asked that she be removed. Thereafter, until she was twelve, she was tutored privately at home by a succession of ladies, none of whom managed to stay for more than six months. Somehow, her parents managed to obtain a place for her at the Wandleford High School for Girls. By the age of twelve, the tantrums had subsided; in their place had come periods of deep melancholy, punctuated by lesser periods of lively excitement. She managed to get through to her matriculation with high passes in both English – at which she excelled – and Geography – which she adored. Asked if she wanted to pursue academic furtherance at university, she replied that she would be bored to death. No job or training seemed to take her interest for more than a few days; she became truculent and easily bored. Alfred saw no alternative but to take her with him into his own business, where he could keep an eye on her. She settled quite quickly into the business, becoming proficient in her own brand of shorthand. Her fantasies had grown with her; they were nowadays peopled with men of stern jaw, perfect physique, silent mystery. She often referred to them in conversation with her parents and colleagues. Her parents knew that they did not exist; her colleagues believed every word, Margaret speaking with the total conviction of one who lived side-by-side with these mythical figures. The girl who did the filing and post was consumed with jealousy for the boss's daughter who seemed to have it all; she was from a rich family, had the most incredible friends, was wooed by the most desirable men. On top of all that was the fact that Margaret could easily have fitted into any one of the film dramas that she seemed to live; she was very beautiful with a figure that most girls would have killed for. She had only one real friend, a plump near-relative who, again not privy to the secret, believed Margaret's stories. Margaret glowed in the presence of her plump, plain friend; was chosen for dances whenever the two attended functions. To her parents, Margaret stayed a constant worry; to her acquaintances, she was 'special', a person of importance, one to be helped and flattered. To her social 'inferiors', she was put on a pedestal, almost to be silently worshipped.

# AN UNLIKELY UNION

John was dazzled by the smile that greeted him, a smile that showed two rows of perfect teeth, framed by a pair of perfectly painted red lips. Deep brown eyes looked directly at him. "Good afternoon to you, sergeant. Is it not a lovely day?" John stammered a polite reply. "Good afternoon miss". Margaret swept past him on her high heels, John just having to turn and look after her retreating figure as it swayed beautifully down the street. She wore a fox stole over a woollen dress, seamed silk stockings showing off a lovely pair of calves. To the sergeant, she seemed perfect, a dream far beyond reach. Margaret, completely aware of her effect on the policeman, smiled to herself; yet another conquest, she thought. In John's case, this was not merely a conquest; he would happily have curled up at her feet and allowed this perfect girl to walk all over him. He was hopelessly in love with a dream, a picture of perfection; whether or not he would ever love her as a person did not enter his head.

The occasional glimpse of his dream had to suffice for the months that followed; no more chance meetings came his way. He would take any opportunity to peer through the windows of the police station in the hope of catching the merest sighting; he was, in the words of the current romantic theme, 'besotted'.

Every weekend, when not on duty, he would manage to get over to his old neighbours, the Kings. Valerie and Peter would greet him with great affection; Valerie, who missed her father dreadfully, would cling to him and cry when it was time to leave; Peter, shy and withdrawn, sat quietly and listened in great detail to his father, seeming to hang on to every word lest he forget one of them. Visiting little Desmond was not so easy as the 'home' had strict rules. The little chap was 'doing nicely', in the words of the matron; John could see that, physically, Desmond was indeed growing properly – in that he was as tall as expected and he looked to be properly nourished. Now four years old, Desmond was still a little backward in his speech, hesitant to the point of stuttering whenever his father tried to draw him into conversation. Desmond was, in fact, losing contact with his father – exactly as he had lost all contact and memory of his brother and sister. He was not happy, that was obvious; John thought long and hard as to ways in which his little son's life might be improved; he came to no conclusions whatsoever.

One bright, sunny morning in October, John was informed that a burglary had taken place in the office block next door to the station. He hurried out, hastily reading the typed report that had come to him from the desk sergeant. He went through the revolving door of the block to be met by a very distraught receptionist. This woman, between sobs, told him that she had found, on entering the building that morning, that a window had been broken in the small kitchen at the back of the ground floor, that a cash box, normally locked in a drawer in her boss's desk, had been smashed open and a considerable quantity of cash taken. The same had been attempted in the offices on the first and second floors. The block, on three floors, was actually owned by the head of the firm of accountants that occupied the ground floor; the second was rented by a company that acted as theatrical agents, whilst the top floor was rented by Alfred's firm of architects. John summoned two constables from the station and went himself up to the top floor. There, he was met by Alfred. John introduced himself and was taken through to a well-furnished office; a large drawing board sat on four metal legs in the large window. A drawer in the desk had been crudely jemmied open. Nothing else in the office seemed to have been disturbed.

"What is usually kept in that drawer, sir?" asked John, feverishly hoping all the while that Margaret, whose name he did not yet know, would make an appearance.

"Well, usually I keep the petty cash box in there. Luckily, I decided only last week to have a safe installed behind that picture there!" He pointed to the far wall on which was hung a photograph of a house recently completed.

"That was a stroke of luck, sir! May I ask exactly when the box stopped being stored in that drawer?"

Alfred pondered a while. "Let's see, now; today is Thursday – well, bless my soul – the box was put in the safe overnight only two days ago!"

"You see, sir; what I'm thinking is that only one drawer was broken open – so how did anyone know that this is the right drawer? Looks exactly like an inside job – or someone acting on information from inside – otherwise, how would chummy know to ignore all the other drawers?"

The two constables arrived and went into a huddle with their sergeant. John turned back to Alfred. "Well, sir – exactly the same with the other two floors; only the correct drawers opened. The window down in the back kitchen has broken glass inside and outside. Definitely someone inside this building – or giving the gen to someone else to do it for him!"

The two constables were sent back to the station, leaving their notes with John. Alfred invited John to sit in one of the visitors' chairs whilst he went behind his desk to occupy the leather swivel chair. "How are you going to set about finding the culprit?" he asked.

"I'm afraid that I'll need a list of all your employees, sir – like I will from the other floors".

"Hmmm – nasty!" mused Alfred. "I'll ask my secretary to get all the details for you".

John had no idea who this secretary might be; he was overcome with stuttering shyness when, being introduced to Margaret, he was shown into her smaller office. Alfred, used to the sight of youngish men reduced to silence (or gibbering nonsense) by his imperious daughter, left them to get on with it. John sat down in front of Margaret's desk and stammered out the request for information. She went to a filing cabinet and took from a drawer a pile of manila folders. Going through each one she dictated the names and addresses to John who entered each carefully in his pocketbook. He appended the ages and dates of commencement with the firm. Margaret, whilst he was still writing, had poured coffee into two cups, one of which she set before John on a corner of her desk. John, who loathed coffee, sipped appreciatively, thanking her for her kindness. He knew that he had to repeat the performance twice more with the other firms but searched feverishly for more questions to ask. He had to make himself tear his eyes away from the beautiful face, to try and concentrate on his notes. Margaret was, as usual, amused by her effect on men of what she considered to be the 'lower strata of 'society'. All the others she had met had been bewitched at first but had been eventually repelled by her air of superiority; something was not right, they thought, hearing of her fantastic 'friends'. But was this one different, she wondered?

John could find no more excuse to delay his departure; he went through the same routine with the other two businesses, made copious notes and went back to the station. He went through the files looking for name-matches – found none at all. Then he tried the old constable who worked in the basement. Modern parlance would call him a 'collator'; then, he was referred to as 'old Bert'. Old Bert was a veteran who knew, or claimed to know, every villain that had ever walked the streets of the 'manor'. Shown the list, he pounced immediately. "Haven't heard of *him* for years!" he pointed at a name far down the list. "Bugger did five years after the last war for breaking and entering!" John peered over the bent shoulder. 'Paul Higgins', he read his own neat handwriting. This individual, fifty-three years old, was employed by the theatrical agents as a clerk, had been for the last decade. "Thanks, Bert!" said John, hurrying out of the station. He ran up the stairs to the first floor and enquired the whereabouts of Mr. Higgins. The head of the firm looked baffled. Apparently, Paul Higgins had called in the previous morning saying that he was very sick, would not be in until the following Monday. John went out again, collected a constable from the front office and set off to the address on his list. It proved to be no more than a ten-minute walk away. Repeated knockings brought no response other than a neighbour who looked up from scrubbing what appeared to John to be an already immaculate front step. "Looking for Paul, dear?" she asked, curlers peeping from under garish headscarf. "Yes, Mr Higgins – that's right!" The woman laughed. "You're too late, ducks!" she chuckled. "Him and his so-called missus left yesterday night – saw them misself, I did, luggin' two heavy cases they were!"

John could do no more than send the constable to the bus and railway stations in the forlorn hope that someone would remember the pair. He went back to the station where he informed his Inspector that, in his opinion, the theft was solved but there was little chance of an arrest. The Inspector agreed and asked John to go back to the offices to tell them the bad news. The theatrical agent was furious with himself and felt that he needed to apologise in person to the other two. The accountant merely shrugged. Alfred took the news as he always did – with a dignified calm. Margaret, when John daringly knocked timidly on her office door, invited him in for more coffee. She hung on every word as he told her, at her insistence, every move of the 'case'. John was taken aback when, making his farewell, Margaret suggested that they meet that weekend in town for a coffee. He really had no idea how to reply, managed somehow, to stutter that 'that would be really nice, miss'. Margaret then said that, as they were to meet socially, he had better drop the 'miss' and substitute 'Margaret'.

He spent the rest of that day in a daze. What could he possibly say to this beautiful girl who looked to him to be about ten years younger than he was? That evening he took pencil and paper and jotted down possible subjects of conversation; each one that he added looked to be more pathetic than its predecessor. He eventually tore the list into fragments and went to sleep.

On the Saturday, he met Margaret outside a coffee house in Wandleford High Street. He had dressed in his best suit, shoes polished to a deep shine, regimental tie firmly knotted. He was shaking with apprehension. Margaret extended a gloved hand for him to take gently and shake delicately, as he would have handled a rare flower. Seated at a corner table, she wanted to know all about him. John found himself pouring out his life story – his poor upbringing, the desperation of the docks, the war in the trenches, service in India, his late wife, his children. Margaret listened in close attention. It was a story to tug at the heartstrings of even the most hardened listener. To Margaret, it seemed the very essence of pathos, almost the perfect film-script. It fulfilled for her all the elements she had imagined her 'lower orders' went through; somehow, to her strange mind, it seemed that her previous imaginings of the privations of the poor were becoming, in this one man, a self-fulfilling prophesy. She determined to see more of this man, learn more about his misfortunes. John was astounded when she suggested a further meeting – perhaps he would like to accompany her to the theatre one evening? John, whose experience of the 'theatre' extended only to occasional visits to the cinema, wondered what she had in mind. Two weeks later, he went with her to the Grand Theatre to see a production of The Winslow Boy, a play that she had come to enjoy. He was entranced both by her and the new world that he was slowly experiencing.

In the months that followed, this unlikely friendship blossomed. John followed every suggestion that she made; Margaret, at last, had found a devoted disciple. She insisted that she pay for nearly all their outings as, 'you do not earn a great deal, do you?' She met and made polite conversation with Valerie and Peter. These two children wondered whether the two might marry – would they, at long last, have a proper home and family, together again with little Desmond? Margaret met that little boy one afternoon when John collected him for a brief outing. Desmond hid behind his father and would not say a word.

Alfred and Gertrude met and liked the sergeant. They had very mixed views of the blossoming relationship. John, to them, was a polite and dedicated police officer; he was smart and honest; he was deferential to what he saw as his 'betters'. But was he the ideal partner for their daughter? Margaret, talking to her parents, said that she would be able to 'get him up to standard'. Her parents knew that this was no basis for a marriage; however, he was the only man who had ever shown the devotion to Margaret that they knew she so desperately needed; he would *never* harm her, would care for and cherish her. Being realistic, they thought that this was probably the best that they could ever hope for. Margaret was sometimes impossible, her fantasies and demands getting more convoluted as the years went by; they needed someone to care for her when they were gone. John seemed to them the only possible choice to have come along. John obviously knew of the fantasies, had experienced for himself the deep depressions; he was in no way deterred. What, they wondered, would happen to his children?


The eventual wedding took place in June of nineteen thirty-six. Valerie and Peter, told some months before, had been wildly excited; they would be back with their Dad again. Desmond greeted the information with his usual quiet acceptance. Then, one week before the wedding, Margaret dropped her bombshell; she would not countenance the inclusion of Valerie and Peter; she would, reluctantly, accept little Desmond. To her mind, the elder two would compete for John's attention; Desmond, being quiet and acquiescent, would simply 'know his place'. John was reduced to desperation; he tried to argue his case but was brushed aside; either Margaret or his children, he was informed. He gave way and spent the night wondering how this news would be received. Valerie broke out into uncontrollable sobs and had to be led away by the kindly Mrs King. Peter looked at his father; eight years old, he knew that he had been betrayed yet again. He said nothing, hated his father from that day forward. It was an inauspicious start to a marriage. John knew that he had abandoned two of his children, had finally betrayed them and his sweet first wife. He felt a deep and pitiful guilt but excused himself saying that 'what else could he have done?'

They set up home in a small semi-detached house rented for them by Alfred. It was in the same road as the big bungalow. Desmond, now six years old, went to school nearby. He quickly learned how to fend for himself, his new mother either reading magazines or 'resting'. He was never told that his own mother had died when he was a tiny baby; Margaret had forbidden any mention of his brother and sister on the grounds that 'it would only unsettle him'. John worked as hard as ever. The threat of war became more positive as nineteen thirty-eight came and went. To the great delight of Alfred and Gertrude, a son was born in the March of thirty-nine. He was called Jamie and was spoiled horribly by his doting grandparents. Margaret, having got over the birth, seemed disinterested – the baby seemed almost a distraction from her own needs and way of life. Desmond, nearly nine years the senior, found himself in the role of substitute parent; he changed the little chap, fed him his bottle, took him for walks in a pushchair. John, now with warden duties added to his police job, was absent sometimes for days at a time. The 'phoney war' of that winter and spring was a strange time; some believing that the shooting would never start; others firmly of the belief that the Nazis would do what they had always threatened - invade both east and west. Late in the spring of nineteen forty they were proved right; bombing started, and the nightmare began.

# AN INCIDENT OF THE BLITZ

Sergeant John Small was barely five feet seven inches tall, quite short for a policeman; he was down to shirt sleeves and covered in brick dust. Around him were three constables, five ARP wardens, the whole of Blue Watch from the nearby fire station; two ambulances and their crews stood by. Many passers by had joined the frantic search for survivors. John had raced from the shelter as soon as the all-clear had sounded; he, like his beat bobbies, had arrived at the smoking ruins just as the fire crew had turned up. The air raid had lasted for well over an hour that afternoon. The crack-crack of anti-aircraft fire had punctuated the screaming descent of the bombs dropped from a mixed flight of Heinkels and Dorniers. There had been one almighty explosion from close by.

The little row of five shops had disintegrated; all there was now to see was a large crater surrounded by brick and timber debris; under the piles somewhere were at least five shopkeepers, plus God alone knew how many shoppers. John, the first of the 'officials' to arrive at the scene had smelt the bad-egg stench of town gas escaping from fractured mains. The first fireman on the scene, alerted by John to the danger, did not bother to wait for any official from the Gas Board to turn up; he quickly located the correct cover in the debris-strewn pavement and turned off the supply, hoping that this served all the demolished shops. That had been two hours ago.

John paused and looked up from the back-breaking task of burrowing through the piles of rubble. He thought that he just might have heard something. He blew a quick blast on his whistle; everyone stopped work, knowing from nearly three years bitter experience just what was required. All noise stopped, voices stilled. Ears strained towards the pile. There – a faint sound from the far left of the site. Still, nobody moved. Would the sound be repeated, would there be a better indication of the precise place to dig? The sound, a faint cry of pain came again from the left. John led his men to the nearest point and started passing back large lumps of masonry. Every few minutes the men would all stop and listen for further indications of life under the huge pile. The man next to John suddenly shouted in triumph. All work ceased as he pointed to the small indentation in the pile that he had just uncovered. A small hand, smeared with blood and dust, waggled filthy fingers. Gently, the rubble around the hand was lifted, passed back; the rest of the arm to the elbow was uncovered. It, like the hand was bare, blood-streaked and indescribably filthy. More rubble taken away, a shoulder dressed in a dirty pink dress and short sleeve came to light. Ten minutes later the little old woman who had attempted to find shelter under the counter of her greengrocery shop was freed. She was barely conscious as the ambulance men moved in to take control. The wound in her scalp bled profusely; one leg was at an impossible angle – smashed pelvis and/or hip, thought John. The crew managed to lift the small frame on to a stretcher; the ambulance sped off to the nearby hospital, bell clamouring for free passage.

A mobile crane arrived soon after. From its jib dangled a huge bucket; into this the burrowers were able to deposit the rubble they were removing; the work speeded up as the pieces now did not have to be passed back down the chain-gang. The bucket when filled, was drawn up, swung sideways and tipped into the road. In the next hour, seven bodies, all dead, had been found. Seven sad heaps covered in grey blankets lined the pavement. John and the rescue crew sat on the rubble, most with heads in hands. Those living nearby supplied mugs of tea; the mugs were sipped in grateful silence. There was just nothing to say.

September, nineteen forty-three saw the fourth anniversary of the start of the war. The bombing, which was primarily targeted on docks, airfields and centres of manufacture, had slowly grown in intensity to take in most suburban areas of population; the carnage had been dreadful. John was still attached to the Wandleford police station, part of the Wandle Division of the Metropolitan Police area. His 'manor' had been on the receiving end of numerous bombing raids, he and his men now well practised in the art of search and rescue. He looked up from his steaming mug to the skyline to the north. Over the City were a cluster of barrage balloons, each tethered to the ground by a cable and winch; the number of enemy planes that they had brought down was negligible. John thought them a complete waste of time and money. Searchlights were beginning to criss-cross the darkening sky – too damned late, as usual. He finished his tea, handed back the mug with words of thanks to the little old man who had been brewing the stuff in his kitchen for the last three hours or more. He would lead his chaps back to the station soon; they to disappear homeward; he to fill in the usual, pointless, report before being at liberty to find a darkened tram to take him south towards his own home.

John arrived back at his house just after midnight; he was exhausted. He crept upstairs to peer into the back bedroom. Desmond and Jamie were fast asleep. In the large front room, his wife slept peacefully, little Robert snuffling a little in his cot by her side of the bed. All seemed peaceful. Having washed – no water to be wasted on a bath – he got into pyjamas and quietly slid into the bed beside his wife. Sleep, he knew, would be some time coming

# A LAME SPIRIT

The Headmistress turned her back to the class, took up a fresh stick of chalk and proceeded to write on the blackboard in bold letters.

Cecily Bedford, Headmistress, had only the previous day celebrated her forty-second birthday, if 'celebrated' applied to a quiet and lonely dinner of rabbit stew and dumplings. The war, now in its fourth year, had taken its toll of the Headmistress in ways that she could never have foreseen; permanent worry lines creased what once had been a smooth and gracious brow. Her husband, Duncan, of fifteen years happy and contented marriage had been called away on permanent service and was commanding a small escort group in the north Atlantic – a fearful and desperate life that had little reward for the days spent awake and fretful on an open bridge.

Cecily, finished writing on the board, turned back to her class; there he was, as usual, gazing forlornly out of the window; her 'problem' pupil.

With Duncan away for months at a time, Cecily had busied herself bringing to fruition a dream that she had long held – to run a preparatory school for local children of what she fondly hoped would be 'promise'. She had never properly defined that word but knew that she would see and recognise it in the little faces when their parents brought them for interview. The fees that she charged would be modest by comparison with other private establishments and she thought that she well might be over-subscribed. The transformation of the large old house into a school had taken six months and it was ready to open by the autumn of nineteen thirty-four. The huge old reception room was now the main classroom, holding thirty-five small desks; the dining room was turned into a cloakroom with benches and hooks around the walls. Above each hook was a pristine rectangle of cardboard, ready to be inscribed with the pupil's name. What had once been her father's study was now a smaller classroom in which she intended that special groups would sit apart from the main body, to be instructed in the skills necessary to pass at the age of seven into other, larger and more prestigious seats of learning.

The little boy, the focus of her attention, continued to gaze out into the faint sunshine with a look of something akin to despair on his freckled face.

During the early summer she had interviewed and engaged an assistant teacher. Julia Forbes had been the outstanding applicant, showing all the dedication to, and love of, small children that Cecily could have wished. Julia had recently graduated and was quietly spoken. Mary Monk, a local woman, was engaged as a part-time helper; duties to include preparing lunches and drinks, setting out classrooms, tidying up and so forth. The staff complement was finished by old Arthur Trubshaw, who would maintain the small sports field (old lawn), the pavilion (old summer house), clean the classrooms and look after the fabric of the buildings. The school was ready and Cecily, with Julia in attendance prepared to commence interviewing prospective little boys.

Boys had come and gone, some now at quite prestigious colleges. Cecily wondered whether her 'problem' boy would ever count among that number.

It was now ten years later. Duncan, on his many leaves before war started in nineteen thirty-nine, had marvelled at his wife's stamina in running the school. It was his firm intention to resign his commission and to join her in this enterprise. However, war had put a stop to all that and, now a Commander, had been given an escort group of two old destroyers, one frigate and three corvettes with which to shepherd merchant convoys from Nova Scotia across the north Atlantic to starving Britain. He still intended to join forces with Cecily as soon as the war had ended but could see no hope of that for a few years yet!

Trying to rid herself of negative thoughts, and with a fierce determination she had written the word, 'Courage' in large capitals in the centre of the board. She turned back to the class to see what effect, if any, her magic word had had upon them.

Thirty-one faces looked back at her. One, belonging to the youngest new boy, was still turned to the window.

"Courage", she said in a quiet and modulated voice, "is something that we must all show to the world at large! Never mind how much we are afraid in these terrible times, with bombs dropping on our towns and cities; with the threat of new and even more terrible weapons that well may come. What we must show is courage. That way, we can survive – indeed, it the only way that we can survive". She, to do her justice, thought exactly that and was secretly ashamed of her temporary and private lapses into pessimism.

Thirty-one faces registered – nothing. The one face registered quiet contentment; it has espied a large ginger cat, crouching under a laurel hedge, thwarted of a kill by a chirpy blackbird that had just hopped to a higher twig. It seemed to look down and mock the cat. The one face grinned to itself. Good old blackie!

The Headmistress quietly broke off a small piece of the chalk and, with an aim perfected over ten years of teaching, unerringly lobbed it on to the unruly ginger curls that surmounted that one face.

"Jamie", she said in even quieter tones.

The unruly ginger head turned towards her. "Yes, Mrs. Bedford", he said, blushing furiously, whilst retrieving the piece of chalk from the floor.

"Perhaps you would be so good as to tell us what we have just been discussing!"

Jamie was at a loss for only a few moments. He had espied, behind the tall and kindly figure the word recently written on the smudged board.

"Courage!" he said. "We were talking about that".

Cecily Bedford never ceased to wonder at the aptitude of very small boys to bounce back from adversity. Clearly, this new little fellow could read; and read very well for one so young.

Jamie Small was, for a little boy, quite pedantically accurate. This was a direct response to his grandfather's prompting. 'Accuracy, first and always!" he constantly reminded his grandson. Therefore, if asked, he would have said that he was precisely four years, seven months and five days old. Born six months before the war had started on the third of September, nineteen thirty-nine, he was stocky and was cursed (as he saw it) with the usual accompaniment to ginger hair, a multiplicity of freckles. Since joining one month earlier the other thirty-one pupils at Brooke Hill Preparatory School for Boys (Infants) he had made one very good friend, one part-time friend and a host of others who called him, 'ginger nuts', 'spotty', or 'measles' according to the degree of animosity present at the time. This last nickname seemed to Jamie to be the most offensive as he had indeed suffered that nasty disease the previous winter but had escaped with neither scar nor mark once the dreaded spots had gone.

Cecily thought back to that day some three months ago when she had received an intriguing letter of application for this little fellow's acceptance as a pupil. It had been written on his behalf by his grandmother. The letter itself was on cream vellum and was superimposed with an embossed address. Both the salutation and valediction were correct, the body of the letter being a model of exactitude and clarity. She had replied immediately inviting them for interview on a Saturday afternoon. Little boy with grandmother had arrived by taxi, although the distance to school from home was a mere half mile. Jamie had appealed to Cecily from the very first moment, being lively in manner but polite when spoken to. He clearly had a very inquisitive mind as she saw him looking around and mentally assessing his new surroundings. The grandmother exhibited all the attributes of a Victorian lady, dressed soberly in light purple velvet dress with diamond brooch. Cecily could recall almost word for word parts of the conversation she and Jamie had shared. Enquiring into his likes and dislikes Jamie had replied without hesitation. 'Hedgerow birds, music and sausages' to the former and 'whale meat and rude people' to the latter. He had, at Cecily's request, written a small essay on a subject of his own choosing whilst the Headmistress and grandmother had exchanged pleasantries and acknowledged mutual acquaintances, since both had lived for years in the same vicinity. Jamie's essay, one short paragraph, had been headed 'The Robin's Nest' and had expressed his admiration for the wonderful and exact creation of that small bird. He had discovered it some weeks before in the privet hedge of a neighbour and had been roundly scolded by that person with dire threats of reprisal for trespass. The 'essay' was short, often mis-spelt, but had correct punctuation and a direct approach to the subject that was almost adult. He had been accepted and the first term's fees paid by his grandfather with a cheque drawn on a rather exclusive bank in the City.

Jamie was still on his feet, looking with some trepidation at the Headmistress.

"Yes, indeed we were discussing courage', she said. "Now, what do you understand that word to mean?"

"Please, Mrs. Bedford", he began. "Courage means being brave when you are really feeling very scared – like when a little bird leaves it to the last minute to hop out of the way of a cat that wants to kill it". This example, he hoped, would earn praise.

"No, no, no! The first part of your answer was very good; but the example you then gave was not correct. Now, who can tell us all why not?"

Inevitably, the first hand to shoot towards the ceiling belonged to Julian Warburton, seven years old and the scourge of all the younger boys. He was soon to be examined for admission to a very prestigious private junior preparatory school and was precocious enough to envisage no hindrance to that next step.

Receiving a nod from the Headmistress he shot to his feet and, leering at Jamie, began to tear the example apart.

"Animals cannot show courage as they just obey their instincts! Only humans can show courage as they are the only living things able to think it out. Even the smallest boy should know that!"

He sat down glowing with self-congratulation. Cecily Bedford, however, was not going to allow such a put-down.

"Basically, Julian is correct", she said. "However, it sometimes looks as if animals are being brave and Jamie, who seems to spend some time studying them instead of attending to his lessons, has seen something that may well be of use to us all – a display of instinctive defiance. Now, what can we learn from that?"

Jamie, even now still on his feet, replied to this without waiting for permission.

"We should hop out of the way when a bomb falls down and pull a face at Hitler at the same time!"

The Headmistress felt that control was rapidly being lost and sought to remedy the situation by altering tack. "Sit down please, Jamie. Courage helps us to feel better and also helps others around us to be brave. They WILL try to copy us. If we do not show courage, we become LAME SPIRITS – and we do not want to be that, do we?"

"No Mrs. Bedford", chorused thirty-two voices. Agreement, whole-hearted agreement, was expected to a question framed in that way.

Cecily's father had been a lay preacher much given to biblical references. He had come up with the phrase 'lame spirit' as his version of the better known 'pauper spirit' that had expressed to that old gentleman exactly the attitude of those who seemed to him to have no faith in anyone or anything – a view he thought was far more prevalent since the passing of the old queen.

"Good! We must never allow ourselves to become cowardly; we must stand up to bullies and be brave and resolute. We must never allow ourselves to show doubt or to lack proper courage. LAME SPIRITS are a bad influence – they will eat into the courage of others and will slowly destroy us all. So, boys, what must we NOT be?"

"LAME SPIRITS Mrs. Bedford!" came the shouted response.

"Right!" said the Headmistress. "And on that encouraging note, as it is now just gone three-thirty, we will bow our heads and pray for courage until we all meet again tomorrow morning".

Receiving her cue, the junior mistress came forward to stand before the class.

Julia Forbes, just twenty-five years old and conventionally pretty, faced the class where with joined hands she started to intone the 'going-home' prayer. "Dear God, as we leave this place, help us to think about what we have learned and to be good and brave people. And keep us safely through the night. Amen".

"Amen!" came the response. Thirty-two pairs of feet stamped and skittered their way out to the cloakroom. Mackintoshes or overcoats, plus scarves and gloves were put on whilst satchels were carried over one shoulder. The boys thronged out of the doorway to greet the waiting mothers or nannies come to collect them. Jamie, being just about the smallest was inevitably the last to leave. As he passed her, the Headmistress looked kindly at him.

"Remember Jamie – do not be a LAME SPIRIT, will you?"

"No, Mrs. Bedford; I promise I won't be!"

Cecily let her gaze linger on the little boy as he went through the door; not for the first time, she found herself in something of a quandary. Most little boys that were in her charge were quite easy to fathom. It took a while in some cases but, in the main they were understandable. Some were loud and boisterous, others were quiet and reserved; some – a very few - proved to be the very model of honesty whilst some few turned out to be anything but. Nearly all, however, were either one thing or the other. Not so, Jamie; he was sometimes loud, wanting to be the centre of attention, making silly jokes to try to prove himself; at other times he was almost in a parallel universe – quiet and thinking of matters far removed from the topic at the time. He was obviously a child of the great outdoors – never happier than when scampering about after birds' nests; being restrained in any way brought on fits of melancholy. He was headstrong, brash and, above all, lonely. He was quite an enigma, thought Cecily – quite a challenge!

Jamie strolled down to the gate. Just as he was about to go through it he was accosted by the old and shambling caretaker, Arthur Trubshaw.

"Here", said the caretaker. "I saw that old moggy miss out on the blackbird. Cocky little bugger!" This confirmed what a lot of the boys suspected; Arthur listened in to the lessons by crouching under the windows. Some boys were forbidden by righteous parents from talking to the often profane caretaker.

Jamie was not one of them for the very good reason that his mother had never even seen the old fellow. Jamie liked the caretaker as the old chap knew the names of all the trees, flowers and birds and also had introduced him to the more colourful aspects of the English language.

"I think that the blackie made his nest in the laurels behind the pavilion. Can I go and try to find it, Mr. Trubshaw?"

Arthur scratched his unshaven chin. "Don't suppose it would hurt", he muttered.

Jamie scampered back around the large house and, crossing the small football field, scraped his way behind the old wooden pavilion. He thrust his head into the laurel hedge and began a systematic search. Emerging some minutes later he had to admit defeat. Despite a thorough search he had not been able to trace even the vestige of a blackbird nest. Several robins' and sparrows' nests had been discovered but no sign of old blackie's.

Some months before, Jamie had come across a small book entitled 'Common Hedgerow Birds of the British Isles'. At first, he had intended only to flick idly through the pages, but the sharp, beautifully coloured illustrations had fascinated him so much that he managed to 'acquire' the book; it now occupied pride of place amongst his hoard of treasures. He was already able to identify all the birds that he came across in his garden, on the walk to school, or on the nearby common. He was beginning to be able to identify them from distance by the manner in which they flew, by the calls that they made. By close observation he had taught himself the differences between some of the nests that they built. Most people meeting this somewhat unruly child for the first time would have imagined his interest lay in destruction of the nests; not a bit of it! Jamie felt at one with the little creatures, would not have disturbed one grass or twig.

Disappointed, Jamie trudged back and emerged into Brooke Hill via the rickety school gate. He did not look around for anyone to meet him; no one ever did meet him, and he started his usual walk down the steep hill towards his home. Brooke Hill descended for about a quarter of a mile and ended, at the bottom, with Derwent Road going to left and right. His way home was then left and then first right into Buttermere Gardens. His grandfather and Grandmother lived in Buttermere Gardens in a large bungalow situated half-way down on the right, whilst Jamie's house was a further hundred yards on the left at number sixty-five.

At the bottom of Brooke Hill, on the other side of Derwent Drive was a large estate belonging to a retired Brigadier General. The house was a large Victorian structure and was surrounded by an apple orchard. It was October!

Jamie scampered across Derwent Drive and turned right instead of left. Some few yards down the estate's fencing was a small opening and, making sure that he was unobserved, squeezed through. He was careful to mind his gas mask, in a cardboard box slung over his shoulder – not that he had ever been called upon to use the horrid thing. He stopped and listened. Nothing. Crawling silently towards the nearest tree he stood, reached up and took down a shiny red apple. It was delicious. Putting two more into his overcoat pocket he retraced his steps and squeezed once more through the gap to emerge on all fours on the pavement. A hand descended on his shoulder.

# THE BRIGADIER

"Gotcha!" said a deep and menacing voice.

Jamie froze, frightened to death by the voice and the strength of the fingers.

The old Brigadier General gazed down at the little fellow and gave a snort of laughter.

"Did the same when I was a lad," he said. "How would you like a slice of cake to go with that apple?"

Jamie stuttered his thanks and was led through the gate and down a drive to the back kitchen. There, he was given a slice of fruit cake which was so delicious that he felt awful at having stolen from the old chap.

"Please sir, I'm terribly sorry and thank you for the cake", he managed to say.

"Just don't make a habit of it and we'll say no more about it, old chap".

Jamie was by now so relieved at his good luck that he became, as some small boys are wont to, quite garrulous. "Please sir, were you really a Brigadier General? Do Brigadier Generals have one crown and three pips? Why are you not in the army now?"

The old man sat down in a Windsor chair that had seen better days. "Yes, I really was", he said, his eyes seeing far-off trenches, smoke and upheavals of mortar bombs. "When I was of that rank we were called 'general' but, since then, brigadiers have ceased to be classed as generals any longer. And, to satisfy your curiosity, I am far too old to be in the army now. I retired nearly twenty years ago and now I grow apples – that is, when the local small population see fit to allow me to reap any harvest from them! So, young feller, what have you been learning today, eh?"

"Well sir", Jamie began. "First, we had some arithmetic, then some grammar, then some reading. Then we had a bit of lunch – I had a corned-beef sandwich – then we started again with a bit of writing, and we ended up with a talk about courage. By the way, I'm a bit of a lame spirit!"

The brigadier tried hard to stop tears of mirth at this dissertation. "I'm sure that you are nothing of the kind!" he said.

"Oh yes sir, I am – Mrs. Bedford said I was, and I have got to try extra hard not to be one!"

"Well, I'm sure that you have bags of the right stuff in you…………"

He broke off as a distant wailing drowned all other sounds.

"Confound it!" he grumbled. "Damned Nazis bombing us in daylight now! Come with me and we'll sit it out in the shelter".

He took Jamie's small hand in his large one and led him out into a yard and down into an underground shelter which he had erected himself some three years before with at least two feet of reinforced concrete over the top. They went in and, before closing the blast door, the brigadier lit a Tilley lamp which gave out a hissing but friendly yellow glow. They sat down on a bench until the attack was over.

Far away came a series of dull 'crumps', felt rather than heard.

"Some poor blighter copping it!" the old fellow muttered.

Brooke Cross, as the old locals still defiantly called the little town south of London, was situated very unfortunately at the centre of a triangle that had three fighter aerodromes at its points. The largest was five miles to the east, the two smaller ones being two miles to the north-west and three miles due south. Inevitably, when these were the targets, Brooke Hill (or Cross) got clobbered by either over- or under-shoots. Jamie was so used to it that he gave it not a second thought. After all, his whole life, except for its first six months, had been wartime. It was his life, and he knew no other,

"My brother took me to see the street in Crosley the other day", said Jamie. "Seven houses were all in bits all over the road. He said that two whole families were wiped out!"

The brigadier was not at all sure that the little lad actually knew what the phrase 'wiped-out' really meant. The small town of Crosley was about a mile distant and close by the southernmost of the three fighter airfields. It was the fifteenth time that damage and casualties had been visited upon it, this latest being by far the worst. Brooke Hill had lost several houses, a few shops and a dairy but had yet to receive any casualties other than minor cuts and bruises.

However, looking at the rather sad little face before him, he revised the earlier opinion. The boy really seemed to know that those families were no more – that they were actually dead and gone. He reflected on the sadness that such a young life should be visited by horrors like that and could actually understand what they meant. But boys were very resilient. Probably he would grow up to forget and to suffer no lasting ill-effects.

Jamie, in his turn, had been studying the brigadier. He was a tall man, very erect of posture and dressed in a check shirt with regimental tie, a mustard coloured cardigan, old corduroy trousers and brown brogues that were shined to a deep mahogany mirror-like surface.

"Please sir", he asked. "Is that a Guard's tie?"

"No, it's me old regiment", came the gruff reply. "Joined in 'eighty-eight' and had the luck to command the second battalion in Flanders in 'fifteen' until the blighters promoted me to the general staff. Shoved out to pasture in 'nineteen' when they had no further use for me".

"Please sir, my dad was in Flanders in nineteen sixteen and got gassed and sent home after third Ypres".

"What the devil do you know about third Ypres?" the brigadier was astounded at such knowledge in one so young.

"Well, my dad told me about the battle and about how many of his mates had copped it on the Gerry wire. He cried when he told me that and said that it was so sad that it was all happening again. Why is it all happening again?"

The brigadier was somewhat at a loss. How on earth to begin to explain to such a young feller the meanness of victory and the humiliation of defeat; the viciousness of reprisals and restitution during the early 'peace'; the inevitable angry resurgence of a beaten and scorned nation?

He was saved as a few minutes later they heard the 'all-clear' whining from the siren atop the waterworks building in Brooke Hill town centre. They emerged from the shelter and with a respectful, 'Good-bye and thank you, sir', Jamie scampered off to Buttermere Gardens and the safety of his grandparents' home.

# NANA AND GRANDAD

The bungalow had been built some years before by his grandfather whose heart condition brought to an end his ownership of a three-storey house and its steep stairs. It spread itself luxuriously amid an acre of ground, with large hall, dining and sitting rooms, kitchen, scullery, morning room, four bedrooms and two bathrooms. Most unusually it had a form of central heating powered by an *Ideal* coke stove and the hot water gravity-fed throughout the house via cast iron radiators. It was home to Alfred and Gertrude Clements, and Daisy, their live-in maid. Alfred was sixty-nine years old and somewhat frail. His wife and adored grandmother to Jamie, was one year younger. They were cousins and had married. Margaret, their only daughter and Jamie's mother, had been born three years later. Jamie was vaguely aware that his grandparents were 'somebody' but was not quite sure how that had come about. In fact, Alfred's elder brother Edward had been, until his retirement, ambassador to various European countries and had retired with the nation's grateful thanks, to the House of Lords with the title of Viscount Caversley bestowed upon him by Stanley Baldwin, prime minister at the time.

He went around the side of the bungalow and entered the open kitchen door with his nostrils assailed by the delicious smell of his grandmother's rock cakes, only just taken from the oven to cool. Dumping his satchel and overcoat on the kitchen table he went to find her. Just past the kitchen door he saw his grandmother reclining in an armchair that was by the morning room window. She appeared to be asleep.

Jamie crept over and took her hand in his. "Hello, Nana!" he said very gently.

Gertrude opened her old eyes and regarded the tousled ginger curls and freckly face that confronted her. "Hello to you too", she replied.

Jamie knew that to even mention the rock cakes would be considered bad manners, as that would be construed as a request. Therefore, he knew that he must wait until he was offered one. His good manners came from the quiet tutelage of the old lady and gentleman who had instilled in him the need to be polite and considerate to everyone. Gertrude herself was an absolute model of rectitude, treating high and low alike with respect and dignity.

The morning room door opened, and his grandfather came in, a tall and imposing figure in wing collar, tie and pearl pin, a grey waistcoat under a black jacket and dark grey trousers. His face lit up as he saw grandson and wife together.

"Hello, young Jamie", he said. Jamie came forward and gave his grandfather a hug.

"Good afternoon, granddad", he said. "Have you had a nice day?"

"All the better for seeing you!" came the expected reply. Turning to his wife he enquired, "Tea a little late today, dear?"

Gertrude shrugged. "Poor Daisy was a little late getting back with the shopping. Apparently, she had to wait for two hours at the butchers and, even then, managed only to get a few scraps of scrag-end of mutton with the coupons. However, she is sure that she can make a nourishing hotpot for dinner tonight. She will serve tea in a few moments. I am sure that Jamie would like to stay to tea and have a rock cake with us".

"Oooh yes please, nana!" came the more than expected reply. Turning back to Alfred, he enquired, "Granddad, what is a lame spirit? Mrs. Bedford says that I could possibly be one and that I must try not to be one as soon as I can manage it".

Alfred settled himself into the only other armchair in the room and beckoned his grandson over to sit on his knee.

"Well, let us see", he began. "I will try to give you an example. Let us say that you get up one morning and know that you have to go for a very long walk to get something that your family really needs. You know that you must go as the things are so important, but you are afraid to walk so far in case you come to harm. Now, a brave boy would go, whatever he feared, but a lame spirit would give in to his fears and stay at home".

"But, granddad, that's what mummy does all the time, and nobody ever calls her a lame spirit!"

Alfred glanced across at Gertrude, both realising that he had to divert this turn in the conversation.

"Your mother has certain problems that tend to make her that way. It is not her fault, and she is as brave as anyone else really. Now, you are usually a very brave boy. Why, you walk to and from school all by yourself; you climb trees that I would not have dared to attempt at your age; you look after your baby brother when you can. I, for one, would never say that you were a lame spirit". "And neither would I", added Gertrude.

One grandparent's assurance would have been good enough, but both agreeing was like having it inscribed in tablets of stone; and he promptly forgot about it as Daisy came through and started to prepare tea in the kitchen.

A little later, it was served on the morning room table. A Georgian silver teapot, a matching hot water jug, milk jug and sugar bowl were neatly arranged together with a fine set of Royal Crown Derby tea plates, cups and saucers. A large platter held thinly sliced bread and butter and a cake stand displayed the delicious rock cakes on a lace doyley. With a little curtsey the maid withdrew to the kitchen, there to enjoy her own tea in peace and quiet. Gertrude handled the heavy teapot with some difficulty; for some years she had suffered the aches and pains of arthritis, the knuckles of her once dainty hands swollen with the knobbly aggregations. She had once tried an old remedy - that of immersing her hands for a time in very warm water. She had ceased this practise when she saw that all it achieved was a reddening of her hands, making her look, in her words, like 'some poor washerwoman'. Gertrude was sufficiently the proud Victorian to abhor such disfiguration. She now put up with the unsightly swellings as simply a part of 'getting on a bit'.

Jamie had to wait for some time before he could begin to sip his tea as blowing on it would not have done at all! Nana would not have approved. So, to eke out the time, he took a proffered slice of the thin bread and started to munch his way slowly, holding a precious tea plate under his chin so as not to spill crumbs, which also would not have done. The bread, to his Nana's chagrin, had been spread for some twelve months now with the hated margarine, butter being in extremely short supply. Even the margarine was on ration and consumed precious food coupons from the three books allotted by the Ministry of Food to the persons living at that address. It was a far cry from her pre-war days.

Arthur was similarly engrossed with his thoughts as he nibbled and sipped. He had retired just eighteen months before the outbreak of war and was, by the standards applied in the nineteen thirties, moderately rich. The bungalow had been built on land that was bought freehold for cash and had been erected to his exacting standards by a local contractor who not only came in on time but also within budget; the builder and his staff had been well compensated. Alfred longed for peace and a return to the days when he and his beloved Gertrude could again live in the manner to which, through his many years of hard toil, they had become accustomed. His younger brother and sister had now come to live nearby. The brother, Frederick, was some two years younger than Alfred and had never married. He had retired from a life of drudgery in a City insurance office and had bought a modest house in a small cul-de-sac just off Buttermere Gardens. The youngest of the siblings, Amelia, had married an Austrian and they had lived happily for some years in Salzburg where her husband, Hans, owned and ran a very successful jewellery business. Although, as the Nazis would have said, of impeccable Aryan stock, Hans had seen the coming disaster and had sold the business in nineteen thirty-three, before the Anschluss took place. He and Amelia had transferred all their funds to London and had left Austria for good. Hans had died the previous year from a cerebral haemorrhage and Amelia, distraught and alone, had agreed to come and live with her brother Frederick. Their pooled resources were more than adequate to afford them a long and comfortable life together. The pair were constant visitors, having to walk a mere two hundred yards to their big brother's bungalow. Alfred thought sadly of the eldest of all the siblings, the new Viscount; childless through thirty-three years of marriage to a woman who was his complete opposite. Edward was urbane and of impeccable manners – indispensable characteristics for a diplomat; his wife, Constance, was rude and hurtful to all and sundry. It often amazed the rest of the family that such a union could have survived a life of diplomatic high-flying where good manners were required. However unlikely, the marriage and the partnership had survived, and the wretched woman was now probably revelling in her new title and the supposed kudos that accrued thereto. Such was the acrimony caused by her that the three brothers and one sister seldom met. Edward, in his retirement from ambassadorial duties, delved deeper and deeper into the political maelstrom of the House of Lords, there to seek new interests and diversions. He had, through his lifelong European acquaintances, been welcomed on to various informal committees, advising on the political situation vis-à-vis allies and enemies alike. He was often aghast and horrified at the dangerous enterprises espoused by Churchill and on more than one occasion had spoken quietly to the Chief of the Imperial General Staff, Alan Brooke (who shared his apprehension), to see if this quietly spoken man could somehow divert those wilder proclivities. Thank the good Lord that the wise Field Marshal was so successful!

Alfred's thoughts turned again to his little grandson who, by this time had finished the cup of tea and was well entrenched into his second rock cake. The old man had agreed with his wife that, on Jamie's birth, they would have to act almost in loco parentis, their daughter Margaret being, they considered, mentally unfit to bring up a small child. Now, with little Robert just a few months old, she had surprised them all by being a doting and caring mother but showing signs of over-compensation by smothering the baby with affection and insisting that he was 'delicate' and needed her constant attention. Jamie was recognised and given effusive cuddles whenever he appeared but was otherwise ignored. It simply was not poor Margaret's fault. Jamie had fallen naturally into the willing arms of his grandparents and, away from either home, had developed an individualistic and protective armour that he would probably carry with him all his life.

Alfred's thoughts were interrupted by Gertrude enquiring if he would care for another cup, to which came the accustomed reply that, 'a delicate sufficiency had been attained so, no thank you, dearest'.

He returned to his reverie, thinking for the hundredth time of the consequences of his family's situation. Oldest brother Edward was childless. He, himself, had a daughter and his brother and sister were similarly childless. Therefore, in the fullness of time, the hereditary peerage would come to young Jamie, the next male relative after himself to be eligible. He had forbidden all concerned even to mention this to Jamie as he was firmly convinced, and Gertrude wholeheartedly agreed, that the little boy's life should be lived unfettered by unnecessary influences; the boy was progressing very nicely and did not need to be weighed down with such thoughts; he was a happy and contented, albeit a self-contained, little chap and should be allowed to continue in this way until he was old enough to deal with the responsibilities of rank and privilege. But heaven forbid that both Edward and he would die too soon to achieve this goal!

Daisy came in to clear the tea things.

"What time would you like dinner served, madam?"

This was pure routine. Every afternoon the same question and each time the considered reply that, 'eight o'clock would do nicely please Daisy'.

# DESMOND

Giving his Nana and Granddad hugs Jamie donned overcoat and satchel and sped off down the road to his own home. He clattered in by the kitchen door just as his elder brother arrived back on his bicycle from school. Desmond, now a tall and gangly thirteen years, attended a school in Brooke Hill town that specialised in the more technical subjects, the boy having exhibited some considerable leanings towards engineering. His bag was bursting with exercise books and textbooks. Leaning the bike against the wall he took off his cycle clips and looped them over the crossbar. He ruffled the ginger curls.

"How was school today", he asked as he dumped satchel and cap on the kitchen table.

"Oh, OK, you know", said Jamie, determining not to mention lame spirits, apples or brigadiers.

"Right then, lets get dinner started", said Desmond, washing his hands before sorting out a couple of carrots, a turnip, a large leek, a few potatoes and an Oxo cube. Jamie, knowing his part in all this, took out the peeler and attended to the potatoes whilst kneeling on a stool so that he could reach the wooden draining board. Soon the vegetables, grown by Desmond in the patch down the garden, were chopped and boiling in water in a large old copper pan on the gas stove. When they were tested with a fork and were soft enough, they were drained, and the hot water kept for future use. Just enough was added back with the crumbled cube to make a vegetable stew. Jamie had set out two places at the table and Desmond ladled stew into two bowls, the remainder to be allowed to cool and set on the marble shelf in the pantry for another day. The two boys wolfed down their meal and set about clearing up. The evening meal ritual followed the same pattern every school day, except for the fact that on two or three a little meat would be added from the precious ration.

Desmond then went upstairs to see how mother and baby brother had fared. His mother never ate with the family, deciding some years ago that her 'delicate constitution' be nourished only with warm milk and cereals, with the occasional biscuit as a treat. She was, as usual at this time in the early evening, reclining on the bed, reaching out and tickling the baby in the cot by her side. Little Robert was gurgling happily but smelt a bit niffy.

"Shall I change little Robby for you?" he enquired, knowing full well that if he did not the poor little chap would stay like it for some time yet.

"Oh, yes dear, that would be very kind", said his mother.

Taking the baby to the bathroom he took off the old nappy, cleaned the little pink bottom and re-clothed it with a muslin liner, a little cream and a clean napkin. He now was expert at pinning it the correct, and secure, way. He tucked baby under one arm and went down to the kitchen to immerse the soiled nappy in the special sterilizing solution in the bucket under the sink. Tomorrow he would attend to the washing.

Jamie then took over his little brother. Laying him on the table he inserted the tiny, pudgy limbs into a woollen suit and drew the hood over the tiny fair head. Then, to the hall to put Robert into the pushchair and strap him safely in. On with overcoat and off for the baby's daily outing.

He wheeled the pushchair down the road and round the corner where little Robert could see the steam trains passing. The tiny chap got so excited whenever a train passed and, on that main London to Brighton line, they were numerous. After five trains had passed, he wheeled back the way he had come and into the small road wherein his great-uncle and great-aunt lived. They both replied to his knock, looking forward to the daily visits with joy. The old couple, bachelor and widow, played peek-a-boo whilst Jamie wolfed down the customary lemonade and biscuits made by Amelia in vast batches every week.

"Nunky", said Jamie. "Might you show me your mickoscope?"

The old fellow took the shiny brass instrument and set it on the table together with a few slides. He inserted one and beckoned to Jamie who clambered to kneel on a chair and peer with right eye pressed to the upper lens. On the slide, superbly magnified, was a dead ant and the little boy examined every enlarged feature, being instructed to look at the tiny join between thorax and abdomen. How small it seemed and yet blood flowed through it and nerves and other fibres were housed in it. A few other slides were examined; one of a wasp, another of a small moth and, most exciting of all, the tiny toe bones of a mouse.

By now dusk had started to descend and it was time to go.

"See you tomorrow old chap", said Frederick.

"Bye-bye Nunky; bye-bye Noony", said Jamie, holding Robert's tiny arm and waving with it. Robert made happy noises and was wheeled back home where Desmond was busy setting the black-out curtains firmly in place. The last thing he wanted was for the peripatetic warden to shout, 'Put that light out!" at *his* house. Robert was given a warmed bottle and returned to the cot where mother awaited him, still reclining on the bed in the gathering gloom.

Jamie wandered into the front sitting room where Desmond was beginning to set out books, papers, pens, pencils and ink for his nightly homework stint. Jamie had not yet reached an age at which Cecily Bedford thought it right and proper that this extra pressure should commence. That would come at about age six. He wandered out again and into the kitchen. Taking an old worn coat from the peg by the pantry, he shrugged into it, turned out the light before opening the back door, passed through it and closed it quietly behind him. He needed no light to illuminate his way down the garden to the fence – in fact, he had proved that he could do it blindfolded by trying this out some weeks before with his eyes firmly closed.

# BASE CAMP

The fence ran along the bottom ends of seven adjacent gardens, the Smalls' being the middle one. Various shrubs and bushes had been planted by it on the garden side of the Smalls' portion. The far-right shrub was the one that Jamie had chosen some weeks before. He had chosen with care. On the left were prickly Berberis and a slightly stunted holly. This, the chosen bush, was a smooth but quite dense Mahonia that did not snag at his clothes or scratched his hands and knees. Pushing the nearest little low branches aside he struggled into the heart of the shrub. Judicious 'pruning' with a 'borrowed' pair of secateurs from Dad's shed had produced a space just behind the centre stem that allowed him just enough room to sit down. He had been careful not to 'prune' his overhead foliage and knew that, once within this space, he was completely invisible from whatever angle. This he had christened his Base Camp.

On the far side of the fence, indeed along the entire length of Buttermere Gardens, rose an embankment. This had been constructed in the previous century as the then London, Brighton and South Coast Railway had probed ever further southwards from the capital. It rose some twenty feet in height at a rough thirty degrees. At its top ran the four parallel tracks of the now Southern Railway – Wandleford some six miles to the north and Brighton over forty to the south. The embankment, before the war, had been meticulously maintained by the railway staff. But now, the war just starting its fifth year, the grasses were high and the stunted shrubs grew unattended. It was Jamie's intention to make a crawl-way, completely under cover, to a large shrub at its top. This would be his Advance Base. Progress had been slow and, as yet, he had achieved little more than the unfixing of two of the feather-edge boards in the fence, leaving the top nails in place so that they could be hinged aside and replaced. It was too dark for him to see what he was doing and so he planned further work for the coming weekend.

He would need a trowel and some thin hazel sticks. He knew exactly where these were to be found as, on the allotments at the end of the road, a fresh load of hazel had been coppiced. The gardeners had scavenged and trimmed the poles for runner beans, leaving a large pile of the side shoots for whomsoever might find a use for them. He would have to borrow the secateurs again and thought that he would be able to bring the thin bendy twigs back in bundles of about thirty at a time. Ah, he would also need some string. No problem! Nunky had masses of it in his greenhouse and would let Jamie have whatever he needed.

Sunk in his thoughts and plans, the little boy dreamed on whilst blacked-out trains passed to and fro along the tracks above, until, with a start he saw the long goods wagons rattling by. This, he knew, passed at about nine o'clock every evening on its way from the coal depots of Wandleford to various shunting yards south towards Brighton; the wagons to be left at each point being unhitched from the rear of the train and puffed into the yard by waiting shunting engines. Reluctantly, he squirmed out of the bush and, with eyes firmly closed again, felt his way unerringly back to the house.

Desmond meanwhile had been hard at work. The intricacies of various metals fascinated him. He had recently mastered the arcane secrets of the slide rule and, with the aid of it and logarithmic tables, just completed a task that demanded he show how a steel bar of a certain thickness and length would respond whilst supported at points X and Y to uneven weights placed at its extremities. Pages of calculations in his meticulous handwriting were strewn about the table top and his fingers, now smudgy from Stephens' Royal Blue ink, gathered them together and clipped them to the back of his summary sheet. He was done and sat back with a quiet contentment. Not only had he completed the task faultlessly but had also fully understood the problem. He heard the back door quietly open and close. Putting homework, books and all the other associated paraphernalia into his large satchel, he went out, turned off the light, and went to the kitchen to warm water for his and Jamie's cocoa. Rowntrees cocoa powder was spooned into two mugs and the heated water (*not boiled*) was stirred in.

Before the war Desmond had enjoyed a spoonful of sugar in his nightly cocoa but now that commodity was in even shorter supply than most others and he had had to get used to the sharp-tasting beverage unsweetened. Still, as the Ministry of Health were at pains to point out, this was only to the benefit of the nation's teeth! Still, he really did not like it, and neither did his little brother, grimacing as usual at the first mouthful.

The mugs were washed and dried and hung carefully on the hooks under the wall-mounted plate rack. From afar came the faint wailing of a siren – yet another bombing raid coming in. It sounded quite a way to the south, and they ignored it. But no matter how many times it was heard, it sent a little wave of apprehension through the teenager as he imagined the devastation being wrought upon some unfortunate neighbourhood. He had taken Jamie to see the flattened houses near the fighter base and, whilst the youngster had seen only piles of bricks and debris, the much older and far more sensitive Desmond had imagined the desperation and sorrow that had been caused to the real people who had lived, and died, there. He had quietly wept on the walk back home and offered a short prayer for his family's safety.

Far off came a series of faint 'crumps' and he shivered, hearing in his mind the frantic struggles and cries of the injured and the desperate shouts of the rescuers as they fought with bare hands to retrieve bodies crushed and, sometimes, miraculously unscathed from the wreckage. But - time for bed.

Desmond made sure that Jamie washed, in cold water, and brushed his teeth before putting on his pyjamas. The two brothers went into the large front bedroom. Mother was asleep and so was tiny Robert. The baby had slept 'right through' from the age of two weeks. Bending over his mother Jamie planted a small kiss on her pale forehead and another on his baby brother's nose. Desmond and he then went into the smaller back bedroom where they had their beds; Desmond's a full size single under the window and Jamie's a much shorter one against the right wall. Jamie climbed in and with a 'nighty-night' to his brother shut his eyes tight and was asleep a few moments later. Desmond made himself ready for bed, deciding that Dad would not be home that night as the raids were coming in more frequently now that the nights were getting longer. Sitting up in bed he read yet again from his favourite book, an account of the Antarctic exploits of Shackleton. He knew that he would never have the strength or the courage to emulate that fiercely determined man, but he could dream, couldn't he?

His eyelids drooped and, setting aside book, hopped out to turn off the light. Sleep came slowly to him as it seemed to every night. Blessed, or cursed, with a fertile imagination, he was sensitive to all around him. He knew from conversations with and visits to friends that all was not 'normal' in his own home. His 'mother' was not as other mothers, laughing, joking, scolding, cooking and shopping. The person he thought of as his mother was different – reclusive, sometimes sad, often deeply miserable, always indoors. She told him of visits made to the house – always when he and Jamie were at school – of famous and important people; surgeons, actors and actresses, bankers and the like – and felt acute disappointment at never having met any of them. When these conversations took place on the rare occasions when Dad's duties allowed him to be also present, his father said not a word but remained tight lipped or busied himself elsewhere about the house or in the garden. It would have been obvious to even the most inexperienced psychiatrist that Desmond's childlike trust in those around him stemmed from a desperate need for security. What had happened to his unknown brother and sister and long-dead mother had certainly bred this need, although he had been far too young for this to register and his memory of it all was non-existent. Slowly he drifted off to sleep. Jamie snuffled a bit in his small bed. Mother and baby slept on. Father wearily plodded with an Air Raid Warden around the streets of South Wandleford. Sirens started up yet again as searchlights probed the blackness over London. All was dreadfully normal for late nineteen forty-three.

# POLICE MATTERS

Sergeant John Small sat at his desk in the old, cramped station, the office being shared by the four sergeants on duty at any one time. Some of his colleagues had adorned their temporary 'homes' with photographs and other memorabilia but he had not, preferring to keep his private life just that.

His shifts alternated by the week; sometimes nights only, sometimes days only, and others that spanned the two. He actually preferred the nights. At times he was in charge of the 'desk'; at others he patrolled round the beats of his constables whilst his most detested role of all was acting as custody sergeant, locking away those drunks and petty thieves that had been caught often red-handed. He saw this as a waste of a sergeant – something that could just as well be left to a senior constable.

When not on police shift duty he spent hours wandering the streets as a relief warden, seeing that as an extension of his civic duty. The previous evening, patrolling the streets, he had met up as prearranged with one of his constables. They had literally stumbled across a shifty character emerging with a small bag from the ruins of a recently bombed shop. The man put up no resistance and was promptly marched back to the station where the bag had been examined. In the bottom were two tins of corned beef. The chap had merely been trying to supplement the rations of his family – wife and three small children. He sobbed quietly after having supplied his name and address. He would be brought before the magistrates later this morning and charged with petty pilfering. The magistrates would doubtless seek to make an example of him as they did all those seen to be 'profiteering' from the war; he would be lucky to see the light of day for another twenty-eight days. And then what would his family do?

John had mixed feelings for the petty thief; pity for him in that he was seeking to provide for others; censure in that he stole to make this provision. There was work enough in these times for one and all – roads to repair, building rubble to clear. However, he had broken the law and that law John had sworn to uphold no matter what his feelings. Duty was duty.

Duty was his refuge; duty to serve his King and Country, to provide and safeguard his family; duty to uphold the law and see that the King's Peace was maintained. Whilst he was able to do all these things, he felt safe and secure. There was never a trace of smug satisfaction or of complacency. He was simply 'doing his bit' and doing it to the very best of his ability. There was only one flaw in all this, and it nagged at him constantly.

Unbuttoning his tunic, he took out the old leather wallet. In it were his warrant card, identity card, one ten shilling note and two slightly faded photographs. His eyes always misted slightly at the sight of his much loved brother Will who had been blown to smithereens during a night attack twenty-six years ago. Will, smart and proud in his uniform grinned out at him, looking much younger than his eighteen years when the picture had been taken in nineteen sixteen. How he had missed him when Will had gone off to Flanders – so much in fact that John had lied about his age and joined up soon after in the same regiment. Their elder brother, Charlie, had risen steadily up the ranks and was now stationed in Plymouth as a Chief Petty Officer, training new recruits on a land-based naval station.

Charlie had been in constant touch with his young brother John after the first war and had followed his marriage to Dorothy and the subsequent births of the three children with great joy. On his peacetime leaves he had been a frequent guest at the small home in Streatham and had been in the Far East when the tragedy of Dorothy's death had torn the family into fragments. He had understood completely John's inability to both provide for and look after his children; after all, there was no help really available, and he knew that the eldest two would be loved and cared for by the couple who had temporarily 'adopted' them. After all, when John had settled down again, he would be able to get them all together as a family once more.

He had been introduced to the well-spoken Margaret but, being an astute judge of character, had seen something in his soon-to-be sister-in-law that disturbed him. Stories of heroes met and daring deeds accomplished by 'friends' simply did not add up; inconsistencies were too frequent to be accidental. 'You will live to regret this, mate', he had said to John. He knew that he was simply wasting his breath; his brother was overawed and entranced by his beautiful fiancée and had no use for criticism of any kind. When Charlie had heard of the marriage and the subsequent refusal by Margaret to entertain Valerie and Peter, he had written a blistering letter to his brother. John had replied that this was probably 'all for the best' and this told Charlie that the cause was hopeless; John would never hear one word against his new wife. He had written one final letter saying that he was absolutely disgusted at the 'arrangement' and that he washed his hands of them both. He feared for little Desmond but knew that he would never be allowed to interfere. From that day he and John had been estranged. He had obeyed Margaret's insistence that they 'did not need anyone poking their noses in, thank you'.

The door opened and his best friend Alan Trainer, also a sergeant, came in and flopped down at his desk. Alan, to be strictly truthful, was not a friend to John in the usual meaning of the word. John was too much a stickler for duty and too private an individual for real friendship to flourish. However, Alan respected the quiet and slightly aloof John and they got on reasonably well.

"Sodding beak's gone all soft on me!" he grumbled. Lighting a foul pipe, he sucked contentedly as his hurt feelings slowly evaporated.

In response to John's inquisitively raised eyebrow he went on to explain the reason for his wrath.

"You know 'Gunny' Flood?"

John merely nodded. 'Gunny' was well known to every policeman within a radius of twenty miles – an habitual drunk and trouble maker.

"Well, I had him up before the bench just now – you know, the usual; drunk and disorderly – urinating in a public place – therefore technically indecent exposure. The soft fart actually let the bastard off with a caution – a bloody caution!"

John, never one to utter the slightest profanity, could well understand his friend's anger. 'Gunny' had a string of convictions going back many years.

"So, the next time I catch the bugger, I'm going to give him a swift kick up the arse and, probably, an even swifter taste of my fist! If all they can do is let the sod off, then I reckon it's up to me to deliver some justice".

"I'd be very careful if I were you; you know what the super did to 'Ponker' Garton when he was caught duffing up that deserter", John reminded the red-faced sergeant.

"Serve the stupid bugger right – he did it in front of three so-called upright citizens. If I do it, it will be in a quiet corner with no prying eyes about. Bloody magistrates!"

Alan took some papers from the drawer in his desk and went out, slamming the door and muttering dark threats about beaks, blaggers and drunks alike.

John smiled. Win some, lose some. It was all the same in the end. His eye was taken by the other picture, a softly smiling Dorothy and three children. Margaret would have torn it up and burnt it to ashes if she had known of its existence. He kept it locked up in his desk drawer whenever not on duty, taking it out and placing it in his wallet only when at work.

Replacing the photographs in his wallet he pocketed it and fastened up the shiny tunic buttons to the neck. Rising, he replaced the chair precisely and, ensuring that the desk was clean and neat for its next occupant, went out in search of the constable who had accompanied him at the previous night's arrest. He found him drinking a mug of tea in the canteen.

Bob Quick was fairly new to the job and had been on the beat only six months. His sergeant had made sure that Bob had done the arrest and had watched and listened both at the scene and back at the station in the custody room to ensure that he had followed correct procedure. His sergeant, short and dapper with immaculate uniform and boots burnished to a guardsman's shine, came over to him.

"Right, Bob", he said quietly. "You're in court in a tick, aren't you?"

"Yes sarge – will you be there – it's my first one", said a somewhat apprehensive Bob.

"No, you'll be OK – nothing to it. Just stick to the facts and don't speak until you are spoken to and, remember this, only speak when they ask you a question. If in doubt, tell the beak that you need to refer to your pocketbook. He will always agree to a copper doing that. But, in this case, stress that he gave no trouble; came quietly and co-operated with us; in fact, go easy on the poor man".

Bob was surprised to hear this from the lips of a sergeant who was noted for strict adherence to all the rules and a staunch believer in the full weight of the law being brought down on the heads of the guilty. However, he was a bit sorry for the chap himself and was somewhat relieved that he did not have to act the 'heavy' – especially in his first solo appearance before the bench. He marched smartly over to the court which was in an adjacent street and returned half an hour later with the news that the man had been given a mere seven days. On hearing this later Alan Trainer, still smarting from his earlier encounter, exploded that 'if that was what the bench were up to nowadays then he might as well pack it in and go down the mines'.

John, meanwhile, was patrolling the centre of the town, checking on his men as he walked with slow dignity past shops and storefronts. Over his shoulder he carried his haversack in which was his gas mask; on the outside of the haversack was strapped his tin helmet with the word 'POLICE' stencilled in white and above which were his three stripes. He reached the spot outside the department store, paused there and slowly rocked back and forward on his heels – to the consternation of a seedy individual on the opposite pavement who had been contemplating a quick foray into that very store to see what quick pickings from the leather goods counter could be secreted in his 'poacher' pocket. He shuffled off muttering to himself of his poor luck and the astounding good luck of 'bleedin coppers'.

John, deep in his own thoughts, had not even been aware of the chap until the moment that the chap started his shuffling retreat. The very shiftiness of the walk brought all his antennae quivering; that and the fact that the man was not carrying his gas mask – strictly against regulations. He might just as well have carried a large sign asking for him to be stopped and questioned. John started to cross the road, stopping a little way over to allow a rattling tram to pass. When he reached the opposite pavement, he saw the shambling figure some fifty yards in front of him. In John's brain was an accurate and constantly updated map of the whereabouts of his constables. Drawing his whistle from his breast pocket he uttered a shrill blast, knowing that the nearest of his colleagues would be appearing any second from a side street ahead. The uniformed figure ran into the High Street seconds later in response to the summons. John did not shout or run; he simply made sure the constable could see him and pointed to the man.

The constable nodded and, reaching out a brawny arm, seized the man by the dirty collar of his old raincoat. The man wriggled and pleaded that 'he ain't done nuffin, guvner'. John came up and the constable searched the pockets inside the coat. Out came an assortment of knicknacks – a piece of string, a ball of dirty and much thumbed putty, a tiny hammer with a spike opposite the head, a glass cutter, five half-crown coins and a variety of pennies, half-pennies and one farthing. John smiled. This was a man 'tooled' for breaking and entering. The constable pocketed the finds and marched the still protesting man back to the station. John went on his way, passing and being greeted by various tradesmen either driving horse and cart, wheeling barrows or simply toting the tools of their trades in hessian bags over their shoulders. He knew them all by name and each was greeted with a 'Good Morning, Mister Green – or whatever'.

Despite being only four days before Christmas, John did not wear his uniform greatcoat; he hated the thing and was usually quite impervious to the cold. He entered his usual tobacconist situated on the corner of the High Street and the road that led down through the bustling street market.

"Good morning, sergeant Small", greeted the plump woman behind the counter. John knew that her husband was away in the RAF at one of the massive bomber aerodromes in Lincolnshire. She had run the shop single-handed since his call-up three years before. Dressed as usual in a flowered fold-over pinafore, worn over a cardigan, blouse and woollen skirt, she beamed goodwill at all and sundry and especially at the dapper sergeant who had apprehended a lad some months before as he attempted to leave the shop with an armful of stolen cigarettes. John had done this quickly and wordlessly, drawing truncheon and whacking the lad on the kneecap as he attempted to burst past him. The lad had sprawled on the floor howling with pain. John had summoned the black maria and the lad had been bundled unceremoniously into its interior. He was still in Brixton Nick with another six months to serve.

"My usual please, Mrs Williams", said John, reaching into his pocket for the one shilling and one penny necessary. A pack of twenty Players Navy Cut was passed over the counter and disappeared into his trouser pocket, well under the flap of tunic where the slight bulge would not be noticed. John thought that this brand suited his rank better than the more usual Weights and Woodbines. With polite 'good day's' John went out of the shop, closing the bell-tinkling door behind him. He walked on.

# MUSIC

Some three miles to the south his fourth child was sitting miserably through a dissertation on the wonders of subtraction and simple multiplication by Julia Forbes, the pretty and slim assistant teacher. Jamie, at his usual desk by one of the large windows, gazed longingly at distant hedges and trees, wanting nothing more than to be allowed to explore the former and climb the latter. Jamie, for as long as he could walk, had been a child of the great outdoors; he hated being indoors except when with his grandparents, his uncle and the fascinating array of wonderful things to see and do, and especially his brother Desmond who explained things so carefully. At all other times he longed for the freedom of the fields and hedgerows. His knowledge of wild flowers and birds was as large as his grasp on arithmetic was small. He simply wasn't interested in the manner by which numbers could be manipulated. They bored him stiff.

The only other thing that could keep him sitting still indoors for any length of time was music, especially the wonderful choral music that came from the local parish church on practice evenings and, especially, choral evensong. He had sat entranced through their rendition one late summer evening of Palestrina's Stabat Mater, the four voice groups blending so beautifully through the often complex harmonies. He had sat and soaked it into his very being, imagining larks and swallows soaring up with the sopranos, thrushes and blackbirds skipping with altos and tenors, whilst rooks and magpies followed the basses. The accompaniment of the organ, mostly subdued with flute and reeds, had been the stream that gurgled and rippled. The choirmaster had noticed the small lad sitting all alone at the back of the church and wondered if there was any hope in recruiting him when his voice was ready. The little chap sat with eyes firmly shut, dreaming his dreams and luxuriating in the waves of perfect sound, lost to all and everything.

Julia, at last aware of the fact that one of her pupils had been lost to her, put down chalk and, dusting her fingers, went softly down the aisle of desks and stopped by Jamie's shoulder. Jamie was quite unaware of her presence, having seen two little fat wrens having what seemed to be a punch-up over the ownership of a worm. Julia bent down to the level of the ginger head and peered through the glass, seeing the miniature war for herself.

"Well, Jamie; who started it?" she asked.

Jamie came back into the classroom with a jolt.

"Please miss, the one on the left found it and started to pull it out of the grass and the other one simply flew down and tried to take over".

"And now that you have sorted that one out, can you tell me what twenty-one minus seven would leave?"

Jamie thought about this. If he had paid any attention at all during the previous twenty minutes, he would have seen this exact sum detailed on the blackboard; twenty-one drawn above a seven (under the figure one), an underline and the answer of fourteen written beneath. However, he had neither seen nor heard and was consequently at a loss. He started with twenty-one and, using fingers started to count backwards until seven fingers had been used.

"Fifteen, Miss Forbes", he announced.

"No Jamie, it doesn't", said Julia, knowing that to get arithmetic into that woolly skull would be a labour of love at best and a nightmare at worst.

"Now, think of taking the seven from the one of twenty-one. It cannot be done, can it?"

"No, Miss Forbes", replied Jamie. It seemed the obvious response to the question.

"So, we borrow a one from the next column, the two of twenty-one, and subtract the seven from eleven. What does that leave?"

That was much easier. "Four!"

"So, we have a four. Now we take nothing from the remaining one and what does that leave?"

That was even easier. "One!"

"Good; we have an answer of one and four, making fourteen. I think that you had better come to see me after class this afternoon and we'll go through it again".

Julia, like her boss the headmistress knew fully well that Jamie was not met after school and would not be missed for the ten minutes that she proposed to keep him.

Soon after, the handbell, wielded vigorously by old Arthur, signalled the end of class for the day. One more and they would break for two weeks Christmas Holiday. Jamie mooched about whilst the other boys shouted and scampered home. He wandered into the classroom and sat on the high stool at the keyboard of the grand piano that was used for hymns in the morning and singing classes once a week. Idly, and using only the index finger of his right hand, he picked out a tune that had been going through his head for some days. Starting on the G above middle C he played quietly through the entire first section.

Julia stopped in mid stride as she came into the classroom. There was no music manuscript on the stand in front of the boy. Had someone taught him this tune?

"Jamie, that was very nice. Do you know what it is?

"Oh yes, Miss Forbes. My uncle played me his gramophone the other day and it is the start of the Rococo Variations by Tchaikovsky. I love the sound of the cello, don't you?"

"But who taught you to play it?" queried the now fascinated teacher.

"Oh, nobody did. I can hear it in my head and can find the right notes quite easily", said Jamie without any trace of bravado.

Julia needed more than this bland assurance. "Do you know the tune of 'Abide with Me?", she asked.

"Oh yes, that's easy", replied Jamie, starting this time in the key of G major at note B and playing a full verse of the soprano tune line.

Julia was quite amazed. Surely, this took at least a year of music lessons. "Who teaches you to play?" she enquired.

"Nobody does", came the unexpected reply. "I just seem to know how to".

Arithmetic was forgotten. Julia sat down on the long stool to Jamie's left. She asked him to play the hymn tune again, accompanying him with the other three voice parts that she knew so well. They reached the end and Jamie turned his freckly face to hers and grinned. She grinned back.

"Off you go - and we must play again some time".

"Oh yes please Miss Forbes; that would be super!"

# MANURE, AND FISH-PASTE SANDWICHES

Jamie got ready to leave and trotted down Brook Hill. At his gate the old brigadier waved to the passing youngster.

"No air-raid today!" he said.

"No sir, but last night's was very noisy", Jamie raised his cap politely and went on his way. Today he would call on his great-uncle and great-aunt. Noony would have made his favourite fish paste sandwiches if he was lucky. He passed the horse and wagon belonging to Mr. Vickery, the greengrocer. Of that worthy there was no sign, probably delivering to the houses thought Jamie as he plodded on. Between the front wheels of the old wagon was a pile of horse manure which would be almost fought over by keen gardeners seeking to force rhubarb and spread over now mainly dormant vegetable patches. Indeed, old Mr. Caterfield, their neighbour in number sixty-three was already plodding towards the prize with trowel and bucket at the ready. Jamie raised his cap to the old man and received only a scowl in return. Mr. Caterfield had made repeated protestations to the Small family about the noise generated by this particular small boy. Behind Jamie, and approaching from a greater distance, similarly accoutred, came Mrs. Philpott. She scurried down the pavement but realising that she would be easily beaten to the prize by the much nearer Mr. Caterfield, gave up and plodded back.

Jamie knocked at the door and Nunky opened it, having spied his great-nephew approaching up the short hill.

"Hello, young Jamie", he said.

"Hello, Nunky", replied Jamie, taking off cap, satchel and overcoat and draping them over the hall chair, the pegs of the coat rack being too far up for him to reach. The terms 'Nunky' and ' Noony' dated back to when he was just about eighteen months old and these were the best approximations he could achieve to the ponderous titles of great-uncle and great-aunt. Neither of them minded at all; indeed, they rather revelled in the affection that these abbreviations implied. Being childless themselves the elderly brother and sister were somewhat flattered by the attention that Jamie lavished on them. The old couple fascinated Jamie and he loved them for their affection and for the wondrous array of things that seemed to sprout from every corner of that magical house. There were microscopes, the gramophone, a tall candle-stick telephone, kaleidoscopes, a whole (uninhabited) tortoise shell, walking sticks with swords inside them, a magic lantern and a host of glass slides – in fact, to the small boy, a positive cornucopia of delights to be explored.

Jamie had always been fascinated by the way in which the couple addressed one another. Frederick addressed Amelia as 'sister dear'. Amelia addressed Frederick as "brother". Very formal and very Victorian. But then, they were Victorian, having lived for the first twenty-five years or so of their lives during the last third of that queen's long reign. Old habits died hard.

Amelia poked her head around the kitchen door and announced to 'dear brother and Jamie' that a small tea of sandwiches was ready for them. They obediently went into the dining room where the table was laid with ironed linen tablecloth, place mats, small plates, cake knives, cups and saucers, milk, sugar and steaming teapot. They sat down in their normal places as Amelia came in proudly bearing a small platter of immaculately squared and de-crusted sandwiches. The crusts were always cut up and put out for the birds, especially in winter. Jamie just knew that they were fish paste sandwiches, and he wriggled in anticipation. His, like most others people's, diet was very bland and monotonous for food was scarce and usually of the same variety for weeks at a time. He took the proffered sandwich but, before munching into it, unrolled napkin from the silver ring beside his plate spread it over his lap in the large triangular fashion that he had learned from his Nana. He bit into the sandwich and Amelia watched with secret happiness as the freckled face broke into a large grin of delight. Shippams Fish Paste – the best of the lot! His granddad had once given him a taste of that most wonderful savoury Gentleman's Relish. It was wonderful and, alas, unobtainable for at least a year. But he had never forgotten the taste! Eggs were almost a delicacy these days and bacon so rare as to be but a fond memory.

"Are you all coming to your grandfather and grandmother for Christmas luncheon?" enquired his great-uncle.

"Yes, I think so, Nunky", said Jamie between mouthfuls. "I heard Dad say something about it the other day when he was home. He will not be on duty for two days!"

This was indeed a treat for all concerned. The most that John usually managed was one weekend in four and one short evening a week at home. Whilst some colleagues managed to wangle time off, John, with his strict observance of duty, never did.

Most nights, when not on police duty, he managed four or five hours of sleep on a sofa in the station restroom. Often, he went for thirty-six hours without sleep, as did many others. There was always a call on his time; police shifts, people to help rescue, crowds to control, unmasked lights to be extinguished or shrouded, ambulances to see safely to the general hospital, bodies to get identified, belongings to be stored and so on and so forth. Never time to rest and relax.

He was, like so many others, war-weary – weighed down with the tears of the bereaved, the hopeless feeling that one bomb site cleared was surely the signal for another to be created.

Nightly he would hear the deep and earth-shaking rumble of the massed bomber raids heading for the industrial Ruhr and the German cities. He wished them Godspeed every time, plus the luxury of a safe return. He cursed inwardly at every air-raid siren and prayed for his 'patch' to be spared until the single note of the 'all-clear' sounded.

It had all gone on for far too long. He had seen his war up close in the trenches and daily recalled the mortars, the flares and the machine guns, the wire and the blood and screams. His new war was being fought at second-hand and he sometimes longed for the closeness of the old regiment where they had the feeling of being 'in it together'. Mates to be joshed and games of cards on upturned buckets played in the wet and festering dugouts. No, this war was different and had affected the whole country. It was somehow, dirtier!

# THE TUNNEL

The next day, being the last before breaking up for Christmas, was a time of jollity for Jamie ending his first term - and a trial for Desmond as he eyed with some apprehension the mound of homework to be completed before going back again in early January. The two boys were home by early afternoon and, whilst Desmond resigned himself to the study of Chaucer, Jamie shot off, muffled to the eyebrows against the cold to start collecting small bundles of hazel twigs. He completed three journeys before he was satisfied that he had enough to create the secret pathway from Base Camp to the Advance Camp that had been his dream for so long. Taking the first small bundle, along with hand clippers and string, he squeezed himself into Base Camp and started work. Wriggling half through the loose fence boards he started to cut a small pathway through the tall grasses and thistles that grew up the railway embankment. When he had completed a section about twelve inches wide and some three feet long, he began to erect his camouflage. Pushing the end of one very long twig into the ground at the left side of the path he then bent it over in an arc and pushed the other end into the soil on the right side, leaving a hoop of hazel. Another six inches further in he repeated the task; then another and another until his new pathway was adorned along its short length. He reached up and drew the long grasses from either side and painstakingly wove them over his hoops, thereby completing the first bit of his tunnel. He calculated that he had another ten similar sections to erect before he emerged at the top of the embankment.

Wriggling backwards, and being very careful not to disturb his work, he ended back at his base camp again where the loose boards were hung straight again. He squeezed out and shot back to the house, up the stairs and into his back bedroom. He looked long and hard at the work that he had done and thought that, after a few days, it would be invisible as the grasses found their own way back to a natural appearance.

So far, so good.

# TRAMS AND JAM TARTS

Christmas Eve morning was bright and frosty. There had been only one air-raid siren the previous night and even this one had been a false alarm, the all-clear sounding after a mere fifteen minutes. As arranged the previous afternoon Desmond, Jamie and baby Robert called at the bungalow at ten o'clock. Jamie wheeled the pushchair in which his little brother reclined, wrapped up in a hooded woollen suit against the cold wind. Desmond walked up the steps and knocked at the door. Gertrude, neatly attired as usual, came out and they started their walk into the town for a few of what she called 'last minute necessities'. At the top of Buttermere Gardens, they turned right down Derwent Drive and went past the shunting yards. Robbie woke up at that point and they all had to wait as the engine pushed a series of wagons in front of it. The shunter had unhitched the first two and, slowing down, the engine parted company with the detached wagons, which rolled on and into the correct siding. Robert was enthralled as the engine reversed to have the next three detached. They walked on. At the end of Derwent Drive they descended a sloping pathway and turned right on the Eastbourne road to go under the railway bridge. A fork in the road went left to the main junction with the Brighton road and right into the High Street.

They went into the Brooke Hill Stores to be greeted my Mr. Stone the manager. He was a tall and slim figure, his immaculate grey overall covered with a spotless, crisp white apron that almost reached the top of his shiny boots.

"Good morning, Mrs. Clements", he bowed slightly and led the old lady and entourage to a stool by the main counter. Ducking behind it he continued, "And what may we have the pleasure of serving you with today?

Nana, perched daintily on the high stool, took out a small notebook from her handbag. Attached to the spine of this little book was a tiny gold propelling pencil. She opened the book and read from her list.

"I will take a quarter of tea and as many currants as you can let me have. Also, have you any of that delicious cheddar you sent last week?"

"How many books would that be for, madam?"

She took her and Alfred's ration books from her bag and placed them on the counter. Mr. Stone clipped out the coupons necessary for the two ounces of cheese per person per week. Calling across the store to the Cheese and Bacon counter he ordered four ounces to be cut with the wire from the fairly small wedge that remained. This was wrapped in paper with immaculate creases and marked with the customer's name.

Mr. Stone made notes of the order so far. "Anything else, madam?"

"I also need two cakes of Sunlight soap, a pound of rolled oats and a bottle of Camp Coffee – and that will be all for today, thank you".

More notes were taken; Gertrude's notebook now contained a small list with, against each entry, a small, neat tick. Pencil and book were returned to handbag. The assistant was busy preparing the remainder of the order; rolled oats being measured into a stout paper bag from a sack on the floor. The items were placed neatly into a box.

Mr. Stone bowed Gertrude and children out of the shop.

"May I wish you and your family all good wishes for the festive season", he said.

"And a very merry Christmas to you and yours, Mr. Stone!"

"Your order will be delivered this afternoon, madam", said the manager, flicking an imaginary speck from the snowy apron. They resumed their walk, passing the small junior school and the dry cleaners. Turning left at the end of the High Street they were on the main Brighton Road. A tram clattered past. Gertrude, to the huge delight of Jamie who had hoped that this would be their ultimate destination, she turned into Woolbridge's Coffee House. A delicious aroma of roasting coffee beans had been wafted towards them ever since the tram had passed. They went through the shop and up a broad staircase at the rear. At the top and covering a large area as big as the shop floor beneath, was the café. Old oak tables for four were separated by high-backed settles; on each of these were flowered cushions, one per seat. They found a vacant 'booth' right at the front and Jamie wriggled into the seat to gaze out of the window at the scene below. Brooke Hill was the southernmost 'terminus' of the trams. There, an arrival from the north, was 'turned round'. Not physically as there was no turntable. A man with a very long pole reached up over the roof of the tram and hooked it over the long arm that took electricity from the overhead wire. He pulled it over to the 'northbound' wire and let the wheel settle delicately on to its new supply. Then he entered the tram itself and helped the conductor to pull the wooden seatbacks over to their 'northbound' position. The driver meanwhile had walked the length of the lower car and had settled himself at the opposite controls. The man descended and, going forward, used his other tool, a heavy lever, to alter the points so that when the tram moved off it would go to the leftmost of the pair of tramlines. All was ready and passengers started to board. Pennies were collected, tickets were punched, and the tram clanked off towards Wandlford, Streatham and, ultimately, the Embankment.

Jamie never ceased to enjoy this spectacle. He knew that his dad sometimes took the tram to and fro from home and work but preferred the bus as being much quieter and a little more comfortable.

He had been so engrossed that he had not noticed that his grandmother's coffee and Desmond's and his lemonade had arrived, along with a small selection of jam tarts. There were the usual red, green and yellow versions and he chose his favourite, the green one. The tarts were munched slowly as treats like this were quite rare and had to be savoured. Desmond, with Robbie beside him in the pushchair, nibbled slowly as he played with the baby's outstretched fingers. He remembered the times before the war when he alone had accompanied the old lady that he knew as Nana. Then they had enjoyed cream cakes and the sugar bowls had been kept filled to the brim by the same waitresses who now served the tables. These ladies were dressed in long maroon overalls over white blouses; small white aprons were around their middles, and each wore a frilly cap perched on her head. Into the rim of these they tucked their pencils whilst order pads dangled on small chains from their belts. Cakes and tarts were never touched but handled with tongs. The manageress, her much taller frilly cap the outward sign of rank, patrolled the tables and spoke quietly to her staff, reminding one for hot water, another for extra plates. Sometimes she re-aligned cutlery to her own insistence upon military exactitude. Gertrude approved this attention to detail and correctness.

Morning coffee over, the bill was paid, and a sixpence left for the waitress under nana's saucer. Down they trooped again, Desmond slowly controlling the pushchair. And then the walk back home with yet another stop to see the end of the morning's shunting ritual.

# CHRISTMAS DAY IN THE MORRISON SHELTER

That afternoon Jamie escaped yet again to his base camp to lengthen his 'tunnel' by a further two yards. He was delighted with his progress and thought that he was the only person in the whole world who knew of the tunnel's existence. In that he was mistaken. Desmond had noticed what was going on and, being a very dutiful elder brother, kept a keen eye on Jamie's doings. He would never dream of telling either of his parents unless it became obvious to him that the little fellow was getting into danger. He just kept a weather eye on proceedings and kept his own counsel. He knew that it would be fruitless to tell mother anyway; she would merely shrug and continue her life oblivious to both Desmond's and Jamie's lives, being truly aware only of Robert's needs. Desmond was, by sheer necessity, a very mature boy capable of cooking, cleaning, shopping and looking after his young brother. He was, in effect, Jamie's brother and father – father John being away for such long periods.

John arrived home on Christmas eve just as Jamie was going to bed. He gave his little son a fond hug and went upstairs to tuck him into the small bed. He longed to talk of the imminent arrival of Father Christmas but knew that it would be a waste of breath as Margaret had told the lad two years previously that this person did not exist. John could never fathom how his wife could live such an imaginary life herself but deny the harmless 'untruths' that would have so enriched the life of a little boy. Oh well; she was *different* and *special*. He would never contemplate mentioning these facts, far less criticise her for them.

Jamie was fast asleep when Desmond eventually went to bed. Just to be the tiniest bit perverse he pushed a tiny parcel under Jamie's pillow. John attended to Robert and eventually collapsed utterly exhausted into bed beside the already sleeping

Margaret. He so looked forward to his two days of peace and relaxation.


Christmas morning arrived wet and dismal with Jamie the first to awake. He tumbled out of bed and crept over to Desmond's bedside to peer at the old wind-up alarm clock on the bedside cabinet. Seven-thirty. He went into the bathroom to have a wash and to brush his teeth with his brush scraped across the block of hardened pink paste that tasted of mint. Then back to his bedroom to change from pyjamas into short trousers, shirt and pullover. He pulled on his socks but wore no shoes. In the house he went invariably without shoes or slippers. Folding up the pyjamas he was about to poke them under his pillow when his fingers encountered the tiny parcel. He took it out and peered in the half-light at the inscription.

'To Jamie. Happy Christmas from Desmond'.

He tore open the paper to reveal a small cardboard box. Inside the box was a badge made from stainless steel and on the badge was engraved a blackbird, Jamie's favourite. Desmond had fashioned this badge, with the pin on its back, during his metalwork classes. It had taken him many happy hours and was expertly made. Jamie loved it and pinned it to his pullover. He was about to wake his brother when the air-raid siren went off. He shouted for everyone to get up and galloped down the stairs and into the dining room. The dining table had long been removed and in its place stood the Morrison Shelter. Roughly the same dimensions as a large table it had a heavy steel top and mesh sides. It was supposed to keep a family reasonably safe if the house collapsed on top of them. John had put some old carpet on its steel floor as the family had to spend hours at a time within its confines. He clambered inside and went to the far-left corner – his usual position – and took up his picture book. Desmond, Margaret and John, the latter clutching the baby, came soon after and they squatted or lay in their accustomed places. Nobody spoke. This was a ritual to be endured, and it was now the sixty-first time that they had done it; the meticulous Desmond had counted! They had each of course spent many hours in other shelters – at schools, at other houses.

Jamie started his book afresh as he did at every air-raid. It was a large book entitled as 'The Pictorial History of the Saints'. His favourite was St. Patrick with his heavy staff, beating the snakes from Ireland and forever banishing them. Of lesser interest was St. George who killed dragons – which did not exist according to his mother. Quite interesting were St. Matthew collecting his taxes, St Luke mixing up potions and medicines, St. Francis leading hordes of strange animals and St. John who looked to Jamie to be rather feminine. John tried unsuccessfully to get a game of 'I spy' started but, after Jamie had baffled everyone with an 'A' for 'atmosphere' – and he had steadfastly refused to divulge this answer until everyone had 'given up' – the game was abandoned and a dull silence returned. There was the occasional far away 'crump' of an exploding bomb but their neighbourhood was to be mercifully spared anything nearer. At last, after a weary two and a half hours had passed. The 'all clear' sounded and they were able to finish dressing and to cross the road for a very belated Christmas breakfast at the bungalow.

The family was greeted, and porridge was re-heated before being served hot and steaming. Only grandfather, John, Desmond and Jamie had the cereal, whilst nana nibbled a piece of toast and Margaret sipped some cold milk. Daisy came in to clear the things away and then it was time for presents.

Amid 'oohs' and 'aaaahs' the parcels were unwrapped to reveal toys, puzzles, socks, ties, scarves and the usual 'thank you so much' and 'just what I needed'. Daisy who was always included got a lovely enamelled brooch and she was so overcome that she had to be comforted by a gracious Gertrude. After all, Daisy had been with the couple since before Margaret had been born and was treated as a part of the household – not quite a part of the family – that would never have done and Daisy herself would have been embarrassed if that had ever been mooted. Then it was time for Nana and Daisy to repair to the kitchen. Gertrude longed for a daughter who would eagerly share the preparation of the celebration lunch but Margaret seemed not to notice and remained in an armchair reading a fashion magazine.

Alfred told them all a ghost story. He was very adept at creating these and did all the spectral voices. Jamie was enthralled and followed every word. Desmond enjoyed the story and John enjoyed his little son's face as each new diabolical twist in the plot was revealed. Robert slept quietly on the long sofa, bolstered in by many cushions. Then it was John's turn. He told a story of an imaginary chase through the streets after a gang of desperate robbers had broken into a bank. It was almost fiction and was based upon the capture of a burglar some weeks before. Jamie again followed each dramatic turn in the embellished chase, with policemen taking cover whenever the gang turned with guns raised, gang members being apprehended one by one after heroic struggles by dedicated coppers, until all were safely under lock and key and the money returned to the strong room. Desmond, who had been practising it for weeks, turned a sheet of blank foolscap paper into a butterfly and was warmly applauded. Jamie was at a total loss what to do when it was his turn. He had known that he would be called upon to perform but had, in his usual way, procrastinated; and now it was too late.

However, he stood in front of them and sang a song about highwaymen, pirates and other less desirable characters; he had heard the old brigadier singing it to himself that afternoon in the bomb shelter. Blissfully unaware of the meaning of such phrases as 'walking the plank' and 'bloody robbery' he sang on and then took a bow. There was at first a stunned silence and then his grandfather started to clap, and the others joined in. They all knew that it was a totally innocent rendition, but Alfred was a trifle shocked, John knew he had to take his son aside one day; Desmond had had his vocabulary enhanced.

And then the gong sounded, and it was time to troop into the dining room for Christmas Lunch. As they were all trooping out of the sitting room Frederick and Amelia arrived and, after greetings and hugs had been exchanged and the newcomers' coats had been discarded, the family sat down to the feast that Jamie for one had been keenly anticipating for some days. Eight places had been set on the snowy linen cloth, eight places resplendent with the real silver cutlery that had been in Gertrude's side of the Clements family for two hundred years. The pieces sparkled and were reflected in the cut glass tumblers and wine goblets that were ranged in perfect line above the place mats. Alfred took his place at the far head of the table whilst Gertrude sat at the other end. Down one side were Amelia, Desmond and Frederick; down the other were John, Jamie and one place left vacant for the moment. Margaret took her glass of milk and placed it on a small table that stood beside an easy chair in the large window bay. She sat down and cuddled Robert to her; she had never, in Desmond's memory, sat at table with either her own or her extended family. Ordinary food had been vouchsafed since she was about sixteen years old and her parents had simply accepted the fact of her 'difference'. Desmond thought this very sad but knew that cajoling or remonstrating would be met equally with either sullen indifference or scornful dismissal. He held, as usual, his diplomatic peace and said nothing.

In covered tureens down the centre of the large table were roast potatoes, parsnips, sprouts and carrots. Sauce boats contained gravy, bread sauce and chopped chestnuts that gave off a delicious aroma. Then, through the curtained door came Daisy pushing the trolley. On its top surface stood a vast platter and thereon lay the wonderful goose, browned, steaming and cooked to perfection. She wheeled the trolley to the far end and, not without some considerable effort, placed it before Alfred, together with the bone-handled carving set that he favoured. Alfred gave a smile of thanks to the maid and asked her, please, to join them. Daisy, for whom the vacant place had already been set, would have waited forever before sitting unbidden in that place. She said her thanks and sat down beside Jamie, who reached over and gave her old hand a squeeze.

Alfred cleared his throat. "Let us all give thanks to the good Lord, and also to my dearest wife and to the inestimable Daisy, for the food that we are about to receive".

A subdued chorus of 'Amen's' preceded the ritual sharpening of the carving knife, Alfred from years of practise being adept at this function. Then the goose was carved and placed in wonderfully thin slices from the plump breast on to plates which were passed down to eager recipients. Vegetables were spooned on to plates and sauces chosen before Alfred allowed 'eating may now commence, good folk'. At this Jamie tucked in with a will, savouring the wondrous delicacy of roasted goose for the first time in his life. A distant relative of the Clements farmed in Lincolnshire, not far from the massive bomber base at Scranton. Every year without fail he dispatched either a brace of ducks or a large goose to various favoured relatives but, for the previous two years had been unable to supply the more popular goose as demands on his time (and the added demands of the Ministry of Food) had allowed only the rearing of the much less troublesome ducks. This particular goose had arrived by carrier only the previous day and Daisy had spent hours plucking, gutting and preparing the bird for the oven. It had taken four hours to cook, the result being generally acclaimed a crowning success by all. Gertrude and Daisy glowed with pleasure.

Happy chatter accompanied the meal, Jamie ever mindful that he kept his elbows off the table and his mouth empty of food before he spoke. As the last forkful was swallowed, he could contain himself no longer.

"Cor, that was absolutely super!" he said, reclining against the chair back.

"Wonderful dinner, thank you Nana", added Desmond.

"Such a wonderful treat", agreed John.

"Dearest Gertrude, a triumph as ever!" said Amelia, whilst Frederick added that, 'as I understand modern parlance, spiffing seems to be the appropriate adjective'.

Jamie, the most ebullient of the assembled company, could bear the suspense longer.

"Will there be Christmas Pudding, Nana?"

Gertrude turned a thankful face to her grandson. "Of course, there will be Christmas Pudding, young Jamie", she replied. "First, let us clear all this away".

Daisy and Gertrude started to pile the tureens on the second tier of the trolley whilst Desmond went around the table collecting plates and used cutlery which he added to the lowest shelf. The laden trolley disappeared into the hall, through the morning room and into the kitchen. The uneaten parts of the goose were placed on a smaller platter that was then covered with a mesh dome that fitted into the rim. This was put on the cold shelf in the larder. Vegetables were heaped together into one of the tureens and similarly placed. Desmond meanwhile piled plates and cutlery on the wooden draining board to await the washing up session that would not happen for some time yet.

Eventually Daisy brought in the steaming pudding and placed it, as the goose before it, in front of Alfred. He went to the massive mahogany sideboard and took from the zinc-lined cupboard, a bottle of brandy and measured half a wineglass full, letting the amber liquid dribble over the exactly spherical creation. Taking a wooden spill from the mantelpiece he lit it from the fire and set the pudding alight. Jamie watched in fascination as the blue flames licked up from the base until the whole pudding seemed engulfed in the softness of fire. The flames died down and Alfred took knife and spoon and started to serve portions which were again passed round. Custard was spooned over the plates, cream being in such short supply as to make it virtually impossible to acquire. Desmond, who had a particularly sweet tooth, ate slowly so as to relish each precious mouthful. Jamie simply wolfed his down and again spoke of his admiration for 'the super pud'. All was restored to harmony except for the one person who had remained apart and aloof from the celebrations. Margaret had finished her milk and was now slowly nibbling her way through an arrowroot biscuit as she cradled the blissfully slumbering baby.

Desmond again helped to clear away the plates, spoons and forks. Jamie crept out to the kitchen to see if his luck was in; would he be allowed to scrape out the custard jug? His Nana had already placed this in the larder when she saw his face.

"Would you like to eat this up?" she enquired.

"Ooooooh yes please, Nana".

Jamie seized a spoon and set to work, cleaning every last little bit from then jug. His attention was drawn again to the larder and the large crockery bowl that contained cold water and a little isinglass powder. Eggs were put into this mixture as it was supposed to lengthen the life of those precious and very scarce items. Jamie knew that if he inserted his hand into the water if would feel 'funny', as if all air was excluded from the liquid. Now and again an egg would bob up to the surface and would immediately be returned to the shop as 'bad'. He surreptitiously dipped a finger into the water. It seemed to go all dead after a few seconds, so he withdrew it and wiped the moisture on his trousers. He galloped back to the dining room where all not concerned with the aftermath of the dinner were preparing to return to the sitting room and coffee. That was again a rarity; Gertrude well knew that the previous day's shopping expedition had been enhanced by the smell of the roasting beans. Before the war the coffee shop roasted beans every day – pale, medium and dark roasts ready for customers' choices before being ground and packeted. Nowadays, roasting took place once a fortnight on average – whenever a shipload was lucky enough to reach Bristol or Liverpool after its hazardous Atlantic crossing. However, today would see a portion of their dwindling supply brewed in the silver pot.

Cups and saucers were handed around and coffee poured and savoured without another precious commodity being added – sugar was in very short supply as well. Jamie drank his lemonade whilst Desmond favoured cream soda.

Then it was time for the next Christmas ritual, a game of pass the parcel. Gertrude fetched this from her own room. It was a very large parcel wrapped in layer after layer of old brown paper. She would never countenance newspaper as a succession of fingers would be smudged in the newsprint and this inevitably transferred to clothes and her precious moquette upholstery.

Alfred wound up the gramophone and stood by, a twelve-inch record in place on the turntable. He had chosen an old favourite – the Road to the Isles by Harry Lauder. He started the record and placed the needle carefully on the outer groove. Round went the parcel until he took the playing head off. One layer of paper was removed – no present! On and on again until, with calculated accuracy, the final unwrapping was performed by Gertrude herself. This revealed a cardboard box, within which were separately wrapped little presents for each member. These were individually labelled and passed round to be eagerly opened. Jamie's contained a little diary, leather covered and with a brass catch and lock. He was delighted and rushed over to give a huge kiss to his nana. In fact, everyone received a similar diary and these were enthusiastically received. Even Margaret had deigned to join in this game and her thanks seemed as genuine as any. Happy times!

By now dusk had fallen and Frederick and Amelia thought that it was time to say their goodbyes. They went down the shallow steps to the road muffled up in coats and scarves for the short, five-minute walk to their own home. John thought that it was about time that his family made tracks as well and dropped the hint to them as they went back to the sitting room. Jamie, who had been looking forward to another of granddad's ghost stories, pulled a long face but obediently went to the hall to fetch their coats. Desmond took his mother's long fur and held it for her as she shrugged into the sleeves. He dressed Robert for the cold and strapped the little chap into the pushchair for the journey down the road.

A full moon greeted them as they waved and said their farewells, adding profuse thanks for a lovely day. There was a quite bitter wind blowing from the north and, as this was their direction, felt quite chilled as they walked in silence. John, on the rare occasions that Margaret accompanied them, took his wife's arm to ensure that she did not stumble. Her self-imposed diet did nothing for her strength and well-being, so he was always ready to support her if necessary. He unlocked their own front door and Desmond hurried to the kitchen to prepare three mugs of cocoa to warm them up. He also poured his mother a glass of milk and put this on the small table by the side of her armchair. Margaret settled herself against the cushions with a sigh of relief; she thought that the day had been rather tiring and wanted little more than to be fussed over before she announced that she was for an early night. Her high-heeled shoes rested on a carved footstool and she was moderately content.

John and the two eldest boys sipped their cocoa and discussed the separate ingredients of that wonderful dinner. Jamie said that his favourite part of all was the roast potatoes whilst both John and Desmond settled on the goose. John went out to the kitchen to warm Robert's bottle which was made up from a tin of baby milk powder and previously boiled water. He took the warm bundle on to his lap and enjoyed the rare pleasure of feeding his youngest. Quiet contentment reigned, punctuated slightly by the gurglings and sucking noises from the baby.

John then indulged himself in yet another rare treat, taking Robert upstairs to give him a change and to put him into his night clothes, a one-piece creation with rabbits dotted all over it. He hugged the child tightly and looked lovingly into the huge blue eyes and marvelled at the little mouth seemingly curved in a happy smile. He thought again of the other photograph in his wallet – of his two eldest that he had not seen for some months now. On rare occasions he was able to hop on a tram or a bus directly from work and go to see them with their adoptive parents. They were always happy to see him, and it tore at his heart to leave them again. Still, they were in a very good home and being looked after by very good people who lavished care and love on them in equal measure. Valerie, now nearly sixteen years old, was doing very well and would start secretarial college after the coming summer break. She was now an inch taller that her real father and was developing into a lovely young lady; she clung to him and was tearful when it was time for him to go. Peter, two years younger, was short and quiet. He deeply resented his father for what he saw as an unforgivable abandonment and kept all his love for his adopted parents. He was showing signs of brilliance at languages and the couple had high hopes for an eventual university place when he had gained the necessary passes. John saw his dead first wife very clearly in Peter's growing features and felt infinite sadness for what had been. He always left with a lump in his throat and deliberately walked back to the bus over Streatham Common where he could weep silently and unobserved. He knew that his devotion to his new wife was far too deep but could not help himself. She was like a goddess to him.

Carrying a full, clean and warm baby in his arms he had reached the foot of the stairs when there it was again, the air-raid siren. The family once again settled into the Morrison Shelter. Jamie opened his book and studied the picture of St.

Peter who was shown holding a massive key and standing on a huge rock. He could never remember why and asked for the fourth time in as many weeks.

"Well", began his father. "St. Peter was chosen by Jesus to be the head of his church and his name really means 'rock'".

"Yes, but what's the key for?"

"It is supposed to be for the gates of heaven", said John patiently. "Jesus apparently chose Peter to open those gates only to people who had lived good lives and were worthy to go into paradise".

"But how would St. Peter know? After all, hundreds of people would have died and would want to get in. How did he know if each one had been good?"

John looked over at his wife, but her gaze was fixed upon distant spot. No help there!

"I suppose all the angels kept a record of each person's life and told him whether that one could get in".

"OK, but what happens to those who can't get in – they would be very cross, wouldn't they?"

"They would have to go into a waiting area; I think it's called purgatory", said John knowing full well that this would not end the matter.

"What would they do there and how long would they have to stay in it?"

"This is a place where the bad and naughty people go so that they can be made sorry for their bad lives and so can earn a place eventually".

"But, if they are dead, how can they do good things and make their lives better. After all, their lives are all done with and they can't really do anything anymore, can they!"

John realised, not for the first time, that he was not cut out for this kind of conversation. He would lose and leave behind an even more confused child. However, it could not be dodged, and he manfully did his best.

"Well, God is very powerful and can read their thoughts and when he saw that a dead person was really sorry enough, he would instruct St. Peter to let that person in".

"Wow!" said Jamie. "Can He read my thoughts now?"

"Of course, He can", John said with all the conviction that he could muster. He was not in the slightest religious but knew that, as his children received instruction in those studies, he could not undermine them. Apart from that, Margaret and her parents went weekly to church - and he was fiercely loyal to her wishes.

"Cor! What happens to me when I have nasty thoughts and do naughty things while I'm alive – are they all put down in my book by an angel?"

"I'm sure that you are seldom naughty enough to warrant that", said John with a laugh.

"I bet I am!" said Jamie, thinking that his courage was being questioned. "I often do naughty things, don't I, Desmond?"

Desmond refused to be drawn and pretended a keen interest in his fingernails.

"I can do very naughty things when I want to!" Jamie thought that he was being dismissed as a 'goody-goody' and that would never do at all.

John realised that he was probably stepping into a minefield but could not help himself enquiring, "What very naughty things have you done, then?"

Jamie thought long and hard, Would the story of the apples and the brigadier get him into trouble? He thought this a bit too risky and chose a lesser misdemeanour with which to prove his point.

"The other day at school I whacked Sammy Hawkins over the head with my ruler!" he announced defiantly.

"Why?" asked John.

"Well, he pinched a pencil out of my satchel and would not give it back; so, I made him!"

"It sounds to me as if Sammy asked for it", said the sergeant judiciously.

"Yes, he jolly well did and I'm sorry that I only gave him one whack. But, will God think that was bad enough to be put down in my book?"

"No, I doubt that", replied John who was feeling somewhat relieved at the relative insignificance of this 'sin'. He fervently hoped that the topic of conversation would change. As if in answer to this prayer came the sound of falling bombs and this was followed by the inevitable question of where they had exploded.

"Sounds over to the east to me", John opined.

"I'll bet that they fell in the beeches again", said Desmond who has seen the craters made by a stick that had fallen the previous week. Many trees had been felled and some were reduced almost to matchwood.

"What would happen if they fell in the pond?" wondered Jamie. The 'pond' was situated about a quarter mile distant and separated the old council depot from the main road. Jamie often watched the dust carts coming and going and thought it would be great to be old enough to drive one of the old steam Fodens that snorted through the streets.

Nobody had a clear answer to that.

The 'all-clear' sounded just after nine o'clock and the family clambered thankfully from their cage. Jamie made ready for bed. He could not wait for the first day of nineteen forty-four when he would start putting things into his new diary. Desmond did the washing up. Meanwhile, Margaret had gone upstairs after giving effusive kisses to all but her husband. John seemed not to notice – he was used to it. An hour later all were in bed and the lights were extinguished as peace settled.

John gave a final and very silent 'Happy Christmas' to his two children some ten miles to the north of where he lay.

Robert slept quietly in his cot and dreamed not at all.

Margaret conjured up the thought of a strong and silent admirer and thought longing thoughts.

Desmond thought about how he was going to construct a sledge for Jamie. Snow was being forecast and he wanted his creation to be ready.

Christmas Day had been super, thought Jamie as he drifted off to sleep. The hours in the Morrison were forgotten.

# NEWS BULLETINS AND BIRTHDAYS

John sat down in his favourite armchair and switched on the Pye wireless set. Early morning light was beginning to filter through the window, and he sipped at his tea and waited for the valves in the set to warm up. Music of a very sombre nature came from the loudspeaker that was situated behind a finely meshed cover. The set, a wedding present to John and Margaret, was quite a large affair, a cabinet nearly three feet in height, and two feet in width and depth. Its case was constructed from a variety of woods with golden oak predominant in the pattern of sunrays that centred on the circle of the speaker. John turned down the volume and waited patiently for the early morning news.

An announcer, after a few last minutes of the music said in the clipped tones of the BBC, '*thet* was 'Moonlight' played on *thet* recording by the BBC Show *Bend*'.

Then, after a longish pause, came the pips of the Greenwich time-signal and the programme that he had been waiting for.

'This is the BBC Home Service; here is the news at seven o'clock', came the deep and perfectly modulated voice of his favourite newsreader.

He listened as the latest from the Italian campaign was explained; the battle for the monastery of Monte Cassino was still raging – apparently the devastating bombing by the Americans had not made the job of assaulting this high citadel any easier and the Polish troops were still massing for yet another onslaught. Still, progress of a sort was being made. Apparently, a large convoy of merchant ships had crossed the North Atlantic with minimal losses – a cause for some celebration. John had met Commander (then a lieutenant-commander) Duncan Bedford before the war and the headmistress's husband had impressed him as a very steadfast chap. He hoped that this was not the signal for an announcement of losses among the escorting ships. The

Russians were, reportedly, making further progress after the miracles of Leningrad and Stalingrad. John took all this with a very large pinch of salt. God alone knew what was the real state of play on the Eastern Front. Most of it, he was sure, was mere conjecture mixed with a heavy dose of wishful thinking. From his own experiences in nineteen seventeen he distrusted the Russians who had opted out of their efforts against Germany to kill their own royal family, most of their generals and a large proportion of the aristocracy – all in the name of so-called socialism. John loathed socialism; some years before, he had literally made himself read Das Kapital and had marvelled at the inconsistencies and rabid stupidity (as he saw it) of its author – a disaffected German who had the effrontery to be memorialised in Highgate Cemetery, occupying a very prominent and undeserved plot. John, although from very humble background – plus his dreadful treatment after World War I by a despicable government – was a staunch Conservative, in his case with a very large capital 'C'.

The litany of war theatres ground on – the Far East theatre where the Americans seemed to be doing everything possible to turn possible victory into vainglorious defeat – the largely supposed situation of German industry, pounded nightly by Bomber Command (more wishful thinking, John mused) – the promise of internal upheaval by the French when the time came. Home front news was sparse; snow predicted for the Highlands, floods for the North East, stricter rationing for some foodstuffs and a slight easing of the rationing on petrol. On the whole, thought John, fairly good news for a change!

A noise like boulders avalanching down a hillside announced the descent of Jamie from the landing. He shot into the sitting room and literally nose-dived into his father's waiting arms.

"Happy birthday, Jamie", said that proud man. It was early March and Jamie was now five years old. His whirlwind progress through life seemed to gather momentum as the weeks went by. Never a lad for quiet and orderly progress, he was now becoming something in the nature of a fast-moving hurricane – a mass of wild enthusiasm and, to his father's and Desmond's minds, wildly impulsive. He was, dreaded John, due for a bumpy passage through life. However, there was never any doubting his good intentions.

He turned his snub-nosed, freckled face up to gaze earnestly and hopefully at his parent.

"Please say you'll be here all day – will mum be down soon? – Desmond has a lot of homework but he promised to play with me – you *will* be here today, won't you dad?"

The words tumbled out in wild confusion.

John patted the unruly ginger curls.

"Yes, old chap, I'll be here all day and your mother will be down soon. Now, how about I make you a special birthday breakfast and then we'll see about getting Robert down as well".

Breakfast was to be a precious boiled egg and toast soldiers with real butter, albeit spread somewhat thinly. Jamie accompanied his father into the kitchen and hopped from one foot to the other as he impatiently awaited his treat. Desmond came in and started to prepare his and his father's porridge.

Jamie sat at the kitchen table and, with teaspoon in hand, gently cracked the dome top of his precious egg. Then, using a finger, detached the small pieces of shell until a tonsure of cooked egg-white had emerged from the speckly brown casing. He scooped the white on to his spoon and ate it with a massive bite from a piece of toast, Mouth full and chomping happily, he surveyed the bright yellow yolk –all runny and wonderful. A new 'soldier' was dipped in, and the resultant sticky toast transferred to mouth. Delicious!

John went into the dining room and brought out a small pile of parcels and put these next to Jamie's plate. There were five of them and had been wrapped in carefully preserved and recycled paper from previous birthdays. Jamie's eyes grew large and he eagerly took the first one. He knew that he had to be careful with the paper and so he delicately unpicked the knot in the string and gave it to Desmond who furled it into a small shank to be stored in the string box. The first unwrapped parcel, the smallest and therefore the top of the pile, proved to contain a small box in which was a perfectly printed card and an object wrapped in tissue paper. It was a viewer , a pocket microscope that folded flat, the two eyepieces when opened being about four inches from the base-plate which would contain the object specimen. The card was in perfectly formed copperplate, 'to Jamie with all best wishes from your Nunky and Noony – I have some slides for you!'

Jamie thought that this was the most perfect present and proudly showed it off to his father and brother.

"You'll have to pop up and see them later this morning and say thank you. Wonder what the slides are?" said John.

"Yes dad, I will". Jamie scampered up the stairs to show off his new possession to his mother. Margaret, most unusually for her at this early hour, was dressed and ready to come down. She tried hard to show interest as Jamie's wild enthusiasm was so infectious.

"Very nice, dear", she said accompanying her galloping child downstairs, the still sleeping Robert in her arms.

Jamie opened the other presents. Next was another, slightly larger, box. Desmond had made this from scraps of wood carefully preserved from carpentry classes. He had fashioned a box for pencils, pens, rubbers and so forth. The top slid perfectly along beautifully routed slots and was etched with Jamie's initials.

"Cor, JAS – Jamie Alfred Small! Thanks Desmond, it is really super!" He shot over to his big brother to give him a fierce, manly hug.

Then came a slightly larger parcel from his Nana and Granddad. It was a new pullover and had been knitted in red with a white 'V' collar – the colours of his favourite football team – Arsenal. On the right breast were his initials again, this time sewn in white silk thread. Jamie was hopping with excitement as he shed his old garment and pulled the new one on.

"Well", said John. "That's another call you must make this morning!"

"Surely, he should write proper letters of thanks!" said Margaret. Desmond noted with some sadness how this remark was addressed, not to her son, but to the world at large – as if someone else should have the chore of carrying the message to its correct recipient.

"Oh, I'm sure that nobody would expect that; after all, he's only five", said John, knowing full well that this would ensure that proper letters *were* written.

"I jolly well can, Dad!" exploded Jamie in self-righteous indignation. How dare anyone think that he couldn't write a proper letter!

John winked at Desmond, who turned away to have a silent chuckle.

Then came a parcel that was even larger. It contained a wooden model sailing ship, complete with halliards, sails and a working rudder. Jamie was overjoyed as his best friend from school, one Matthew Hartley, had one and Jamie had been ferociously jealous ever since they had gone to the nearby pond to sail it. Jamie hugged his Mum and Dad.

"That couldn't be a better present", he stuttered between embraces. "Matty will be ever so jealous as mine has two masts and three sails. I bet it will beat the pants off his little boat!"

The final present had been prepared by John some weeks before. It was a large, flat parcel and contained a huge book of outline pictures for Jamie to colour in. John had addressed it as coming from little Robert. Jamie went over to his mother and planted a small kiss on Robert's slumbering head.

"Shall I write letters to you and mum and Desmond and Robert?" he asked, sensing a rather large task ahead of him.

"No, we will not need letters. Just write a quick 'thank you' to Nana, Granddad, Nunky and Noony and take them with you. Just two letters will be quite enough", John replied.

Managing, but only just, to stifle a massive sigh of relief, Jamie shot up the stairs to get two pieces of paper and a pencil. He shot down again and sat himself at the dining room table. He managed to produce two almost identical letters of thanks (complete with two identical spelling mistakes) and asked for envelopes. Desmond fetched them for him and these were correctly addressed, the letters inserted and gummed down. There, he had done it - and all accomplished in under half an hour!

He went out to the shed to look again at the sledge that Robert had made for him. His brother had managed to salvage the timber and had fashioned two curved steel runners.

Unfortunately, snow had come at the end of January and had lasted a mere three days. Still, Desmond had taken him one weekend to Hartley Down, an area of common land about a mile distant. It had one very long grassy slope and the two boys had taken it in turns to career down the snowy expanse amid a host of other excited children – and not a few equally excited fathers! Desmond had presented the splendid sledge to Jamie and had painted a name on its side – 'The Small Flyer'. Desmond had fashioned the runners so that the fronts hinged slightly inwards when the cords were pulled – thus acting as a brake. He had thought this design out quite carefully and had created a set of blueprints that were now in his folder to be presented as a part of his body of work later in year. Jamie thought it quite wonderful. How many other boys had such a clever brother, he wondered?

It had been planned some days before that Jamie would have a small birthday party and he had readily accepted with the proviso that, as he had only two special friends, these would be the only guests. John, ever mindful of the expense and the scarcity of food, had readily agreed. The two boys were expected at about three o'clock, air raids permitting. He also thought about a proposal made by Alfred and Gertrude some weeks previously. Julia Forbes had heard Jamie play the piano a few more times and had been so impressed that she had written to the grandparents. She had deliberately not written to Margaret as, after consultation with Mrs. Bedford, had been told that the old couple paid the school fees and also that writing to the mother would be a waste of time. Alfred had called on them and had suggested that, as Jamie showed such promise, they would be more than happy to fund proper piano lessons and had already found a good tutor. John had mentioned it to his wife and Margaret had appeared uncharacteristically enthusiastic at the prospect; perhaps, John thought with a twinge of guilt, Margaret saw some kudos in it all. He hated himself for such disloyal thoughts – but they came to him from time to time.

Never for an instant did he think of mentioning it to Jamie; he imagined the pleasure on that freckled face and the keen anticipation to get going now!

When Jamie came in from the shed for a drink of water John said that there was something that he and his mother needed to tell him. Jamie, with thoughts of a possible extra present or treat, galloped into the sitting room and sat cross-legged on the floor. Desmond, privy to the secret, stood by the window. Robert tried to crawl around the carpet and made funny noises.

"Look, old chap", started John. "Miss Forbes has told us that she thinks you have a gift for music and that you need to be professionally taught. So, your grandparents have agreed to pay for lessons for six months to see how you get on. Now, what do you think of that?"

Expecting a whoop of joy, they were all a trifle amazed at Jamie's response. His face puckered into a frown. He loved playing the piano but was not at all sure about the regimentation that 'proper' lessons would impose. After all, he loved reading but hated the confines and discipline of the classroom sessions. He could already read, so why did anyone need to teach him? Similarly, he could find his way around any tune and could pick it out for himself; he did indeed have a gift for music, but it was a gift of absolute harmonic recall – an ability to reconstruct the notes of a tune once he had heard and remembered it, and to hear in his head the accompanying harmonies. He, of course, did not know all this; he simply knew that he could do it.

"Who would I have to go to?" he asked.

"Well, you know the Worthys at number 61?"

Jamie nodded. Mr and Mrs Worthy were about the same age as his own parents and had two children – Tina who was two years older than him and Ronald who was just one year older. He thought that Tina was beautiful, and that Ronald was a swot.

"Mrs Worthy is a music teacher and takes the occasional private pupil, So, it wouldn't be all that far to go, would it?"

Jamie thought some more. It could be quite fun, he supposed – and he would be able to see seven-year-old Tina of the long, blonde ringlets and the sparkly blue eyes. Yes, that clinched it!

"Thanks Dad, that would be super!" he said.

After lunch, a plate of meagre sandwiches 'filled' with scrapes of Marmite and bloater paste, Desmond and John repaired to the kitchen to prepare the birthday tea. Jamie scampered off with his two letters. John made a jelly from a packet of crystals that had been in the cupboard for a short time – not long enough, he hoped, to stop them from setting once he had poured them into a metal mould and added the boiling water. After vigorous stirring he had covered the mould with a piece of muslin and placed it on the cold marble shelf in the larder. Desmond made 'special' sandwiches from a jar of fish paste (provided by nana) and from a pot of raspberry jam (made and provided by great-aunt Amelia). That strict and upright lady had also provided a sponge cake which Desmond spread with a mixture of icing sugar (a rare commodity) and water. He kept back a small amount of the icing and added a drop of the raspberry jam. The resultant pink paste he used to fashion 'Happy Birthday Jamie'. This was also set on the marble shelf.

Jamie arrived first at his grandparent's house. He was admitted by Daisy who gave him a hug and wished him 'many happy returns'. Gravely he offered the little letter to his Nana who, with Alfred looking over her shoulder, just as gravely opened the envelope and withdrew the small piece of writing paper. She read the letter aloud.

'Dear Nana and Granddad', she said. 'Thank you ever so much for my luvely puulover – it is a super present and I luv it so much. Yor luving grandson Jamie'.

"What a very gracious letter!" she exclaimed and offered her thin arms for the expected hug. Alfred was still able, just, to lift the stocky little chap and to clasp him to his chest.

"And now, I suppose", continued his Nana. "You would like nothing better than a rock cake!"

Jamie took the proffered object and nibbled at it, words of thanks being slightly muffled through the crumbs. Gertrude decided that, as it was his birthday, to overlook this lapse of manners for once. Jamie munched contentedly. Life was quite super at times, he thought.

Saying a polite 'goodbye' he shot off again to see his Nunky and Noony. As usual, he arrived breathless and beat a loud tattoo on the brass knocker. He presented his second letter to the old couple and listened as Amelia read it out.

'Thank you ever so much for my luvely vyooer – it is a super present and I luv it so much. Yor luving Jamie'.

Amelia, to her everlasting credit, refrained from comment upon the spelling – after all, he *was* only five years old! She supposed from her long life of inexperience with children, that it was not *too* bad an effort! She almost gasped aloud as her spare and ageing frame was crushed in a fierce hug of thanks. Nunky, more generously upholstered, suffered less and was once more amazed at the exuberance of this small boy whom he had come to love and cherish.

Nunky handed him a small packet and Jamie opened it to reveal ten delicate slides to put into his new 'vyooer'. He was very excited and, wrapping the tiny packet carefully in a not-too-clean hanky, thrust it into the inside pocket of his jacket. He would spend a happy hour later that evening looking at them. His Nunky had stuck a miniscule label on the bottom of each slide that told of its content.

Bidding the old pair farewell Jamie shot off again. Instead of going down the short hill directly to his home he turned left and went up the remainder of the short road to where it did a sharp left turn before ending in a wooded path. Jamie slowed down and sauntered along the path, hands thrust deeply into pockets. Horse chestnuts were starting to show their 'sticky buds'; hawthorns were showing various beginnings of pink and white; lime trees had a greeny-yellow tinge. The sun shone and Jamie was blissfully happy. His friends would be coming soon for his small party and all was right in an all-right world. At the end of the path the way descended to Farthingdown Road by means of a set of steps constructed from old, tarred railway sleepers. Jamie hopped down them, trying to keep balance on his right leg. Somehow, this dangerous manoeuvre accomplished, he arrived at the bottom and, turning left again, walked past large villas set detached in their grounds. Laurel and privet hedges abounded and Jamie thrust his ginger head into each, looking for signs of the new season's nest building. He was rewarded at last by a pair of thrushes busy fashioning their cosy home. He was squawked at as the birds beat a hasty retreat. Not wishing to disturb their efforts he withdrew his head and noted the place. He would come back in a few weeks time to see progress; perhaps by then there would be a clutch of speckled eggs for him to see.

Jamie was only truly in his element outdoors. Being confined to a classroom for hours at a time frustrated him. Mrs Bedford and Miss Forbes knew this only too well; but to have moved him from his window seat, would have only exacerbated the problem and they were reasonably content to let him gaze longingly through the glass whilst, at the same time, apparently able to absorb the minimum of instruction to satisfy a slow progress through the mysteries of his lessons. His knowledge of the basics of arithmetic, English, history and RI were perfunctory. His knowledge of the flora and fauna was, for his age, quite exceptional. To get him to utter a coherent sentence on the Norman Conquest was virtually impossible; to hear him talk excitedly on the differences between the nests of hedgerow birds was a small education in itself. He knew the habits of hedgehogs, rabbits and foxes; knew the various hunting characteristics of owl, hawk and falcon; could read the spoor marks that traced through a wood – and all from direct observation, driven by an insatiable thirst for such knowledge. He had little or no interest in the subjects that he was told would 'benefit' him in later life; they were *boring*! He was becoming a bit of a 'loner' as his interests were not shared by most of his friends – some of whom thought him a bit 'weird'. They had all-consuming interests in football, guns, cowboys, Indians and the host of other distractions for the more 'normal' of their age-group. Admittedly, Jamie had a love for the Arsenal – he had no idea why this team! Similarly, his father had a love for Tottenham Hotspur, although being brought up much nearer to West Ham and/or Charlton Athletic. John could not have explained his infatuation with the North London team any more than Jamie could elucidate his fascination with the Gunners.

At the junction of Farthingdown Road with the north end of Buttermere Gardens was the pond that Jamie frequented and on whose surface he was determined to demonstrate the superiority of his newly acquired boat. He wriggled through the metal posts and started a clockwise examination for frogs and newts. He was barely half -way round when the air-raid siren started its miserable wailing.

"Bugger it!" he said – an unfortunate phrase picked up from his frequent conversations with old Albert, caretaker of Brooke Hill Preparatory School for Boys.

What to do? He was about equidistant from his own home and the house of his old Nunky. He decided that his father and brother would be somewhat happier to see him safely home and he started to run thither as he heard the far off droning of what he knew to be Dornier bombers. He was well able to differentiate between the engine sounds of these and Heinkels, Wellingtons from Halifaxes and Lancasters, whilst Hurricanes and Spitfires were easily told from Messerschmitts.

He shot past the pig bin, into which the good citizens were exhorted to put any food waste. This was collected by a local farmer who mixed it with water and fed it to the litters of piglets that would eventually be sold for good money to the butchers/slaughterers who could then charge even more for their delicacies.

He arrived at his home and flew through the back door and nose-dived into the Morrison shelter. His father gave him a look of relief and Desmond asked him where he had been.

"Went to Nana's and Nunky's to give them my letters", Jamie gulped in air.

Margaret, cuddling Robert, seemed unaware of Jamie's presence, indeed had not even remarked upon his earlier absence.

Jamie remembered his new slides and took them out to show his brother. Desmond was quite interested as, among the tiny bones and feathers, were two of slivers of wood. He wondered what they would show him when greatly magnified. One was labelled 'Indian Teak' and the other 'Elm'. He was very interested to study the fibres as his knowledge of the various stress characteristics of different woods was minimal. He *needed* to know more. He wondered if Nunky had other examples.

Margaret *had* noticed Jamie's absence. She had long thought that this self-contained little boy needed little or no help from her. She was quite proud of her son and his, at times, hare-brained exploits. She saw him growing up as an intrepid explorer – a romantic re-birth of one of her imagined heroes.

However, she was totally absorbed in her baby, who she saw as 'delicate'. In fact, Robert was as healthy a baby as anyone could have wished. Margaret 'wanted to be needed' and looked upon her youngest as the perfect outlet for this. Her thoughts for her husband were dichotomous to say the least. She knew perfectly well that he saw her as a goddess, was slavishly devoted, and could not help feelings of both contentment and contempt at this manifestation.

She was immensely proud of the 'breeding' from which she came; the expensive education, the perfect manners that emanated from comparative monetary comfort of her parents and relatives. She knew her 'place' in the great scheme of things and had little respect for those whose 'places' were even slightly lower down the ladder. She had long disregarded Desmond as being the product of one of these 'lower' echelons and treated him with the same aloofness with which she had always treated Daisy, her parents' maid. Her mother and father *never* treated Daisy, or anyone else for that matter, with anything other than kindly affection. Margaret had interpreted this as well-meant condescension! She had forbidden mention of John's previous marriage and its offspring. John, miserably aware of his failings in that quarter, had acquiesced and her parents and other relatives had, to their shame, done the same lest the fractious young woman do something that they might all regret. It seemed to them to be the lesser of the two available evils.

The raid proved to be of mercifully short duration and the family resumed their 'normal' life as the all-clear sounded.

Soon after this there came a knock at the door and Jamie's two friends presented themselves for the party.

Matthew Hartley and Tommy Allen, respectively best and second-best friend, solemnly shook hands with Margaret and John and thanked them politely for being asked. They were shown all the presents.

"Cor, that new boat will beat my old one!" said Matthew, determined to seek an update of his own, superseded, possession.

Tommy, a very studious boy who had no interest in boats, water or other sporting pursuits, was bored. His only interest was in reading the exploits of adventurers and explorers. In that, he had found some common ground with Jamie who loved exploring for himself.

They all tucked into the tea and, faces smeared liberally with jam and icing, were ushered to the sink for a thorough clean-up. Then it was time for games. Desmond had made two props, the first one being a pointer that whizzed round on a small vertical shaft. The three boys sat down on the carpet, the pointer in the middle. Desmond gave it a twirl and it stopped pointing at Matthew. This lad was then given the second prop. It was another revolving pointer that had an octagonal base, on which were inscribed eight different subjects. Matthew spun it and it came to rest at the legend, 'a game that I like'. So, Matthew had to speak for two minutes on that subject, Desmond consulting an old pocket watch and, as its second hand came to twelve, said 'GO!'

"Well", began Matthew. "The game I like is cricket. It is for two teams and each team has eleven players. They toss up for who bats first. The other side is put into the field. The first two of the batters come in and the bowler bowls six times for an over".

Tommy, by this time, was totally perplexed. He started to form a question but Desmond 'shushed' him so that Matthew could finish.

"Well", that lad continued, with a fierce look at the unfortunate Tommy. "If the batter hits the ball, they run between the wickets to score runs. Then they change ends and another bowler has a go. If the ball hits the stumps the batter is out. If a fielder catches the ball straight from the batter then he's out too. If the ball hits the batter on the leg and his leg is in front of the stumps then he's out LBW".

Tommy had completely given up by this time.

"If the ball goes over the boundary on the ground then it's a four; but, if it goes over without bouncing, then it's a six. When all the batters are out then they swap and the batters are the fielders and the fielders become the batters. When all of *them* are out then they tot up the runs and the winners are the side with the biggest score. The end!"

Matthew sat down to receive polite applause from John, Margaret (who had understood quite a bit of it), Desmond who had understood it all (but had no love for that arcane pastime), Jamie whose thoughts had been elsewhere and Tommy, who was a well-mannered lad.

"One minute and forty-seven seconds", announced Desmond.

The pointers were again put to use. This time it alighted at Jamie and the subject was 'how to make a cake'. Jamie stood up and prepared to give what to him would be a piercingly funny performance. He gave a slight cough.

"First, you get a very big bowl and put some flour in. Then you get some margarine and start to mix it all together". He knew that he was on safe ground with this opening as he had watched his Nana do it on numerous occasions. Before the war she would have used butter, never the dreaded margarine. But Jamie did not know that.

"Next you get some currants and mix them in as well. Now comes the really nice part. You go out into the garden and get some slugs which you squash flat".

Matthew and Tommy pulled faces and went, "Yuk!"

Desmond, not for the first time, experienced a sense of disappointment with his brother. He had thought out a very sensible game and had fondly imagined that five-year-olds would treat it with the gravitas with which he himself approached every task – and, whilst Matthew had had a very good go at it, here was his own brother playing the fool.

Margaret had not been listening; she was on all fours playing with her crawling baby, for Robert had at last mastered this elementary method of perambulation and was, as she called it, 'into everything'.

John had turned away to smother a chuckle. He knew that Jamie suffered from a sense of the ridiculous; he had no trouble with that as his own brother, long dead under the soil of Flanders, had exhibited exactly that same sense of fun. He saw a lot of his departed brother in his son. What a waste that they could not have known one another; they would have formed a wonderful bond – uncle and nephew getting up to all sorts of mischief!

"Now you can cut up the squashed slugs and mix them in too – plus some jam and a bit of Marmite. You can put it all into a cake tin and bake it in the oven for five or six days. You will need a saw to cut it up with, but it'll be delicious. There!"

Jamie sat down whilst Matthew and Tommy hooted with laughter. Margaret was still playing with Robert. John gave a short burst of applause whilst Desmond tried not to exhibit the affront that he felt welling up.

He consulted the watch. "One minute and five seconds. Not as long as Matthew's story. Now, we need not spin to see whose turn it is. Tommy, would you like to spin the other one and select your subject?"

Tommy obediently spun the pointer and could not resist a shout of delight as it came to rest on the legend, 'Where I would like to go'. Right up his street! He sprang to his feet and began.

"Where I would like to go is the South Pole!" he began. Jamie and Matthew, on cue, hugged themselves and shivered.

"I would get a crew and sail down from Australia and across the Southern Ocean and land on that bit that sticks out". He was mortified that he could not remember the name of the vast promontory that pointed up in the general direction of the South Atlantic. However, he soldiered on.

"We would have tents and sleeping bags and have sledges and a team of dogs and plenty of meat for the dogs and lots of food for us and compasses and Primus Stoves and billycans and pointy sticks to test the snow and funny shoes like tennis racquets and heaps of very warm clothes". He gulped in a huge lungful of air.

"We would try to go about twenty miles a day and it would take us about two months to get there and put a large stick in the ground with the Union Jack on it to show that we had been there and it was ours! Then we would have to come all the way back again. The dangerous bits would be crossing the ice where it had cracked – it think that the crack is called a crevice – and we would have to put long pieces of metal over the crevices and go over very carefully 'cos they can be very deep and you can fall miles and miles down to the bottom. When we got back to the boat everybody would have a party and we would sail all the way back to England and the king would make me a Sir!"

To wild applause he sat down again. Margaret had actually listened to this story and was fulsome with her praise.

"Tommy!" she said. "That was a wonderful speech. You have a brilliant imagination and you will be a great success when you grow up!"

Tommy blushed a deep red at this somewhat over-generous outburst.

"Yes, indeed", added John. "A very good talk".

Desmond looked at the watch. "One minute and fifty-seven seconds! Tommy is the winner!"

Just then they all heard the wail of the siren.

"Bug....................!" began Jamie. Thinking very fast he stammered a hurried explanation for that truncated expostulation. Pointing to the far corner of the floor he uttered, "Bug – just seen one on the carpet over there!"

John, not fooled for a minute, had to smother a laugh. Desmond, not fooled either, was shocked but said nothing. Everyone else seemed blithely unaware as they all tried to cram into the Morrison. Just as they were settled came the all-clear – surely just another false alarm or, thought John, some blithering idiot accidentally pressing the button. They clambered out shouting with laughter.

The three boys scampered out into the late afternoon sun and played with an old tennis ball whilst Desmond set about clearing up the remains of the tea and restoring the room to its normal neatness.

Jamie did not mention his Base Camp or the 'tunnel' that he was constructing. It was his secret, and he did not want to share it with anyone else – not even with Matthew who was his very best friend. He had constructed the covered crawl-way almost to the top of the embankment and planned to reach Advance Camp the next day. He had aimed it at the base of a large Buddleia shrub with which the top of the embankment was liberally dotted. It looked quite dense at the base and would make a super place from which he could spy on the trains and passengers that clattered past. He could not wait to get there.

However, he took his turn with the tennis ball and sent it in what he firmly believed was a spinning trajectory towards Tommy. He would never catch that one! Tommy caught it one handed and sent it on its way to Matthew. After a while they tired of this and went back into the house to see if there was any more food to be had. They were in luck as a few sandwiches remained. They wolfed these down.

Soon after this came a knock at the door. John opened it to admit the slim and elegant figure of Mrs Hartley, Matthew's mother. John was always slightly at a loss when confronted with this alluring person. She was quite tall and had a wonderful figure that she had dressed in a tight grey sweater and a black pencil skirt. She was a few years ahead of fashion. Her legs were encased in seamed silk stockings, and she wore quite high heeled shoes. She looked, to John's eyes, very lovely. Margaret, no mean fashion plate herself, cast an appraising eye over the visitor. She knew that she could hold her own with any woman, but this particular specimen gave her pause; she had a somewhat sardonic smile and exhibited a sense of wit and perception. John hurried away to get the two visitors.

Margaret walked over to shake hands. "They will only be a minute", she said. "So good of you to fetch Tommy as well".

Virginia Hartley smiled back. "Oh, not too far out of my way and poor Tommy's mum is a little large to undertake long walks!"

Margaret was amused at this not-too-subtle put down. Tommy's mother was a lady of generous dimensions that she did nothing to decrease with a prodigious daily calorific intake. Where she was able to obtain these foods remained a complete mystery to one and all. What Margaret failed to perceive was the other interpretation that Virginia had intended – that, as Margaret was known hardly ever to go out at all, she would have been similarly disinclined to undertake the errand.

Mrs Hartley had suddenly espied a tiny head, not far above floor level, suddenly emerge from the sitting room.

"Oh look, Robert is crawling! How he has grown!"

Margaret scooped up the child and cooed at him. "I will never understand where he gets the energy from", she said.

"He's very delicate really and needs constant attention. Doctor Talbot is always having to come round to see to his ailments".

Virginia, who was an extremely shrewd judge of character, thought that this was either an overstatement or a need by Margaret to consult the good doctor on her own behalf. She was actually right on both counts.

John came back with a now coated and gloved pair of small boys. They solemnly thanked John and Margaret for 'having them' and went off with the stately Mrs Hartley. John could not help staring after her for seconds longer than necessary before closing the door. That walk was amazing! He felt quite ashamed of himself as his own wife was equally beautiful but, in some senses, unobtainable. There was no meeting of minds; no shared laughter; merely a lifetime of devoted service. Sometimes he longed for the fulfilment of a true relationship, such as he had enjoyed with poor Dorothy.

The birthday was now coming to an end and John was due on duty at eight that evening. He went upstairs to wash and to change into his uniform. Being a soldier of the first war he was allowed to wear the medal ribbons that he had earned – the blue, white and yellow of the nineteen fourteen-eighteen medal and the rainbow colours of the medal for the 'Great War for Civilisation'. These were stitched above his left breast pocket. He gave his immaculate boots a final flick with a duster and went downstairs to say goodbye. Jamie knew better than to hug his dad's uniform. Desmond called out his 'goodbye' from the dining room where, as usual, he was busy with homework; Margaret allowed a small peck on her soft cheek. John kissed baby Robert's head and was rewarded with a huge smile and a little chuckle.

# BLACK MARKET

Folding his greatcoat neatly over his left arm he walked down the road, past the pond and crossed the main Brighton road at the pub, there to wait for either bus or tram. To his annoyance he saw that the winner that evening was a rattling tram that swayed along the rails from its terminus in Brooke Hill. He got on and sat down on the nearest wooden slatted seat. He showed his police pass to the clippie and stared moodily out of the window as the tram made its noisy and uncomfortable way into Wandleside. He alighted at the stop opposite the massive theatre and walked up a side street to cross another main road to the police station. As usual, he was fifteen minutes early.

He was the duty sergeant that night and he assembled the fifteen constables in the parade room for their briefing. He called the parade to attention and turned to salute his Inspector. That officer was just about to address the parade when the door opened and in came the tall figure of the Superintendent. Most unusual!

The Inspector turned and saluted his superior who had an announcement to make.

"I have received a report this afternoon that a gang of black-marketeers is due to arrive on our manor any time soon. The info comes from a source that we have always found reliable in the past – so – eyes peeled and I want the lot of them inside as soon as they appear!"

John thought that this would be a near certainty. These characters always seemed to dress in sharp clothes and slouch trilby hats; they might just as well carry banners stating, 'please arrest me as I'm up to no good'. They were mostly of military age and were, to John's mind, contemptible.

However, he maintained a strict silence until, Superintendent and Inspector gone, he gave a final briefing.

"Stay near the middle of your beats so that we all know where each other is – ready to come to the whistle. You know what to look for. Keep in shadow if you can and let's round these bastards up! Right; parade to your duties, dismiss!"

The constables crowded out to walk to their respective beats and to relieve the off-going duty men who would tramp back to the station for tea and 'wads' before going home for a well-earned rest. John decided to join the beat of the two constables that were nearest to the mainline railway station. He felt that this could well be the most productive hunting ground. He signed out, donned his greatcoat and walked purposefully towards the railway. Just by the entrance to the booking hall was an empty kiosk that was used morning and evening by a newsvendor. He hid in its depth and peered out at the main doors. He was ready for them if and when they arrived, assuming, of course, that they came by train.

An hour passed, an hour in which John became more and more cramped. The local beat bobby had passed some minutes before and had looked, as he was supposed to, into every nook and cranny. He had seen the lurking figure in the shadows and knew from the shine from the stripes that his sergeant was lying in wait. Being an old hand at the game he had passed on without revealing the slightest sign. John nodded – good man! The minutes dragged by as the infrequent trains were heard to come and go. Being an important station, each passenger train stopped; the only trains that went through were troop trains – now becoming more frequent – and goods trains. It was common knowledge that troops were massing at various points along the south coast; perhaps the invasion was not too far distant. This had been expected for more than a year now and John, as most people in England, heartily approved the delay until the manpower and materiel were available in sufficiently large numbers. He well remembered going 'over the top' in response to half-baked plans and bland assumptions. This time it should be done with proper planning and meticulous detail. The newly appointed allied ground force commander seemed to know what he was doing. John approved of the quietly spoken and thoughtful Eisenhower – such a change from the usual brash and loud-mouthed American. He even approved of the choice over Montgomery, who he considered to be far *too* careful, despite the advances he had made in the North Africa campaign. However, his thoughts were wandering, and he dragged himself back to the matter in hand. Black market spivs!

Another southbound train chuffed to a stop. Doors opened and slammed shut. Much shouting and blowing of whistles. The train belched smoke and chuffed off again. Nothing and nobody of interest!

Then he heard the unmistakable shrill of a police whistle. It had come from the direction of the bus station – about a quarter of a mile northwards up the main road. He shot out of his hiding place and was joined at the first corner by two other coppers as the three ran as fast as they could to the repeated calls.

Arrived at the bus station they found five constables struggling with three men in raincoats and hats. Two had hold of cardboard suitcases. With the new arrivals the three men were quickly subdued and handcuffed. John then took the suitcases and walked over to the bus inspector's office. He went inside and quickly shut the door behind him to exclude the light. He nodded to the inspector and put the cases on a table. Opening the first one he was not in the least surprised at its contents. Small rolls of silk cloth and packets of nylon stockings – the usual!

On opening the second case however, John realised that they had hit the jackpot as, under layers of packets of cigarettes, were books of clothing, food and petrol coupons! This was contraband indeed and the three were looking at a very long stretch. If many people had their way this would be accompanied by severely hard labour!

Taking the cases, he went to the nearest blue police call box and asked for transport back to the station for three prisoners and two cases – plus escorts. The three were huddled miserably on the pavement, surrounded by a very cheerful posse of coppers – John telling them of his finds. Busses came and went until, with bell ringing, the Black Maria turned up. Both other sergeants on duty had wangled places and had come to join in the 'fun'. The prisoners, cases and two constables, with John, piled in and the short journey back to the station was accomplished slowly as the vehicle was fitted with shutters on the headlights to exclude all but the tiniest downward beam on to the immediate road surface. However, the driver celebrated with bells ringing as he turned into the station yard. The three men were hustled into the charge room and were duly processed by the sergeant. They were stripped of laces, ties, coats, belts, braces and any other 'dangerous' item and were locked into separate cells. The Superintendent himself came down to examine the suitcases and there was an overall sense of satisfaction among the policemen at a job well done.

The constable who had first spotted them had been very canny. Instead of raising an immediate hue and cry he had quietly gone back to the nearest corner and had summoned help via the telephone in a sweet shop. This had resulted in calls being made to the nearest three police boxes where the blue lights flashed. Other coppers, answering the calls, had arrived and the five had torn back to the bus station and set about the men. This first constable was brought into the Super's office and was warmly commended for his actions. He would be rewarded by acting as arresting officer and would certainly have to appear in court. John, being nominally in charge of the apprehending, was also to appear as he had been the one to seize the suitcases and discover the contents. He went to the canteen in very high spirits to enjoy a cup of tea.

# ADVANCE CAMP

Back at Brooke Hill Desmond was ready for bed – Jamie long since tucked up after his birthday celebrations. He put away all his books, having ruled neat lines under his work and dated the entries. His slide rule was polished and put away into its case; dividers and compasses were boxed in velvet linings; pencils meticulously sharpened for their next use; ink bottle carefully screwed tight, and pens wiped. He crept upstairs and, having ascertained that his mum and Robert were fast asleep, went to the back bedroom. He undressed and put on his pyjamas and then went to the bathroom to clean his teeth. He climbed into bed and found that sleep, usually the easiest of states to assume, was unattainable. He tossed and turned and ruminated on the antics of his younger brother, the behaviour of his mother and the demeanour of his father. He found, not for the first time, that he was totally unable to fathom any of them.

Why, for instance, did Jamie have to make a game of everything? Why could he not, just once, be sensible?

Why did his mother stay for days in her room? Why did his dad say that this was because she was 'having one of her bad spells'? Why did his dad always excuse this sort of behaviour when it was obvious that there was nothing physically wrong with her? After all, when she was 'well' she was good company and talked with a great degree of intelligence upon a wide variety of subjects. She loved music and could sing very beautifully. She was a very pretty lady and Desmond could see no reason at all for these periods of 'unwellness'. He sighed and lit the little night-light at his bedside to try and read himself to sleep.

Jamie woke up early for school the next morning and was surprised to see his brother sitting up in bed, fast asleep, with a book on the floor and the remains of the night-light in the little saucer of water. He shrugged and went to the bathroom for a quick (and in his case, perfunctory) wash; he cleaned his teeth (almost) and got dressed in his shorts, shirt, tie, blazer, socks and shoes. He shot downstairs and started to hack off a slice of bread to spread with marg. and jam. He wolfed this down, accompanied by gulps of water from the tap.

Desmond, awoken by the stomping from downstairs, came down and prepared his usual porridge. He got dressed and, before seeing his brother off to school, went upstairs to find his mum getting Robert up. He kissed both goodbye and cycled off on the three-mile journey to his own school.

Jamie had shouted his farewells up the stairs and was walking up Buttermere Gardens when he was met by Matthew who lived at number one, very near to the shunting yard. The two greeted each other.

"Hello Jamie, great party yesterday. I loved your silly story!"

"Wotcher Matty. When can we go and sail the boats do you reckon?"

This salutation had again been copied from old Albert. It would have been frowned upon by his grandparents and resulted in severe reprimand from his mother.

The two boys trudged up Derwent Drive and then the hill to the school. Satchels and coats were hung in the cloakroom, and they trooped into the large classroom for morning assembly.

For reasons of her classical education Mrs Bedford demanded the answer 'Adsum' to the calling of names, rather than the English version of 'Here, Mrs Bedford' that would have sufficed in most junior establishments. Neither Jamie nor Matthew (nor most of the other boys) had the first idea what the word meant; it was ritual and was accepted that it was the thing to say. So, they duly responded as Julia Forbes read out the alphabetical list of attendees.

Then it was time for the first hymn of 'assembly'. That day, Cecily Bedford had chosen the rousing hymn 'He who would valiant be'. The opening notes were played on the grand piano by Miss Forbes and the whole school broke out into a cacophony of sound. Jamie, who had a very good musical ear, sang lustily in tune but thought it rather funny to 'be a penguin' instead of a 'pilgrim'. Matthew had to stuff his hanky in his mouth but could do nothing about the tears of mirth that rolled down his cheeks.

Jamie still had not started his music lessons with Mrs Worthy. He was still in two minds about it and, had it not been for the attraction of the alluring Tina, would have backed out long ago. His first lesson was due after the Easter break, and he thought of it with some apprehension.

Mrs Bedford led the prayers after the hymn had ended and exhorted the boys to seek the guidance of the Spirit in all they did that day. Then, with a final 'amen' the assembly broke up and they all sat at their desks to undergo a session of the use of the full stop, the comma and mystery of mysteries, the semi-colon. They dutifully copied out the sentence from the blackboard.

'Peter and Paul, followers of Jesus, went to Jerusalem; they brought the good news'.

Mrs Bedford then went on to explain how each of the punctuation marks was applied and how it enforced a correct reading of, and emphasis upon, the words.

Jamie drifted off.

He followed the school cat's progress across the small playing field – once the big lawn of the back garden – to the far-off laurel hedge. The cat sat and then crouched down in its shelter, its eyes fixed upon a point half-way up the dark green foliage. In there, to Jamie's certain knowledge, was a robin's nest. Was the cat after a bird? Surely too early for fledglings to be present! He saw in his mind's eye the pair of little birds flying hither and thither collecting grasses to mould, with the occasional soft feather, into the perfect, cosy cup in which the mother would soon be laying her tiny eggs.

He was still deep in his own thoughts when, forty-five minutes later, the first lesson ended, and books were taken out for arithmetic. As the first sum was dutifully copied out Jamie still had his English book open.

Julia, who was taking this lesson, came quietly over to his desk. She tapped the ginger head with her knuckle.

"The rest of us have moved on, Jamie!" she said.

Jamie came to with a start. Looking hurriedly at the next desk he put away the English exercise and took out his arithmetic book.

"Sorry, Miss Forbes", he said with what he hoped was his most winsome smile.

"Please pay attention!" Julia, despairing, went back to the blackboard and proceeded to show how to divide seven into thirty-five.

Jamie drifted off again. This was no deliberate act of defiance, simply an inability to concentrate upon anything for more than a few minutes that did not hold his interest.

The cat had obviously given up and had wandered off to try his luck elsewhere. The robins continued to fly in and out. The sun shone weakly through a hole in the grey clouds. He wanted nothing more than to be allowed to wander free among grasses and hedgerows. Beastly school!

During lunch there was an air-raid warning. Gas masks were collected from the cloakroom and held in readiness. Another short-lived interlude as the all-clear sounded.

The 'going-home' bell sounded at three-thirty and Jamie shot off homewards, eager once more to get to grips with his 'tunnel'.

The brigadier saw him pelting down the hill and came out to greet the little lad who had so interested him months ago.

"Hello young feller-me-lad", his moustache bristled as he spoke.

"Good afternoon, sir", replied Jamie, ever hopeful of cake and lemonade.

"Rushing home to help, are you?"

"No sir. I've got to finish my secret hideaway", said Jamie, unthinking.

The brigadier was amused. Some foolish notion, he supposed.

"Well, mustn't keep you from work of national importance!"

Jamie raised his cap and shot off again. He arrived home and quickly changed out of his school clothes and into his ordinary home dress. He put on an old coat, noticing that the house seemed unusually quiet. Peeking into room both down- and upstairs, he saw that his mum and baby brother were not in – with granddad and nana, he supposed. He went out into the garden and through the fence and up the tunnel, taking with him the last six (he hoped) hazel twigs. The ground was a bit damp under his knees, but this had never deterred him before. Jamie fondly imagined that the 'tunnel' was invisible from outside and fairly weatherproof. In fact, it was neither; It was perfectly possible from a small distance to follow the line of the humped passage and it was also possible to see, in places, through the woven grasses. Added to which was the fact that the hazel twigs were quite prominent. However, at a distance of over one hundred and fifty feet, it was quite well camouflaged – and this was the distance from which he gauged it – his bedroom window.

Crawling up the tunnel he proceeded to cut, brace and weave the final short distance to the top. He reached this goal about an hour later. He was triumphant and did a small war dance on his knees. He had arrived at the dense buddleia bush. Slowly he started to cut back the small shoots that populated the centre trunk and could soon see right through it and along the railway tracks to both right and left. Advance Camp had been achieved and he was so excited that he uttered a piercing yell. This was unfortunate for, working quietly in his greenhouse at the bottom of the garden of number 67, was their elderly neighbour Brian Norris. Kate and Brian Norris were well into their seventies and had spent all forty-eight years of their childless marriage in this house. The greenhouse was old - Brian's pride and joy, where he produced all his own bedding plants from seed and also started off his normally bountiful supply of vegetables.

Just on the point of setting down a small flowerpot of geranium cuttings, the shriek caused him to start violently, dropping the pot to the floor where it shattered. He rested against the shelving and tried to quieten his suddenly racing heartbeat.

"Dear, merciful heavens!" he gasped. "What on earth was that? Is someone hurt?"

He opened the greenhouse door and peered out, waiting to see if the yell of what he thought was agony were to be repeated. Nothing. Silence.

Jamie had heard the crash and went very still. The last thing on earth he wanted was for his 'secret' to be discovered – especially as he had only just achieved his goal. He froze and remained invisible.

Peering through the foliage he was just able to see the old, bent figure scuttling up his garden path to disappear around the house. He carefully made his way back down to the fence, crawled through and replaced the two slats. Making sure that the coast was completely clear he shot as silently as he could back into the kitchen and went out the front door, which he was careful to keep ajar with an old shoe in the jamb. He peered out. Mr Norris was in the road looking anxiously up and down. He could see nothing, certainly no cause for the shriek of what he still believed was acute pain and anguish.

A few doors down were the horse and cart of Charlie Vickery, the greengrocer. It was parked by the kerb and the horse had its head buried deep into the nosebag which Charlie attached whenever he thought he would be some time with a customer. Mr Norris, feeling a little better by this time, walked down just as the greengrocer emerged jingling the coins that he had just received.

"I say", quavered old Mr Norris. "Did you hear a cry of pain some moments ago? Quite a shriek, it was!"

Charlie Vickery, who had been deep in conversation with his customer on the subject of spring greens, scratched his chin.

"Fort I 'erd sumfin – didn't know what it were!"

"Oh, it was a terrible cry!" asserted the old man. "But there is no accident in the road and there has not been a train past for some time. I wonder from whence it came".

"Might'er bin from over the railway – or p'raps from annuver 'ouse".

Mr Norris, now almost fully recovered, decided that enough was enough and went back indoors to fortify himself with tea and biscuits. It never occurred to him to mention it to his wife Kate as she had been almost stone deaf for many years; she would not have heard anything. He gave it up as being one of life's mysteries and went back out to clear up the mess in the greenhouse.

Jamie crept back indoors and went up to his bedroom. He decided that having had one very narrow escape, he would not go back up to his advance camp until the next day. Instead, he made himself presentable by transferring the mud from his knees to a dampened flannel and went over to see his Nana and Granddad.

# A DEATH SENTENCE

He went round the side of the bungalow and opened the kitchen door to find Daisy sitting in her old rocker and nursing a cup of tea. Her plump cheeks were stained with tears as she turned a sorrowful face to see who had come in.

"Oh Jamie", she sobbed. "Such sad news!"

Jamie was at a loss. "What bad news, Daisy?"

"I'd better let master tell you himself – t'aint my place really".

Jamie went through into the lounge and found his grandparents in a similar state of distress. His mother, cuddling Robert, looked very sad too. What could have happened?

He went over to Margaret and tugged at her sleeve. His mother looked at him and he saw that the great big brown eyes were glistening with unshed tears.

"What's wrong, mummy?" he asked, fearful to hear the reason; It must be quite serious for them all to be so upset.

"Poor Aunt Amelia is going to have to go into a nursing home", she managed to say before the first tear stole down the soft, powdered cheek.

"But why?" asked Jamie. He did not really know what a nursing home was but feared that it was not very nice as it was causing so much unhappiness.

His grandfather, wiping his eyes on a snowy handkerchief, came over to him and knelt down so that his head was on a level with Jamie's.

"The poor dear is very sick and needs to be properly looked after", he explained.

With the innocent simplicity of a small child, Jamie looked at his granddad.

"Is she going to die?" he enquired. He could think of no other reason for the deep distress.

Alfred longed to say a simple 'yes' but felt that this would be just too brutal for the little chap to accept. In fact, Jamie would have accepted this as a simple statement as dying was something that he *could* understand. He knew that people died, had seen where they had lived in the bombed-out houses and accepted that they were no more.

They had heard only that same morning that the headaches that the old lady had been experiencing were brought on by a tumour of the brain; that it was inoperable and certainly terminal with a prognosis of weeks rather than months. It had come as a fearful shock to Frederick who was at that moment in his own home trying to arrange for his sister's transfer to a nearby nursing home. She would need round-the-clock attention as the pain would soon become intolerable and the necessary drugs would have to be administered in doses that responded to her constant and changing needs.

Margaret, who had little or no understanding of a child's mind, was upset.

"That is a very cruel thing to say!" she admonished her son.

Alfred looked painfully at Gertrude. It was direct and to the point but was not cruel in the slightest. It was simply the working of a small brain where one was alive or one was dead, was awake or asleep, was black or white. He decided to try an explanation.

"Poor Amelia has a nasty illness that is not going to get better. There is nothing that anyone can do except to pray for her. Perhaps we could all say a short prayer now and hope that God will let her rest".

Jamie closed his eyes and put his hands together.

"Dear God", Alfred began. "Please look with kindness on poor Amelia. Please do not make her suffer and let her have peace. Amen".

"Amen", agreed Jamie as Gertrude and Margaret added their own private thoughts.

Alfred held out his arms and clasped the little boy to him. Jamie, finding that such grief was contagious, wept too and his face was soon as wet as the others were. Alfred rocked him silently. Amelia would be the first of that generation of the family to leave them and the shock had been severe. All right, any of them could be blown to bits at any time; that was simply to be accepted in this dreadful war but, to know that it was going to happen – and imminently – was very hard to bear.

Jamie went over to his mother. "I didn't mean to be cruel, Mummy", he said. "I just wanted to know!"

Seeing her father and mother nod, Margaret was mollified. She still did not really understand the directness of her child but accepted that, as her parents accepted it, it would have to do. In a rare display of affection, she reached out and ruffled his curly head. Jamie started to cry again so Margaret took his hand and, with Robert in his pushchair, said goodbye and led the little boy back home.

Desmond was home by the time they got there. He took one look at the doleful faces and sat his mother down in her chair. He received the news with his customary stoicism.

"She will soon be at peace", he tried to assure his mother. Margaret was not so sure. She was a regular churchgoer but had never actually come to believe unquestioningly in the existence of a Creator. If she had ever taken the time to sit down and analyse her thoughts, she might have come to the conclusion that she was just another in the vast army of those who thought that it would be 'nice' if there actually were a God and Saviour. She believed the stories but had never once probed their authenticity. As to their relevance to her own life she, like so many others, had not an inkling. Desmond, on the other hand, had thought deeply about it and believed wholeheartedly in the goodness of God and the purpose of the life that he felt compelled to lead.

Jamie was still at the stage where he knew that he was alive; was on this earth to enjoy himself and have fun. Eventually, he would die and go to heaven. Desmond knew how his little brother thought and quite envied him the simplicity! Life had become more and more complicated in the last few years. Sometimes he longed for the peace of quiet acceptance but knew that it would never come; his brain was just too active seeking reasons and motives, answers and paths to follow. He hardly even set foot inside a church and was convinced that, to lead a good and fruitful life, it was unnecessary to follow blindly the rituals and customs of organised religion; he led his life by learning what he knew to be useful and by being of service to his family. That was enough for him for the time being. He also knew that it would be up to him to break the news to his dad. His mother would get far too emotional and would probably embellish the telling with fanciful versions of the diagnosis and the family's outpourings of grief. No, he had better do it himself. So, for the time being, he sought comfort in the usual.

"I'll go and start getting the tea ready", he said and made for the kitchen.

"Why don't you lend a hand, dear", said his mother to Jamie, wanting nothing more at that time than to be alone with her baby.

Jamie obediently went out as well. Desmond put a brotherly arm round his shoulders as toast and crumpets were made ready. This was one of the two days every week that meat was not on the menu. Sometimes the greengrocer would have a rabbit that came from a source known only to that good man and the old fellow who poached them. Other days there was some poor quality meat and, occasionally, the joy of a sausage or two. But today was a no-meat day.

John arrived home soon after the meal was started, and Desmond was grateful that his dad had chosen to arrive by the kitchen door. He took him aside and gave him the news about Aunt Amelia. John was shocked and immediately went into Margaret to comfort her. Margaret, however, had already accepted the situation and was not too eager to have the matter reopened. So, before joining his sons at toast and crumpets, John played with Robert. He felt slighted that his sympathies had been almost rudely rejected. Margaret had simply put it to the back of her mind; she had *not* forgotten but had just wanted it all to simply go away. The world to her was sometimes a horrid place and she withdrew from it as much as possible, taking her baby with her into that comfortable and secluded corner that her mind had created – a corner inhabited with niceness and good, handsome and, above all, well educated people.

John munched on his toast and watched fascinated as Desmond carried on with the everlasting homework. He had a suspicion that his son was doing far more than the work set by the teaching staff, was pushing himself to learn and absorb every scrap of information that it was possible to glean. He had a great admiration for this type of relentless drive and regretted the paucity of his own education; still, he had not done too badly for the start in life that had been his lot. He thought back to the year nineteen-sixteen; he had left school at just fourteen, three years earlier and had accepted that he would have to settle for the menial tasks that were at that time available – errand boy, coal merchant's labourer – all very poorly paid and seemingly without future. When his two brothers had left to join the war, he had felt a desperate loneliness, a sense of empty futility – so lonely that he had 'fudged' his age and joined the colours. His basic training had been brutal, supervised by sergeants and warrant officers who seemed hell-bent on the total demoralisation of the young soldiers; they were told tales of slaughter at the front line, of the probability they would be maimed for life, if not killed in their first few hours. It seemed a joke to the battle-scarred veterans; they did it to 'toughen them up', little realising that all they inculcated was fear and dread. The officers were aloof, distant to the point of seeming to belong to a totally separate race. You never spoke to an officer. If one spoke to you, it was not the done thing to look him in the eye. That could well be interpreted as 'dumb insolence'. No, the correct thing to do was to stare well past the aristocratic face and to frame answers in staccato; 'yes sir' – 'no sir'.

Those officers, or the young ones lucky enough to have survived the first war, still reigned supreme. He thought of the clipped diction, the haughty manner, the supercilious arrogance of their modes of address whenever one spoke on the wireless – as if theirs were the only ideas that carried any weight, theirs the right to command, theirs the inheritance of riches and influence. He remembered well the very few exceptions that he had encountered; his battalion commander in Flanders who instructed all his junior officers that the only true and legitimate order for an officer to give was 'follow me!'; the old quartermaster who had gently tended the wounds of his comrades, be they officer or lowly private. It should have all been different when that bloodbath had ended in nineteen eighteen. It had not; the same rules applied as before except that jobs were even scarcer, pay more pitiful for those who had managed to find work. No 'homes fit for heroes'; no levelling out of the social strata; no universal franchise for the women who had taken the place of their menfolk on the home front.

John was a prime recruit for the burgeoning socialist movement except for one thing – there is nobody quite so conservative as the working man. His inbred sense of duty and loyalty to king and country saw the havoc being wreaked by strikers in nineteen twenty-six and he shied away from it – was appalled at the sheer 'disloyalty' but, at the same time knowing that these men were simply striving to attain the dignity of a living wage. To his mind they were going about it in entirely the wrong way. They should have fought whilst maintaining the discipline of work, not by abandoning their principles to follow those he felt were little more than traitors.

He went into the sitting room and warmed up the old wireless set. After a few minutes the strains of a dance band eased his tensions; they were playing the tune of the moment and one that he particularly enjoyed, the Moonlight Serenade. After the 'pips' came the news headlines. The Russians were making slow and steady progress on the eastern front; Cologne and Dusseldorf had been bombed yet again; the allied armies were progressing nicely in Italy and the tonnage of shipping lost was slowly lessening. All in all, quite good news. After the bulletin had ended, he listened to a wordy but almost incomprehensible talk by an official from the Ministry of Food in which this plumy-mouthed individual exhorted even greater sacrifices be made and tighter restrictions accepted. And then, thought John, probably went off to enjoy a four-course dinner at a posh restaurant. He even *sounded* well fed – damned hypocrite! He turned off the wireless and sat quietly in the dark. Would things change after this war, he wondered?

Desmond had listened to the news and the talk as well. At one point the official had said that his words were being beamed 'through the ether' to his listening public. Desmond snorted with derision. Didn't the oaf know that ether was not a gaseous component of the darkness of space? He could cope with ignorance when such was freely acknowledged; he could not stomach plain inaccurate stupidity. He returned to his calculations.

Jamie sat in bed and worried about his secret camps. He knew that something was amiss but could not pinpoint just what this 'something' could be. He might just ask Desmond when his brother came up to bed. He read a book and waited until he heard footsteps climbing the stairs. As Desmond prepared for bed Jamie broached the subject in what he fondly imagined was a roundabout way.

"Des", he started. "Des, if someone was (his knowledge of the subjunctive was years distant) to push a tunnel through some long grass and used twigs to make it stand up, would it all fall down?"

Desmond came over to Jamie's bed and sat down.

"If you mean that 'tunnel' that you've been making up the embankment, then there is certainly a danger that it will collapse!"

Jamie was aghast. "How do you know about it – it's a secret!" he objected.

"I've been watching your progress for weeks and I know how you've been making it", he replied solemnly.

Jamie was tempted to utter his favourite (and also secret) 'bugger it' but restrained himself just in time. He remained silent, hoping that his knowledgeable brother would help him out. He was not disappointed.

"Listen", said Desmond, his engineer's hat firmly in place. "You have been using hoops of twigs pushed into the ground, haven't you?"

Jamie nodded.

"Well, you've been very lucky so far – no very heavy rain or high winds. If either of those had happened each hoop with its grasses would have been flattened – see – there's nothing holding them all together, is there?" He paused and was rewarded with a shaken head.

"Right then, what you've got to do is to get some string and some long straight twigs and bind two of these long pieces along the hoops. That way you will give the whole thing a lot more strength!"

Jamie nodded; he saw exactly what Desmond was getting at. Unfortunately, he would have to find the long twigs from somewhere and knew that the original pile of hazel was exhausted. Where could he get some?

"Do you promise faithfully that you'll never go on the railway lines?" said Desmond.

Jamie nodded. "Cross my heart!"

"Then", said Desmond. "It'll stay our secret – but remember – no going further than the bushes on the top – OK?"

"Promise!" replied Jamie. Could anyone anywhere have a more super brother, he wondered?

# REINFORCEMENTS

He quickly fell asleep as Desmond finished his wash and cleaned his teeth. Baths were a bit of a luxury as there was a restriction to no more than six inches of water to be used at any one time. How in heaven's name the authorities thought that they would ever be able to enforce such a prohibition was totally beyond his imagination – still, it *was* an instruction and both he and his father obeyed it scrupulously.

He hopped into bed and put out the little night-light. Laying there under the blankets he first said his prayers and then thought over the happenings of the day. The war was ever so slowly beginning to turn in their favour, but the day had been spoiled by the terrible news about great-aunt Amelia. What agonies must she be suffering and how much worse would it have to get? He turned over on his side and gently fell asleep.

The very next afternoon found Jamie down at the allotments. He had 'borrowed' a pair of secateurs and was foraging for straight sticks. Running along the side of the furthest vegetable patches was a hedge of various plants – hawthorn, ash, elder, privet and laurel. Surely, he would be able to find something there! Hawthorn was out – it was far too prickly; ash was a bit too tough for his small hands; privet was useless, as was laurel. However, elder was very strong and bendy. It would have to do. He managed to find and cut about twenty straightish shoots, each some four feet in length and, with these bundled up, struggled back home under their weight. He was quite puffed as he secreted them under the cover of 'base camp'. Then he started to do as Desmond had advised and was soon making excellent progress up the 'tunnel', fastening the new sticks to the 'hoops' until he was sure that he had made an excellent construction. He paused half-way and gave the portion behind him a shake. He was delighted to see that the small movement he was able to induce made no appreciable difference to the structure; it was so much stronger now!

By late tea-time his work was at last complete, and he sat in 'advance camp' to watch trains come and go. A lot of those going southwards towards the coastal ports contained flat cars on which were loaded trucks, armoured cars, tanks and artillery pieces. Each military train had, behind the engine and at the rear, anti-aircraft guns that were constantly manned throughout the journey. There were also many trains containing soldiers in full gear.

He had his small diary with him and made funny notes in it, noting the types of trains that passed. He thought of himself as carrying out very important work, keeping a record of the movement of men and materiel.

He had come to recognise the various anti-aircraft guns and his spelling of 'Oerlikon' and 'Bofors' were not too far off! He knew all the types of lorry and tank; his little record was sprinkled with Bedfords, Jeeps, and Humbers.

As he went backwards down the tunnel, he thought how important his book was and how it must never fall into enemy hands! Not even his closest friends would *ever* be permitted to know of its existence. He was satisfied and fulfilled; he was now able to 'do his bit'.

# PROMOTION

John was about to finish his shift behind the tall desk in the custody room when a message was brought to him by one of the newest constables. For the first six weeks of their active service these men were assigned to menial duties in the station, not thought yet ready to face the wicked world outside. They would carry messages, bring tea to the sergeants and watch as the older coppers wrote up their pocketbooks, prepared statements to be given under oath and generally learned the tradecraft.

"Sarge, super wants for to zee 'ee when you'm done!" The new copper was from somewhere west of Winchester and was a constant source of amusement to the others in the station. His references to 'varmints' and other unlikely titles for criminals were soon in common usage, a policeman entering with a ruffian in handcuffs saying, 'caught this varmint breaking into old mother Sweetings' place. He used a bloody great vizgy to get his entrance'. Apparently a 'vizgy' was a West Country dialect word for the head of a grubbing mattock; it had taken some hours of patient questioning for the older hands to elicit this from the novice who had spent the time using other incomprehensible words and phrases to get his explanation across. He was a source of much good-natured amusement and seemed to take it all in very good part.

John finished the hand-over to his colleague, walking the cells and going through details of each occupant, marking off in the custody record as he went. He straightened and brushed his tunic, polished his immaculate boots and trudged up the stairs to the top floor where the superintendent had his office. Outside the door sat the super's secretary, a mousy and permanently flustered lady who, despite all appearances, had never been known to lose a file or even a paper.

"Good afternoon, Miss Riley. The super wanted to see me?"

Thus addressed Gwendoline Riley raised her greying, untidy head and peered at the visitor through tortoiseshell rimmed glasses containing thick and permanently grubby lenses. She blinked at him.

"Oh yes, Mr Small!" To her all the sergeants and the older and more experienced constables were 'mister'. "Please go right in – he's expecting you".

John knocked at the door and entered. The super was sat at his desk, a massive old oaken affair strewn with papers, files, copies of charge sheets and the like. He looked up and sat back.

"Ah, yes, Sergeant Small. Come in, come in – sit down. Won't you" He relaxed in his old leather chair, took out his gnarled briar pipe and filled it from a battered leather pouch. His favourite Virginia tobacco had been almost unobtainable for years now and he had to make do with what he considered a vastly inferior 'Empire' blend that came through the supply routes from Rhodesia. Clouds of blue smoke curled up to the yellowed ceiling as John sat down in a 'visitor' chair that faced the huge desk.

"Please, light up if you want to", urged the super. John obediently took out his cigarettes – he had recently tried Capstan Full Strength and had found them to his taste – and lit one with a match from a box of Swan Vestas.

"How are things going?" enquired the tall and imposing figure with its one shiny crown on each shoulder. "Been with us a few years now and doing a very remarkable job!"

"Fine, sir, thank you", replied John. "Took me a while to learn the manor but I think I've got most of it now".

The police-speak word 'manor' implied a great deal more than a simple cartographic knowledge of the streets; it included known haunts, regular villains, weak points, vulnerable people and premises and a whole host of other 'intelligence' that would have surprised (and alarmed) the law-abiding population. Of course, whilst the war ground relentlessly on, the 'manor' was complicated further with profiteers, black-market, bomb sites, dereliction and homelessness. Thank the Good Lord, John often thought, that the umbrella of 'family' was still in good enough shape to shelter those whose own homes had disappeared. Heaven alone knew what would have fallen to the 'authorities' if such social cohesion had not been available!

"I'm going to speak quite frankly!" said the super. John felt an 'Oh-oh' coming on; what had he done to merit a 'frank' speech? He had worried for nothing as the super continued in a very friendly manner. "Your work here has not gone unnoticed; you are always punctual, your beats are always properly supervised; your appearance and bearing are never short of a shining example! Making you blush, am I?"

John had indeed started to redden as he listened to this eulogy. All he ever tried to do was his *best*! Surely, that should be the aim of any policeman and he expected no praise at all for having attained what re regarded as the absolute minimum.

"Perhaps I'd better get to the real reason I've asked to have this chat. There is soon going to be a vacancy for Inspector – Paul Withers, as you must all know, was quite badly injured when that bomb caught him in January. He's been given a medical board and the poor chap is going to have to pack it in. So, what it all boils down to is this. You've sat the Inspectors' exam and your results were quite good; I know that you would bring all the necessary qualities to the post and, if you want it, I'm ready to back your application. You'd make an excellent fist of it, and I'd like you on my senior team. So, what about it?"

John had listened to this with almost open-mouthed astonishment; he had *never* imagined himself going beyond his present rank – was so thoroughly indoctrinated by training and experience to 'know his place' that such an elevation was nearly beyond his imaginings. He was, not to put too fine a point on it, flabbergasted!

"I'm absolutely amazed!" said that simple and honest man. "Honestly, sir, I never thought for one minute that you would have me in mind for the job. Surely Fred Taylor is much more experienced than I am?"

"Yes, but Fred is only three years from retirement, and he would never accept anyway - sees the 'orficers' as he calls them as the enemy. You, on the other hand, have quite a few years of service left and the men actually respect you. Some may not actually *like* you, but they all have a deep respect for you – as do I! Otherwise, your name would not have come to mind in the first place. So, again, what about it?"

John knew full well that, in some quarters, he was not liked. He was a stickler for immaculate turn-out and for following 'proper' procedure. Some others, he equally knew, saw sloppy conduct as a disgrace and backed him to the hilt. Would the dislike of some be deepened by what they would see as his 'defection' to the upper echelons – and would his job be all that harder as a result? On the other hand, would he not be in a position to further enforce his own standards on those unwilling to 'toe the line'? These few were not at all bad coppers; they simply rebelled at what they saw as his insistence on enforcing pettifogging, meaningless regulations; they would never mutiny. Was he beginning to be tempted, he wondered?

"Sir, I'm gratified that what I've done has brought my name up for the post. But it will mean a big difference to me and, with your permission, I'd like to think it over!"

"Of course – but I'll give you no more than twenty-four hours. Must get this post filled soonest! Paul is struggling and needs to rest, poor blighter. So, come back tomorrow and give me your answer – and mind it's yes! Off you go and have a chinwag with the missus".

John got up and stood to attention for a second before bidding the super a 'good night, sir and thank you'. He went back to the locker room, his head a whirl of thoughts. First was the money; the considerable rise would be a blessing. Then there was the severing of close relations with his fellow sergeants; he would never be able to function properly using the familiarity with which he now operated – they would *expect* him to maintain a proper distance. Did he really want this? Then, of course, came the doubts; Was he, a poorly educated man, fit to command respect among what would be his far more erudite peers? Would he be able to 'fit in'? Constant reminders from Margaret of his poor background – both to his face and before others – had so seriously undermined his own self-respect that he felt that he had no option but to fulfil her prophesies; he had to turn it down, didn't he? After all, he was comfortable doing what he was doing and being where he knew his place. He decided to call on his father-in-law, a man whom he respected above all others for sage advice and thoughtful comment. He caught a hated tram back to Brooke Hill and eventually knocked on the door of the bungalow.

Daisy announced him and he sat down in an easy chair opposite to where this mother- and father-in-law were sitting together on the sofa, deliberating on the final two words of that morning's crossword.

"Hello John, what brings you here? By the way, do you happen to know the answer to 'palindromic pick-me-up' – seven letters?"

Almost without thinking, John replied, "Reviver"

"God bless my soul, so it is. Clever of you old chap! Now, what can we do for you?"

John started to explain his dilemma; the offer, his need for the extra money, his own supposed unsuitability for the post and so forth.

Gertrude interrupted. "Of course, you must accept, John. You owe it to your family but most of all you owe it to yourself! You are smart, honest and probably the most hard-working man I have ever come across. You will make a wonderful Inspector and I, for one, will be proud to tell everyone of your success. You have earned it – so grasp it with both hands".

Alfred nodded enthusiastically. "I know what has brought the doubts into your head, but you must ignore them. Present Margaret with a fait-accompli – say to her that you know that it would please her, and you are doing it for her sake and not your own!"

Not for the first time, John was grateful for the counsel of this man. Here he was, elderly and proud, but still able to get to the root of the problem, still able to identify where the problem *really* lay; to know his daughter so well as to be able to formulate an escape route that would satisfy that ego *and* achieve the result that was actually only just and proper. He made his mind up; he would accept.

Sipping the proffered cup of cocoa, he sat with the old couple until it was obvious that they needed their bed. Taking their old hands in his he thanked them; Planting a soft kiss on Gertrude's soft and wrinkled cheek he bade them a good night.

He went home to his family. Alfred and Gertrude went to bed and chatted before sleep came. Both were thrilled for John; they thought that it would likely be the making of that honest but self-doubting man – despite his admitted 'poor' background.

Desmond was still at his homework but stopped and pummelled his dad on the shoulders. "Great, dad – you've earned it", he beamed.

Margaret, reading in bed, received the news somewhat differently. John, remembering his father-in-law's advice, told of his reluctance (absolutely real), but his acceptance for her sake, her correct status. Margaret mulled this all over for a while. "I suppose it will all be for the best", was all she could manage. John, used to the hurt and the put-down, accepted that he would never hear words of delight for his sake, encouragement or praise. He thanked God for little mercies and fell asleep, mind made up.

# LITTLE BUDDY

Three days later saw the start of the Easter Holidays, at least as far as Desmond and Jamie were concerned. Two long weeks stretched ahead of the little boy, a fortnight of no school and the freedom to do exactly as he pleased. The day saw the end of a period of cold drizzle that had blanketed the south-east for the past week or more. Military movements along the railway line had intensified recently so he was really looking forward to getting up close to the action. The previous year he had been exploring the various nooks and crannies of the house. In the under-stairs cupboard he had found, lodged far back under the lowest tread, an old school satchel. It was made of very dark leather and, under a thick layer of dust, he had discovered the initials 'TLB' and the year '1931'. Who, he wondered, was TLB and which school had he attended; more to the point, where was TLB now? Inside the satchel had been an old Oxo tin that had once contained a gross of beef cubes. He had given the satchel and tin a bit of a clean with a fairly clean duster, secreting the bag under his bed for future use. Now, he had the ideal use for it. So, making a small marmalade sandwich and corking up a small bottle of water, he put both these into the tin. This, along with a pencil and his precious diary, were put into the satchel and he made his very quiet way down the garden and into Base Camp. Carefully removing the two fence slats, he crawled into the tunnel, closing the fence up behind him. He crawled up to Advance Camp where he squatted under cover. He peeped to right and left – no trains in sight. He opened the satchel and took out his notebook with the pencil. He opened the diary and found the correct day – Maundy Thursday.

Coming from the north was a slow-moving troop train. It was pulled along by a fairly large locomotive that Desmond would have recognised as a 'King Arthur' class, resplendent in the green of the Southern Railway. Behind it was a flat car with the inevitable manned anti-aircraft guns that pointed to the blue skies. Behind that were some eight carriages. The train was proceeding very slowly and seemed to be coming to a stop. Jamie wondered why but made no movement to give away his position. The train did come to a halt; gusts of steam blew from the engine. Jamie could see that the carriages were filled with soldiers, some of whom were lowering the windows on their heavy leather straps so that they could peer out to see what was going on. Right opposite Jamie was a huge black face surmounted by a fatigue cap. Jamie had never seen a black face before; he wondered where this one had come from.

In the rearmost carriage of the train a door opened and a man in light khaki fatigues jumped down on to the ballast; he was festooned with pouches and had a bandolier of ammunition over one shoulder with a short carbine in his right hand. He started up the train in Jamie's direction, making the boy squeeze further into his hidey-hole. As he came level with Jamie, the huge black man called down to him, "What's up, cap'n? – why we stopped?"

"Something to do with a hold-up further down – we'll be here for a bit so you can let the boys down for a smoke in small groups".

"Aye-aye, sir", the black man grunted and, opening his door, jumped down with a crunch on to the hard, sharp stones. He crossed over to Jamie's bush and crouched down. Calling over his shoulder he beckoned to the next man to appear in the open doorway. "Look-at here, you guys. We have a spy!"

Jamie was horrified for he knew what happened to spies.

"I'm not a spy – I'm English!" he stuttered in fright. "I'm making notes so that I can write my story for next term!"

The black soldier, now seeming more vast than ever, thrust out a massive hand. "Well, hi there, little buddy!" he said, a huge grin breaking the face in two to display the most perfectly white teeth that Jamie had ever seen.. He called over his shoulder again, "You guys, this little fella's making important notes here – so, covering fire needed! Take up a defensive position!"

Three figures dropped down and squatted in a semi-circle around the bush, short rifles at the ready. The black man looked at Jamie again. "And who might you be?" he asked.

"My name's Jamie Small and this is my Advance Camp", he announced proudly.

"Master-sergeant Amos Wilkes at your service, li'l buddy!"

The penny dropped. "Oh, you're American!" said Jamie.

"Indeedy!" came the reply. "The US Marine Corps will keep you covered while you make your very important notes. So, you carry on and rest easy. We'll see you come to no harm". He turned to one of his marines. "Got any candy for the little fella?" he asked.

The marine groped in a pouch and came up with a chocolate bar; he reached back to give it to Jamie. "Cor, thanks!" Jamie gasped; he had not seen such a massive bar of chocolate for months – sweets being severely rationed. Slowly he took off the wrapper to expose the dark chocolate. He took a tentative bite through the delicious covering; within was a layer of soft toffee surrounding a crisp biscuit. Jamie loved it.

The immense master-sergeant stood up. He was well over six feet tall, with biceps that were as thick as Jamie's waist. He took out and lit a cheroot, puffing contentedly as he watched the little boy devour the candy bar. The Limeys had had a hard time of it, he knew. Having been met with nothing but kindness since arriving in England some months before, he had a fond regard for these resilient, stubborn people. The little freckled lad seemed to him to personify all that was best, cheerful and courageous.

The train held eight hundred marines, bound for billets near the port of Newhaven. It was no secret that the allied armies were massing on the south coast, everyone predicting an invasion across the channel in about a month's time. The master-sergeant viewed the prospect with some keen anticipation; time to really get to grips with the German army, for which he had the greatest respect. It would not be easy, he knew. But it had to be done and the sooner the better he reckoned. His unit had been training in the eastern States until before Christmas; they had come over in troopships that had been escorted by vessels of the Royal Navy – for whom he also had the highest regard.

As time went by the 'guard' around Jamie was changed, those going 'off duty' lolling about and lighting cigarettes from soft packets that seemed unfamiliar to him. Daddy's cigarettes came in stiff boxes. After about half an hour a small contingent came down the track, stopping at every group to deliver a large steaming billy-can of coffee – plus a greasy paper bag filled with something that Jamie had never seen before. The nearest marine took one out and offered it to him.

"Say, kid, wanna do'nut?"

Jamie took the proffered item and inspected it. Round and slightly flattened, it was coated in sugar. He took a bite. He had never tasted anything so good in all his life.

"I say, thanks. They are super!" he managed with mouth crammed full. The marine chuckled and handed over another which rapidly disappeared down the same route as its predecessor. The marines filled their own water bottle cups from the can and sat around sipping scalding coffee, which to Jamie's ears sounded like 'cawfy'. He wondered what it could be. It was obviously very nice as all the marines drank it down with relish.

The morning dragged slowly by; the engine continued to hiss steam; the marines continued to rotate their 'rest' breaks; Jamie continued to watch all their comings and goings with awe. Never had he been so close to so many armed men, who seemed to take it all for granted, sitting easily about whilst surrounded by a positive arsenal of weaponry. The way that they handled the rifles was almost nonchalant and Jamie vowed there and then to become a soldier when he was old enough. He would simply have to make his own rifle and learn to handle it with such ease. He watched their movements and made mental notes.

Then came the inevitable wailing of the siren. The marines sprang into action, all piling from the train to lie along the top of the embankment, rifles loaded and pointing to the sky. Coffee was drained and the metal cups screwed back on the tops of water bottles. Jamie realised that all this had been accomplished with not one shouted order being given. Far off came the drone of the daylight bombers of the Luftwaffe – vastly reduced in numbers now. Jamie wondered if he should crawl back down his tunnel to seek the sanctuary of the Morrison in his house. But he felt so safe among these men that he stayed where he was. He didn't want to miss a minute of it. A couple of the bombers came slightly nearer, prompting a deafening barrage from the anti-aircraft guns at the front of the train. The bombers sheered off, dropping their loads to the east; they disappeared from sight as seven loud explosions came from the direction of the distant beech woods. Jamie found himself almost smothered by the immense form of the master-sergeant who had dived to protect the little lad as he heard the bombs start to fall, He knew full well that they would land at quite a distance; but the movement was completely automatic. Apart from that, one never quite knew – so always better safe than sorry.

Jamie gasped as the large body lifted from him; some of the small branches had been bent under the weight; Jamie was covered in little bits of twig and leaves. He brushed himself down as the great face broke into a grin.

"OK, little buddy?"

Jamie squinted up at his personal bodyguard. He has been taught that it was always correct to offer one's hand when giving thanks, so he held out his diminutive, grubby one that was engulfed by the massive black one. "I say, thanks!" he murmured, rather self-consciously.

"Don't mention it old chap!" came the reply in a fairly close imitation of Burlington Bertie.

"I'd better be getting back now, my mum will wonder where I've got to", said Jamie, knowing that his mother probably had not even noticed he was missing from the house. Still, it really was about time that he put in an appearance. He waved to all his new friends, especially the do'nut man.

"You keep up the good work, you hear!" were the last words he heard as he squirreled back down the tunnel. He crept under cover as much as possible until he had reached the kitchen door. He went in, sat down to eat the sandwich, which had been so readily forgotten due to the coming of do'nuts into his life. Did all Americans eat them, he wondered? Finishing his brief lunch, he went in search of his mother and little brother.

# KRIMSHANKERS

John was at the police tailor, having just collected a new tunic and peaked cap. Gone was the high collared version and in had come a jacket with lapels, over a shirt and tie. On the shoulders were the wonderful two 'pips' of his new rank. He had suffered the inevitable joshing from some of his colleagues, whilst appreciating the wholehearted congratulations of others. Notice of his promotion had been posted on the board. He had secretly taken a copy from the file and had folded it into his wallet; a childish failing, he knew.

Now it was time to attend his first parade and to give his first briefing. He walked into the station and went to his new office. No longer did he share a desk; his own office with one desk and his name on a printed card on the door, 'Inspector J. Small'. How glad he was at that moment that he had accepted the promotion.

As the moment approached when he would walk into the parade room, he started feeling nervous – all the old suspicions of self-doubt returned. Was he really fit for this office? He gave himself a mental talking-to, put on his cap, took up his black gloves and short leather covered cane and strode down the corridor. He turned the door handle and went in, to be amazed at the spontaneous burst of applause that greeted him.

"Parade, 'shun!" called the duty sergeant who then turned to John and saluted. "Parade all present, sir".

John returned the salute. "Thank you, sergeant", he managed. Clearing his throat he started on his speech, rehearsed for many an hour.

"You, or most of you, have known me for quite a few years. You therefore know that I insist on three things. The first is a proper turn-out. You wear this uniform with pride at all times! The second is proper discipline. Most of you, thank the Lord agree with this already, but I am sure you know that *I* know those very few of you who don't!"

There was a burst of laughter; all of them knew who was being referred to.

"Last of all", continued John. "Respect for the public! They pay us to uphold the law for them. They need us and we are their servants!"

This was a trifle pompous, and he knew it. However, it was one of his firmly held beliefs and he had wanted to stress it.

"Now, what's on today's 'menu'? There will be a need for extra vigilance around the market as we seem to have been invaded by a new plague of 'dippers'. Next, take a good look at the power stations, those of you on that beat. We have had complaints from the manager there that some of his coal has been going 'walkies' – similarly the coke from the gasworks. I think that's all. Please carry on sergeant".

As he went back to his office the parade was dismissed 'to its duties'. He closed his door, took off hat and gloves and sat down with a sigh to start on the small pile of paperwork that required his attention. It was all so different. Perhaps he would take a walk later and visit the patrols – just to keep his hand in and to prove that he was not now totally remote from the 'coal face'.

First job was to interview two deserters who had been apprehended whilst trying to board a bus for London. He picked up the 'phone and was connected with the local military police. "Captain Regent here", came a very clipped voice.

"Inspector Small, Wandle Division", he announced himself. "We've got two chaps here that match the descriptions of a couple of men on your 'missing' list. We caught them this morning, apparently. No documentation on them – no I.D. cards, no pay-books, ration books or anything. I am going to interview them and wondered if you would like to send someone down to give a hand".

"I'll come myself", came the reply. "Nothing doing at the tick – be with you in about thirty minutes if that's OK".

John withdrew the two arrest sheets and clipped them to a copy of the army's latest 'gone AWOL' list. He wandered down to the custody sergeant and asked to have a peep at the two men in question. The sergeant took his huge bunch of keys and opened the barred door to the cells. John looked at the blackboard. 'Anon –susp AWOL' was chalked against cell five. He raised the peep-hole flap and peered in. Sitting on the hard bunk and glaring balefully at him was a youngish chap. John looked long and hard at him and referred to the descriptions on the list. A very good match, he thought. He was exactly what had been called in his war, a skrimshanker.

The second, resident of cell nine, was not so clear cut; nearly, thought John but enough room for doubt. But, in that case, why had the fellow been without papers of any kind, why the refusal to identify himself? No, he had to be interviewed as well.

As he waked back to his office he passed by the front desk where a very tall and imposing figure was leaning. He had on an immaculately pressed uniform and Sam Browne belt that gleamed. On his head was the red covered peaked cap of the Military Police.

"I've come to see your Inspector Small. Seems like a couple of your johnnies picked up a couple of my johnnies!"

John walked over to introduce himself, trying to suppress the old feelings of inferiority. In his last few days in the army he had been apprehended by the military police. He had actually been trying to stop a couple of soldiers stealing food from the cookhouse and had been dragged into the guardroom, there to face a lieutenant from the 'Redcaps'. He had been humiliated and called every sort of derogatory name by this member of the upper classes. Luckily, the other two had exonerated him and had admitted their guilt. But - those feelings persisted.

John went to a vacant interview room with his papers, the captain following. The first, sullen individual was brought in, and John was determined to seize the initiative; after all, this was a police station and his policemen had caught the man. Before the man could sit at the table opposite the two officers, John sprang to his feet.

"Name, rank and number!" he shouted.

The fellow automatically came to attention, his hands darting from his pockets to form into fists with thumbs in line with trouser seams but caught himself before he gave the automatic answers. It was, however, enough for John. Also, it seemed for the Captain. That immediate response had given the game away. This was a man with military experience.

"Look lad", said John. "Don't make things worse than they already are. We all know you are AWOL from your unit so do us all a favour. Tell us who you are, and we can all get on with our lives".

The man resumed his former slouch, his face showing disdain for the two who faced him. John referred to his notes.

"Are you 2477195, Private Henry Williamson, absent without leave from Salisbury?"

No reply. The man stared back and spat deliberately on the floor. Such disrespect was far too much for John to stomach.

"Right! I suspect that you are that person and am now handing you over into the custody of Captain Regent here. Have you anything to say that would cause me to reverse that decision?"

More silence and a look of sheer malice that had no effect whatsoever on the Inspector.

"Might I ask your constable here to hop out and get my two corporals?" asked the captain. John turned to the constable guarding the door; he nodded, and the policeman went out to return shortly with two beefy military policemen.

Formality was called for in situations like these. John addressed the captain. "I have reason to believe that this person is a deserter from his army unit and am formally handing him over to your custody!"

The captain, equally formal, signed for the 'body' and told his two men to take the man away in handcuffs. He was to be put into the staff car outside and was to be guarded by one of them until they could all leave. As one corporal approached, the man dropped into a fighting stance. He really should not have wasted everyone's time, thought John. He knew exactly what would follow. The captain aimed a blow at the back of the man's neck and down he went. He was jumped on by the two redcaps, handcuffed and dragged to his feet to receive a crippling blow to the stomach. He slumped between the two and was dragged out.

"Sorry about that", the captain said. "Got to let the blighters know who's boss, don't you know!"

The second man was brought in, and John repeated the abrupt question that elicited such a give-away response from his mate. This time the result was entirely different.

"2175189, Private Crooks W", came the answer. John was surprised; those details appeared nowhere on his list. Seeking further clarification he asked for the man's unit.

"First battalion, Berkshire Rifles, Sir!"

John raised a quizzical eyebrow at the Captain, who shrugged.

"Do you have permission to be away from you unit?" John asked.

"No sir; absented myself without leave", admitted the man who seemed to be stifling some very deep emotion.

"When and why?"

"Sir, yesterday at eighteen hundred hours. I got a call from my old mate that my house had been bombed and that my wife was missing. I asked my Company Commander if I could have a forty-eight-hour pass but we are under orders to move soon and he said no".

"What is your home address?" asked John. He was fully aware of all addresses in his 'manor' that had been bombed.

"Seventeen, Francis Street, sir".

John excused himself for a moment whilst he went to his office for his copy of the 'known casualties' list. There she was. He went back to the interview room to carry out that worst possible job in a policeman's life.

"Is you wife Patricia Ann Crooks?" he asked.

A look of dread passed over the face. The man nodded.

"I'm sorry to have to tell you that a body thought to be that of your wife was dug out of the ruins at that address two nights ago. As yet we have had no formal identification and I would like you to go to the morgue with one of my sergeants. You never know, there just might have been a mix up!"

The chap wept silently as he went out to a police car. Captain Regent told his two chaps to hop off with their prisoner and to come back for him in about an hour. John took him to the canteen for a cup of tea whilst they waited for the return of his sergeant and the other prisoner.

"Probably not up to the standards of your officers' mess", John apologised as they took the watery brew to a small table.

"Don't you believe it, old chap! Some of our messes are just that – a complete shambles. We don't have the fancy silverware that some of the county regiments have collected over the centuries. Why, my breakfast was served only this morning by a mess waiter who forgot the mushrooms".

John was not exactly sure whether this was a joke or a slight put-down. He decided not to share army reminiscences with his companion in case further disparaging remarks were forthcoming. After some desultory conversation about the expected invasion, they both went back to the interview room. Questions were superfluous, the sergeant giving John a quiet nod.

"I'm very sorry for you loss", said John, quietly to the defeated man. "But I have no choice in the matter. You have admitted absenting yourself without leave and I must therefore transfer you to military jurisdiction".

The chap looked as if he would not have minded if John had told him he was to be taken out and shot. Again, the 'body' was signed for and was taken, this time quite kindly, to the waiting staff car. Taking the officer aside, John enquired what was likely to happen to the soldier, now slumped in misery on the back seat. "Well, given the circumstances, he'll probably be given some compassionate leave and, if he reports back properly after that, no more will be said about it. I'll make a sympathetic report; that might help the poor sod – looks as if he could do with all the help he can get". John was very glad to hear this, contrasting it to the treatment of deserters from his own war. He bade farewell to the captain, received gracious thanks for his help and hospitality. The new Inspector went back to his office to sink down in his chair. Not too happy an introduction to his new duties, he thought looking with distaste at the new mound of paper that awaited his attention. Still, he reflected, there would always be time for a brisk walk about the streets to get a whiff of fresh air, to keep his finger on the real pulse.

# SHUNTING ENGINES
# AND BROKEN BISCUITS

The next day was Good Friday. Desmond declared his intention to attend the three hour-long service at the nearby Catholic Church. He had been reading about this two-thousand-year-old religion; he was fascinated by the rituals and had decided to go to see it for himself. He had chosen this particular service as it was the longest in the year, eclipsing by far the midnight mass of Christmas. It would help him to observe at first hand those people whom some in his own Anglican Church *still* regarded as the blasphemous enemy. John was off for duty at noon, whilst Margaret intended to visit her old uncle. Jamie volunteered to look after Robert.

This offer from a five-year-old would have amused some and horrified others. This family saw nothing strange in the arrangement. Jamie took his little brother for walks in the pushchair, fed him his made-up meals, knew how to mix the concentrated orange juice for the 'sipper' beaker that had recently been enthusiastically accepted, made a very good job of changing nappies. All in all, he was a very competent carer. He had learned all of the above from Desmond, who had patiently gone over the various skills time and time again; Desmond was at school for long periods in the day and had determined that another pair of hands be available in his absence. John had seen the little fellow in action; he knew of the love and care that Jamie lavished upon little Robert; he had absolutely no qualms. Margaret, whilst being devoted to her baby, took every opportunity to avoid what she saw as the 'messier' side of his care; she was only too happy to delegate on occasions, leaving her free to pursue other matters.

So, when breakfast was over, Jamie saw to Robert. Dressing him warmly in his little rabbit suit, he strapped him in the pushchair. Having obtained two pennies from his mother he waved good-bye to the rest of the family, wheeled Robert out of the house and up the road; he knew exactly where little brother would want to go! Various residents were outdoors as the weather was sunny, but with a brisk wind blowing. The pair was greeted by everyone who saw them. 'Hello, Jamie – giving little brother a breath of fresh air?' Jamie nodded and replied, 'Yes, Mrs (or Mr) Philpott (or whomsoever)'. To him such questions were rhetorical – not that he knew the meaning of the word; he regarded them as a waste of breath; he could not see them for what they actually were – polite utterances of friendly people. He was becoming slightly intolerant!

Round the top corner they went to be greeted by the sound of the regular shunting engine. "Uff-uff!" shouted Robert in glee. Jamie pushed him a little further to a point where the chain-link fence was unobstructed on the other side by bushes or piles of pallets. There was the best view. Robert clapped his hands happily at every pass of the locomotive, pushing long lines of trucks or pulling them back for yet another shunt into a waiting siding. Up and down walked the shunter with his pole. Eventually, the last wagon had joined its correct fellows; the driver reversed the engine to a point opposite Jamie whilst his stoker raked out the firebox ready to replenish it with coal from the six-wheeled tender. Steam wisped from the escape valve; brown smoke curled from the chimney. The driver climbed down and came over to the fence.

"The little'un likes this, don't he?" he said, waggling grimy fingers at Robert.

"Oh yes, I bring him whenever I can. He loves to see your engine and to watch the trains shooshing by on the main line".

"He goin' to be an engine driver, then?"

"Oh, I hope so!" said Jamie. "I'm going to be a soldier; when I'm home on leave I will be able to come and see him doing the shunting as I suppose you'll be retired by then!"

"Cheeky little bleeder, ain't yer? I'm not *that* old yet!" The driver delivered this with a chuckle to show that he took no offence. He sat down on a nearby pallet and took from his trouser pocket a tobacco tin. He wore what seemed to be the universal engine driver's apparel, a flannel shirt open at the neck with a 'sweat rag' tied round his neck, a jacket and trousers in faded blue, a battered and extremely oily peaked cap on his head. Jamie watched fascinated as the driver opened the tin. He took a cigarette paper from a packet, pinched out a measure of dark brown tobacco and teased it into a loosened sausage along the length of the paper. Licking the gummed edge, he rolled it into a cylinder and stuck it in his mouth, lighting it from a match taken from a box of Swan Vestas. He gulped in a lungful of smoke and snorted it out in twin streams from his nostrils. Robert and Jamie were fascinated at this, Jamie vividly calling to mind the similarity between this and the picture in his book of Saints, the dragon breathing fire just before expiring from the lance thrust of St. George.

Robert bounced up and down, pointing to the smoke issuing from the driver's somewhat bulbous nose. "Uff-uff!" he shouted. "Uff-uff!"

The driver burst out laughing, a laugh that turned almost immediately into a bout of coughing. Jamie grinned. Wiping his eyes, the driver looked at the little boy in the pushchair. "Finks I'm an engine, don't 'ee! Well, s'pose I am in a way". He took in another lungful of smoke. "Now, watch this!" he said. Jamie watched as the driver tilted back his head to puff out five perfectly formed smoke rings. "Wow!" he said, greatly impressed; he would have to try and do that himself one day.

The driver finished his cigarette and went back to the locomotive to help his stoker top up the tender's water tank. The boys watched as the stoker climbed on to the heap of coal to get at the domed lid. He hinged it back, reached out for the dangling canvas hose to feed its end into the opening. The driver went to the chain and pulled it downwards. The hose filled, straightened, water gushing from the circular tank mounted on four high steel legs. The stoker shouted. "'Nuff!" so the driver let the chain loose from his grip to dangle as the water was shut off.

The engine manoeuvred a guard's van on to the end of a long line of trucks that were standing, coupled together, in the nearest siding. The shunter attached it to the first wagon so that the whole length of twenty trucks was pulled backwards on to the main shunting line. Uncoupling allowed the engine to go a bit further back whilst the shunter positioned points that allowed the locomotive to pass down a parallel track and take up its position once more at the other end. The wagons, heaped with coal, were then taken at slow speed through Brooke Hill Station, then via a branch line to a station nestling on the North Downs. Robert waved his good-bye to the 'uff-uff' as it disappeared. "Uff-uff gone, 'Amie! Uff-uff gone!" Jamie assured his brother that it would be back again the next day; he wheeled the pushchair past the shunting yard, down the sloped path, to arrive at the bridge under the railway. He headed for a corner shop. Entering, he went straight to the small counter where his goal lay. There, aslant, was a glass barrel of broken biscuits. The hexagonal 'barrel' had a large bakelite screw top that pointed towards the old shopkeeper. In the barrel was a heap of assorted biscuit pieces, broken either on receipt or during transfer to customers' paper bags. The miscellany included Digestives (Jamie's absolute favourite), Rich Tea, Osborne and the *very* occasional Ginger Nut. These last were eschewed as he resented his school nickname!

"Please may I have two penny-worth of broken?" he enquired. The old man gazed fondly through rather grubby spectacles at the little boy and the baby. "Of course you may, sonny!" He reached for a brown paper bag and ruffled the end so that the opening parted. Unscrewing the jar, he reached in a hand that was adorned by a frayed, grey woollen mitten; The hand went in five times to fill the paper bag which was then flipped over and over until the top was closed, a screw of paper at each side. Jamie handed over the two pennies and took the filled bag which was placed carefully on the wire tray under the seat of the pushchair. Bidding the old shopkeeper a polite farewell he wheeled his brother out again, under the bridge, up the slope, to arrive once again at the sidings. There he stopped to allow Robert to watch as the occasional train came past – either slowly, preparatory to stopping at the station (or going north having already stopped there) or flashing past on its express journey. Each was categorised by little Robert as 'Big uff-uff' (the expresses, invariably), or 'Li'l uff-uff'. Jamie, meanwhile, munched his way through all the bits of Digestive biscuits that he could find. Unfortunately, these were in a distinct minority. He handed Robert a piece of Osborne which was eagerly seized in tiny fingers and inserted into mouth to be sucked. "Um-um, bikky!"

He arrived back at home, parked the pushchair by the hall stand, took Robert upstairs to change his nappy. Robert, by this time, was on his third piece of biscuit and needed his face and fingers wiped to remove the paste that resulted from biscuit crumbs mixed liberally with saliva. Clean and happy, the little boy was carried down to his mother.

Margaret looked up from her reading. "Had a lovely walk, darlings?" She took Robert and gave him a cuddle before setting him down on the floor. Robert immediately wriggled over to crawl to his first 'climbing post', the side of the sofa. He waddled round from 'post' to 'post'. Jamie sat down by his mother and peered at the leather binding of the book that she held before her. "Is that a good book, mum? What is it all about? Would I like it?"

Margaret shook her head. "I doubt it", she replied. "Its an anthology of poems by William Wordsworth". Jamie was puzzled. "What's an anfology?" Margaret, eager to continue her reading, tried to be patient. "The word is an-*th*-ology and it means a 'collection', I suppose". Jamie was not finished by any means. "Who is William Wordsworth?" Margaret sighed, marked her place with a book-mark, put the closed book in her lap. "Not who *is* – who *was*! He died a long time ago and he lived in a lovely cottage in the Lake District – before you ask, that is a beautiful part of England up in the North-West, near to Scotland. He walked for miles and wrote the loveliest poems about what he saw". "Did he write poems about the bombing?" Jamie enquired. Margaret struggled to answer that one. She took her son's hand in her soft one, looked into the green eyes that gazed into hers, eager and agog for more information. "No, he didn't write about the bombing – there wasn't any when he was alive. You see, this war hadn't started then!" Jamie was at a loss. "But the war has *always* been there!" he spluttered; he had known nothing but war all of his short life.

Margaret was a highly intelligent woman, marred – if that was the right word – by her origins and preferred, reclusive lifestyle. She knew that to try to explain the concept of 'peacetime' would be lost on her son; he had no experience of this state, nothing at all with which to compare his entire life-experience. She changed tack. "Did you get your broken biscuits?" She knew that this would most easily divert his attention.

"Oh yes, I got a big bag full. Robert had a couple as well. Would you like one?"

He scampered out to the hall to retrieve the bag. Margaret never ceased to be amazed that any son of hers could not just *walk* anywhere. Whenever motion was called for it was accomplished at the fastest speed possible. She took the bag and rummaged through the contents, selecting some bits of Rich Tea. She allowed herself only the plainest of biscuits. She took up her book again. Jamie, seeing this, knew that the short interlude was over. He took himself off to his Advance Camp, armed with diary and pencil.

# RELIGIOSITY

Some time later, Desmond arrived back from church. "Desmond!" Margaret called – "Please come and tell me all about it". She was fascinated by the mechanics of religion. Desmond came in and sat down opposite her in the old armchair. "Well, it was *very* long and really very sad!" he began. "First, there was a big procession, all done in silence. There was no music at all for the whole service. There were three priests and they all wore just their white things; they came to the altar and lay down on their fronts with their arms out to the sides and just stayed there for ages while nobody said a thing! What do you call that thing on the altar where the bread is kept?"

"I believe it's called a tabernacle", said Margaret.

"Oh yes; well, its door was open and there was nothing inside it. Suppose that was meant to show that Jesus was dead and in his tomb. Anyway, then they started the Way of the Cross – you know, going round the fourteen stations on the walls of the church. They stopped at each one and said what it was. Then everyone said lots of prayers and it took ages for them to get to the last one. We all had to stand and I saw several old folk getting very tottery – one just had to sit down at one point. Anyway, then there were loads more prayers and readings. You know, I just don't get it! Jesus told everybody to love one another and had really a very happy life. Why are people made to feel sad when his death was the whole *point* of his being here. Why can't they feel happy – after all, he achieved what he came to do, to save us all. So why does everybody want to cry when they think of the crucifixion? I know it was a terrible way to die, but it was *meant* to be, wasn't it?"

"So, will you go there again?" Margaret asked. "I just don't know", replied Desmond. "I might give it a try on Easter Sunday at what they call High Mass – after all, *that* should be more cheerful, shouldn't it? Oh, I meant to ask; how's great-aunt Amelia?"

"I went to see Nunky this morning and he was just about to go to the nursing home when I left. I'm afraid that she is sinking fast. He said that the doctor had told him it can't be much longer. He was dreadfully upset, poor darling".

"Well, I'll hop up to see him this evening, try to take his mind off things for a bit. I know, I'll show him my latest plans for making a dynamo; that will interest him!"

Desmond went to get his work from his bedroom, spread the plans over the dining room table to make the minute alterations in detail that he knew were necessary. His old great-uncle *would* be interested; he was fascinated by everything mechanical. Desmond wondered what the old chap would do when he found himself all alone once more; would he retreat into his shell, or would he be able to 'snap out of it' as he had heard it expressed? He somehow doubted it and determined to do all he could to divert Nunky's attention to other, fascinating matters.

As he had left the church that afternoon, he had picked up a small booklet entitled, "What must I do to be a good Catholic?" He finished his alterations and started to read the text. He became more and more drawn to the strict observances that were demanded. He was a boy of tidiness and method; he lived by his own rules and regulations. He brushed his teeth night and morning for exactly five minutes; he chewed his food thirty times per mouthful; his bicycle was cleaned after every use, dirty or not; homework was done every time and on time. Now he read that Catholics were *ordered* to attend Mass every Sunday and on every Holy Day of Obligation; to confess their sins on a regular basis; to take Communion; to pray night and morning – oh, ever so many things. He approved this ordered existence, contrasting it with the rather loose arrangements of the Anglicans. He *knew* that there was a Creator God who had made Heaven and Earth; with a Divine purpose. Therefore, didn't it make absolute sense to live one's life by a set of firm rules that coincided with that purpose?

He put the pamphlet away; he would think again after he had attended the Easter Sunday service.

# RAILWAY GANGS AND A DEATH

Jamie, meanwhile, was engaged in an entirely different dilemma. Approaching him along the railway tracks was a gang of men. One held a long-handled hammer with which he tapped each length of rail. Another had a shovel whilst another held a massive spanner. Now and again the spanner was applied to the huge nuts that held the rails to the fishplates. The nuts were tightened as necessary. The man with the shovel took ballast from the side of the track to replenish any area that showed signs of a hollow. Should he attract their attention or remain hidden? His curiosity would always get the better of any remnant of discretion, so the question was meaningless.

As the three came level with them he poked his head out of the bush. "S'cuse me, what are you doing?"

The man with the hammer had been on the point of tapping the rail when Jamie asked this question. Quite startled, he dropped the hammer on his foot and hopped about on the other leg. "Bleedin' 'ell!" he muttered. The man with the spanner looked over at Jamie and laughed. "Wot you doin' there, lad?"

Jamie told them of his very important mission to plot all the trains that passed so that, one day, he would be able to make a full report.

"Strewth!" said the man. "You mean every train, do you?"

"Well, only those that go by when I'm actually here. I can't do those that go by when I'm not here!"

The man, a father of five children himself, knew how seriously such an obsession appeared to a little child. "No, well obviously not when you ain't here. How many have you got so far?"

Jamie did a quick calculation. "Seventy-nine!" he said proudly.

"By 'eck. You must have been here for ages to get that lot. Now, we must get on".

"But what are you doing?" said Jamie, still needing information.

"Right – old Bert here taps the rails to see if there are any breaks or cracks. If he hears a nice ring, then it's all right. If he hears a 'clunk' he marks the bit for the gang to change it. It'd be dangerous, see. Now, these 'ere rails are bolted to the sleepers, so I make sure the bolts are tight – plus the bolts that join the bits of rail together. Willy looks for gaps in the ballast and fills them up. There, that's what we are doin'. We are called permanent way inspectors". He grinned at this description, whilst Willy and Bert (now recovered) hooted with laughter.

"My dad's an inspector too!" he said proudly.

"What, a bus inspector?" asked Willy.

"No – he's a police inspector. He's very important now!"

Bert, who had no love of the police for reasons that he kept to himself, grunted. Willy, whose own brother was a policeman, wanted more information.

"Me bruvver's a copper! Where is yer old man stationed?"

"At Wandleford", replied Jamie. "P'raps he knows your brother!"

"Yes, p'raps he does", replied Willy. The gang moved down the line, tapping, bolting and shovelling as they went. Jamie noted down three more trains – soon he would reach the hundred train milestone. He started to feel hungry, so wriggled back to the fence. He entered the kitchen to wonderful aromas of sausage and mash with Bisto gravy. Sausages were indeed a rare treat, despite the fact that his father suspected and voiced that suspicion, the sausages were probably over fifty percent sawdust!

Desmond had browned the sausages nicely and had mixed a little margarine into the mashed potatoes. Jamie made a castle of his mash, spooning his gravy into the middle to form a small pond. He ate the sausages first and then set about the remainder, trying to diminish the 'castle' carefully so that the reduced 'pond' never burst the potato banks. The last few mouthfuls were all forked together to make a thick puddle.

After washing up the dishes, Desmond took his plans to Nunky. Jamie spent the evening playing with Robert whilst Margaret watched the antics of her two children.

Robert, now old enough to be manhandled a little, was held aloft by Jamie who lay on the floor. Robert wriggled above him as he was lowered to his brother's chest, hoisted up again. He giggled with merriment for he loved this game. Every time he was lowered, Jamie planted a big kiss on the little snub nose. Robert thought this huge fun as he went up and down.

Becoming bored with this game, Jamie set Robert down on the floor and crawled after his brother. Round and round they crawled, out into the hall, into the dining room, into the Morrison shelter, into the kitchen. Jamie deliberately led him away from the stairs, these being much too dangerous yet.

Tiring of this quite quickly, Jamie picked him up and sat him down in the old armchair and started to tell him a story. Taking the smallest toe in his fingers he began his made-up tale.

"This little pig liked sweets and ate them every day". Taking the next toe, he continued. "He ate and ate and ate and became as big as this little pig". This continued until, grasping the largest toe of all he ended, "And he became so big that he was as fat and huge as this great pig!"

They both dissolved into peals of laughter. Margaret looked on and marvelled at Jamie's imagination. Where on earth had it come from, she wondered? She never for a moment thought that her own vivid imagination could have anything to do with it!

There came the sound of the front door opening and closing. Desmond came in, quietly took the two young ones upstairs and made sure they were ready for bed, tucked them in. He returned downstairs to his mother as the tears started to roll down his face. He sat down next to his mother and took her hand.

Margaret knew what was coming, had been prepared for it for days past. "She's gone, hasn't she?"

Desmond nodded unhappily.

"I went to Nunky's but there was no reply, so I walked up to the nursing home. Nana, granddad and Nunky were all there in the sister's office. Noony died about eight o'clock!" It was too much for him as sobs shook his body. Margaret reached impulsively for the teenager and hugged him to her, a very rare occurrence indeed.

"There, there, dear", she said quietly. "The poor darling would have been in terrible pain, so it's a merciful release really!"

Desmond, old enough to understand the terrible agonies the old lady had suffered, nodded. "Yes, she's at peace now. God will look after her".

The two sat for some time side by side, hands touching. It was a very long time since Desmond had received such warmth and affection. Margaret broke the silence.

"Did anyone say when the funeral will be?"

"Granddad said that it will probably be next Friday", Desmond replied, dreading the coming event.

"I must ask your father to make sure that he can have the time off. I will have to ask Nancy to look after the wee ones". Nancy O'Brien, long standing home help would do this gladly, she knew.

Desmond took himself off to bed whilst Margaret waited up for John to come back from his 'shift'. One blessing of his recent promotion was that his hours were now a lot more regular than before. He came in fairly punctually at three minutes past midnight.

"How's Amelia?" he enquired. Margaret could not cry; she had many years before been unable to express grief. Quietly, she told her husband the news. John took her hand and said that he would definitely attend the funeral. Only a direct hit on the station would prevent him from coming!

A sad day drew to its end, Margaret sleeping as soundly as ever.

# PIANO LESSONS AND A FUNERAL

The following Tuesday was the occasion of Jamie's first piano lesson with Mrs Worthy. He arrived spick and span, hands washed and fingernails scraped; hair brushed into some semblance of order. He was ushered into the front room by Victoria Worthy and asked to sit on the piano stool as she adjusted the height to make sure that he could reach the keyboard with forearms horizontal. Jamie's day was irretrievably ruined when Tina, seven years old and pretty as a picture, poked her head round the door, uttered and exasperated, "Oh no, mother! Not *another* noisy little boy!" before flouncing upstairs to her bedroom. The door was heard to slam. Jamie sat quite dejected.

"Now, Jamie. Let's start at the beginning, shall we? Can you show me where middle C is?"

Jamie unerringly laid the tip of his right index finger on the correct key.

"Very good! Now, use your right thumb on middle C and play me a scale upwards".

Jamie started going upwards until he had used his little finger on the G. Now what, he wondered? He had run out of fingers!

Mrs Worthy showed him how to do it by using thumb, index and largest fingers to get to E, double his thumb under to hit the next F, so to progress up to the top C, ending correctly with his little finger. He was made to practise this over and over until he thought that his poor fingers would drop off. His first lesson ended with a downwards scale from middle C using the same technique with the left hand. Jamie had never been so bored in all his life. He simply wanted to play a *tune*! Not only had he been made to do horrid scales; he had been made to follow the written notes as well. It was immeasurably worse than arithmetic.

Margaret was eager to see how he had got on and made him recite, blow for blow, everything that he had done. Jamie, realising that many peoples' feelings would be hurt if he told the simple truth, expressed false pleasure. Margaret was delighted; she would like to have a musician in the family.

Jamie had not been told of Amelia's death, his parents fondly supposing that it was kinder to shield him from the truth at his young age. He had walked the previous day to his Nunky's house, finding that dear old gentleman tearfully writing at his desk, answering letters of condolence. Jamie had immediately guessed the truth and had asked outright if she had died.

"She will be happy now it's all over, won't she?"

Frederick had taken his great-nephew into his arms. "Yes, she's at peace now, nothing hurts her anymore."

Jamie thought this to be good news but, as his parents had not said anything about it, thought he had better not reveal his knowledge. Perhaps mummy would be made very sad if he mentioned it. Similarly, he said nothing to his nana and granddad. He simply accepted that Noony had gone to heaven and was happy.

The funeral itself was a severe disappointment to Margaret. Dressed, like all the family in black, she sat just behind her parents in the parish church. She could feel nothing as the flower-bedecked coffin was carried in, to be set on two trestles before the altar rails. The vicar began by welcoming all the mourners to this 'sad occasion'. His voice assumed a solemn timbre that he had always adopted for funerals. Alfred read the first lesson in his wonderfully modulated tones. Margaret listened with pride to the words so correctly pronounced. The senior member of the family, the Viscount, then offered the eulogy, stressing the essential goodness of his sister, her many works of charity and kindness, her marriage to Hans and their abandonment of his native land due to his loathing of the Nazis. He spoke fluently and well, pausing only once to turn aside, blowing his nose into a cambric handkerchief to hide the wiping of a stray tear.

Margaret listened as the vicar went through the rest of the service. She stood to sing in her clear voice the hymns that had been chosen, wincing at every false note played by the ancient soul at the organ console. Then it was time for the recessional, the pall bearers taking out the coffin as the mourners, front pew first, followed in train. The coffin was borne round the side of the church with everyone following to the far corner of the adjoining graveyard. A new hole had been dug, the two parallel mounds of soil covered with green cloth. Margaret joined John, Desmond and the rest at the sides as the vicar started the ritual of committal. This he intoned with even deeper solemnity than before. Not one mention of the joy of her life, no thanksgiving for it, it was all so deeply depressing. Desmond sobbed quietly as the coffin was lowered but managed, in his turn, to take a handful of earth and drop it on the highly polished lid.

Then it was all over. Frederick had arranged for a breakfast to be served in the splendidly vaulted church hall. Waitresses circulated with small schooners of sherry, glasses of fruit juice. People, at first somewhat subdued, began to greet one another. Relatives, strangers for years at a time, renewed acquaintanceships, old friends reminisced. Desmond was quite surprised to see his mother sitting apart from the throng, his father standing in his splendid uniform protectively behind her chair. Was she avoiding the other members of the large family, or were they avoiding her? Certainly, apart from her mother and father, none of the other relatives came over to speak to her. Margaret sat with eyes downcast.

Alfred, seeing Desmond standing forlorn and alone, went over to his 'grandson'.

"You have never met my eldest brother, have you? Come and say hello". He took Desmond by the arm and led him to where a small group had congregated by the buffet table.

The Viscount broke away and came over to Alfred. "This, I suppose is Desmond", he said, holding out a large hand. Desmond took it and shook formally. What did one call a Viscount, even when a relative? He decided to play safe.

"Yes, sir", he said.

"Heard marvellous things about you from my brother here!" boomed Edward. "Says you are a budding engineer – going to set the world on fire. We will need all the engineers we can get once this little lot's over; lots to rebuild and remake".

Desmond decided to take the plunge. "I've been designing a new sort of dynamo, sir; one that produces about twenty percent more output than the ones we currently make – and it will be made from materials that have a far longer life!"

"Bless my soul!" said the Viscount, taking Desmond by the shoulder. He had only the sketchiest idea what a dynamo was but was taken by the lad's obvious enthusiasm and earnestness. "You must come and see me some time and we'll see what can be done with these ideas of yours!"

Desmond was thrilled at the prospect and regarded this important figure with great respect.

"I'd love that, sir!" he said. He sensed that his time was up, so he strolled back to his own parents, a plate of rolls in his hand.

"Damned good mind he's got", Edward said to his brother. Alfred agreed. "I have seen some of his drawings. Frederick, who knows far more about it all than I suspect either of us does, says that he will go far. He's a thinker and, God knows, we need all of those that we can lay our hands on!"

No other member of the large family came to speak to Desmond; only his Nana and Granddad, Edward and Frederick acknowledged him. This was simply because none of them knew what to say to him. After all, he was not a blood relation. All of the older generation knew this, his father's background; they had all taken a vow of silence on the subject, entreated by Alfred not to mention the past and so upset his daughter's precarious balance. Therefore, they stayed away. Desmond knew nothing of this and was slightly puzzled. John knew all about it and was sad. He was by nature a gregarious, friendly man; he desperately needed to talk to them, to seek their approval. He stood quiet and resigned.

The younger cousins, nephews and nieces, had never been told but followed the lead set by their elders. They assumed that that branch of the family was somewhat aloof, reserved. Yet another opportunity for truth and understanding was missed.

Eventually, those with long journeys to make, started to drift away. All made their final farewells to the principals; none came near to Margaret, although one of them, a distant old cousin from Liverpool, waggled his fingers in a friendly manner in her direction.

Soon, only those principles were left. The Viscount (mercifully without wife, thought Alfred and Gertrude), made his own good-byes, reminding Desmond once again of his promise. He shook John's hand to congratulate him on his new position, The Viscount, like brothers Alfred and Frederick, thought very highly of this man, were always taken with his steadfastness, his sense of right and wrong. All were perplexed by Margaret's inability, or unwillingness, to see his very obvious good points, her obsession with the poor and bad. They were all too close to see the real problem – her desperate need for perfection, her self-loathing for having failed to achieve it; her need to lash out at those nearest to her who had failed to 'measure-up'. They saw only the outward signs, never the deep unhappiness that was the root cause of it all. The family parted company at the doorway to go their separate ways.

As the walked back home, Frederick accompanied Desmond.

"I hear you have a new dynamo under design", he said. "I'd love to see it!"

Desmond said that he would happily bring the plans the next day. He had a great respect for this old man, for his thoughtfulness, his judgement.

Alfred and Gertrude walked home, arm in arm and in silence – a companionable silence that was the product of thirty-nine years of marriage and deep friendship.

John followed behind with Margaret on his arm. He never tired of being seen in public with his lovely wife. Margaret, for her part, thought that John's new appearance was a distinct improvement on previously. He was now an 'officer'. He would, in her opinion, never be a *gentleman*, but it was a step in the right direction.

Jamie and Robert had spent the day at Nancy's little cottage. She adored the two and spent a happy time amusing Jamie with stories of her life, the people she had 'done' for, the great houses that she had cleaned. Jamie particularly liked her description of an old lady she had worked for; Nancy described her as looking like an 'old heron, squatting on a branch looking for fish'. He thought it hilarious as squatted on the table, head hunched down between shoulders and a miserable expression on his face. Nancy's massive bosom had wobbled alarmingly as she shrieked with laughter.

At five o'clock she walked the two back to Buttermere Gardens and handed them over to John. A couple of half-crowns were pressed into her fat hand, not that she had asked for or sought payment. She saw it as one of the great perks of her job. She loved the two children.

# A SHOPPING EXPEDITION

On the Tuesday after Easter Jamie was collected by his grandmother. They were to go into town to have Jamie fitted for his new school uniform as he had suddenly shot up about two inches and outgrown the originals. Gertrude, practical with needle and thread, had declared that the hems of the old garments were too short to accommodate the necessary alterations; the old shorts and blazer would have to be abandoned; also, Jamie needed new shoes as these had been suddenly outgrown as well. Jamie viewed his new stature as something of a mixed blessing. First and foremost was the distinct improvement in the attitude of his friends; no longer a short, squat boy, they now treated him with a little wariness. Jamie liked this. On the other hand, he had found a bit of difficulty squeezing through the fence and up his tunnel. Did he have the patience to enlarge it a bit?

Outings to town with nana were always viewed with glee; each one ended as sure as fate at a restaurant or café for juice and delicious cakes. Almost any indignity suffered at the hands of condescending shopkeepers was worth the eventual outcome of the expedition. As the pair walked down Buttermere Gardens to the corner by the pub where busses and trams stopped the sun came out. It had been an indifferent Easter, alternating between short showers and watery sun. This was different today, the sun shone from a bright sky, full and strong. It, to quote Frederick's saying, 'warmed the old bones'. Before the war Gertrude would have travelled to Wandleford by their own car, driven by their own chauffeur. Petrol rationing had put paid to that; that and the fact that Clive Tyson, the chauffeur, was now serving king and country in the uniform of a sergeant in the Royal Army Service Corps. The car had been laid up for the duration in the large garage that had been built at the same time as the bungalow. The bungalow was built some thirty yards from the road and was approached by a long path of shallow, up-slanting steps. The garage was just back from the road, on the right of the property as seen from the road. It had a very strong flat roof of twelve inches of reinforced concrete. Double hinged doors were now hidden behind two blast walls, each over six feet high. The car inside was one of Jamie's delights. The maroon and black Morris Ten smelt of leather and petrol; he loved squeezing into the garage to sit behind the wheel and make 'motor' noises.

First to arrive was a bus, to Gertrude's relief, for her thoughts on the rattling trams were very akin to those of her son-in-law. They boarded and sat at the front so that Jamie could peer through the front left window and steal occasional glances at the driver who was perched in his cab in front of him to the right. Jamie loved to watch how the massive gear lever was moved and mimed each shift. They passed the next pub on the right, behind which a road forked back and up the hill to the North Downs; just past this was the bus depot, then onwards to another pub at yet another fork in the road. Gertrude saw with dismay that there were even more houses covered with tarpaulins, more heaps of rubble, more smashed lives. Then they were in Wandleford itself, going slowly up the High Street. There were some delivery vans about, some horses and carts, but very few cars. Passed on the right was the strange domed theatre that staged musicals and the occasional concert of what was now quaintly called 'light music'. Then they were getting ready to alight as the other theatre came into view, the famous Hammond Theatre in which was a mighty organ. It was not what Margaret had called 'one of those horrid, wavery, quavery Wurlitzers', but a real pipe organ, four manuals, on which famous players had performed recitals, had accompanied huge choirs in such works as Bach's Mass in B Minor and Margaret's all-time favourite, the Crucifixion by John Stainer. The theatre also, of course, staged plays and concerts. It had miraculously been spared from the bombing so far.

Just up from the Hammond Theatre was a branch off the High Street where the ancient open market thrived. Jamie loved the place; to wander past the stalls of fruit and vegetables (now quite sparse), leather goods, flowers and various household goods was his idea of bliss. He tried to copy the raucous cries of, "T'marters – frippence a poun!", "Luvverly dafferdills an' toolips!" Gertrude had ceased to remonstrate with him over his aping when she came to realise that his normal speech was not being affected; he was simply absorbing the sounds, loving each and every new experience. However, that day, there was no time for the market. They walked on until they came to the rather superior department store that she favoured. Probyns Store had been there since eighteen seventy-one, as witnessed on the front wall, chiselled into a red brick plaque that matched the fine Victorian façade that was four storeys high. There were five sets of double glass doors into the store, each attended by a doorman resplendent in his brown and gold uniform. The door was opened inwards with a polite, 'Good morning, madam'. Gertrude smiled her thanks and preceded Jamie into the sweetly scented hinterland. Small counters were set at all angles, each supervised by a young woman in brown skirt, brown blouse with gold edging. Gertrude, unlike her daughter, did not use proprietary scents, preferring her favourite lavender water. The two went to the back of the ground floor where the lifts were stationed. Jamie loved these as well. Each had funny concertina doors made of steel bars and was attended by yet another old man on a stool. He would grasp the brass handle, slide open the doors, both outer and inner, to allow entry and egress of the shoppers. Jamie followed his grandmother into the opened cage. The doors were slid shut. "Which floor, madam?" asked the old chap. "Menswear, if you please!" "Going up!" announced the man as the cage rattled on its guides. They arrived at the second floor and found themselves confronted by a very tall man in a morning coat. He gave a slight bow. "How may we be of service, madam?"

They were led to a far counter that specialised in school uniforms where they were introduced to 'our Mr Carter' who would 'attend to all their needs'. Gertrude, seated at the counter on a stool supervised the proceedings. Jamie's new short trousers and blazer were brought out and he was led off to a small cubicle to try them on. He returned to stand before his nana who gave the new garments a very critical inspection that clearly passed with flying colours. "Very neat and tidy, and with the requisite room for future growth!" To Jamie, the things seemed impossibly large; the blazer sleeves almost hid his hands whilst the trousers completely covered his knees. Discussion, never mind objection, would be utterly useless he knew from bitter experience. So, he said nothing, went back to change again into his own old, comfortable clothes; he went back to his nana as the new garments were parcelled up in brown paper – and what a parcel it was. The paper was folded back so that the ends could not cut fingers. Each fold was immaculately straight, the whole tied with white string that was eventually secured with a double bow knot. Gertrude opened her handbag and withdrew her cheque book as her bill was prepared. Jamie loved watching the process. Bill and cheque were folded into a cylinder and closed; the cylinder was attached to an overhead wire; a lever was pulled to allow the cylinder to shoot over to the central cash desk where it was detached, bill and cheque entered in a ledger, a copy of the bill was stamped as receipted, all to be returned to their counter by the same means. It was fascinating. Folding her receipt into the leather purse, Gertrude thanked 'our Mr carter', gave the delivery address for the parcel and led Jamie back to the lifts. To his joy he heard the request, 'restaurant, please'. Up they went to the top floor where a trio of old ladies – violin, cello and piano, struggled with a rendition of Strauss waltzes. They were led to a small table and attended to by a waitress, again in the familiar brown and gold.

Gertrude had ordered coffee, orange juice and a selection of pastries. Jamie could hardly wait to see what delights this 'selection' would comprise. He uttered a short prayer for his absolute favourite, a Viennese Whirl and to his utter delight there were two of them among other cakes atop a linen doily. Gertrude, seeing his face, took one and put it on his plate. "I know you love these, Jamie dear. Eat up and mind the crumbs, won't you!"

Strauss had given over to a selection from Gilbert and Sullivan. Gertrude found herself quietly humming along to The Gondoliers; she stopped, embarrassed that others might have heard her – that would never do; how common! Jamie had no such inhibitions and hummed to himself. Gertrude was quite amused to hear him still humming the tune as they left the store. Was he really as musical as reports claimed?

By the roadside outside the store stood a large, covered van, its rear doors opened wide so that the whole empty interior was visible. At the far end was a large white screen on which was being shown a newsreel. Mr Churchill was seen in the uniform of an Air Chief Marshal inspecting rows of Lancaster bombers that had returned from one of the thousand bomber raids. His unmistakable voice blared from a loudspeaker mounted on the roof of the van. Next came a series of moving pictures taken, presumably, by an observer on one of those raids. Blackness of night, flashes and bursts of anti-aircraft fire, desperate jigglings of the aircraft to try to dodge them; the ground below, a darker black than the night sky, suddenly lit up with flashes of bomb bursts; fires started to rage. Gertrude felt sorrow for those poor wretches caught by this devastation. However, the Germans had brought it upon themselves with their arrogance, their blind obedience to that maniac with the silly moustache! She took Jamie's hand and walked to the big shop next to the department store. This was her favourite shop, a bookshop that had the reputation of being able to find and sell any book that had been printed in the last hundred years. Duffy & Hawk, Booksellers, had been in existence since the golden jubilee of eighteen eighty-seven. Gertrude went to a far counter marked 'Reservations' and waited patiently for her turn to be served by a lady with quite impossible red hair piled high on her head. This individual peered down her nose at lists of books through tiny pince-nez that seemed in danger of falling from the tips of her thin nostrils. They also gave her voice a distinctly nasal twang.

Gertrude, at her turn, gave her name to this lady; lists were examined, names sought, titles examined. Eventually, satisfied with her search, the lady turned to a face peering from a hatch behind her. "Mrs Clements – Homas Hardy – Yude The Obs'hure", she called out. The face withdrew. Jamie struggled not to laugh. After a very short time the requisite book was thrust through the hatch to be neatly wrapped and tied. Again came the business with little cylinder, overhead wires, cash desks. Gertrude put receipt and change from her immaculately crisp white fiver into her handbag. Holding her precious parcel she took Jamie out and across the road to catch a return bus. She had been collecting Thomas Hardy for years; she loved his work, its perfect descriptions of a countryside and age now long gone. She had wanted a copy of Jude The Obscure for some months; now, at last, her collection was complete.

To her disgust, the first to arrive was a tram. Reluctantly, she got on, Jamie hopping up behind her. A penny fare plus a ha'penny half were purchased, the punched tickets given to Jamie to swell his collection. Back they rattled until they arrived at the terminus at Brooke Hill. They had passed the tram depot, yet another establishment that fascinated the little boy. It was next to the large dairy from which the milk carts daily emerged to go on their rounds. At one side was a long row of stables for the horses, whilst a strong smell of manure emanated from the premises.

The walk home, past the pond, under the railway bridge, was accompanied by Jamie still humming the music that the trio had played. He was trying to master the art of whistling but, as yet, had managed only a thin sound that was completely unacceptable. However, with his Nana so close by, he dared not utter such sounds. To her they were 'common' sounds, indulged in by costermongers and the like. So, he forbore and hummed instead.

Margaret was waiting for them. Most unusually, she had prepared a plate of delicately cut sandwiches and a pot of tea for her mother. Gertrude was very happy to see this and, although not in the least hungry, ate two whilst the others disappeared into Jamie's mouth.

"Was the uniform all right?" asked Margaret.

"Oh, very nice dear. It will be delivered tomorrow".

Margaret knew that she and John, with his increased pay, could well afford the clothes but she also knew that it gave her mother great pleasure to take her grandson shopping, to provide the 'necessary' as she had had to do in years past.

"I hope you said a big thank-you to Nana!"

Jamie, who had forgotten to do anything of the kind, smothered his little grandmother with a big hug. "Thank you

Nana for my new uniform and for the cakes!" came somewhat muffled inside his Nana's fur stole.

Gertrude had needed the diversion. Following a week of sadness, the loss of her dear sister-in-law, she had enjoyed the company of her grandson. The little lad brought happiness to her and to Alfred, a freedom of thought and lightness of spirit that would have been impossible in the days of her own childhood. She still retained the prim and proper behaviour that had been drummed into her but saw only good in Jamie's mad antics and, occasional, wild escapades. The little fellow seemed to her to be simply a mass of good intentions that went wrong, more often than not, by being so impulsively pursued. There appeared to be no malice or anger in him, just a wild and impetuous nature that, sooner or later, would have to be properly directed. Desmond was the ideal brother to do this. Jamie, she knew, idolised him. Perhaps she should have a quiet word in that lad's ear.

Gertrude and Alfred had a very high regard for Desmond. He was quiet, thoughtful and patient. They believed that he deserved every chance in life and had little sympathy for Margaret's dismissal of his talents.

Sooner or later this young man would have to be told, or – heavens forbid – would find out for himself, the true story of his birth and the fact that he had an older brother and sister. What on earth would that do to the boy? How would he react? What would then be his feelings towards his father? Would he curse him for his duplicity, or would he find some way to understand and forgive?

Gertrude tried to think of other things, to escape back into her own happy world. She knew that this was sheer cowardice and hated herself for it. But it was out of her hands. Her daughter ruled the situation – after all it *was* the business of that family, not her own. It was a dilemma for the future. She dreaded its happening.

# INVASION AND A RED NOSE

There was huge excitement in the classroom; Cecily Bedford could hardly make herself heard over the noise that erupted from the children. Still, she thought, she had only herself to blame. Two days earlier the allies had mounted the biggest invasion in history, crossing the English Channel in hundreds of ships and planes. She had told the children of this momentous news, plus the fact that her husband was in command of an escort group, safeguarding the vulnerable landing ships, shelling the German land-based gun emplacements and making sure that the way was clear for the mass of supply vessels that were waiting patiently miles offshore.

Some boys were convinced that the allied armies would simply walk all over the German army, would in a few days be in Berlin. Others, from overheard conversations between their parents, thought that it would be very tough going. None of these boys was much over the age of seven; all had opinions as all had lived only during war, knew the regimental badges of the British Army, could identify the planes and ships. Jamie was no different but soon tired of the buzz of rumour and wild conjecture. His thoughts ranged to the great outdoors; he still sat at his favourite desk by the window and gazed out into the early June sunshine.

Mrs Bedford took the large pointer and rapped loudly on her desk. This elicited no response, so she rapped louder. Still no result.

"Silence!" she bellowed in a voice that her husband would have found useful from his bridge against a force eight gale.

Quiet, utter quiet, descended. Faces looked forward to the board; postures were made more erect and attentive. Even Jamie was woken from his reverie. Mrs Bedford had been known to use that pointer on things other than her desk!

"Now", she said, gazing at the silent mass before her. "Let us look at the map".

She unrolled the large map of Europe that had seen so much use the past few years. Its wooden roller was propped over the top of the blackboard so that the Channel formed the centre of the part visible to the class.

She pointed at the Cherbourg peninsular and to the marked landing beaches on the Normandy coast. She then pointed at the south coast of England.

"Who can tell me why the invasion came as such a surprise to the Germans?"

As was inevitable, the hand that reached to the sky and waved pleadingly belonged to Julian Warburton. He was almost gibbering in a frenzy to be asked. Mrs Bedford allowed her gaze to switch from this perennial nuisance to his neighbour.

"Well, Alan?"

This little boy stood up, trying to disregard the furious looks of his neighbour. He knew that Julian would try to take it out of him in break-time. He swallowed.

"Please, Mrs Bedford. The Germans thought that we would take the short route and try to land at Calais or somewhere near there. They never expected that we would go such a long way across".

"Very good, Alan. You can sit down now. See, children, how far it is across to Normandy and how short a journey it would have been to Calais. That is only just over twenty miles, but we chose to go much further. They *expected* us to go the short way and it must have come as a nasty surprise to find that we had not. They were simply not prepared. Now, who can tell us who is in command?"

Hands immediately shot up again. Cecily chose a normally quiet boy from near the back. "Yes, Frank?"

"It's General Eisenhumber!" he said confidently. He was drowned out by a gust of laughter.

"Nearly, Frank! His name is General Dwight Eisenhower and he is an American".

"Why is he American, Mrs Bedford? After all, the invasion came from England – so why isn't the commander one of ours?" This came from Matthew Hartley, Jamie's best friend.

"Think about the size of America and the size of Britain", said Cecily. "America has five times the number of people and their army is much bigger than ours. It seemed only right that General Eisenhower should be put in charge. After all, General Montgomery is in charge of the British troops".

This still did not satisfy Matthew, a stickler for detail.

"But we have been at war with Germany much longer than they have!"

"Yes, but the Americans have been helping us with ships and food – and they have lent us money to keep going".

Matthew subsided, still muttering that he thought it unfair. Quite a few of the boys agreed with him, echoing their parents' thoughts of 'those Yanks'.

However, the lesson scheduled for that morning was reading. Cecily had instituted a method of ensuring that all the boys got a fair turn to read aloud to the class. She had made them all memorise their place in the 'queue' which was arranged in alphabetical, surname order. On her order the reading books were taken from desks and opened at the right pages. She consulted her little aide-memoire that she kept in the deep pocket of her tartan skirt.

"Right, we start today with Peter Reason. From the top of page thirty please, Peter!"

Jamie simply could not afford to let his attention wander. After Reason came Sanders and then came Small.

Peter Reason, six and a half years old, began.

"King Arthur sat at the round table and looked at his knights. He was not happy. He had been told that one of them had killed a farmer who had not done anything wrong. The king was very angry and asked who had done this terrible deed".

"Very nicely read, Peter. Next boy!"

Adam Sanders stood up.

"Not one of the knights would own up; they all sat quietly and looked down at the table. Not one would look up at the king. They were all very scared of what the king would do. King Arthur asked them again, this time in a much louder and more angry voice".

"Excellent, Adam. Next!"

Jamie stood up and cleared his throat.

"Again, there was silence round the big table. King Arthur then drew his mighty sword and went round to each knight in turn. He made the knight look at him and asked, 'was it you who killed the farmer?' He knew that the knight who had done it would not dare to lie to his king. Each knight answered, 'no'. Then he came to Sir Beddingvere".

Hoots of laughter greeted this. Cecily looked hard at Jamie; had that been an innocent slip, or had it been deliberate, playing the fool?

She waved for silence. "That knight's name is Bedevere!" she corrected, looking closely to see what reaction it provoked. She was reassured as Jamie went a deep red.

"Sorry, Mrs Bedford", he stuttered. Obviously, a slip, thought Cecily. He would pay for it by being ragged by the others. If it had been deliberate, he would not have been able to suppress a grin.

Readers came and went as the story unfolded. Bedevere admitted his guilt, was banished for a month from the round table; the somewhat moralistic points of truthfulness and honour were rammed home.

Then it was time for the lunch break. Jamie went out to the cloakroom, followed by a motley assortment of boys. "Who's Beddingvere – the knight who makes the beds?" "I say, Jamie, is a Beddingvere the man who looks after the flower beds?" "Hoy, spotty, did Beddingvere wet his bed like I bet you do?" This last came from a boy named Graham Jones, not much bigger than Jamie and one of Julian Warburton's hangers-on. It was too much; Jamie launched himself at the jeering face and landed a punch on the snub nose. Graham went down howling, to be surrounded by a large throng who urged him to get up and fight. Graham, nursing a swelling nose, stayed where he was.

Julia Forbes was first on the scene. She quickly identified the assailant and dismissed all but Graham and Jamie to the playground. Then she started to enquire why Jamie had thought it wise to punch Graham on the nose.

"He called me 'spotty' and said I wet my bed – and I *don't*!"

"Is that true, Graham", asked Julia. Graham thought quickly. Enough of the rest of the boys would back up Jamie's version as Julian and his small band of cronies were not very popular. He simply nodded. Julia satisfied herself that Graham's nose was not bleeding, merely swollen and quite red. She sent him out as well and took Jamie to see the headmistress.

Cecily listened as the story unfolded. She had to try very hard to keep a straight face; 'well done, Jamie' she wanted to say. However, discipline must be maintained.

"I will *not* tolerate fighting in my school. I shall have to report your conduct to your father. Meanwhile, go back to the classroom and write fifty times, 'I must not fight'.

Jamie slouched disconsolately back to his desk to get a sheet of paper. He dipped his pen into the inkwell only to find that some wag had filled it with little balls of blotting paper. He reached across to the next desk and began. The first twenty lines were quickly finished; thereafter, the second twenty dragged. The last ten seemed to him to take a week. He was miserable and quite hungry when at last the task was finished. He took the 'lines' to Mrs Bedford and was upbraided for slovenly penmanship. However, he was allowed to grab a quick sandwich before joining the others for the first lesson of the afternoon. Beastly arithmetic – how he hated it. He sat looking out of the window, longing to be free, to be allowed to do what he wanted to in the fresh air. He did not actually suffer from claustrophobia but hated being indoors when the sun was shining. That afternoon Jamie was a very unhappy boy.

As he left school later that day Cecily put a letter into his hand. "Now, mind you give that letter to your father. I shall check!"

Jamie was in no hurry to get home. He hoped to see the old brigadier, but that gentleman was not outdoors. There was nobody to speak to, nobody in the road or in front gardens to delay his homecoming. He went in the back door, hung up satchel and coat; he went up to his bedroom to read. Mother and Robert were obviously out somewhere. However, pangs of hunger drew him back to the deserted kitchen. He took the loaf of bread and sawed off a couple of slices on which he spread some dripping from the bowl in the larder. Taking these back up to his room he buried his head in a book all about the Boer Wars. He had absolutely no idea who the Boers were or what the war had been all about. What he liked were the stories of individual soldiers, flying on horseback over the veldt (whatever that was) to take vital messages to field commanders who were in desperate situations. He saw himself astride a white stallion thundering over wide grasslands, arriving just in the nick of time to save the situation. Slowly his mood lightened until, with a start, he heard his father arrive home. Still no sign of mother and Robert; Desmond, he knew, was not due home yet. Taking the dreaded envelope, he went down the stairs.

"Hello, Dad. Mrs Bedford said to give you this letter".

John took the envelope and opened the flap, took out the single sheet of school headed notepaper. The body of the letter caused him some amusement which, of course, he took great pains to conceal. After the customary salutation Mrs Bedford had written in her immaculate copperplate, 'I have had to punish Jamie today for fighting with one of his school- mates. Apparently, this other boy made some remark to which your son took quite violent objection, resulting in the other boy suffering a swollen, painful nose, although showing no signs of any real injury. I had occasion to reprimand your son, to impose fifty 'lines' which were duly delivered, albeit of increasingly poor penmanship. I am always loath to write parents concerning the behaviour of their children but, in this case, thought that I had no alternative other than so to do. I am sure that you will endorse, even reinforce, my lecture to Jamie upon the unacceptability of violent conduct even, and I suspect this to have been the case, in the face of some real provocation. I remain yours very sincerely'.

John folded the letter back into the envelope and thrust it into his pocket. Jamie, who had been hopping from one foot to the other, stared at his father; would he get a whack? John crouched down until their faces were only a few inches apart.

"Well, old son, what did this other boy do?"

"Dad, he said that I *wet my bed – and I don't*!"

"So, what happened then?" asked John.

"I punched his fat nose! I know I shouldn't have, but I did and I'm sorry I didn't make it bleed. He is always picking fights and bullying – him and that other Julian – they nearly always pick on the little boys. I'm not really sorry at all!"

John could not help but smile at his little son who, since his last growth spurt, no longer thought of himself as one of the 'little boys'.

"What he said was very rude, as well as being untrue". Jamie was very pleased to hear this. "However", went on his father. "You really must not take the law into your own hands and lash out at every remark that you find offensive. Perhaps you could have thought of something to say that would have offended *him*?"

"But Dad, I can *never* think of clever things to say quickly enough. I can think of them miles after, but not at the time! Anyway, he is always doing it and I'm not sorry I slugged him!"

John was not sorry either. "Well, old chap; let's say no more about it, shall we. Just remember to think hard before you start punching all and sundry. When you get to a more senior school, you can always ask for three rounds in the ring with proper boxing gloves on?"

Jamie was not at all sure about this. But, as it seemed that he would escape a whack from his dad, nodded and said that this was indeed a very good idea. The incident passed; the boy went upstairs feeling relief for his escape; the father went out to the garden feeling some pride in his son. No mention would be made to any other member of the family; it was kept between the two of them. As a result, Jamie, sensing his father's pride, felt closer to a father for whom he already had love and respect.

# THE DOODLEBUG

The next day, another mild and sunny late spring day, Jamie was due to have yet another music lesson after school. Therefore, instead of loitering down the hill to examine trees for birds' nests, he hurried down the hill. This steep road had, for some wholly unexplained reason, been ignored some years before when the Urban Council had decided to plant trees in its residential roads. Derwent Drive was a mass of horse chestnuts (their pink and white 'candles' long fallen), whilst Buttermere Gardens had been planted with Jamie's favourite trees – graceful silver birches. He hopped down the hill, five hops on left leg and then five on right. The object was to avoid any joins in the large paving slabs. His record to date was one hundred and seventeen hops before infringing this rule. Today, to his great joy, he passed this by a considerable margin but stopped well before the steep hill ended or he would have no challenge left for another day. As he resumed what for him was a steady walk, he heard the unmistakable spluttering from on high of a dreaded V1 flying bomb. He shuddered.

These indiscriminate missiles had been 'sent over' from the continent for some days now and were the latest manifestation of what the politicians called 'the terror tactics of a desperate and evil foe'. They were filled with fuel that was calculated to run out just short of the intended target, thus causing gravity to bring it down somewhere near the selected spot. The nose was packed with one thousand pounds of high explosive, the motor being attached in a pod above and to the rear of the body of the missile. Everyone now knew that when they were heard roaring overhead, all was safe. Danger came only when the motor started its final splutterings. Those in the know had also warned of more sinister missiles to come; they had hinted darkly of the possibility of rocket-powered bombs. The development site of Peenemunde, on the German Baltic coast, had been identified some months previously and had been repeatedly bombed.

Jamie looked over his shoulder and distinctly saw the terrible thing already starting to wobble as the lack of fuel and forward motion destroyed its aerodynamics. The motor stopped; the bomb tilted over. Jamie screamed in terror and started to run. Thinking quite clearly, almost it seemed to him in slow motion, he shot into the open gateway to the brigadier's house, hoping to reach the Anderson shelter where months ago the pair had sought refuge during a conventional bombing raid. He was within twenty yards of this sanctuary when the bomb hit the ground, the ground-contact fuse igniting and setting off the main charge. It had fallen directly on a house opposite that of the brigadier. That house, large and sturdily built, lay a good fifty yards from the road. Jamie, when the explosion occurred, was a good hundred yards from it. There came a thud, a split second of terrible silence, a massive explosion. Jamie was picked up and hurled sideways to land in a tangle of arms, legs and satchel in a rhododendron bush that was in full, deep red flower. He was dimly aware of a choking cloud of brick dust swooshing over him, small pieces of stone and splintered timber spiking his back and legs. He saw quite clearly a huge piece of chimney stack soar overhead. Then his eyes dimmed over and he lost consciousness.

Neighbours, shaken and trembling, were first on the scene. Their natural focus was on the shattered remains of the large house. One old lady who had suffered the Zeppelin raids of nineteen sixteen, was far more aware of the correct procedure than the twenty or so others who were milling around.

"Quiet, everybody! Let us listen carefully, see if anyone cries out!"

Silence fell. The soft spring wind stirred the young leaves, made small eddies of dust above the dreadful crater. Not a sound other than this was heard. Instead, from afar, came the strident clanging of bells as two fire engines hurried to the scene. They were followed more sedately by an ambulance. By the time these three vehicles had come to a stop in the long driveway the crowd had started to speculate again. The old lady came over to the fireman who had a white stripe around his black helmet.

"I asked for silence some time ago", she explained. "We could hear nothing at all. I hope to God that means they were all out!"

"Amen to that, madam!" said the station officer. He had attended well over a hundred bomb sites and was inured to the sight, and collection of, shattered limbs, broken bodies, pathetic remnants of possessions once cherished. He held up his hand and called for another period of silence. Nothing. He was just about to drop his arm again to signal his men to start the search when one of the ambulance crew, hovering at the gateway until needed, heard a faint whimper. He shouted again for silence. Again the faint whimper. He was sure that it had come from somewhere across the road. He walked very quietly across and stopped at the torn remains of the brigadier's gate posts. There, a faint whimper nearer the now pock-marked house. He stepped as lightly as he could down the gravel, stopping every five strides to listen again. The whimpering was louder and guided him to a row of bushes that were covered in dust and debris. He found the little figure huddled deep within the foliage of a bush at the far end. The ambulance man noted the open door of the Anderson shelter that seemed to gape in mockery.

"Over here!" he called, kneeling by the small figure. He laid an expert hand on the thin neck and found a strong pulse.

"Lie still old chap. Help is coming. No, don't move!" This as Jamie, his sight slowly returning, started to wriggle upright. Strong hands restrained him; he struggled in terror. Was the devil trying to keep him from escaping to heaven? He was terrified, sobbing in frustration. The man, now joined by his colleague and the fireman, told him again to keep still until they had made sure that he was not seriously injured. He was quite new at the job and had little or no understanding of children. However the fire station officer had.

"Look, old man", he said, taking one of Jamie's little hands in his calloused grip. "You have had quite a nasty bump. You are quite safe but we need to see where it hurts. Can you tell us if anything is really sore?"

His quiet and authoritative voice seemed to do the trick; Jamie calmed down a bit; perhaps he was not dead after all. He tried to blink his eyes clear of the dust. His back and legs seemed to be a mass of little fires. The other ambulance man took over. He started on the usual injury assessment.

"Ok, old chap. Lets start with your right hand. Can you wiggle your fingers for me?"

With some difficulty Jamie thought this one through. He slowly waggled the fingers and thumb of his right hand. Then came the left hand, followed by right toes, left toes, right leg and left leg. All moved without Jamie screaming with pain; but he did start whimpering again as the movement started the little flames dancing in various places.

"Well, there don't seem any real bad injuries!" said the ambulance man. A stretcher was fetched and Jamie was lifted gently on to it, covered with a red blanket and carted into the waiting vehicle. Just as it was about to reverse into the road, a policeman arrived on the scene. He was a war-time 'special' and had the officious bearing of one who relished his part-time authority.

"What's going on here, then?" he asked of all and sundry.

The station officer waved around generally, encompassing the crater, rubble, the general scene of destruction. "Have a wild guess!" he said contemptuously. The other firemen laughed, even the neighbours had a quiet smile. The 'special' pointed at the ambulance. "Who's in there then?" he asked, trying to retrieve the situation, to attain some dignity after what he saw had been a crass utterance.

"Little lad, obviously caught in the blast. Found him in the bushes in the garden over yonder".

The 'special' took out his notebook and started to make notes whilst everyone else simply ignored him. The ambulance drove off to the cottage hospital, bell ringing for its demanded free passage through what was nearly non-existent traffic. Before the war the little hospital carried out routine operations on tonsil removal, the occasional appendectomy, minor breaks and so forth. Since the bombing its staff had become well versed in serious trauma care, amputations, compound fractures. The learning curve had been steep and achieved with dedication and speed.

# HOSPITAL

As Jamie was carried on the stretcher into the little Casualty Department his eyes had blinked out the last of the masonry dust. He saw a bright overhead light and the serene face of the sister in charge looking down at him.

"Right, little man! Let's see what we can do for you, shall we?" She took a pair of large scissors, starting to cut off his blazer, shirt and shorts, talking all the while to reassure her little patient. Jamie suffered in silence until he was gently rolled over by the nurse who was assisting. He started to whimper again. The sister looked at the marks on the little back and on the backs of the legs. None was in the least serious but, together, must be causing considerable pain. She took a ball of cotton wool, dipped it into a basin of mild antiseptic, began to clean the cuts and bruises. Jamie felt the soothing coolness and calmed down a little until all the little fires settled down from flames to a dull smouldering. Gentle fingers applied a cold ointment to the bruises, gauze and plaster to the cuts. He was beginning to feel better, if a little woozy! The doctor on duty came in and expressed admiration for the treatment so far administered to the small patient. He took a pencil torch from his pocket and examined Jamie's eyes. One gave him a small concern, the pupil being a trifle dilated. However, he gave the order to put Jamie into a pair of pyjamas and to have him transferred to the children's ward on the top floor. Jamie, cleaned and dressed in pyjamas far too large for him that smelt of carbolic soap, was wheeled to the lift and taken to a bed in the far corner of the ward that contained twelve beds, six on each side. The ward sister welcomed him and gave him a drink of orange juice, sending one of her nurses to fetch him a slice of bread and butter. She then closed the curtains around his little bed and told him to try and sleep, explaining that of all medicines available, sleep was the most efficient. He would feel much better when he woke up, she promised.

Meanwhile, the ambulance men had looked through Jamie's satchel and pockets. They found a label in the back of his ruined blazer that gave his name and address. One of them went into the sister's office and 'phoned the Brooke Hill police station so that an officer could be dispatched to Jamie's home and his parents informed. The duty sergeant took the call and, to make sure that needless anxiety was avoided, called the ward sister to be appraised of Jamie's condition. He recognised the name and 'phoned the much bigger station at Wandleside. Although Brooke Hill was in the area covered by the Surrey Constabulary, whilst Wandleside was in the 'Met' Jurisdiction, he had known Jamie's dad for some time. He asked to be put through to the Inspector's office and spoke briefly to John. He explained as much as he knew, telling of the relatively minor nature of his son's injuries. John thanked the sergeant; he went up to the Superintendent's office and explained the situation. That kindly man told John to 'Hop off and comfort his family' He would see John again in the morning. Any help or assistance required, just give 'me a bell'. John thought about commandeering a squad car to take him home; he dismissed the idea as being a waste of precious resources. However, the Superintendent had outguessed his subordinate officer; a police driver approached John, saluted and told him that he had been told to drive him home, collect his wife and take them all to the cottage hospital. Then he would have to get back to the station. Uttering a short prayer of thanks, John climbed in the large Wolseley which, with bell clanging, set off at great speed southwards. John climbed out of the car and went in to break the news to Margaret.

She expressed horror and could not wait to get to see her son. This surprised and gladdened John; he had not thought that such feelings for the boy really existed. On the way, baby Robert was left with his grandparents; they arrived at the cottage hospital in a record four minutes. Thanking the police driver, John followed Margaret into the reception area to be told that Jamie was on the top floor. Up they went in a shaky old lift to find his little bed enclosed behind curtains. The sister came from her office and put an admonitory finger to her lips.

"Shhhhh!" she whispered. "The little lamb's fast asleep – do him the world of good. He's got some nasty bruises and cuts, but they will all heal up quickly. He also had a mild concussion, or so the doctor thinks. He's, all in all, a very lucky boy. It seems he got caught in the blast from a Doodlebug while he was on his way home from school. You can sit with him if you promise to be quiet!"

Margaret and John found hard chairs and sat one each side of the tiny bed. Margaret took her little son's hand in hers and bent forward to plant a soft kiss on his ginger curls. He looked quite angelic as he lay there, eyes closed, chest rising and falling regularly. John wondered, not for the first time, why on earth she could not show him that love when he was awake. Surely, she knew that Jamie needed that love and care just as much as Robert.

They stayed sitting there for about an hour before Jamie started to awake. He opened his eyes slowly and took in the unfamiliar surroundings. Memory came back in a flood as his eyes filled with tears. Margaret stroked his head.

"There, darling; no need to worry any more; mummy is here!"

Jamie tried manfully to stop the tears. John reached forward and tweaked his nose. Jamie looked over to his father and gave him a watery smile.

"Hello mummy; hello daddy. I got blowed up! It hurt a lot but I didn't cry much. They took my school clothes off with a big pair of scissors. They took me to the 'hostipal'. Does it mean I won't be going to school tomorrow?"

"I doubt if you will be back at school for some time!" replied John. He could not mistake the angelic smile that spread over the freckled face; apparently that was the best news that he could have imparted. Margaret continued to fuss over him. She beckoned the sister over and asked what was the prognosis.

"Oh, I expect we will keep him here overnight, just to keep an eye on things. Nothing very serious that you would not be unable to attend to at home, dear!"

Margaret, to John's amusement, bridled a bit at the 'dear'. To his great relief his wife decided to ignore it and thanked the sister politely. The door to the ward opened to admit an elderly, tall military gentleman who had a typical army moustache. He peered round and came up to Jamie's bed. He stood at the foot and regarded Jamie, who stared back at him with a smile of recognition on his face.

"Hello, young feller! I hear you took a 'blighty one'. You the little chap's parents, eh?"

John stood up, erect in his uniform; he knew senior officer-like authority when he saw it. He had not heard the expression 'blighty one' for many a year. It was used by the soldiers at the front who had been wounded just severely enough to be sent home for convalescence to 'dear old blighty'.

"Yes, sir", he replied. "Jamie is our son. I am John Small; may I present my wife, Margaret". This, he also knew, was the correct form. Margaret gave him a quiet smile and held out her hand to be lightly shaken.

"You have a plucky little chap here; tells me all sorts of stories. You caught a packet at Ypres, I hear".

John nodded. "Yes; I was with the Rifles then. Phosgene attack put paid to hundreds of us."

The old brigadier shook John's hand. "Was a staff wallah then; commanded my regiment in 'fifteen' but they took me away from them – blast their hides! Never knew that a little feller like this would have ever heard of 'Third Ypres' – told me all about it, didn't you?"

Jamie tried to look suitably modest at this fulsome praise. He was about to say something when the door opened again to admit the 'special' constable, seeking to complete his report of the incident. He recognised the brigadier immediately; he began by saying how sorry he was at the damaged caused to the big house.

"Damage? What damage?" asked the brigadier, moustache quivering. John recognised the signs and sat back to enjoy what he knew was coming.

"Damage is what has happened to my neighbours' house. Thank the good Lord they were all away for the day. *That* is what I would call damage!"

"Quite, sir", agreed the somewhat abashed 'special'. He tried to remedy this gaffe.

"This lad was found on your property, sir. Do you wish to institute proceedings for trespass?"

# A DAMNED DISGRACE

The brigadier seemed quite speechless for a moment. His face, usually a ruddy shade, deepened to a rich puce.

"Trespass, you say? *Trespass*? I'll have you know that this plucky little feller is a good friend of mine. We have had long yarns together. You come here and have the bloody effrontery to ask me to sue for trespass! A little boy gets blown up and all you can think of doing is to have him charged with a crime? You, sir, are a disgrace. Personally, I would have you flogged! I shall inform whoever is unfortunate enough to be your superior that you are unfit for your position and, moreover, have the manners of a warthog! Now, be-gone with you!"

The 'special', red as a beetroot, scuttled from the ward.

"Bloody cheek!" exploded the brigadier. John and Margaret regarded the old warrior with awe. Recovering slightly, John thanked the brigadier for his dealing with the situation.

"Think nothing of it, my dear chap. Can't have idiots like that ruling the roost, can we?" He turned to Jamie who had been listening with astonishment to the explosion from the brigadier. If only he could learn to say things like that; he wouldn't have any more trouble from Julian and his cronies if he could! The sister had been about to remonstrate with the brigadier but had been just as transfixed as had everyone else by the sheer force of that personality. 'Don't suppose we'll see that idiot again', she thought.

"Now, you get better as soon as you can. When you've recovered, please bring your mother and father to tea. We'll have a fine time, won't we?"

"Oh yes, sir; thank you, sir", said Jamie, delighted that his mum and dad would see him for the fine, upstanding pillar of society that he thought he had now become. John and Margaret thanked the brigadier for his kind thoughts and for the invitation. With hands shaken all round, the old gentleman departed, still muttering darkly about horsewhips and jumped-up jacks in office.

"I'll get the Brooke Hill Inspector to have a quiet word with that oaf", John promised as he and Margaret departed. They would come again later that evening they promised. Jamie, feeling much better, settled down for another nap. His bruises still hurt but, no school for ages! Utter bliss! He slept soundly throughout the night, to awaken to a breakfast of porridge, boiled egg and buttered toast soldiers. He wolfed the lot.

John walked home with Margaret; they stopped off at the bungalow to give the good news to her mother and father, also to collect little Robert. Margaret went home with the baby whilst John reversed his steps to go to the Brooke Hill police station. He wanted some answers. He was greeted by the duty sergeant who showed him into the Inspector's office. The two officers exchanged greetings and, over coffee, went through the sequence of events. Why, asked John, had there been no air-raid warning?

His opposite number had wondered the same thing. Apparently, this one was a single missile and had thus crept under the screen. There had been no warning received from the authorities. John also mentioned the crass behaviour of the 'special'; the Inspector threw up his hands in a gesture of despair.

"That idiot will have to go!" he said darkly. "Do you know what he did about a week ago after the bomb fell on Rokeby Terrace? Well, an old couple had been bombed out and were staying with some friends a few doors down the road. Because a part of the road was still covered with rubble the next morning, the daft fart actually threatened to arrest the old pair with causing an obstruction! I hauled him over the coals for that one; obviously doesn't seem to have done the trick. He's got to go before I strangle him myself!"

John sympathised; some of his own 'specials' were fairly crass but, thank heavens, nothing quite as bad as this. He walked home thanking the powers that be that his family was still intact. This caused the usual pangs for his other two children; he still regarded them as his 'family', would always do so. He resolved to go and see them whenever his next weekend afforded him the opportunity to catch them not at school; he was careful always to make sure that absolutely nobody knew of these visits – Margaret because of her jealousy, Desmond because of the need to keep him unaware, Alfred and Gertrude because they would see it as a betrayal of their own daughter. He was always in this quandary; he wondered where it would all end.

# RECUPERATING

Jamie arrived home by ambulance the next morning, the doctor having satisfied himself that the concussion had been only temporary. The bells were ringing as the vehicle drew up outside his home. He had specially requested that they were rung; he felt terribly important! To his utter horror he was sent up to bed to rest for the day. Rest? He wanted nothing more than to change into his old clothes and spend some time at Advanced Camp to make notes on the trains. He grumbled, changed into his own pyjamas, was reminded to say a polite 'thank you' to the ambulance crew, climbed with muttered rebellion into his bed and sat there with his book of saints. When Desmond came home that evening, he very kindly abandoned his everlasting homework and research, to sit with his little brother. Jamie told him all about the V1 Doodlebug, how its motor had stopped, how he had seen it falling to earth. Desmond uttered a silent prayer of thanks for Jamie's deliverance. He knew that there were even worse bombs to come. He had read a lot about the dreaded V2 missile. At least, with the V1, you could hear it and try to take cover when it ran out of fuel. The new one would be a ballistic missile travelling above the speed of sound. Anyone hearing the blast of the explosion would then hear the uncanny passage of the thing overhead, like the tearing of a cloth. He had satisfied himself that he understood the principle. Indeed, his physics teacher had taken the small class out to the playing fields for a demonstration. At a distance of three hundred yards, he had signalled to an assistant who had taken two dustbin lids and smashed them together. Indeed, the sight of the lids meeting had preceded the sound of that metallic coming together. So, light (that conveyed visual imagery) travelled a lot faster than sound. The master had then gone on to explain that light travelled at approximately six hundred and seventy-five million miles an hour, whilst sound travelled only at seven hundred and fifty. Desmond calculated that light travelled nine hundred thousand times faster than sound – but was that all correct? He wondered if he had got it all right. Inaccuracy could be measured in factors of very high numbers, and he recoiled from talking about it until he was absolutely sure of his facts.

He had, on his great-uncle Frederick's advice, taken his new dynamo drawings to his grandfather. After all, Alfred had spent a lifetime designing buildings, using metals and so forth. Alfred had expressed a quiet admiration for the drawings, the intricate and meticulously detailed design work. He then asked, what was to him, the most pertinent question; was it actually feasible? Had Desmond worked out the cost of making it in large numbers. He had set Desmond the task of costing out just one unit, for materials, tooling, labour. Desmond had done this and had been shown that the tooling was a one-off cost, that the materials would be mitigated by economies of scale, etc. Then Desmond had done the sums again, added twenty percent for the manufacturer's profit and a further twenty percent, compounded, for the profit of the retailer. Desmond had come out with a figure of £12.17.6 as the end selling price, assuming a production run of ten thousand. He knew that quite a few (inferior in every way, he thought) were already on the market for under £8. Therefore, Alfred asked again, was it really feasible? By this one simple exercise the old man accomplished what a battery of theorists would have failed to do – to give the young man a valuable lesson in the realities of business life. Machines, he told Desmond, were not just things of design creation; to come to fruition, they had to be commercially feasible as well. Desmond was a sadder if wiser young man!

Jamie was due the very next day to attend yet another music lesson with the unforgiving Mrs Worthy. Desmond had already taken a note from Margaret to apologise for his enforced absence. Apparently, he was quite the young hero; whilst he dreaded the grinding monotony of scales, arpeggios and key signatures, he looked keenly forward to displaying his 'war wounds', hopefully to an admiring Tina. But it was not to be. He got up and was allowed to mooch about the house. He passed a pleasant enough couple of hours playing with Robert but pined for the sunshine. All the trees had been in full leaf for ages now and he was missing it all. The oak that year had preceded the ash into leaf; according to the tale he had heard, this presaged the coming of a 'splash', rather than the 'soak' had the reverse happened. He was bored, nothing to do except draw silly pictures; his drawing was, he knew, awful. Somehow, what he wanted to depict in two dimensions on paper, never in any way resembled the object that he tried to depict. Circles came out irregularly ovoid; squares turned into wavery trapeziums, straight lines into mere squiggles. If only they had a piano, he would be at least able to sit and pick out real tunes. Those gave him no problem at all!

He tried to interest himself in a story book about olden times. He gave it up; he had not the foggiest idea what a 'quartern' was, had never heard of trebuchets or codpieces. Margaret found him standing at his bedroom window, looking disconsolately at the big outside world. She marched him off to the bathroom where she re-dressed his deeper cuts; all seemed to her to be healing nicely. She then suggested that he read to her and picked for him a copy of Palgrave's Golden Treasury. She reclined on the sofa, Jamie squatting on the floor. He began with a poem on the page at which the book had naturally fallen open.

"I wondered lonely as a cloud", he began. Margaret stopped him; 'wandered', she corrected. Jamie went on. "That floats on high o'er vale and hills. When all at once I saw a crowd, ------- why did he see a crowd – were they going to a football match?"

On being told not to be silly, he went on, "A host of golden daffodils. But daffodils aren't gold, they're yellow!" Poetic license meant nothing to a pragmatic five-year-old, especially when explained by one who had very little understanding of the young mind. Margaret, resignedly, took back the book and found a poem in a volume of 'nonsense' rhyme that better suited the reader.

"The owl and the pussycat went to sea in a beautiful pea-green boat. They took lots of food and plenty of money wrapped up in a five-pound note. That's silly – why wouldn't they put it in a purse? Can I have a five-pound note for Christmas? I could buy about twenty tons of broken biscuits if I had a fiver! When's Dad coming home – would he give me a fiver now that I'm wounded?"

Margaret gave up; she could cope with, readily enjoyed, the baby talk and antics of Robert; could even enjoy the very grown-up conversations of Desmond. Jamie utterly defeated her. He was at that extremely (to her) tiresome age where everything was taken in its literal sense or, worse still, made silly jokes from. She suggested that, if he went very carefully, he could go to his Nunky for an hour. This, she knew, killed two birds with one stone; Jamie would be happy, and Uncle Fred would be diverted and, poor old chap, needed all the diversion he could get.

Jamie limped out of the house until, believing he was now safely out of sight, broke into a limping gallop. He knocked at Nunky's door; the old boy was very pleased to see him and made a great fuss, wanting to hear all about the bomb and Jamie's injuries. He said that Jamie deserved a medal for bravery. His idea was that he would quietly ask Desmond to fashion the medal, then take it to the local jewellers to have it engraved; his sister-in-law would make the ribbon. He himself would make a nice wooden presentation case lined with an old piece of velvet. Frederick was pleased with the idea. For the next hour he went through various slides under the 'mickoscope' with Jamie, explaining the intricacies of moths' wings, bee stings and tiny ammonites. Jamie was enthralled. He went back home much chirpier and insisted on regaling his mother with all his new-found knowledge. To do her justice, Margaret listened patiently, smiling at the mispronunciations, the wrong assumptions. She told him that, should the weather be clement (his mother's expression), he would be allowed out to play the next day. Wondering, not for the first time, why the weather should have a name at all - especially Granddad's name - he went to bed much happier with life.

July brought rain and dark clouds; the allied armies were bogged down in Normandy by fierce resistance; the news from the BBC, usually upbeat, seemed quite pessimistic. Jamie had not yet been able to get back to Advance Camp; his cuts and bruises had healed within a fortnight – there had been no repercussions from the very temporary concussion. But, as soon

as he was pronounced fit for the outside world again, down
came persistent drizzle; as he now had to attend school again,
he was not a very happy boy at all. However, school would
soon be over, and he would have seven weeks of summer
holiday to look forward to. In his short life he had never
experienced the joys of travelling to a special holiday
destination; the war had stopped all that. There had been no
more flying bombs falling near Brooke Hill, the Germans
concentrating much more on the East End of London,
especially the docks area. But everyone knew that targets could
change, indeed *would* change at the drop of a hat, plus there
were the new V2 rockets that were anticipated from various
intelligence sources. The prospect was bleak.

# BITTERNESS AND RECRIMINATION

On the third Saturday of July John was at long last able to get an afternoon to himself by switching a part-shift with a colleague. He had four hours in which to go and see his 'other' family. This often gave him pangs of conscience – he had not been to see them for some months; as well as feelings of guilt there was a deep longing to see them. He changed into civilian clothes in the locker room and managed to jump on a bus which took him fairly swiftly to the stop at Streatham Common. Alighting, he walked briskly up the path on the side of the open common land to where a tree-lined avenue branched to the left. Down this street lived the couple that had 'adopted' his two eldest. Chrissy West had been a lifelong friend of poor Dorothy; when she married her husband Sam and had come to live near to John and Dorothy, the four had been very happy. When, eventually, Valerie, then Peter and Desmond had come along, Chrissy had been delighted for her friends; she had also been devastated by the news that she and Sam would never be able to have children of their own. Thereafter, Chrissy had become a second 'mum' to the three, minding them when Dorothy was at work, looking after them with tenderness during their mother's brief, terminal illness. It had been Chrissy who had cared for and comforted the children after the funeral, John being so deeply committed to the police force, he had little time during the day or evening to spend with the children. Desmond had been eighteen months old when his mother died; he had no recollection of her at all. Sam and Chrissy had agreed without hesitation that they would take Valerie and Peter until John could sort 'something out'. Dorothy's mother had agreed to take Desmond as she had never worked and had ample room and time on her hands. John grieved for his lost wife whom he had loved deeply. He was not able to miss his children as he had never been allowed the opportunity or the time to bond properly with them. Soon after this had come John's opportunity to transfer station with promotion. Dorothy's mother had become sick, so little Desmond had then become two, then three and four, in the care of a succession of different, often indifferent, child-minders. He had not been seen by his siblings since the day when his father had moved to Wandleside. Margaret had agreed to take Desmond immediately they were married but had refused absolutely to have anything at all to do with the 'other two', had refused to allow any mention of them at all. John, infatuated with his new bride, had meekly agreed. So it was that Valerie and Peter grew up separated by some ten miles from their little brother.

John knocked at the door and was welcomed in by his old friend. Sam had never really forgiven John for what he saw as his abandonment of the two children. He had never understood how on earth anyone could do such a thing. His wife Chrissy was more understanding, knowing of the pressures that John had been under, his eagerness to see that the two were lovingly cared for.

"Long time!" said Sam shaking John's hand. "Far too long", agreed John, sensing the reproach. "Chrissy got your letter the other day; she's laid on some tea for you three in the front room. We'll leave you for a bit to catch up!" John was very grateful for this kindness. He went into the front room to see his children.

Valerie, now seventeen, was growing into a very attractive young woman. She was short like her father but had her mother's eyes. John looked at that shy face and felt a pang of instant recognition; the older Valerie became the more she resembled her dead mother. The girl jumped up from the chair and ran over.

"Hello, Daddy", she said, burying her head in his shoulder. John hugged his little girl desperately. He looked at his son, standing in the bay window. Peter regarded him coldly. "Hello, father", he said.

Valerie had been five when her mother had died and remembered that soft, loving person with a sense of huge loss. The two had been inseparable. Although Peter had been three, he also had fond memories of his mother, the stories she had told them at bedtime, the warmth of her smile. Both remembered their little baby brother.

"How's Des?" asked Valerie, taking John's hand to lead him to the small table where tea things had been laid. "Oh, as usual; terribly busy with schoolwork. He's designed a dynamo! I don't begin to understand it, but Margaret's father thinks very highly of the thing".

"How are Jamie and little Robert?" John always had difficulty with this question; he was never sure how to answer. Too much enthusiasm would, perhaps, be interpreted as a preference on his part for his new family; too little could appear indifferent. He told of Jamie's experience with the flying bomb and of Robert's continued interest in trains. He kept to facts. Valerie listened to the tale with keen interest, Peter with thinly veiled scorn. John had always been aware that his daughter had inherited her mother's sweet, understanding nature – her ability to forgive anyone almost anything – as well as her looks. Peter had grown into a withdrawn, resentful lad. He loved his sister as well as Sam and Chrissy. They were his family, and he wanted no other; after all, the 'other' family had not wanted him!

Valerie could not help saying, "Oh how I wish we could all be together!" She invariable gave vent to this longing on the rare occasions that she saw her father. John had said more than once that such a thing was just not possible; Margaret had been unable to cope with three new children and would not now want her own two 'upset' in any way. He shied from the real truth that his wife had forbidden any contact at all with them; he lived in dread of her finding out about his occasional visits. Valerie longed to believe that her father's explanation was the true reason; Peter thought that his father had married again into a family that was 'far above' them, that his father was secretly ashamed of them, had deliberately abandoned them in his search for 'betterment'. He deeply resented John; utterly despised his new 'stepmother'; detested the mere mention of his two new half-brothers.

Valerie acted as 'mother' pouring tea and handing round a plate of biscuits. On being asked how she was progressing, she told John the latest news; she would start secretarial school in the coming September, would spend her days in the office of a local solicitor carrying out general clerical duties whilst spending her evenings on the course. She hoped to be fully qualified in two years time. Peter, after pleading glances from his sister, said that he had passed all his exams so far and wanted to become a doctor when he was old enough. John was delighted at the news and tried to pat his son on the shoulder; Peter shied away on the pretence of going to the lavatory.

Valerie snuggled up to her father. She had thought out the next speech very carefully, indeed had practised it quite a few times.

"Daddy, what would you say if I came over to Brooke Hill one afternoon – it would only be for an hour or two. I'd love to see Des again. You could ask him to meet me anywhere you might suggest – say a café or something?" She looked desperately at him.

John had known that this would come some day; he wanted exactly the same thing himself. But.............

"Look, sweetheart", he faltered. "Margaret is not strong; she would be very upset if Desmond were to be confronted by this........."

Peter, who had reappeared, came and stood in front of his father. "What you really mean is that little Des doesn't know anything about us, does he? You've never actually told him about us, have you?"

John's silence was eloquent. Valerie recoiled, looked bitterly hurt. "Please, Daddy, that isn't true, is it?"

John found himself utterly at a loss, could say nothing.

"There, you see!" Peter said to his elder sister. "I bet nobody except the sainted Margaret and her parents know anything about us at all. He's disowned us – is ashamed of us. We wouldn't fit in with his new lifestyle. He probably thinks we would actually embarrass him!"

John was stung into a reply. "Of course, I don't! I have tried to explain how things are many times. The situation is very delicate, but you must *never* think that I'm ashamed of either of you. I love you as much now as I did when you were born".

"But you don't love us enough to let us meet our own brother?" snapped Peter.

"Oh, dear God, some day you might understand", John was near to tears. Valerie was sitting apart from him at the other end of the sofa. Her eyes were downcast; to John she looked completely devastated.

Peter had not finished. "If I'm not good enough to be allowed to see my little brother, not good enough to meet your precious Jamie and Robert, then I never want to see you again. You are ashamed of me, and I hate you for it. Sam is my real father – you obviously don't want that part anymore. So much for the love that you say you have for us. It's a *lie – it's all been a pack of lies*! Val has stuck up for you all these years. I've tried to tell her that you aren't worth it – perhaps she'll see now that I was right all along"

Peter strode out of the room; they all heard the front door slam. John sat, his head hung in absolute misery. Valerie sobbed quietly. "Please tell me that Des remembers us", she begged.

"He was far too young when it all happened", he faltered. "He could never have remembered anything at all."

"But you could have told him, couldn't you?"

"Yes, I could have", John was trying to be as honest as he could. "But the situation has never come up. Margaret does not want anything to upset her children and I must respect her wishes".

"But how could telling Des and the kids upset them? They might be very happy to know that they have a bigger family. I know I would if I were in their shoes!"

"Margaret is absolutely against it", said John.

Valerie was so bitterly upset that she burst out, "What you mean is, you're scared of her. She rules the roost, and you all have to scuttle about obeying her wishes. I'd like to meet her – give her a piece of my mind. If you really did love us, you would try and get us all together, not do everything you can to try and keep us apart. It's cruel!"

"You must never ever try to see Margaret or the children; it would simply make things worse!" John really believed that, hoped that one day his daughter would see the sense in it too.

"Oh, don't worry; I know when I'm not wanted!" Valerie was crying bitterly now. "I'm going to find Peter. I always believed in you, but you've made me see that there is never going to be a future for us all. If you want to write to me, I suppose it's OK – I'll write back, but it's better if we leave it at that. Oh, and don't worry about me upsetting your cosy little world. I won't try to come and see anybody. Peter would never dream of it and now, neither would I!"

Valerie went out of the door, wiped her reddened eyes and went off in search of her brother.

Sam and Chrissie came in a few moments later. Sam regarded his old friend. "Well, that went well, didn't it?" Chrissie sat down by John and took his hand. She had always understood John's weaknesses, his infatuation with the beautiful Margaret. Although she had never met Margaret, John had told them all about her; had told of her background, her fits of depression and tantrums.

"Why couldn't you talk to Margaret about it all? Try telling her that your life is incomplete without all your children. Say that you would be much happier if you were all together some way or other. Surely, she would understand?"

John shook his head. "You really don't know her at all, do you?"

"That's crap!" said the forthright Sam. "If you really wanted any of this to happen, you would make it – stand up to her! Look mate – you're forty-five years of age, a bloody police inspector – not some snivelling down-and-out! For Christ's sake sit her down and make her listen to what *you* want, *you* need!"

John had no reply to any of this; he sat and sipped the cold remains of his tea.

"Oh, what's the use – what's the *bloody* use!" Sam slammed out of the room, went to potter in his greenhouse, perennial refuge when he was exasperated.

Chrissy had watched John while her husband had been remonstrating with him. She knew that there was a lot of truth in what Sam had said. "John", she decided to add her own thoughts. "Sam *is* right, you know. You simply can't go through life blaming Margaret for it all. OK, she's not strong, she's got to be humoured now and again. But this can't be all her fault. You must see that!"

John saw it only too well; he knew that on this one subject he was as weak as a kitten but could not bring himself to contemplate the possible disaster that any confrontation might bring. The risk of losing his precious wife was far too horrible to contemplate.

Chrissy saw the defeated look; she got up and started to clear away the tea things. John knew that it was time to go. He called a soft good-bye and walked down the common again. His heart was filled with lead; had he ruined once and for all the chance of remaining reasonably close to his lovely daughter who he had loved for her own sake as well as for her resemblance to her mother? Peter, he knew, had been lost to him for years but, to lose his little Val was nearly more than he could bear. His journey back to Wandleside was the most miserable he could ever remember, far worse than the trembling terror he had felt on his journey to the 'front' in nineteen sixteen. He wished desperately for a chance to start again, to keep the love of his three children, the closeness of his sweet Dorothy. But that would mean never meeting the lovely Margaret, feel the glow of her presence, the pride in his beautiful wife. Also, it would mean that Jamie and Robert would not be.

Like many a man before him, he found himself in a quandary to which there was no answer. He would simply have to learn anew to accept life as it was; no good hoping for the unobtainable, that happy resolution that would for ever remain far beyond his reach. The bus trundled on, coming at last to his stop. He carefully deposited his ticket in his jacket pocket; it would be added to Jamie's collection. What that lad intended to do with the hundreds in his bedroom drawer was anyone's guess.

John did the only thing that he could. He immersed himself in his work, trying to be the best that he could. He resolved to earn the respect of his colleagues for, sure as hell, he had no respect for himself.

# A LUCKY ESCAPE

August of that year had started damp, much to the annoyance of one small boy who itched to spend every waking hour out of doors, especially during the long summer break from school. After a few days the weather had cleared up; many days had been spent happily in his Advance Camp, noting the number and variety of trains that passed. Many of those going south were filled with troops rushing to be ferried across the Channel to reinforce the invasion that had at long last, broken out into the Normandy Plain. Fighters from the three nearby aerodromes flew constant mission to supply air cover and to strafe the defending German positions; Jamie lost count of the number of Spitfires and the much more numerous Hurricanes that buzzed by overhead, their unmistakable Rolls Royce engines growling. Now, another recent addition had been added; Jamie had to refer to Desmond who told him that it was a twin-engine Mosquito, had really been around for some time.

At night the northern sky was crossed by a mass of white pillars of light as the searchlights in and around the capital probed for bombers; mercifully, these were now quite rare. Instead, there had been a massive increase in the number of flying bombs. The V1 'Doodlebugs' had wreaked carnage in the capital, the odd one now and again coming south to try and destroy fighter installations. Jamie, on advice from his father, now jumped as high as he could whenever one of these was heard for, as his Dad had told him, if you jumped they would not hit you. Jamie was also reassured by his grandmother's assurance that 'lightning seldom strikes twice'. So, on hearing a V1 nearby, Jamie jumped as high as he could, pulling faces and sticking out his tongue, yelling 'Missed me!' as the missile passed by.

A very few of the fighter pilots who flew their Spitfires at great speed, had tried to parallel the course of a V1 flying bomb, had tried to get a wing tip beneath the stubby aerofoil on the missile and tip it over as it crossed the sea. On a few occasions, this had succeeded; many and lurid were the stories of drunken revelry at local public houses whenever one of these attempts was successful. The local population viewed these escapades with kindly toleration; the fighter pilots had alone prevented an invasion of England; they were feted, would be remembered as 'the few'.

The V2 rockets were another matter altogether. Flying faster than the speed of sound, there could be no audible warning of its approach. It drove at full velocity into the ground; its crater was massive as it erupted from so deep underground; the carnage one of these ultimate 'terror weapons' could inflict was truly horrendous. In one instance twelve houses were flattened, twenty others damaged, eighteen people were killed outright and over a hundred were moderately to severely wounded. The prayer, much repeated both in churches and elsewhere, was, 'Please let us finish the Germans before these V2's finish us!'

Desmond had had a lucky escape on the very last day of his one-week bicycling holiday. He had packed a large saddlebag with clothes and had set off one late July morning to stay at the uncle and aunt of a school friend. This couple lived the far side of Guildford. Desmond and his friend had spent happy days cycling along the famous Hogs Back, watching the massive troop movements at nearby Aldershot. On his journey back home, he had just passed Leatherhead and the River Mole when there came the most colossal explosion. He threw himself off his bike, slithered into a muddy ditch and prayed. Then came the ripping-cloth sound of the passing of the rocket. A V2 had landed not a mile in front of him. He slowly emerged, covered in mud and weeds, collected his bike from the roadside and continued his journey. As he pedalled onwards, he started to recite his rosary, without, of course, being able to finger his way along the beads. One Our Father, ten Hail Mary's, one Glory Be. He dedicated this to his deliverance from the bomb. Then another set for his family. His conversion to the Roman Church was not yet formalised; he had attended mass every Sunday and classes with the local priest. He felt safe and secure in his beliefs, took great comfort in the fact that his God had kept him safe throughout this terrible war.

He arrived home, washed and changed; he never said one word about his escape to anyone, feeling that this was between God and himself. He knew that his father would be sceptical, would put it all down to 'the luck of the draw'; his mother would make a terrible fuss, would dramatise the incident out of all proportion. Jamie needed no reminder of his own lucky escape.

# QUITE A FORMAL TEA

One afternoon in mid August saw the occasion of the visit of Jamie and his parents to the brigadier's house. At Margaret's insistence, cards had been left; this paved the way to a formal written invitation being sent, a formal letter of acceptance being returned, and a date and time set. John, Margaret and Jamie walked the very short distance to the brigadier's home, leaving little Robert with Margaret's parents en-route. Jamie insisted on pulling the chain at the front door, hearing from the far regions of the large house, the tinkling of a bell. Slow footsteps approached, the massive door creaked open. An old man wearing a brown waistcoat with brass buttons over a shirt and bow tie stood there. He gave a short bow of his head.

"Good afternoon, madam, sir" he said in a voice that would have been the envy of any priest solemnising a funeral. "If you would care to come in, the brigadier is expecting you". The three were led into a hall decorated with old panelling, two stags' heads and a hall stand that was large enough to accommodate the coats and paraphernalia of a small regiment. Margaret's light coat and gloves were placed delicately on a hanger; John removed hat and gloves which were put carefully on the top. They were led to a room on the right; the old servant opened the double doors and announced, "Inspector and Mrs Small and Master Jamie Small, sir!"

The old brigadier came towards them, hands outstretched. He bade them all a very good afternoon and invited them to join him on deep sofas around the empty inglenook fireplace. He nodded towards the now re-closed doors. "Splendid feller, old Jenkins; been with me for longer that I care to remember; was me servant-cum-valet in the last lot – what they now call a batman – God alone knows why! Me wife loathed him, of course!"

"Is you wife no longer with you, brigadier?" Margaret asked, delicately. Clearly, the lady was not in residence, or she would have been the one to greet them first; the framing of the question covered all other possibilities. Margaret's very expensive education had not been wasted!

"Memsahib died years ago – cholera of all damned things – out in Africa when I was with me regiment on a short stay! Miss the old gel terribly!"

It behoved John and Margaret to look at the floor and mumble almost silent condolences; outward shows of grief would not be appropriate. The brigadier, dressed in plaid shirt, regimental tie, corduroy trousers and highly polished brown shoes, lumbered to his feet and went to the door. He opened it a bit and shouted, "Jenkins!" The servant, older than his master by quite a few years, stuck his head through the door a few moments later. "You bellowed, sir?" he enquired. The brigadier took absolutely no notice of the familiarity of the remark. "Yes, Jenkins – tea, when you are ready!" The old chap nodded and withdrew. The brigadier clearly thought that some explanation was due. "Been through a lot together, Jenkins and me; saw out three years in Flanders and the Somme; still, don't suppose I need to tell you anything about that, do I, young chap?"

It was many a long day since John had been called 'young chap'; he was quite pleased at the soubriquet! He shook his head. "Saw enough of that to last me a lifetime, sir!" The awfulness of it would never leave him, would ever bring back nightmares of mud, barbed wire, machine guns. The brigadier clearly thought that enough sadness was enough. He looked over at Jamie who had been squirming a bit in the depths of a massive club armchair.

"Now, young feller-me-lad; hear that you like the great outdoors. Ever seen a badger?"

Jamie, woken from a dream about snails being dropped by thrushes on to rocks to smash the shells, shook his head. "No, sir, I never have".

"Well, if yer parents have no objection, I'll show you some. There are two old'uns living in a sett at the far end of me garden, where a small bank borders me property. Have to watch for 'em at night 'though; they are nocturnal as I suppose you know".

"Oh yes, sir, I know that!" said Jamie, agog at the prospect.

"Thought so! Well, if you two agree, the little feller can come one evening and we'll spend a few hours in me hide that Jenkins and I made last year. Lots of room in there, binoculars on stands ready for the blighters".

Jamie looked pleadingly at his parents. "Oh please, mum, dad!" he said.

Margaret and John exchanged glances. To John's mind, it would do his little boy the power of good to spend time with this splendid old chap; Margaret was delighted to have her son and, by inference, herself accepted into the upper strata of Brooke Hill's society.

"Well, if you promise to behave and do everything the brigadier tells you."

Jamie was overjoyed; a whole night away from home and badgers to see. How his friends would envy him when he told them all of his exploits when the new term started.

Jenkins staggered in with a butler's tray laden with tea, scones, jam and a small pot of clotted cream. God alone knows where he got that from, thought John.

At the brigadier's invitation, Margaret acted as 'mother', taking for herself only a cup of very weak tea and a half of buttered scone. John knew that he had to restrain his normal healthy appetite; manners forbade him from taking more than one cake. However, the Brigadier was amused at Jamie's performance, urging the little lad to pile on the cream, not to 'spoil the ship for a ha'poth of tar'. Jamie obliged and wolfed it down; he had never had clotted cream before. Margaret prayed that her son would not disgrace her by being sick! She need not have worried; Jamie seemed to have the digestion and the constitution of an ox. After further pleasantries and a conducted tour around the large garden, it was time to go. Thank-you's and good-bye's were made. Jamie would appear the next evening to spend the night; he danced home in a fever of excitement. Margaret, as soon as she arrived back, set to writing a polite 'thank-you' note to the brigadier which she asked Desmond to post through the letter box. She wrote the salutation as 'My dear Brigadier', the valediction as 'Yours very truly, Margaret Small'. She even addressed the envelope with the clear message 'By hand'. Everything correctly done!

# BADGERS

The next evening Desmond walked Jamie up to the brigadier's house. In his little case were a set of pyjamas, slippers, a toothbrush and a change of socks. Old Jenkins took him up the massive staircase to a bedroom that contained a full bedroom suite of mahogany framed bed, wardrobe, chest of drawers, washstand with huge bowl and jug, a bedside table and an armchair. Was this really all his, wondered Jamie in awe of such opulent surroundings?

The brigadier greeted him as he came down the stairs. The old chap was as pleased as punch to have a child about the place; his own two sons were at that very moment in France, one commanding a tank troop whilst the other served his old regiment as its padre. He had almost forgotten what joy a small child could bring; he had looked forward to this visit for hours.

Taking a torch he led Jamie out of the scullery door, making sure that his young visitor had enough clothes on to counter the slight nip in the evening air. He led the way very quietly past rose beds, currant bushes, until they arrived at a very low contraption that looked like a wooden hut that had been sawn down to stand but four feet high. The brigadier put his finger to his lips, opened the little door, went down on all fours and crept into the hut. Jamie followed. The floor had been covered with an old rug to keep out the cold. The two side walls were of unbroken timber whilst the front end had one large pane of glass in a wide frame. In front of the window were two sets of powerful binoculars set on tripod stands. The brigadier motioned Jamie to the right-hand pair, he taking the left and lying full length before it. Jamie could sit cross-legged at his set. He was shown in silence how to twiddle the eyepieces to suit his eyesight. The bank, some thirty feet in front of the window, came into sharp focus showing the entrance to the sett. The brigadier whispered to him, "Now we just sit and wait, old chap".

To Jamie's mind, there was absolutely no need for the binoculars; they were near enough to the bank for his young, strong eyesight to function with absolute clarity without the need for any mechanical aid. However, the old brigadier had reached a time in his life when the same could not be said for his eyesight, or for any of his senses, as he often told himself. So, he had set up the binoculars on their tripods. He was a man to do things 'properly' and had unearthed them from a trunk that contained, among other things, a Zulu spear, a German pickelhaube helmet, his own Sam Browne belt and a host of militaria from his past life. The binoculars were of nineteen sixteen vintage, with lenses by Carl Zeiss, sheathed in well oiled leather cases. He knew that he needed the aid of these wonderful lenses, but had thought he must offer the other pair to his very young guest in case the little chap felt 'out of it'.

They lay for some minutes in a very companionable silence; the old war-horse, now well into his seventies; the young boy slowly approaching his sixth Christmas. As the dark outside the hide began to deepen, small wisps of mist, like thin gossamers, scrolled up and over the blades of the long grass; The recent rains had left a residue of surface moisture which cooled rapidly in the night air; this colder atmosphere clung to the ground, only to be warmed slightly by the residual heat in the grasses, warmed by the autumn sun, and so cause the tiny tendrils of white mist. It all gave the prospect in front of the hide a slightly ethereal appearance. A large moth fluttered by, hovered for a few moments, but was gone before Jamie could focus his lenses on it. Another (or was it the same one?) came from the opposite direction; Jamie, being ready for this one, focused on the insect and marvelled at the speed of the wing beats that kept the heavy-looking body suspended before it too flew off. Jamie turned to his companion.

"My Nunky showed me a lot of slides of moths' wings", he whispered, conscious of the warning to move only slowly and to keep noise to an absolute minimum.

The brigadier, who had been appraised at the recent tea-time visit of the various members of the family, was aware of the identity of this Nunky.

"You are such a lucky lad, you know. Never had the luxury of such things when I was a whippersnapper – had to find out a lot of things all by me'self. Studied the birds and the insects; fascinated me; still do!"

"Do you know that a moth's wings are attached to his body by little strings that are thinner than my hair?" asked Jamie.

"No, I didn't know that. You seem to know a hell of a lot about it for one so young!"

Jamie, keenly aware that his mother and grandmother would be appalled at his hearing such language, grew even more fond of the old man; with him he found that he could really be himself, had no need to pretend or to hold back. Somehow, he sensed that the brigadier felt exactly the same way, liberated by his acceptance by a very small child. The highly unlikely combination lay and sat in silence for a few more minutes. Not a sign of movement from the sett. From a distance came the sound of a hoarse coughing.

"Blasted old fox out again!" mumbled the brigadier. "Still, he won't get at me chickens; Jenkins had seen to that. Damned resourceful feller, given his head! Want to know how he keeps old Reynard off me birds?"

"Oh, yes please!" Jamie was very eager to hear anything to do with this remarkable servant who seemed to be allowed to speak his mind whenever he so pleased.

"Well, put a four-foot high chicken wire fence round the birds and their coop. Big area really. Then put another wire fence a foot or more outside the first fence. Wired the outside fence to a load of car batteries that he keeps 'topped up' during the day. We both watched the fox the first night; nearly gave the bugger heart failure when his nose caught a shock; raced orf like the very blazes! Yet, silly old Reynard comes back every damned night to try his luck. You'd think he would learn, eh?"

Jamie laughed quietly at this wonderful story, could hardly wait to tell his mum and dad. He would have to keep the expletives out of the recitation, of course! The old man rumbled on very quietly.

"Remember a couple of old foxes that tried to scavenge the trenches in 'fifteen. Me sergeant major wanted to shoot them, but I said that they were doing no harm; live and let live, what?

Daresay the old Alleyman had his share of vermin to deal with too!"

Jamie had never heard that expression. "Who were the Alleymen?" he enquired.

"Ah, comes from the French language, that does. They call the Germans *les Allemands*. So, of course, we called them 'Alleyman', like we called Ypres *Wipers*!. Most of the rank and file could not be doin' with foreign pronunciations, so they made up their own words that seemed to sound about right!"

"My dad was in the trenches, but he never likes to talk about it. I wish he did, though; must have a lot of good stories, killing Germans and so on!"

"Don't you believe it, my lad! Most old soldiers don't like to talk about it at all. D'ye know, most of the time we were scared out of our wits. The noise, the shelling, the machine guns; never knowin' from one minute to the next if one of the bullets comin' in had your name on it. Germans were the same, scared witless just like us! Saw loads of the fellers taken prisoner; spoke to some who had a bit of English. Said they were only fighting for Kaiser and Country, doin' their duty. Just like we were supposed to be fighting for our King and Country, doin' *our* duty! Makes yer think, what?"

"But we're still fighting the Germans, aren't we", Jamie was puzzled.

"Yurs, started all over again just after you were born. First war was all about trade and this one is all about hatered. Silly buggers should have buried their differences; had every chance to do so – buggered it up, as usual! Now we fight Nazis and Nips, alongside the Americans. Thank God for the Empire – splendid chaps from Canada, Australia, New Zealand, South Africa and the rest. Don't know what we'd do without them!"

Jamie knew quite a bit about the 'sides' that had been fighting for years now. "What about the Russians? Aren't they on our side, as well?"

"Russians are on the side of Russia; always have been, always will! Can't trust a load of peasants led by a murderer. You mark my words; when this is all over we'll have to start all over again with the Reds – damned Bolshies will want to take over most of Europe once Hitler and his henchmen have been beaten. Can't have that!"

Jamie felt the need to enquire further into this damnation of what he had heard described as 'our plucky Russian allies'; who or what were Bolshies? However, he was stopped by a gentle nudge from a bony elbow.

"Here comes Brock!" came a sharp whisper.

Jamie focused on the opening to the sett. Indeed, movement was visible just inside; grey, white and black movement. A paw, with long, very sharp claws pushed at a lip of soil to clear it to the side of the opening. It was withdrawn and, for some minutes, there was complete stillness. Then it appeared again. Jamie watched, breathless. The claws moved a little more of the spoil, was joined by the other front paw; a black head, white striped, emerged from the gloom. Small black eyes glinted in the faint moonlight; the body followed the head until the complete animal was outside on the grass. Another head appeared; soon the two were both outside, sniffing the air. Surely, they would soon move off to hunt for food, grubbing up their meals from under the earth with those huge claws. But something was not quite right, was not exactly to their liking; after slowly circling the area they lumbered back to the sett and disappeared underground once more.

"Blast! Thought they were going foragin'. Still, never mind – saw the blighters!"

"They are much bigger than I thought they would be", Jamie had been startled at the size of Brock the badger.

"Yurs, they are quite a size. D'ye know, there is a cat goes on his nightly walk; belongs to some damned fool of an old woman down your road somewhere. That cat keeps well clear, I can tell you. Old Brock would tear it to pieces if it came anywhere near the sett. Huge beasts, wonderful to watch. Now, young man, I think it's time to get you to bed, don't you?"

Jamie thought nothing of the kind, wanted this special night to go on and on. But good manners demanded that he obey his host. Together, they crawled out of the hide and made their way to the scullery door. From within came the delicious aroma of cocoa. Jenkins, still in his part livery, set down two thick mugs of the steaming brew.

"The Navy wallahs call this 'gunfire' I believe!" muttered the brigadier, dipping his moustache and long, beaky nose into his mug. Jamie sipped the hot liquid which tasted different to that which Desmond prepared most evenings.

"Rum taste, Jenkins", the brigadier raised his eyes from the mug.

"Run out of sugar, sir; had to use saccharine instead".

"Bloody awful muck! Still, beggars can't be choosers, what?"

"Indeed sir! Beggary has been thrust upon even the highest in the land. I'll bet even the king, God bless him, has to make do with the bloody awful muck, as you so eloquently phrase it!"

"One of these days, Jenkins, you'll go too far; then, where would you be?"

"Oh no sir; I always stop just the right side of the line. But, if I did cross it and you fired me, then where would *you* be?"

The old man nodded; indeed, he would be utterly lost without his old manservant; together, they had survived campaign after campaign, had dodged the same bullets, had so many shared experiences. Besides, Jenkins had been devoted to his late wife, had helped nurse her through her last days. No; life without Jenkins was totally unthinkable. But sometimes his barbed tongue grated the nerves. Both knew that they were acting out their respective parts, were following some unseen script that was familiar and damn it, comfortable. No, he simply could never part with his old servant, whatever the provocation.

Jamie was by this time yawning, his head drooping. The brigadier bade him a good night; Jenkins saw him up to his bedroom and Jamie, dressed in pyjamas, fell into the massive bed; he was asleep in minutes. Sirens clamoured at three in the morning. The brigadier opened one eye and cursed; Jenkins awoke and ignored it; Jamie did not even hear it.

He awoke at about nine the next morning. Strong autumnal sunlight lightened even the thick curtains; he hopped out of bed and went to the windows, pulling the heavy blinds aside. He looked to the top of the garden, some two hundred yards away. There was the hide, the bank of soil; some distance to the right was the chicken run protected in its double fence where old Reynard still had not learned his lesson and there was a ginger cat, crawling past the chicken wire on his daily patrol. Jamie wondered how far the cat had to detour to keep him at a safe distance from the badgers. He saw that the flowered pitcher on the nightstand was filled with water. He stood on a chair and somehow managed to pour a little into the matching bowl. He washed his face, hands and neck, brushed his teeth, combed his hair – a hopeless task at the best of times; those unruly curls stood out in all directions whatever he tried.

Dressed in his day clothes, he descended the huge stairs, literally following his nose to the dining room. Two places were set at the long oaken table; chafing dishes stood on the long sideboard. He peeped under the covers; mushrooms under one, bacon under another, eggs under a third. Could he help himself, or should he wait for someone to invite him to? He hopped from one foot to another as he pondered; he was ravenously hungry. On the table was a small rack of toast with a dish of real butter, a pot of marmalade. A Georgian silver teapot steamed by the side of twin containing hot water; a silver milk jug stood ready; his tummy rumbled.

He had just decided to help himself when the door opened. The brigadier, folded newspaper under arm, came in. "Good morning, young feller – sleep well?"

"Oh yes, sir, thank you", replied Jamie. The old man walked briskly over to the sideboard. "Well, don't stand on ceremony – tuck in!"

Jamie waited patiently as his host loaded eggs, bacon and mushrooms on to a warmed plate. Jamie did the same, wondering what the mushrooms would taste like. He sat at the vacant place, his host occupying the one set at the head of the table. "Eggs from me own hens, mushrooms from me own fields; bacon by special arrangement, what?"

Jamie was by now quite used to each statement ending on the up-tone of a question, knew that he was not expected to make any answer. He tucked it with a will, finding the gently sautéed mushrooms were absolutely delicious. Trying not to make too much noise, he buttered a triangle of toast, adding a small quantity of the precious marmalade. Did he dare ask if this was made from the brigadier's own oranges? He had some idea lurking in the back of his memory that oranges were not grown in England, but was not absolutely sure. He waited for his tea to cool before sipping it, making sure that he did not make any sucking noises. The brigadier took his breakfast in silence, for the most part buried behind his copy of his paper. Jenkins entered near the end of the meal and silently started to clear the things away, using the large oval butler's tray that Jamie remembered from his parents' visit.

At last, the brigadier folded his paper, put it beside his cup. "Damned rot, most of it!" he grumbled.

"What particular rot did you have in mind, sir", asked Jenkins, fussing over teapot and milk jug.

"Some damned fool in Parliament says we should offer the Germans what the idiot calls 'an honourable peace'. Never heard such rot! If we stop now, all that'll happen is that the damned Reds will march right through Poland, Germany, Czechoslovakia, the Balkans, the whole shooting match. We'll be faced with having to shoo them out as well!"

"What a great pity it is sir that the Prime Minister is devoid of such wise counsel, has to make do with mere professionals!" Jenkins shuffled out with another laden tray.

Jamie listened to this crossfire with interest. "Damned cheek!" huffed the brigadier, draining his third cup of tea.

Soon, far too soon, it was time for Jamie to collect his small case from his bedroom. He found his host in the garden, muttering darkly about weeds and blackflies. Jamie thanked him for a wonderful stay, knowing that 'good form' would require him to pen a letter when he got home.

"Don't mention it, old chap. Now, you come whenever you like; just bang on the door; don't wait for an invitation; glad to see you whenever you want. Oh, and if you get any cheek from Jenkins, just tell me and I'll boot the bugger's backside. Kindest regards to your mother and father, what?"

Jenkins was oiling the hinges on the front gate, now replaced after the bomb blast. He paused to say farewell to the young guest. Jamie politely thanked the old chap for his kindness and went on his way home. He entered, as usual, via the kitchen door and was about to take his case up to his bedroom when he was summoned by his mother from the front room; she wanted to hear all about it. Jamie sat down and eagerly described the whole evening, night and morning. In his excitement to relate the exact details he totally forgot to edit the brigadier's utterances; thus, Margaret listened in amazement to her little son using words like damned, blasted, buggers and the like.

She worked hard to keep from laughing out loud as her little son related the interchanges between master and servant. She knew full well that that was just how the brigadier spoke, meant no harm by any of it; was just living and reliving his life in the military where such modes of expression were commonplace. Jamie unpacked his case to flee out of the house, to climb up to Advance Camp and watch for troop trains, always keeping a weather eye out for flying bombs; not that he would ever actually *see* a V2 rocket, of course.

# A HOMECOMING

Whilst the brigadier was tending his roses, Jenkins was very surprised to see a battered taxi draw up at the kerb, one of three that plied for hire on the forecourt of Brooke Hill station, built the same year as Jamie's dad had been born. Out of the cab came a figure in khaki battledress, white dog collar in place of usual tie. The old servant went forward to help as the figure manoeuvred a pair of wooden crutches to the pavement. He struggled to gain his balance on the one good, left leg, Jenkins without a word took the valise from the seat and helped the young man into the house where he collapsed on a deep settee with a groan of pain. He raised a mournful face at Jenkins.

"Well, here I am, or what's left of me!" he joked. Jenkins saw at once that it was no joke. Neither he nor his master had had the faintest idea that Master George, as he would always be known, had received any injury at all. "I'll go and inform the master that you are here, Master George". He hurried out to the garden. George relaxed against the cushions, closed his eyes as a fresh wave of pain shot up his right leg. He had been commissioned into the Army Chaplains Corps at the outbreak of war, having been ordained at Southwark Cathedral as an Anglican priest at the age of twenty-six. Now, aged thirty-five, he knew that his army padre days were over. With luck he would heal up, perhaps obtain a parish not too far from the old pater. The brigadier hurried in.

"Caught a packet, old chap?" he sat down, eyeing his younger son in distress.

"Got caught just outside Caen, father. I was with a mixed Anglo-American force – hell of a mix up, as usual. The chaps were clearing the last few houses in a small village when a grenade came lobbing out of a window; bounced on the cobbles and went off. Lump of shrapnel went right through my thigh, tore quite a hole, blood everywhere. Still, it took the head off the poor fellow near me, so I suppose I should thank the Lord for small mercies! Still, was carried back to the dressing station, then back to the same beachhead and on to a ship home. Spent a couple of days at Pompey being patched up, then sent home to convalesce. Don't suppose they will have much use for me after this; will probably have a limp for a bit!"

"Up with the advance, eh?" He need not have asked that question; George was a chip off the old block. Priest or not, he would always be in the thick of it, beside the chaps who, at any moment, would need him most.

"Yes, if you can call it an 'advance'", replied George with a grimace. "More like a series of ill-coordinated leaps, really. Once we had got off the beaches, we were led to believe that it would be fairly easy going for a bit, until Gerry got his act together. All that eyewash about hoodwinking them into thinking we would land at Calais or somewhere – catch them with their pants down. Rubbish – took the Gerry no more than three days to rush his armour south. We are taking one hell of a beating; the Yanks have lost thousands already! Our generals want to consolidate and wait until we have overwhelming numbers and materiel – you know, the old Montgomery theory, whilst the Yank generals seem to want to be all 'gung-ho' and try to finish the war yesterday. How Eisenhower manages to control them all is beyond me!"

"Must have the patience of a saint!" agreed his father. "Still and all, we *are* advancing, I suppose?"

"Oh yes, we're advancing all right! Maybe not always in the right direction, but we *will* get there. I think everyone knows that Germany is finished; I'm sure that their General Staff do. But we're taking massive losses for every mile gained!"

Jenkins came in with two pewter tankards and a couple of bottles of Whitbread Pale Ale. He unscrewed the stoppers and expertly poured, not a drop of liquid spilling, just the correct amount of 'head'. He set a tankard down by George's elbow, another by the old brigadier. Both took a first draught; both sighed in contentment.

The brigadier muttered something about 'seeing to yer room' and went out, blowing his nose into a large handkerchief. Both George and Jenkins knew that he was saving them from a show of embarrassing emotion; just wouldn't do. They heard him calling for 'Mrs Pratt' who came in daily to wash and clean. Jenkins perched his old frame against a side table.

"Hurts a bit, Master George?"

"Just a bit!" agreed George, wriggling painfully to ease the constriction of the bandages.

"Had lots of experience in the last lot; shrapnel and bullet wounds. Got a load of sulphur powder somewhere, so I can look after your dressings. Probably seen far worse in the trenches!"

"Yes, I suppose you have", agreed George, recalling his father's stories of the work done by those volunteer servants. According to the brigadier, Jenkins had applied a tourniquet to the leg of a wounded lance-corporal, thus saving the man from an unnecessary amputation; had himself used ordinary twine to stitch up wounds. He would willingly let the old chap tend to, what was by comparison, a minor injury.

That evening, after George had been put to bed for a good rest, the brigadier knocked on the door of Jenkins' sanctum as he called it. Whenever he felt the need to converse with the old servant he would go to Jenkins' quarters. There, he could sit and chat; Jenkins would never take the liberty of sitting down in the brigadier's rooms; just wasn't done. He found the old servant reclining in his old armchair, a glass of beer at his elbow. Jenkins made to rise but was waved back as the brigadier sank down into the other armchair. He accepted a glass of straw-coloured ale and sipped the top appreciatively.

"Poor chap, looks quite exhausted!" said the, by now, much relieved parent.

Jenkins nodded. "Probably lost a lot of blood; does horrible things to you when you bleed a lot; takes time to recover, sir".

"Remember that young subaltern who had his arm taken orf on the march up to Albert? Screamed like a baby when you bound it up so tight!"

"Only way, sir; have to stop the bleeding – pressure is the only way to do it. I remember him very well – young Mr Tompkins; only been 'out' three days. Some of them young officers lasted just a few hours. You and I, sir, we're the lucky ones!"

The brigadier seemed to mull that over for a while. Were they, in fact, the lucky ones; spared a horrid death only to see the country that they had fought for brought to its knees by wastage, unemployment and general decay? Only to have to see it all slide once again into the nightmare of a further war? He was not so sure. He was deeply concerned for his other son, presently commanding his unit in the thick of it; and not a word from him for weeks now. At least, George was home and safe; pray God for the safety of Thomas. What he desperately longed for was his two sons home again, war over, safe. Then he might have his own grandchildren to spoil. Jenkins was fully aware of this aching void in the old fellow's life – his wife gone and his sons in danger. The prospect of grandchildren was ever present in the brigadier's mind but, with George almost 'married' to his church and Thomas clawing his way up the ranks to lieutenant colonel (hopefully), that prospect seemed as far away as ever. All right, Thomas *was* married to a lovely young woman at present awaiting his return from the war in a flat in Knightsbridge; but she was one of the new breed of career women; she held a quite important position in the editorial office of a society magazine, was herself wedded to her career. So, would she even want children?

Jenkins stretched out a hand to the wireless set. "Want the news, sir?"

"S'pose so – lets hear the latest, what?"

When the valves had warmed there came the usual 'messages' that made sense only to those who had originated them and to the recipients, hopefully safe and sound in the remainder of occupied Europe. 'Mr Green's tomatoes are ripening under the light of Venus'; 'The purple frogs take a big leap over the moon'; 'Caterpillars are eating my uncle's potatoes'. They both imagined excited agents folding away aerials, hiding wireless sets and setting forth to blow up bridges or railway lines. It all seemed like some ghastly game. Then came the usual 'pips'.

"This is the BBC Home Service. Here is the news. Heavy losses have been inflicted on German units as Allied forces break through. Some of our units are pushing towards Rouen and report meeting little resistance." 'Tommy rot!' said the brigadier. "There are reports coming in that our Russian Allies are pushing harder and are inflicting crippling losses on the Germans; the Eastern Front appears to be crumbling".

"Turn the damned thing off!" Jenkins did as asked, tacitly approving the command to silence the drivel coming from the wireless.

"At least the Germans have the honesty to issue their lies from what they acknowledge to be a Ministry of Propaganda. We, on the other hand, deal out our lies with a perfectly straight face; pap for the Home Front. Was the same throughout the first lot – politicians telling their despicable lies while the poor Tommy has to exist in mud and bullets, unable to scream the real truth back at them. Bastards! Why in God's name can't they say, quite honestly, that we are taking a beating; that we will probably win through; that the cost will be heavy? Why don't they tell the *truth* just for once?"

"When has any politician told the truth, sir? Moseley tried that at one time, and look where it got him! Ended up telling different lies. They know that the truth would make them unelectable!"

"Glad I was a soldier then; simple really! Here we are and there they are; kill lots of them and we've won; lose lots and we've lost, Think I'll take up farming after this is all over. Honest folk, farmers – have to be. Have to face the weather, diseases and what not; no time for making up stories or excuses; have to face facts and deal honestly with them. Fancy coming to farm with me, Jenkins?"

"If it's all the same to you sir, I think not. I'm a bit too old to trudge along with half a county stuck to my boots. If you'll pardon the liberty, so are you, sir – too old I mean to contemplate fighting the rain and the snow. Damned stuff always wins!"

"Suppose you're right, as usual. Still, nice dream, what?"

The two old men sat in companionable silence, sipping ale, thinking their thoughts as the night drew on.

"Good to have young Jamie here, eh?"

"Indeed; a breath of fresh air sir; and such a lively young boy".

"What happened to that old pair of binoculars we took off that Prussian colonel? Thought we put them with the others. Couldn't find them the other day"

"I believe they are still in one of the spare bedrooms, perhaps even in Master Thomas's old room. Do you wish me to locate them, sir?"

"Yes, try to find them, like a good chap, will you? Thought young Jamie would like them. Perhaps we could get a nice new case for them, give them to him for Christmas".

The two parted company and went slowly to their beds. The brigadier looked in to see how his son was doing. George was sleeping peacefully. When Jenkins rose about four in the morning to answer a call of nature, he also looked in to find the young master tossing about and muttering in his sleep. He sat quietly by the bedside until George settled once more into a regular breathing pattern. He went quietly back to his bed. Rising again just after eight o'clock, he went to George's room to find the young master sitting up. He gently unwound the bandages to expose a tearing gash on the outside of the thigh. This he dusted with sulphur powder before putting a new thick lint dressing on it. He wound on the bandages. Some time in the future, he thought he would try an age-old remedy; he would put some maggots to eat the decaying flesh, so speeding up the formation of new, healthy tissue. He went downstairs to prepare breakfast.

# BADGER PATROL

When he had arrived back home, Jamie had been reminded by his mother that he must write what she termed a 'bread and butter letter', thanking the brigadier for his hospitality. She seemed far more interested in observing the proper procedures than in what her son had been up to, what he had done. So, Jamie had retired to the kitchen table with pen, paper and ink; had written a quite long – to Jamie, anything over one paragraph was long – letter of thanks. He had signed it with a flourish, this being now the fifteenth attempt to produce a signature that was both illegible and flowery. He had seen numerous examples of signatures on letters and cheques that most were indecipherable; his would be just as obscure. The letter, inserted into envelope and addressed 'by hand', he delivered in person to Jenkins who promised the 'young master' to hand it to the brigadier as soon as that old gentleman had awoken from his, as Jenkins put it, 'post-prandial snooze'.

It had been on Jamie's mind for many months to gather together his two best friends, to form them into a 'patrol' that would roam the countryside looking for and studying the flora and fauna. Now he had a really good name for his patrol; they would become 'The Badgers'. The size, strength and sheer force of these animals had impressed him as had no other; previously, his favourite had been the fox; the disdain of the old brigadier for this animal had put paid to that! Now, all he had to do was to contact Matthew and Tommy, to tell them of the great plan; he never for one moment thought that this would not be to his friends' liking; he was so excited by the idea that he naturally supposed that they would be just as thrilled. His father had suspected for some time that Jamie's single-mindedness would lead to upset; he seemed to have no thought for the feelings or needs of others, that what he thought desirable was automatically what they would find desirable as well. Was he selfish or merely headstrong?

So, Jamie went to call on both his friends and told them that they must attend a meeting by the pond that afternoon; matters of great import would be discussed; a new and thrilling adventure was in the offing. Of course, with such a build-up, neither Matthew nor Tommy could refuse; both were quite agog to find out more. Consequently, three little boys huddled that afternoon in the shelter of an old alder tree that grew by, and partly in, the pond. Jamie could hardly contain his excitement as he outlined the Great Idea. He spoke at some length; they would start on the common as they were all allowed to go to and from this area unsupervised.

"Well, OK", said Tommy, a boy of few words. His enthusiasm was not as keen as Jamie would have hoped. Still, one convert was worth a thousand pressed men!

"What, spend all our time looking at mouldy old flowers, silly hedgehogs and daft sparrows?" Matthew was disappointed with the prospect. He had been looking forward to something more in the line of a twentieth century crusade. He was a boy of action, forever climbing trees, scaling small cliffs; to him, this seemed very tame stuff indeed!

Jamie was quite taken aback at Matthew's response; it had not occurred to him that his best friend would not be as wildly enthusiastic as he was. However, he persevered.

"We'd be able to look for their nests or homes; not to take any eggs, of course. We'd get to know all about them – watch where they go, see what they eat. It's what I've always wanted to do!"

"Yes, but it isn't what *I've* always wanted to do", muttered the intransigent Matthew.

After much pleading and promises that Matthew could borrow his penknife, the matter was settled – more or less. Matthew agreed to 'give it a go'. Tommy would go along with anything agreed to by the others. They arranged to meet the next morning and to set out on their first 'patrol', bringing with them water bottles and sandwiches to sustain them for the day ahead. They had only one more week until school recommenced in early September; Jamie was determined to wring the most possible from the remainder of the summer break before, once again, the school walls hemmed him in.

The next morning saw Jamie at his bedroom window looking with unconcealed glee at the sunshine; what a good omen that was for the first day of the 'Badgers'. His father noted the barely suppressed excitement and, after subtle probing, was told of the momentous day ahead. He simply warned his son to 'take care'; he had far more pressing matters on his mind. Margaret had been showing signs for a few days of the onset of another of her 'episodes'. When these occurred, she would take to her bed – sometimes for two or three weeks, lying in the darkened room with only the occasional interruption from other members of the family calling in to wish her a speedy recovery. There was nothing really from which she needed to recover, nothing whatsoever physically the matter with her, apart, of course, from the chronically poor diet that she had imposed upon herself. She just declined into a sort of mental limbo, thinking her fantasies, dreaming her dreams. During these 'episodes' she was scathing in her comments to her husband, oblivious to her children – even to the needs of her beloved little Robert. She withdrew into herself to such an extent that any talk had to be about her, the state of her 'health', her aching disappointment with all that surrounded her. This morning she had said that she must 'rest' for a few days. John knew exactly what that meant; she would lie in bed for days on end, being comforted, pandered to, waited upon. He dreaded these 'episodes'. Therefore, when Jamie and Desmond had left for the day, he had to wait patiently for Nancy to arrive at ten o'clock for her daily chores of cleaning and polishing. This sweet-natured woman would always step into the breach, would stay at the house until either John or Desmond came home. Margaret would be in completely safe hands. He explained the problem as Nancy huffed and puffed her vastly overweight body around the kitchen.

"Oh, the poor dear! Never you mind, sir; I'll look after her, don't you worry!"

Nancy had listened time beyond recall to Margaret's stories of the wonderful acquaintances that she had 'just missed' yet again. She, a simple and trusting soul, believed every word of it as, indeed, did Desmond and Jamie. John had never once betrayed his wife; he, along with Margaret's parents, were the only people that knew otherwise, were conversant with the sadness of the lies and deceits. John had an uneasy suspicion that Doctor Talbot knew that all was not well with his most persistent patient. He went off to work knowing that Margaret was in good hands but worrying about the coming days; how bad would it get this time, he wondered?

The Badgers proceeded to the old common by way of a small wood. Jamie insisted that they stop under a beech tree to try and spot any inhabitants. There were none visible; they went on until they emerged upon the common itself, a series of rolling hills atop the North Downs. Mostly, this land was of open grass, long and waving in the late summer breeze. Occasional small shrubs broke up the landscape; the east side being bordered by a dense wood; the north came to a point that ended in the road along which the three had approached the common. To the south the land sloped slowly downwards to a steep chalk cliff; to the west it sloped precipitously to a row of small houses bordering the road to the coast. Jamie led his patrol into the eastern wood and declared that this was where they would set up their permanent camp. He chose a thicket of hazel for this purpose; using his penknife, he cut three lengths of wood for thumb-sticks which he proudly presented to his friends. Walking with these, he led the patrol through the wood to where it overlooked the southern end of the common. Peering over the edge of the cliff they were surprised to see a party of khaki-clad figures at the bottom.

"Let's squat down here for a bit and see what they're doing", said Jamie.

"Well, OK" came the inevitable response from Tommy. Matthew merely shrugged.

They lay under a small bush and peered down the cliff. Two of the figures detached themselves from the others and started to free-climb the loose surface. As they ascended, pitons were hammered deep into the chalk; ropes were threaded through the eyes of the pitons; the climb continued until the two had reached a small ledge that was still some twenty feet below the top where the boys were hiding. They beckoned down and others started their climbs, using hand- and foot-holds previously pointed out for them by the two leaders. The boys noted that all the figures wore rubber boots rather than the black leather normally used by the army; each carried ammunition pouches and small haversacks; Sten guns were slung behind them on webbing straps. On each head, rather than a beret or a steel helmet, was a woollen cap comforter; faces and hands were smeared with irregular patterns of camouflage cream. The two leaders started climbing again and were soon spreadeagled at the top, peering downwards to direct the efforts of the followers. As each man slithered over the top he was directed to a point along an imaginary semi-circle; he crawled to his allotted position, lay full length behind whatever cover was available and faced 'outwards', thus forming a defensive perimeter. Soon, all were atop the cliff, each in his allotted place. The two leaders then crawled to the centre of the semi-circle where they carried on a whispered conversation. The boys had frozen into their bush, far too excited to move a muscle. This was much more like it, thought Matthew.

After a few minutes, one of the leaders stood up to call the men together. They arose and sat round the tall figure.

"Right; well done everybody! A little less noise next time, please! Perhaps we could do a repeat this afternoon *without an audience*!" He pointed to the bush. The three boys shrunk back; so much for their belief of invisibility!

"Come on out, lads; we won't bite!"

The three wriggled out to be beckoned into the circle, to sit down among these hard-faced men.

"Well, let's make use of our visitors, shall we? Did you hear us climbing, any noises that might have given us away?"

Matthew, by far the boldest of the three, replied. "No, I didn't hear anything – oh, perhaps there was a 'clink' now and again, but nothing very loud!"

"There!" said the other leader. "Told you clodhopping buggers to keep anything metal well wrapped up. Anything else?"

"Well, no, not really!"

"Thank Christ for that!" said the second man. Matthew decided to push his luck a little further.

"Are you Army; are you practising for a special mission?"

"No, not the usual Army; we're commando, and what we may or may not be practising for ain't none of your business, young feller!"

Matthew subsided. However, the men of the commando unit made them quite welcome, breaking out their rations to share around. Out came the inevitable bully beef and Spam, the tasteless beans in tins. The boys shared the crude meal, taking in the equipment and the very silent, disciplined manner of these men.

"That's a Sten, isn't it?" queried Jamie, stuffing another wedge of Spam into his mouth. He didn't actually like this stuff, had eaten more than enough of the spicy, compressed meat in the last few years to last him a lifetime.

"Sten? Right!" said the second leader who was addressed as 'sarge' by the others. "Useless bugger, the Sten – more dangerous to us than the Gerry; goes off 'alf-cock whenever it feels like it! Give me a Thompson any time!"

Growls of agreement greeted this remark. The Sten was notoriously inaccurate and unsafe, prone to jam at the slightest provocation; the Thompson submachine gun, or 'Tommy', was far more accurate at close quarters and infinitely more reliable.

"OK, you lot; on yer feet!"

The men left not one scrap of evidence that they had ever been there; formed up roughly into two ranks and trotted off on their silent rubber boots. They disappeared round a fold in the ground, presumably to descend to the bottom of the cliff for another practise climb. The three members of the Badger Patrol, thinking that they had better make themselves scarce, also trotted off. They entered the wood, to regroup at their hazel-bound HQ, as Jamie had taken to calling it. Whilst they were having a drink, Jamie started to point out all the trees that he knew, hoping to enthuse the others with his love of the countryside.

"That's an ash; ash-prongs make the best catapults, you know! Now, that is an oak; see the leaves, they are all lumps and bumps; that one over there is a beech – it's got a smooth grey trunk and its leaves are all hard and shiny; that one hiding behind the ash is a silver birch; the one beyond that is a rowan – my dad calls it a mountain ash".

Matthew thought that Jamie was simply showing off; he had absolutely no desire to know any more about the types of trees; the only thing he needed to know about any tree was whether or not it was climbable. He had had enough.

"I'm off home; coming, Tommy?"

"OK, then", replied that most obliging of boys. The two trudged out of the wood, leaving Jamie all alone under his hazel HQ; he minded not the slightest at being alone as he spent a good part of his life in his own company. He was a bit disappointed at Matthew's lack of keenness for the new 'patrol', but could envisage himself having endless adventures. He would have preferred to have their company but could manage almost as well without it. He settled down in the warm shade and nodded off for the 'forty winks' that Nunky enjoyed every afternoon.

When he awoke, the sun had slipped far down the western sky; it was long past the time he should have reappeared at home for his supper. He gathered up his sandwich wrappers, hid two of the hazel thumb-sticks in the HQ and set off home. As he joined the road at the northern end of the common he noticed that the commando unit was 'doubling' down the carriageway a short distance ahead. He decided to keep pace; so, with his stick held at the 'port' position across his body, he jogged behind them. The back marker turned his head and grinned at the little figure, already starting to perspire at the pace he was forced to maintain. Jamie puffed after the unit, quite glad to turn left and stop as the commandos ran straight on past the end of his road. He leaned on his stick, gulping great draughts of air into his lungs; the commandos, being young men and extremely fit, ran at what to them was a slow pace; however, they could keep this pace up for hours. Jamie was used only to walking long distances. Frantic bursts of sprinting were his normal way of covering short distances. He was not yet equipped physically for endurance running. He wondered what he should do about that!

Arrived back at his house, he parked the little thumb-stick behind the kitchen door to find Desmond already eating the supper that he had prepared some time before. He sat down and, between mouthfuls, told his big brother all about his day.

Desmond told him that their mother was in bed and that Robert was spending the night at Nancy's home – probably would stay there for some days to come.

"Mum in bed again, then?" asked Jamie. He was very used to this state of affairs – so conversant that comment was superfluous. Desmond nodded. "Had another one of her bad turns", he replied. Desmond had lived for many years with this phenomenon, had come to regard it as a normal part of their 'family' life. He went upstairs, creeping into the front bedroom to check on his mother. Margaret raised a wan face from the heaped pillows.

"All right, mother? Do you need anything?"

Margaret shook her head. In her 'ill' voice – husky and subdued – she replied that 'Oh, I'll be all right, you know; just need some rest".

Desmond nodded, went back downstairs to carry on with his latest idea to make Jamie a go-kart from pieces of wood he had found on a nearby dump. The old pram, a relic of Jamie's babyhood, would supply the wheels and the brakes. All he needed to find were some screws; he would be able to make the metal brackets to hold the wheel axles to the frame when he had returned to school. It was to be a 'super' version, with proper steering and a footbrake; no cutting corners with bits of string or nails. He drew up his plans as Jamie got ready for bed. The little lad felt quite tired for some reason; despite the fact that he had slept for three hours that afternoon, his eyelids were drooping already. He was in bed, fast asleep, when John at last came home from yet another day organising patrols, seeing to the never-ending mounds of paper, supervising interviews and the like. He was as tired as his little son, not really able to appreciate the supper that Desmond had saved for him. John ate his meal quietly, then went over to his son to peer at the plans.

"Wow! That'll be quite some go-kart when it's done!" he said in admiration. He put a kindly arm about Desmond's rather bony shoulders. "You know, I don't know what we'd all do without you, son", he said. "You cook and shop, do more homework than any boy I've ever come across, keep the whole place going for us. I know I don't often say this, but – thank you for all you do. You're an absolute marvel!"

Desmond blushed; he was not used to thanks from any quarter and did not really know how to respond. Jamie was always full of praise for his 'wunnerful' brother; his dad always praised him for the meals he prepared. But, as to being actually *thanked*, well – that seldom happened. He was pleased that his efforts were noticed but had never regarded it as anything but his duty to carry out all the tasks needed to keep the household going. In that, he was very like his father.

"Oh, that's all right, Dad. I looked in on mother a little while ago; she said she was OK for the time being. Robert is down with Nancy for the night. I know he loves the old soul, but he misses his mum!" John knew this as well; but, how in blazes did you explain to a tiny child that his mother would always put her own needs before those of others; was blind to the real needs of her children for love and affection and, above all, time! All right, she attended to Robert with devotion when her own needs were not paramount; if only this damned war would end, he would be able to do a normal shift of normal hours and so be available at home whenever he was needed. Perhaps it would not last much longer; the reports on the wireless were hopeful. Being an old soldier, he was able to sometimes read between the lines, not always believing the up-beat phrases, the euphoric statements from their leaders. He lived in hope of easier times, not for himself as he knew that the more time he was at home the more opportunities Margaret would have to belittle him, to make her incessant demands. He stopped at that juncture, feeling deep remorse for such disloyalty; he was indeed lucky to have such a beautiful wife, to enjoy a standard of living that came partly from his increased salary, mostly from the generosity of her parents. How else could he have afforded the school fees for Desmond and Jamie. He should try to be positive, think of the good things to have come out of this liaison. He went up to bed.

# A GREAT PLAN IS HATCHED

Jamie had wanted to give up his music lessons; he was heartily sick and tired of the constant scales and theory; as he had said to Mrs Worthy, 'I just want to play tunes!' That lady had been horrified at the mere idea. She had replied that 'tunes, as you call them, can only be permitted when you have learned the essentials, the proper groundwork'. To Jamie, this had sounded like a death sentence. That, coupled with the disdain he received from Tina (whom he now loathed) prompted him one day to say that he thought that the lessons were a waste of his valuable time. This phrase had been overheard by him on one occasion when he had been an unwilling audience at a slight altercation between his granddad and an unwelcome canvasser from the local Labour Party. The words had stuck as they described exactly how he felt about music lessons and beastly arithmetic. He uttered them when asked how his latest lesson with Mrs Worthy had progressed. His mother had called him an ungrateful little brat, not to be so unkind when his grandparents had gone to so much trouble on his behalf. Jamie had stormed out of the room, slamming the door; he had sulked for hours in Advanced Camp, even forgetting to note the trains that passed. How, he wondered, could he extricate himself from those horrid lessons? They forced him to do things that, to him, were an absolute waste of time; he *knew* how to play the tunes that he actually wanted to play. The fact that the lessons would equip him to play *properly* was lost on him; he was being made to do what he did not want to; he was sufficiently arrogant to resent being told that he was not yet good enough. He knew different – he *was* good enough.

Stuck with the hated lessons, he resolved to do all in his power to make Mrs Worthy realise that she should give *him* up, to make so little progress that the whole affair would grind slowly to a halt. So, on his next appearance, he went hesitatingly through a scale in D major, followed by a total mess of the next in succession – E flat major. The whole lesson was spent in him making more and more mistakes, being careful to correct the previous one but to add yet another, new one immediately after. He knew that he was beginning to succeed when, near the end of the allotted hour, Mrs Worthy threw up her hands. "You are *hopeless!*" she wailed. Jamie made himself look downcast whilst smothering a satisfied smirk. It was working! A few more like that and the poor lady would ask for him to be removed as unsuitable. It never entered his young head that he was being unfair to that poor lady, was wasting his grandparents' money; all he could think of was ending the torture, being allowed to go his own way as, indeed, he had been forced to do most of his young life. He had been forced to find his own amusement, to be a detached, independent being ever since starting to walk. Devoid of the love and attention of his mother, the enforced absence of his father, he was slowly growing into an isolationist – despite the love and care shown to him by his elder brother who did what he could, when he could. Jamie was, at heart, a sad and lonely child who gave off an air of devilment and bravado to mask his basic unhappiness.

Now, he had to face the fact that his new venture as leader of the Badgers was likely to come to nothing. Matthew did not really want to join in; Tommy would follow, but half-heartedly. What could he do to bring the excitement that he so desperately craved? He thought that his best bet was to take up the brigadier's offer to call in whenever he wanted; that old gentleman was a source of super stories, had been all round the world. Surely, he would find something exciting there?

On the first day of the new term, Jamie found himself no longer in the youngest group of children in the school. There arrived a new intake of eight little boys; Jamie, at five and a half, felt distinctly superior. Much to his astonishment, he was appointed by Mrs Bedford as one of two ink monitors. His job every day was to make sure that the porcelain inkwells, sunk into the tops of the desks, were empty of rubbish and filled with ink. Each desk had, at its top-right corner, a brass ink holder that was covered when not in use by a sliding metal plate. When pushed back, this plate revealed the inkwell itself. Jamie was told to use a piece of blotting paper when taking the well out so as not to make too much mess of his fingers. Despite this good advice, his fingers soon became a dark blue. Pieces of rolled up paper were removed with a length of wire, then the well could be reinserted into its hole and filled via a small funnel. The first two desktops were quite awash before he mastered the technique. This exercise was carried out between assembly and first lesson. He had perfected his knack of paraphrasing the lines of the most favoured hymns; his neighbours in assembly were now informed of a Trinity comprising 'Father, son and holey toast'; were told that, 'There is a green bus far away'; were comforted that they 'Be of good beer', instead of cheer. He saw absolutely nothing sacrilegious in any of this; he loved to be the centre of attention for a short while, to make people laugh at his wit. After all, it was funny, wasn't it?

On his way home he called in, as he had been invited to, on the brigadier. His son George, now supported by only one cane, answered the front door, Jenkins being busy somewhere on the property. He had been told all about this young lad and was quite eager to see him. His father, he explained, was attending to the chickens and would be in shortly. He sat Jamie down at the scullery table and poured him a glass of ginger beer – Jamie's favourite.

Jamie could not refrain any longer. "How did you hurt you leg?" he enquired, hoping that it would not cause embarrassment. George laughed and went on to explain all about the shrapnel and his evacuation from the front line of the attack. Jamie listened enthralled, only memories of 'good taste' lectures by his grandmother making him refrain from asking to see the actual wound itself. Jamie had noticed something else, as well; George wore a 'dog collar'. "Are you a vicar?" he asked.

"No, not actually a vicar; I'm what the army calls a 'padre'", he replied. Jamie quite astonished him by stating, "That's Latin, isn't it? It means 'father'!"

"Well, sort of! It's an old name used by soldiers. We go with the troops right up into the battles; but I act more like a nurse or a doctor, most of the time".

Jamie sat talking to George for quite a long time; he told him all about the visit to the hide, the sighting of the two badgers; he told him of the formation of the 'badger' patrol, the reluctance of his two friends to participate with the necessary degree of enthusiasm. George was particularly interested to hear about the cliff-climbing exercise that the boys had observed, the quiet efficiency of the commando unit. What, he wondered, were they practising for – or, rather, *where* were they practising for? The brigadier came in and sat down, just as that particular episode was being discussed.

"Commando, eh?" he muttered. "Yes, sir – struck me as odd, too!"

Jamie had never heard a son refer to his father as 'sir' before; perhaps, he thought, as they were both officers, the son called his father 'sir' because he was of a superior rank? Most of his friends called their fathers 'Dad' or, in one case, 'Daddy' – this was rather silly, in Jamie's opinion. The same boy called his mother 'Mummy'; this he thought as equally silly. Oh, he had just remembered; Julian referred to his parents as 'Pater' and 'Mater'. He would, thought Jamie!

Father and son had not yet finished ruminating over the commando. "Would have thought that they would have practised for the beach landings back in the summer – you know, bit down the coast to outflank a part of the defences. Wonder what cliffs they are going to climb – don't know of any in Normandy – not inland, anyway".

"Perhaps they are practising for another 'front', one we don't know about – say Norway or somewhere". The brigadier shrugged his bony shoulders. "Don't suppose we will know until it's all over; nobody tells me anything anymore". This lack of intelligence seemed to his son to worry his father more than anything else; he had been 'in the loop' for so many years that, to find himself suddenly cut off from information was like being thrust into the middle of the Sahara Desert with neither map or compass. The old man fretted, felt useless.

That evening John, early home for a change, decided to take Desmond and Jamie for a walk. He overrode Desmond's excuses of a 'mound of homework', insisted that they did not do anywhere near enough as a family. Desmond heartily agreed with this; funny, he thought, no mention of mother – wasn't she and little Robert a part of the family as well? Margaret was still 'recuperating', Robert still spending more time with old Nancy or his grandparents than with his mother.

The three set off for the beech woods that had been growing on a nearby hillside for over three centuries. It was one of Jamie's favourite haunts, full of wonderful birds and insects. He had seen his first woodpecker some months before, drilling into the bark of a massive trunk; he had sat for over an hour in absolute stillness watching the bird drill, stop, listen, drill and drill. He had marvelled at the sheer strength, comparing his ability to peck with forward thrusts of his neck to the speed and force of that feathered body; what muscles that small bird must have! They walked through the wood, feet rustling over coppery fallen leaves that gleamed with a metallic sheen in the rays of the setting sun filtering through the trees. It was all so quiet in the woods, so peaceful. Desmond was not unaware of the beauty of the place, the majesty of the smooth, grey-barked giants; his interests, however, leaned towards the more prosaic aspects of his surroundings. How many cubic feet of timber were contained in the trunks? What was beech wood used for? He had heard somewhere that it made the best furniture frames; so, how many chairs could be obtained from one of those huge trunks? John, meanwhile, simply revelled in the peace and quiet. His days were, for the most part, mundane with paperwork interspersed now and again with the excitement of arrests, the formality of court appearances. He missed the cut and thrust of what he still considered to be the main purpose of policing – interfacing with the public, being visible on the streets, knowing the haunts and habits of those whose interests were as anti-social as his were social. Yes, an hour or two with his two sons in the quiet of the woods was just what he needed.

They sat down on a fallen tree. It had toppled over during a storm the previous winter, victim of its previous inability to reach enough of the sunlight to form sufficient growth and strength, victim of its neighbours which *had* succeeded in their fight for *lebensraum*. Jamie squatted down to see what was growing and living between the fallen trunk and the ground beneath; ants in profusion, of course; small beetles a-plenty.

Lots of food for birds there! Desmond was beginning to fidget at the thought of the homework as yet not begun. He said that he really ought to get back to it and, saying that he would see them both later, went back down the lane, head full of formulae that needed to be used for solving the problems set that afternoon by the physics master. John and little Jamie stayed sitting on the trunk; neither saw the least necessity to talk. Far away came the drone of bombers forming up for yet another night raid into the Ruhr Valley, or somewhere. Such a nightly occurrence called for no comment at all. Then came the wail of a siren, again some distance from them – over towards Bromley, thought John. The light was fading rapidly, would be gone completely in another hour. A slight chill rose from the woodland floor, heat of the autumn day leaching up to the colder air above. Neither Jamie nor his father noticed the slight drop in temperature; John because his thoughts were elsewhere; Jamie because he never really felt the cold at all. John was thinking for the thousandth time of his other two children, hopefully safe and sound with their adoptive parents. He had written twice to Valerie, trying to explain, begging for her understanding. No answer had been received at the police station – she knew that she would never be able to communicate with her father at his home; letters might well be intercepted by an ever vigilant Margaret. He felt sometimes near to despair; maybe the time had come for him to acknowledge the fact that his dual life was over, that he had only three children, that he abandon for ever the other two so as to achieve some partial harmony in his life?

# NIGHTMARE

A slightly louder droning came from the same direction as the siren had sounded earlier. The drone altered slightly to a splutter, then back to a steady drone. The noise came nearer, changed back to a more pronounced splutter, cut out completely for a few seconds. Jamie looked up at his father in puzzlement; what was happening?

Three miles to the east of the beech woods a German bomber was fighting for its very life; the port engine had been peppered over its supposed target by a burst of ack-ack fire; had caught alight, flames licking fiercely along the nacelles, streaming back across the aerofoil of the wing into the darkening sky. It stopped altogether after a period of intermittent firing and missing. The pilot knew that his chances of getting back to his airfield in France were about zero; he struggled for height, pushing the remaining starboard engine to its maximum. It screamed a protest at him that had his nerves jangling. The co-pilot sat as if transfixed beside him; in the nose lay the bomb-aimer, calmly calling out landmarks to his pilot. The altimeter showed that he had attained just over three thousand metres when the starboard engine started to misfire, to stutter. Immediately, the pilot eased back on the throttle, levelling out his flight; his height would just have to do. He scanned the ground ahead, looking for places that he might land the wallowing, ungainly craft. He saw the open common land about ten kilometres ahead, the same common land that Jamie had roamed with the 'badgers', seen the commandos. Between the plane and this possible refuge was a small town, then a dense wood. The starboard engine faltered again, caught, misfired, packed-up altogether. He nudged the co-pilot, made the gesture of a parachute descent, left it to this frightened youth to get the bomb-aimer out as well. He knew that his war was coming to a rapid end but was determined to land his plane as safely as possible, destroy any papers and then set fire to the aircraft before making his way to the south coast and possible escape back to France. Some hope, he thought!

A fierce gust of air told of the opening of the mid-section hatch, the dropping of his two crew members. He was alone; struggled with the controls as the unwieldy machine tried to glide. He dared not depress the nose quite yet, needed all the height he could maintain; but, without forward propulsion, this was a losing battle. The plane lost height increasingly as speed dropped off. He would have to dip the nose soon, he knew, otherwise the plane would go into a stall from which he had little hope of recovery at this low altitude. He realised with a sick feeling that he was not going to reach the open common land; tentatively, he attempted a little pull on the stick. Could he gain a few more metres in height? The plane nearly stalled; obviously not! He was a bare hundred meters above the treetops as he crossed the eastern boundary of the beech woods. His only hope now lay in trying to skim the tops of the trees as gently as possible, hoping that this would slow his progress sufficiently that, when forward motion was stopped altogether, he would be going slowly enough to settle somewhere in the canopy. The belly of the plane scraped the first twigs and leaves. It sunk a bit lower, the scraping becoming louder. Speed had dropped off alarmingly until he guessed it to be no more than sixty kilometres per hour. Was it going to work? The pilot, a young man barely into his twenties, prayed to God, to his mother, to his girlfriend in far off Hamburg. A slightly thicker branch slewed the craft to the right, tipped the nose, started the last downward plunge. The plane, slowing all the time, seemed to the young pilot to be going in slow motion; he saw branches pass by, could notice the cracks in the bark; the starboard wing sheared off to be left supported by two thick branches. There, in front of him, was the thick carpet of leaves, the detritus of the woodland floor. It came up at him so slowly, arrived in front of the Perspex, seemed to open up to welcome this strange visitor. Unknown to him, one bomb remained in the racks that had supposedly emptied over their target. Like its fellows, it was fitted with an impact fuse. As the plane crumpled to a halt at no more than twenty kilometres per hour, it juddered free at last, fell forward and exploded as the nose cone touched the bomb-bay bulkhead. The pilot heard the massive explosion just behind him, seemed to have an age in which to make a final prayer before he lost consciousness as flames erupted all around his strapped-in body.

Jamie and his father heard the first scrapings above their heads, the tearing sounds, the sudden screech as the wing was torn off, the shuddering fall, the deafening explosion from which they were mercifully shielded by the massive intervening trunks. Instinctively, they both ran to the seat of the fire that had started to rage. There, sitting quietly in the cockpit, they saw the pilot. He sat quietly as if waiting for death, or a lift home. The heat of the fire was searing, causing them both to retreat to a safer distance. Fearing that other bombs were about to explode, John dragged his little son down behind the bole of a huge tree. Jamie hugged the ground, peeping round the trunk to watch in horror as the flames licked into the cockpit. The pilot, roused by the deadly inferno, raised his head, opened his eyes. He seemed to struggle for a moment with his harness, his open mouth screaming silently to the little boy. To Jamie, it seemed as if the man looked directly at him, begging for his help, terrified as he saw his ghastly end approaching. Jamie started to scream himself. John reached across to his son and hugged him fiercely, trying to get the little eyes away from the awfulness.

The cockpit was now a mass of white flame, the pilot invisible and burning; he had mercifully lost consciousness again so was spared waking knowledge of his final immolation. The aircraft burned, setting fire to the dry tinder of the woodland floor so that John literally took Jamie up into his arms and ran to a safe distance, the little boy hugged to his chest, sobbing with terror. John ran from the woods, into the lane, stopped at the top of the road that led to the town. There, he knew, was a police call box. He set Jamie down on the pavement and opened the door to the box, took the handset from its cradle and waited for a response. "Brooke Hill Police Station", came the crackly voice.

"There is a German bomber down in the beech woods, just off Sandy Lane", said John. "One occupant that I could see; well on fire when I left the scene". He was succinct, years of training coming to bear on the limitation of the report to absolute fact; no opinions, no frills.

"Right, sir. Fire brigade only, then?"

"Yes, I'm afraid so", John put down the handset, closed the door, sat down beside his little son, said nothing. Jamie felt the strong arm round his shoulders, snuggled into his father and saw again the face begging him for help. He shuddered with terror, was barely conscious of being carried back home, of being cleaned up and put safely into his bed. Desmond, appraised of the evening's tragedy, went up to his little brother; he sat down on Jamie's bed and took his hand. "All over now, old chap!" he soothed.

John climbed wearily up the stairs to the front bedroom. Margaret was awake, sitting up against her usual mound of pillows. John sat down on the bed, removing his shoes and socks as he told his wife of the crash, the explosion, the fire. Margaret was horrified. She turned a face contorted by fear to her husband. "What would have happened to me if you had been killed?" she gasped. John said nothing, merely took the soft hand in his, put it to his face, kissed the open palm. "I'm here, love! I'm here to look after you!"

In the back bedroom, Jamie lay under the blankets, his small body convulsed with shivers and shakes. He kept seeing that terrified face, the open mouth pleading for assistance. He should have been crying for his 'mummy'; it never once occurred to him to do so. Instead, he gripped his brother's hand, refusing to let go until Desmond had to pry the little fingers loose, gently so as not to upset the little chap. He got ready for bed, carried his little brother in his arms and cuddled him tightly until the sobbing and shaking had slowly stopped, the boy at last falling into a deep sleep of utter exhaustion. Twice in the night he was woken by little cries; twice he hugged his brother asleep again.

The clock by Desmond's bed showed seven-thirty as the alarm went off. Jamie woke beside him with a start, tears immediately starting from the puffy eyes. He struggled upright, cramped at being snuggled beside his brother in the single bed. The horror returned. Desmond knew that he had to let Jamie talk it all out. He asked questions in whispers to receive a choking summary of the crash, the explosion, the fire. "He wanted me to help him, Des! He was calling me to help him, and I couldn't!" Desmond was at a loss how to comfort the little boy. "You couldn't have done anything, Jamie. It was *not your fault*!"

Slowly, Jamie fell silent, the horrors still playing in vivid colour across his mind; the heat; the flames; that face. Just as slowly, his normal ebullient nature took control once more. At length, with Desmond now ready dressed for school, he muttered, "S'pose I couldn't, really!" He got up, washed, dressed and went downstairs for his breakfast. John had had to leave before six that morning as he had a full schedule of work to get through. Looking in on his two boys before he left, he was relieved to see Jamie fast asleep under his big brother's protective arm. He had left a fearful Margaret, promising to be back by five that afternoon. She would be alone that day; Desmond and Jamie would be at school, Robert still with dear old Nancy. He knew that she would have all day to brood, to fret, to fear for her safety. Despite all the denigration, the put-downs, she needed him as desperately as he needed her. The children needed her as well but, Robert apart occasionally, had had to make do without. Desmond, sensible and utterly reliable, had become almost completely self-sufficient. Jamie was slowly becoming a 'loner', with the occasional outburst of silly jokes whenever he felt the need to be noticed. Robert was still too young to notice anything but the absence of his mother; he longed for the tickling, the romping, the fun. He was growing to love old Nancy, but he missed his lovely mother.

Jamie walked slowly to school that morning. It was another sunny autumn day, birds twittered, a soft breeze disturbed the leaves that were turning into their deep colours. It was a morning that would normally have seen his whistling (trying to) and skipping along, looking for nests.. Today, music was far from his thoughts; even the total exasperation of Mrs Worthy at his last lesson that would, he was sure, lead to his final removal from her pupilage, did not even enter his mind. All he could see was the terrified face, the silent pleading; no matter what he did to direct his thoughts elsewhere, this image returned time and again.

He stood during assembly, unable to make the slightest variation in the words of the two hymns that were performed; he sat miserable through two interminable lessons, staring as usual into the far distance but unable to focus on the wildlife that flitted past his field of vision. That face, that open mouth – pleading for his help. Tears started to roll down his cheeks unchecked. His face was so turned away from the front that this was not seen by either of the teachers. He wiped a sleeve across his eyes and tried to concentrate; but the words all blurred into one unintelligible monotone, a background hum to his thoughts. After nibbling at a sandwich at lunch he was sought out by the ever persistent Matthew.

"You're quiet today – no jokes for us, eh?"

Jamie could keep it to himself no longer. "Saw a German plane last night crash. Fell in the old beech woods. My dad and I were out for a walk. Saw it tumble through the trees and explode!"

"Wow!" exclaimed a very impressed Matthew. "What did you do?"

"Couldn't do anything! The pilot was still in his cockpit – he burned up!" Jamie started to weep again.

Julian, school bully, happened to overhear this. "What, another of your fancy stories?" he scoffed.

"It's true, did see it!" snuffled Jamie. "You ask my Dad; he was there as well!"

Julian had been meant to leave this little school, to go to his prestigious prep school that term. For some reason, inexplicable to him and a matter of fury to his parents, he had failed the entry examination, had been told to try again next spring. His failure rankled with this proud and boastful only child; his spite had increased since the rejection.

"You'll be telling us next that you fired a catapult at it and made it crash!" he scoffed.

"I *did* see it – I *did*!"

"Liar, liar, pants on fire!" crowed Julian, dancing round the miserable Jamie. He urged others to join him in mocking the little boy. Jamie's usual reaction to this sort of provocation was to launch himself at the opponent, no matter the size and strength of that person. This time, to everyone's amazement, he ran through the chanting circle and into the cloakroom, to lock himself into a lavatory cubicle.

Julian could not restrain his glee, his triumph over an opponent. He rushed into the classroom where Mrs Bedford was setting out the books for the first afternoon lesson.

"Mrs Bedford! Mrs Bedford!" he shouted. "Jamie has been telling one of his stories again; how he saw a German bomber crash and explode!"

"One *did* come down last night", said Cicely, stacking the remaining books on her own desk. "I wonder if that is what he is referring to?"

Julian, seeing his triumph beginning to leak away, needed to reinforce his own side of things. "Jamie says he saw the crash and the pilot burning in the plane!"

Cecily could imagine nothing worse. Could it be true? If so, the little lad needed all the help he could get. She hurried upstairs to her office and dialled the number of the Wandleside police station, asking to be connected to Inspector Small.

"Jamie seems very upset today", she said. "Did he witness anything distressing yesterday evening?" She phrased the question obliquely so as to get either a confirmation or a denial without her having to prompt.

"Yes, I'm afraid he did!" replied John, seeing again the little distressed face. "We were out for a walk in the beeches when the plane came down. We both witnessed the explosion. I'm afraid Jamie saw the pilot die in the flames. It upset him a lot, cried all the way home!"

"Yes, I can well imagine that he did", agreed the headmistress, her heart going out to the small boy. "I'll look out for him, see he gets home safe and sound this afternoon".

After mutual 'good-byes' she hung up and went down to find Jamie. He was just emerging from the lavatories when she literally bumped into him.

"I've just been speaking to your father", she put a gentle arm around him. "He says you had a terrible experience last night!"

"Yes, Mrs Bedford", snuffled Jamie. He followed the headmistress into the classroom, already starting to fill with boys summoned bank inside by the bell for first lesson. She took him to the front of the class, turned and addressed the boys.

"Last night, a German bomber crashed near here. The pilot died in the plane; he was burnt. Jamie saw this and I've just spoken to his father who was there as well. Now, as you all know, Jamie's father is a police inspector and, if he says that this is what happened, then it did. We would now all like to say how sorry we are for you having to see this dreadful thing, Jamie – wouldn't we, class?"

"Yes, Mrs Bedford", came the response. She had not finished. "Some boys also want to apologise for not believing you, Jamie!" She shot a look at Julian, who was looking open-mouthed in astonishment. Whatever outcome he had envisaged, this was certainly not it! However, he was in a deep hole and had to extricate himself.

"Sorry, Jamie", he mumbled. Cecily knew that this was the very best she could get and left it at that. Jamie resumed his seat by the window, receiving a squeeze on his arm as he passed Matthew's desk. He felt a little better; at least, others now knew about it, could share his misery.

As school ended for the day, Mrs Bedford had a quiet word with her assistant, Julia Forbes. She appraised her of the situation, asked the ever patient Julia to see Jamie home as her way passed his house. Julia agreed without a moment's hesitation. She wanted to take the little boy's hand, to comfort him; she refrained as some inner sense warned her that he might be ragged about being 'teacher's pet'. They walked together down the steep hill but stopped right outside the gate to his grandparents' bungalow.

"I'll go and have tea with my Nana", said Jamie, leading the way up the shallow steps to the large porch. He knocked, timidly for him, at the door which was opened by the maid. Jamie led Julia into the sitting room where his grandmother was busy arranging some flowers. To his surprise, he saw his mother sitting quietly on the long sofa.

"Hello, Nana; hello, mum!" he said ever so quietly.

"Why, whatever's the matter?" exclaimed Gertrude, dropping flowers and scissors to hug the silent little boy. She raised a questioning face to Julia, whom she had met on a couple of visits to the school. Julia explained all about Jamie's ordeal, both the previous evening and that day at the school. Gertrude cuddled her grandson, aghast at the possible damage done to the quite sensitive lad. She looked gratefully at Julia, for whom she had a great liking and respect.

"Miss Forbes", she said. "Thank you ever so much for bringing Jamie all this way; it was very good of you!"

"Well, no trouble at all, really. I pass by the top of Buttermere Gardens myself. I just couldn't see the poor little lad making his way home all alone".

She excused herself and was seen out, Gertrude's thanks following her down the steps. At least, she thought, he is in good hands there. But fancy her not even knowing about it! Hadn't Jamie's mother (whom she had recognised) ever bothered to tell his grandmother of her own son's experience? She had noticed with concealed distaste that Margaret had made no move to comfort, to reassure, her son; had left all this to the kindly little grandmother. 'Poor little mite', she thought.

Gertrude's natural practicality took over; she summoned Alfred from his pottering in the garden and sat him down in a deck-chair, telling him the story, whilst Jamie held her hand with a fierce determination.

"What you both need is a rock cake!" she said. Daisy was summoned and asked to bring the necessary out into the garden where Jamie sat on his grandfather's knee, quietly telling that wonderful old man of the death he had seen, his misery at not being able to do anything to help that screaming face. Alfred held his little grandson close, rocked him gently, watched as a little colour came back into the wan face as bits of rock cake disappeared.

Gertrude left them to it; she went back indoors wondering how to broach the subject with her daughter, Margaret sat as before, a far-away look in her wide, brown eyes. Gertrude knew that she had been 'recuperating' for the last three weeks, isolated in the darkness of her bedroom. "What a terrible thing to happen!" she began. Margaret looked up.

"John saw it too, was ever so near the explosion!" she replied. Her mother knew exactly what this meant, how her daughter's first thoughts were for her own safety and wellbeing.

"But why did you not think to tell me all about it, dear?" she enquired as gently as possible.

"Oh, it's all over now and no harm done, mummy!" Margaret seemed quite happy at the prospect.

Gertrude thought, 'No harm done? What about the harm to that little mind out there?' Instead, she capitulated as usual, gave way to that selfish, self-centred demand for attention. "Yes, I suppose it's a case of 'alls well that ends well'", she said, sadly.

She went out again to see how things were progressing. Jamie was listening with all his usual rapt attention to another of Alfred's made-up ghost stories. His face had perked up considerably, to her great relief. She offered Jamie the last rock cake and watched happily as it disappeared with the usual speed and urgency.

"Thanks, Nana; they are super, as usual!"

She went back to her daughter. "Look, why not leave Jamie with us for a couple of days. He can have the spare bedroom and we can feed him up. I know John and Desmond never come home until quite late, so it will be good for him and good for us, as well. You know how we love to have him here!"

Margaret looked as if a load had been lifted from her mind. "Oh, yes please, mummy; that sounds marvellous!" she replied. "I've got Robert coming back to me this evening, so I'll be quite happy!"

Gertrude regarded her daughter. 'Yes, I suppose you will', she thought, adding, as Julia had done, 'Poor little mite!'.

# A DREADFUL CHRISTMAS

Christmas at the Small household passed almost unnoticed; nineteen forty-four became nineteen forty-five almost by accident. John had drawn Christmas duty as, being the newest of the three inspectors, subtle hints from the other two had convinced him that it was only 'right and proper'. Therefore, he had been missing from the family home for nearly all five days of the festive season; he had also been working on the eve of the new year and the day itself. Desmond, as usual, had been exceptionally busy with his homework, plus the manufacture of Jamie's go-kart. He had begged the use of Alfred's shed for this work as he did not want his brother to see his splendid new conveyance until it was completely ready. Jamie had gone back to his Advance Camp, noting trains and their contents as before. He had nearly forgotten the dreadful episode of the burning airman, suffering only the occasional flashback or the odd nightmare. Margaret had returned quite happily to her self-imposed isolation, amusing her baby son whenever she felt the need to communicate with another human being. Little Robert was taken out for 'walks' on a daily basis, mostly by Jamie – who had the time – and sometimes by Desmond – who tried hard to make some time for what he considered a very pleasurable task. To the five members of this family, all seemed back to normal; to any observer, it would have appeared utterly bizarre.

Desmond had started to take a great interest in the progress of the invasion by the allied armies; he had found an old map of mainland Europe, had pinned it up on the wall beside the huge old valve radio. Every night he would faithfully trace in pencil the movement of the advance. John, on the rare occasions that he was there when the nightly bulletin was broadcast, was proud of the care and precision that his son took over this task, would comment on the daily variations, would discuss the implications with a young man who appeared to be capable of the most intricate analyses. The whole country had felt depressed when, just before Christmas, the Germans had sprung a surprise counter-attack in the forests of the Ardennes. They had taken the swiftly advancing Americans completely off guard, pushing deep into their front, driving a massive wedge, threatening to break out into the plains beyond. Winston Churchill, not wishing to alarm people, referred dismissively to this offensive as the 'Battle of the Bulge', hoping to minimise its significance, its detrimental effect on morale. Few who really thought about it were taken in by this; it was serious; it could well spell disaster if it was allowed to go much further. American losses by the middle of January were considerable; allied reinforcements were rushed to fill gaps, to cover flanks. Slowly, almost by inches, the offensive literally ran out of steam, the Germans unable to re-supply from their hugely depleted reserves. Desmond had daily altered his map which now looked quite complex. The German advance had been pencilled in and marked with each day's date until a massive 'bulge' had developed. Now, at long last, this bulge was being flattened out; surely, soon it would be obliterated. By the time it was completely repulsed the Americans had lost some seventy-five thousand dead, wounded or taken prisoner. It had been, in the words of a previous general, 'a damned close run thing'.

German bomber raids had almost stopped but had been replaced by a great increase in the number of V1 and V2 attacks. John was kept furiously busy co-ordinating the efforts of his patrols with helping the fire brigade, the wardens, the ambulance service and the mass of volunteers struggling to cope with clearing debris, finding bodies and scattered possessions. It was a daily, nightly, never-ending task; he was becoming exhausted. It seemed that, as the invasion neared the German border, Hitler was making a last frenzied effort to turn the tide by destroying and demoralising the home population.

Christmas, the sixth of this interminable war, had begun with dark skies that threatened either rain or sleet; even the weather seemed to be set against any festive spirit lightening the general mood of depression. All during the night of Christmas Eve, flying bombs and rockets had rained down on London and its suburbs; fearful damage had been caused; many had lost lives, homes, possessions. John had been out of the station for eighteen hours, sitting in a patrol car, his driver rushing him from scene of carnage to another; he, like his policemen, was exhausted. When eventually he managed to return to the station at four o'clock on Christmas morning, it was to find that a part of the building had been severely damaged by a flying bomb that had landed in the next road. The Superintendent was in his shirt sleeves, among his men as they feverishly dug into the piles of bricks, desperate to find colleagues known to be under there somewhere. John and his driver pitched in, forming part of a human chain that passed bits of masonry and timber back to a growing pile of debris. Civilians of all ages came to help, once it was clear that no more could be done for those under the collapsed houses. One old chap, well into his seventies, joined the chain gang. "You lot are always there for us", he said to John. "Now it's our turn to help the old bill". John clapped the old chap on the shoulder, passed him the next handful of shattered bricks and mortar. Some of the local women volunteered to 'man' the police canteen, to brew gallons of tea, butter bread for corned beef sandwiches. It was not until well after six that morning that the first body was found; an elderly civilian clerk was slowly brought out of the rubble, handed gently to the ambulance crew. A short, curt shake of the head was sufficient to galvanise the burrowers to continue. By eight o'clock, all missing personnel had been found. Five constables, one sergeant, one inspector and the chief inspector all pronounced dead; mercifully three constables had been found alive. One had a broken leg and pelvis, another severe lacerations, whilst a third seemed by some miracle to have merely a black eye from contact with his own knee as he was blown under a massive oak table. The police and their crew of volunteers sat down wherever they could and drank tea; almost no-one was able to eat anything at all. The Superintendent came over to where John was sitting, slumped down beside him, lit his foul-smelling pipe. A warden was just about to issue a stern reprimand about the possibility of fractured gas pipes when he caught the baleful eye above the bowl of the fuming pipe; thought better of it; sat down and took up a mug of tea.

"Just me, Paul and you to run this motley crew now", he said. His face, like all those around him, was streaked with perspiration that had made ragged channels through the layers of grime and dust. The other remaining inspector joined the 'council of war', summoned over by a tired wave of a hand that was blistered, filthy, covered in smears of blood. Paul English, not far from retirement himself, slumped down. He was one of the very few who seemed able to eat anything; indeed, his appetite was both prodigious and famous throughout the Division; he was on his fifth doorstep sandwich. "We'll have to run two management shifts until I can get some replacements", the Superintendent said wearily. "Although, God only knows where we are going to get them from!" Losses throughout the police force were running higher than in most other disciplines. Paul spoke up through a barrage of corned beef and pickles. "Norwood is short, so is Forest Hill – so I dunno where you're likely to get any!"

"Only way, as I see it, is that you two will have to head the shifts, acting up as Chiefy; senior sergeants to act up as Inspectors; most experienced bobbys to act up as sergeants. Paul – you look just about done in. Sod off home for some kip! John, can you draw up a temporary roster while I carry on here?" John nodded wearily, stood up, plodded over to the undamaged portion of the station to where his own office, totally unscathed, seemed like an oasis of peace. He collapsed into his chair, sipped the rest of his cold tea and started to draw up a list of suitable personnel to 'act up'.

# ACTING CHIEF INSPECTOR

As soon as he had completed this he put through a call to the Brooke Hill police station, asking that, as a favour, the local beat bobby could call in at his home to say that he was all right. His old acquaintance, the desk sergeant, said that it would be no trouble; his shift was ending soon, would call in himself. He asked about casualties at Wandleford, cursed bitterly at the losses. John took his list to the Superintendent's office for approval; not that he thought he might have made any mistakes, but to observe the hierarchical niceties. His superior officer glanced through it, put it down on his desk.

"Somehow thought those names would come up", he grunted. "OK John; I'll see these chaps – you've got enough on your plate at the moment. You go and get yourself settled into the CI's office and I'll send Sergeant Plumb up when I've told him he's acting Inspector. I'll let him handle the acting sergeants; you never know – we might just find a gem among all of these! Right, can you handle things here for a while; I've got some very unpleasant calls to make!"

John agreed without hesitation. He had in the past handled this woeful task himself, having to call on a family to tell them that the husband, father, son, brother, had been killed in the line of duty. It was horrible but, somehow, not quite as horrible as telling distraught parents that a little child had been killed. He wondered at the distinction – gave it up as he was just too damned tired. He entered the Chief Inspector's office, barely able to look at the framed photographs on the desktop; the man himself, wife, two beautiful little girls – all wearing Sunday Best for the studio portrait. He found a small box and carefully placed all the personal items in it; he would deliver it personally, probably the next day. He sat down in the deep leather chair, could barely stop his eyelids closing. Taking paper and pen, he started to draw up lists for the revised shifts that had been so savagely thrust on them.

There came a knock at the office door; it opened, and Terry Plumb came in. His uniform was in tatters, covered in dust and grime; he had been one of the officers that had squirmed into the mounds of rubble to try to find the bodies. Sergeant Plumb had been a police officer for just about the same time as John; he was a massive man, well over six feet tall, hugely muscled as a result of years of weight training in the police gym, hence his volunteering immediately for the backbreaking task of burrowing into the collapsed building. John waved him to a seat. Terry Plumb almost collapsed into the visitor chair, his vast weight making the frame creak and groan. He sat there as tears started to streak the grime on his face. "Shit, shit, shit!" he said, wiping his face with a blood-stained handkerchief. John knew that there was nothing useful anyone could say, felt exactly the same himself, wanted nothing more than to curl up somewhere and sob himself to sleep. He had not felt this deep emotion since his time in the trenches, having to come to terms that, once more, he had survived the shelling, the machine guns; seeing around him the remains of his mates who had not survived. The need to rant and scream in anger and frustration was always the first reaction, followed by the collapse into tears of sadness and hatred. He waited patiently as the Sergeant tried to compose himself.

"Wanted to do that, myself – kick the furniture, the cat, anything! Find myself a corner and shut the whole business out. Happens every time!"

Terry Plumb knew that John had, like himself, been in the trenches, knew all about violent loss of life, of friends. He looked up at John. "Well, suppose we've got to carry on! Super's told me the news; wants me to act up as Inspector until this mess gets sorted. I've got your old shift by the way".

John knew that the shift was in the best possible hands; knew, also, that to say anything of the kind would be superfluous as well as crass. "What do you make of my suggestions for Acting Sergeants? You've got to work with them, after all. Better to have who you want from the outset".

Plumb simply nodded. "They are the ones I would have picked myself – but you know that, don't you? Those two have already passed their Sergeants' exams, put the time in. No, they'll do nicely, Guv!"

John was startled to hear this nickname for his acting rank, had never thought in a million years that he would be addressed in that manner. The fact that he was now so addressed was due to the violent death of the original post-holder; this caused him to have yet another choking feeling, almost of guilt. This simply would not do, he told himself. Back to business. He asked his new Inspector to round up the two and to get them started as soon as possible; the streets needed patrolling; the public needed to see policemen doing their duty, protecting them. He wondered if there would be yet another influx of 'specials' recruited to fill gaps; hoped not, if that oaf at Brooke Hill was a typical example. He immediately regretted this slur on a group of, in the main, deeply dedicated men and women who simply wanted to help out; this in addition to working full time at their own jobs. Terry Plumb had obviously been thinking along the same lines.

"S'pose we'll get more 'specials'", he muttered. He brightened a bit. "Lots of good folk come in that way. Need their hands holding, of course, but that's what us old war horses are for, isn't it, Guv?"

"Yes, Terry, I suppose it is. On your way, old son – rally the troops!"

When Terry Plumb had left, John started once more to draw up rotas. He was just about to go in search of a typewriter when he realised that he now had a secretary to do this for him. He poked his head round the door to find, in the outer office, that that lady had returned. Like everyone else, she was covered in dirt and grime, her smart suit probably a write-off. She was about John's own age, normally smartly dressed, super efficient; she was sitting with her head in her hands, sobbing quietly. John went silently back into his office. The damned lists could wait! Everyone needed some short time to come to terms with the disaster, to grieve. Sooner or later their sense of duty would kick back in; they would then want nothing more than to bury themselves back in their work, to toil furiously as if to try to sweat it out. After half an hour had passed, John again looked out of the doorway; there she was, sitting upright, compact in one hand, powder puff in the other, repairing the mess that she realised her face had become. She looked round and managed a tight smile.

"Sorry to disturb you, Mary", John began, holding out his hand-written notes. "No, no trouble – need to get busy!" She took the papers, threaded foolscap and two carbons into the carriage of her Olivetti. "These the new rotas?" she enquired. John nodded. "Yes, it's make do and mend, I'm afraid. Terry Plumb will be taking over my old shift for the time being".

Mary had been looking through the lists. "You and Paul are taking twelve hour shifts each, I see. Your poor wife will take a dim view of that!"

John thought that Margaret would probably not even notice. Desmond would, of course; he, at least, would understand. He smiled a tight smile but said nothing, leaving his secretary to get on with the typing. *His secretary*, he thought. Even if proved to be a short, temporary appointment, he would enjoy having someone with whom he could share the burden. He went down to the canteen for more tea and a bun that had a scrape of jam inside it. The room was still crowded with policemen and the remnants of the volunteers; smells of stew and dumplings made him realise just how hungry he really was. So, taking a wooden tray, he stood in the line to collect a bowlful. A very new constable came over to him. "I'll take that up to your office, sir", he offered.

"No, you won't, son", he said firmly. "I'll take it myself to that table over there, thanks for the offer!" He thought how Margaret would scorn such behaviour – plebeian, she would term it. He should take all the perks on offer, should relish the trappings of rank and position. After all he and his men had been through, he simply could not do that; could not bring himself to create a false distance that would be deeply resented. No; his place, at least for the time being, was here with the troops. He sat down and wolfed the delicious stew, not caring what discarded parts of the unfortunate animal had been used in its preparation.

Later that afternoon, he attended the first parade under the new arrangements. He spoke quietly to them all, urging them to appear calm, solicitous, polite. He paid tribute to his predecessor, to their comrades now lying in the morgue. He noticed a few tears being shed among these toughened characters, wanted to share the grief but knew that he could not. What he said should have come from the Superintendent but that poor man was still on his rounds, visiting and holding the hands of the families concerned. John sent them all on their way, holding his Inspector and his Sergeants back for a final word. "Look out for odd conduct", he warned. "Some of them might need a bit of hand-holding; some may well be over-zealous – you know – take a suspect behind a bush and give him a going over!"

He went back to his office. Mary had gone for the day leaving the new perfectly typed rotas on his desk. He sat down to go over them once more. They seemed OK. Next, with a slightly shaking hand, he opened the desk diary. There, pencilled in for the next day were two entries. 'Meeting Councillor Clarke – 10 am', said the first; 'Penny's birthday – supper!' read the second. The second entry stopped him in his tracks. Was Penny his wife, or one of the daughters? He felt deeply ashamed that he did not know the answer to that question – knew that he *should* know! His own tangled home life, the need to keep Margaret away from his colleagues so that she could not denigrate him in front of them, had meant that he knew little or nothing about *their* home lives – a fact for which he felt a deep shame. There came a quiet tap on his door. "Yes?" he called.

The young constable, assigned to front desk duty, popped his still grubby head into the office. "Your sons are here to see you, sir!" Behind the young man John could see the anxious face of Desmond. He smiled his thanks. "Thank you, constable", he said. "Oh, and by the way; see the duty Sergeant and tell him that you've got to go and smarten up; can't have the public being greeted at the station by a ragamuffin, can we?"

"Oh, no sir; immediately, sir!" The young man galloped off. John beckoned Desmond and Jamie, who had been hiding behind his big brother, into his new office.

"Had to come and see you're all right, Dad. Your friend from the local nick gave us the message a couple of hours ago. Saw the damage as we came in. Looks nasty. Lose anyone?"

"Too many, son; too damned many! Still, how's you mother?"

"Oh, Ok, you know", replied Desmond. "I gave the little ones their tea and brought Jamie up on the tram to see you, see when you might get home. Suppose it'll be a while yet!"

"Afraid it will, old son. I've got the job here until they can get a replacement – me and Paul, that is".

Jamie had been looking around the office, rounded the large desk and jumped on to his father's lap. It was exactly the right medicine; John hugged this strange, mischievous little boy to him, looked with great fondness to Desmond, his rock.

"Thanks, son", was all he could manage. Desmond knew that there was a wealth of meaning behind these two simple words; nodded to his father. "That's OK, Dad", he said.

Jamie jumped down again and started to explore the office. In one corner he found his father's peaked cap; he put it on and laughed as his head almost disappeared. John and Desmond burst out laughing at the spectacle of the small boy prancing around and bumping into things. Jamie had, for a few precious moments, acted unconsciously as a tap by which the tensions were released. He took off the cap and gave it solemnly back to its rightful owner. John placed it on his desk. "Tell your mum I'll be back as soon as I can; when Paul gets here to take over. Shouldn't be too long now". He took Desmond's hand in his. "Thanks again, son!"

After the two had left him, he went the rounds of the remaining parts of the station, went outside to see how the emergency covering of the collapsed part of the building was coming on. Tarpaulins were stretched and anchored in place; it looked fairly secure. Just after eleven o'clock, Paul came into the office and slumped in a chair. He looked even worse than he had when sent home for a 'rest'; his uniform was dishevelled; his face, washed and shaven, looked old and grey with fatigue. However, he gave John a weary smile as he received a briefing of the current state of play. He stood before John's desk, straightened up, gave a proper salute. "I relieve you, sir!" he grinned. John stood, donned his cap, forced a weary grin and replied, "I accept your relief, sir!" he said. He said good night to the duty men in the front office, went to the door only to find a car and driver waiting for him. Just one more thing he had forgotten; the Chief Inspector rated a chauffeur! He sank back into the leather and was asleep before they had reached the main road. Christmas day had passed almost unnoticed in the Small household.

John was not due back until eleven o'clock on Boxing Day morning, Paul having relieved him for a twelve-hour stint at eleven the previous evening. He determined to make the most of the time, so had set his alarm for seven o'clock. His car would collect him at half past ten. Desmond hurried about preparing breakfast whilst Jamie scuttled about in great excitement. Would he get his presents today, he wondered?

# BELATED CELEBRATIONS

They all sat round the Morrison shelter, which sometimes doubled as dining table. Margaret had joined them with Robert, sitting and wriggling in his highchair by her side. Food was quickly gobbled down; so, by eight o'clock, all was cleared and ready for the presents. Desmond had asked for a new slide rule, one far superior to the old one that he had used for the past two years. He opened the parcel, and his grin of happiness was more than enough; hugging his mother and father, he sat there and performed complex calculations. John received a tin of fifty of his favourite cigarettes which Desmond had managed to buy with the money his mother had given him. He had had no difficulty acquiring them from a tobacconist in the High Street, a fact that would have troubled John more than somewhat had he been aware of the fact. Margaret opened a delicate tissue-wrapped parcel to find a beautiful silk scarf in pale blue. She could not stop herself peeping at the label. Whatever she found inscribed there was obviously enough for her to offer a soft cheek to John and Desmond, who had conspired together after seeking Nana's advice. She was delighted with her present. Robert received a spinning top that he could not wait to try out. With a laugh, Desmond un-strapped the little fellow from the highchair, set him down on the carpet and showed him how to put the top upright, press down on the threaded plunger to get the top revolving. Squeals of happiness told of a new skill mastered. Desmond hurried out to the shed and came back in, steering the go-kart through the door. Jamie gave a wild yell of delight. "For me?" he asked – as if it would be for anyone else! Desmond received a fierce bear hug. He had fetched it across from his grandfather's shed the day before, having made it over a period of weeks. John had chipped in with the cost of the fixings. Desmond showed him how the steering worked; he had salvaged an old wheel from a disused van, had made an open rack and pinion. The brakes worked off a foot pedal that, via a series of levers, worked pads on the rear wheels. Jamie was, as he said over and over, 'funderstruck'". Getting permission, he put on a thick coat and manoeuvred the super-kart to the road. Being Boxing Day there was no traffic about; only the trams were working on the main road, the busses having been stopped for the Christmas break. Buttermere Gardens had a very slight slope from south to north; Jamie clambered aboard and settled himself into the padded seat. Desmond gave him a push and stood with his father as the little boy steered an erratic path down past the houses. By the time he had gone half-way he was doing well over fast running pace; he gently put his foot on the brake pedal and was quite relieved to find that the kart slowed nicely until, arrived at the end of the road, he had come to a gentle stop. Desmond had showed him how to pull it back up a hill; he turned the kart round and settled the steering so that the front wheels were straight; a small metal bar dropped into place locking the steering in that position so that he was able to go to the front, using the small rope attached, and pull it back past his father and brother to the very top of the road. "It's super!" he yelled. They left him to it and were soon to see him flash past the house uttering whoops of joy. Margaret said that they really should get him to 'moderate his tone' if they did not want complaints from the neighbours. John, in a very rare moment of coarseness replied, "Bugger the neighbours!" His wife stared open-mouthed at him, as if he had uttered the most disgusting profanity known to man.

Jamie was still outside with the 'super-kart' when John's driver called for him on the dot of ten-thirty. Jamie was at the kerbside using an old sock to polish the wheels, removing the merest trace of dirt that had accumulated. The young constable driver got out of the car. "That's a super kart!" he said. Jamie bubbled over with eagerness to explain. "My brother Desmond made it for me; it's got real steering and rear brakes; it goes like stink!" He ran to the open front door. "Dad, you've got a car! You've got a car! You didn't tell me you've got a car!"

John, dressed in uniform, as immaculate as ever, came out. "Only while I'm acting Chief Inspector, son!" he laughed. The young constable drove off, Jamie waving until the black vehicle was out of sight. "Wish I had a brother, sir!" he said. John leaned back in his seat. 'So do I', he thought.

Desmond prevailed upon his young brother that the kart should be put away in the shed whilst they ate an impromptu Christmas lunch, put back from the previous day. He had prepared sprouts, roast potatoes, a somewhat tough leg of mutton with gravy made from a strange brown powder. However, it all tasted quite delicious to the two boys. Jamie put a bit of each of the ingredients in Robert's little bowl, cut them all up and smothered the result in the gravy. He fed little Robert with a spoon, chuckling as the little face became more and more obscured. Having wiped the chubby face with a flannel, he helped Desmond with the washing up, eager to get back 'on the road', as he put it. Margaret had sat quietly beside the table, managing her usual glass of milk, a miniscule bowl of cereal and two plain biscuits. She seemed as far away as ever, thought Desmond.

# THE KNIFE GRINDER

The next day brought even more excitement into Jamie's young life. Desmond had left quite early to visit a friend, had cycled off for the day. Jamie was in the front room when he heard a sing-song voice from the road. "Knives to grinda; scissors an' knives to grinda!" He shot out of the front door to find out what on earth was happening. A weird contraption was slowly being pedalled along the road. It came to a stop by him, and he was able to examine it closely. It consisted of an old bicycle towing a small wooden trailer that held a large stone wheel, amongst other strange things. A small, battered figure wearing a huge black beret was sitting on the saddle.

Margaret, who had realised from years past what it was, came out with a pair of scissors. "Gooda morning, Senora!" said the little man. "Luigi he a'back again! Issa terrible time I have; they put me in large camp up in north by big lake, maka me work on farm. Now, we all friends again". He took the scissors and put them in the pocket of his ragged jacket. Margaret realised why she had not seen the little old Italian for a few years. He had obviously been rounded up and incarcerated whilst Italy was at war with Britain. Since the Italians had hanged Mussolini and declared peace many months ago, the little chap would have been released. Jamie watched fascinated as the man set up his machinery. He uncoupled the small trailer, wheeled it round to the front of the bicycle; he lifted the rear wheel of the bicycle on to a stand that allowed the tyre to revolve clear of the ground. He attached a long spare chain from the sprocket on the back wheel to the pulley on the cart so that, when he sat on the saddle and pedalled, the sharpening stone revolved in front of him. He took the scissors from his pocket and started to grind a perfect edge on the blades. He tested the result, declared himself satisfied and handed the scissors back to Margaret who gave him a shilling for the work. By this time, neighbours had arrived and formed a queue. The little Italian busied himself with carving knives, shears and scissors; tiny sparks flew from the wheel. Jamie took it all in, utterly fascinated; was this a job he would like when he was grown up, he wondered?

When the queue had been served, the trailer was returned to the rear; the man cycled on up the road uttering his cry. Jamie tried to copy it under his breath as he walked by the side of the contraption. Another queue had formed at the top of the road; the machinery was set up again; more showers of sparks issued from the wheel. Jamie calculated that, when this lot had been done, the man would have taken over a guinea from this one road in the space of an hour and a half. 'Cor!' he thought.' Not bad going!' Perhaps this *was* a job he would take up.

He waved goodbye to his new friend as the combination was pedalled into the next road. "Gooda bye; gooda bye!" "Toodle-oo, old fruit", said Jamie, aping a comedian he had heard on the wireless. He went back home to collect the go-kart; he spent the rest of the afternoon whizzing down the road, puffing back up again. He managed to perform that afternoon without the accompaniment of 'wheeeeeeeeeeeee!' as his mother had asked him not to 'show her up, please'.

He eventually tired of the constant repetition; he took the go-kart back home and parked it in the shed, the old sock once again being used to clean the wheels. He went into the kitchen and helped himself to a thick slice of bread and dripping. Munching this, he went in search of Robert; perhaps he could take him for a walk, he thought. He found Robert in his usual place, waddling around the furniture in the front room whilst his mother looked on. Margaret frowned as she saw Jamie eating bread without the nicety of a plate to catch the crumbs, as she had repeatedly told him was the proper behaviour of a gentleman. Jamie had only the sketchiest notion what a gentleman actually was; he thought that his granddad must be one; his mother always harped on about his father, John, who was no gentleman and 'never would be whilst he had a nose on his face'. Jamie thought the idea of his dad without a nose was absolutely hilarious; he was too young to recognise the meaning behind the actual words.

# FALSE ORIGINS

"You will never live up to my expectations, will you?" Margaret said, having again remonstrated with him at the absence of a plate. Jamie was confused; what were 'expectations', he wondered? "I named you after one of the most perfect gentlemen I have ever known and look at you! Holes in you socks; muddy knees; dirty face! I sometimes wonder how on earth you can be a child of mine!"

Jamie was even more confused. Whose child could he be if not his mother's? Prudently, he decided to say nothing; he sat on the floor, plate strategically held under bread; the plate that he had hurried out to the kitchen to get.

One sentence in his mother's remonstration had intrigued him; he decided it *would* be prudent to enquire further, perhaps divert attention from his face and knees.

"Who did you name me after, mum?" he asked.

"Oh heavens! You do not name a child *after* anyone; you name a child *for* someone. I am sure that I have told you all about him before".

"No, mum; I can't remember anything about that!" Jamie was absolutely certain on the point; that was one thing that he would certainly have remembered.

"I have asked you a million times *not* to call me 'mum'; it is *so* common. 'Mummy', if you must, although I would prefer 'mother'".

"Sorry, Mummy", mumbled a chastened Jamie, remembering to take the next bite *after* speaking.

"Well, to answer your question; I named you for a man whom I met long before I met your father. He was tall and very handsome; he had wavy red hair like you will have when you are older. I was with your Nana and Granddad at a very nice restaurant in London and this man was sitting all alone at the next table. Somehow, your Granddad got into conversation with him during a break between courses; it appeared that he was a

Canadian and had a large farm up the Fraser River. He bred horses especially for the Royal Canadian Mounted Police and was extremely rich. I was very happy when he asked me to dance with him after we had finished our coffee. Well, after a week he had been invited to visit us; he took me in his very expensive car to all manner of wonderful places. He was over in England for about six months and had asked me to marry him. Of course, I accepted! Nana and Granddad were delighted at the prospect of such a wonderful son-in-law; they both loved him dearly. Well, he went back to Canada because he had business to attend to; he would be coming back again in about three months, when we would plan a wonderful spring wedding. He was coming back over by ship when they ran into bad weather as they were going along the Saint Lawrence Seaway. The ship struck some sort of obstacle and started to capsize. Apparently, some passengers had been trapped behind a big steel bulkhead door so, naturally, he volunteered to help free the poor souls. As they were prising the door open, the ship lurched suddenly and the door crashed back, trapping his arm in the frame. By the time he was freed he had lost a lot of blood; another ship took everybody off later and he was taken to the nearest hospital. It was all too late; blood poisoning had set In and he died a few days later. He was a wonderful man, the absolute love of my life. He was called Jamie – Jamie Marcus".

Margaret was weeping as the story came to its grisly end. Jamie, moved almost to tears himself, clambered up to give his mother a hug. "Never mind, Mummy", he said softly. "You've got Dad instead!"

Like most of Margaret's fantasies, this one was based upon a small grain of fact; there *had* been the initial meeting at the restaurant; the man *had* been a Canadian; the rest was pure invention. How she absolutely *longed* for it to have happened that way; how tragic it all was. John had heard the story many times, as had Desmond. John, having checked diplomatically with Alfred, knew it was a tissue of lies; yet another manifestation of her incomplete life, her longings. Desmond believed it implicitly, as did everyone else to whom it had been told over the years. Margaret was so utterly convinced that it *should* have happened that way that her narration carried total conviction. So sad, everyone thought; so *very* sad. How brave she was to have borne up under the strain of such a loss!

Jamie was, unknown to him, absolutely right that he had never heard the story in his life before. For some reason, Margaret had kept it from him until now. It never entered her mind that, if and when he ever found out it was untrue, he would discover he had been named for a person who had never really existed; a figment of a tortured imagination. It was an act of cruelty perpetrated upon a little boy by someone who really did *not* know better. However, he put it to the back of his mind as he prepared to take his little brother for a walk to see the 'uff-uffs'. By the time the two came back home, he had forgotten all about it. They had seen a very new type of engine, one that had a tender in front as well as behind. Jamie waited impatiently for Desmond to get back home to find out what on earth it was. To Robert, it had become the 'big, big, big uff-uff'.

# ACTING LIKE A MAN

Just over a week later saw the start of the new school term; Jamie went back with bad grace, hating the thought of being cooped up yet again. Desmond, of course, went back with a song on his lips. It was now nineteen forty-five and he would be fifteen that summer, starting on his last year at senior school. He longed to get an apprenticeship in an engineering firm – a safe bet, thought Alfred and John as they discussed his prospects over a rare Sunday lunch. Jamie himself would soon be six years old; he had already thought of a few ideas for his birthday present; a bike would be nice; but then, so would a piano of his own. Thinking about pianos brought back the thoughts of his continuing battle with poor Mrs Worthy. That lady was being slowly driven to distraction as her pupil corrected one mistake only to make several more; and then to make the original mistake again. She had, at the last lesson, told him that she was going to ask his parents that he discontinue the lessons. Jamie was *very* careful not to whoop with joy until he was well out of earshot. It did not enter his head that his Nana and Granddad had wasted valuable money on those lessons; all he could think about was one more hour of freedom every week; no more nasty scales!

He got into the habit, one afternoon a week, of calling in to see the brigadier and his son. The routine was always the same; Jenkins would answer his knock, would greet him with the exact same words, 'Ah, good afternoon, young sir!' Jamie was quite taken with being a 'sir' all of a sudden. He would be shown into the brigadier or taken out into the garden if the old man was pottering about. George, now healing up nicely, still walked with the aid of a stick – probably would for the rest of his life. He was in the process of, as he put it, 'making himself available for parochial duties' – was already helping out the local vicar with the occasional service. Jamie, to his huge excitement, had been presented with the old German binoculars, now held in a new leather case. They, along with the go-kart, were his pride and joy. When not whizzing down slopes he would spend hours happily in his Advance Camp taking notes whilst scanning the railway tracks in both directions with the aid of the powerful lenses. His association with Matthew and Tommy had almost petered out; he somehow felt more *complete* when doing his own thing in his own way; nobody to gainsay him; nobody to convince that what he wanted to do was the most desirable.

Now and again, especially at night, he would get a flashback of the burning aircraft, the screaming face. Then, he would actually *need* someone else, would start to tremble and whimper. Desmond, who was usually about when this happened, would realise immediately what was wrong, would comfort his little brother. John filled that post just once before being told to 'leave the boy alone; tell him that he's old enough now to snap out of it! It's about time he started to act like a man!' Jamie had heard these words from his mother, trying herself to get to sleep. His father had patted him on the head, whispered in his ear, 'there, old chap; just forget all about it'. John had never attempted to comfort him after that episode, thinking that, perhaps, Margaret was right. Curiously, knowing her as well as he did, it did not occur to him that she might just have been exasperated at the interruption to her rest. Jamie, still far too young to comprehend why he was treated this way, felt scorned, inadequate. Therefore, he attempted to jut his chin out, lower teeth in front of upper teeth; to act like a 'man', when what he needed most of all was the kindness and love of a complete family, to know that they all really *cared* about him. Apart from Desmond's unselfish attention, he felt isolated. Gradually, he withdrew further and further from his friends, spending hours on his own every day.

He little realised that the visits to the brigadier, his weekly tea at his grandparents' house, were of vital importance. When he was with his Nana and Granddad – sometimes also with Nunky – he felt secure; with the brigadier and George, he felt included. At home, with Desmond always so busy, his father absent for so much of the time, he felt alone. Sometimes he thought that, perhaps, only Desmond would notice if he ran away. This thought used to make him quite sad; as time passed, it started to dawn on him that it was quite an exciting possibility until, one sunny spring morning, he decided that it would really be quite a good idea. His Dad would be working through the night; Desmond was staying for a few days with a friend. His day at school was even more tedious than normal; why, oh why, would the day not hurry by, he wondered. He galloped home, went straight up to his bedroom. His mother and Robert were in the front room; she was reading him a story. He took the top blanket from his bed and rolled it up as tightly as he could; found his satchel and managed to cram the blanket in. Then he went to the kitchen to cut slices of bread and dripping which he wrapped into a sheet of greaseproof paper. This and a couple of bottles of water joined the blanket. He put on an extra pullover on top of his beloved Arsenal sweater, hoisted the heavy satchel on his shoulder with the binoculars hanging from their strap around his neck. He went downstairs as quietly as he could, found his mackintosh and draped it over an arm. He left the house via the back door and, looking a little like a diminutive pack mule, started to walk away from his home.

His steps turned naturally up the long road that led to the common. By the time he had got there, his shoulders were aching. However, he forced himself to carry on, to enter the beech woods, to find once again the old 'Badger' camp within the hazel thicket. There were the two thumb-sticks he had left there months before; obviously his friends had never been there since. With a huge sigh of relief, he shed his load and squatted down in the 'camp', invisible to anyone unless that person went right up to the thicket itself. Feeling hungry, he munched just one half of his first sandwich, sipped at some water. As evening fell, he scanned the woods through his binoculars, acting as he thought a secret spy would. He noted people walking their dogs, a young man and girl tripping along hand-in-hand. From afar came the occasional whistle of a train. When a siren went off, he remembered with a start that he was quite close to the place where the bomber had come down. Indeed, had he walked just a hundred yards further, he would have seen the stumps and blackened remains. Suddenly, he felt alone but, remembering his mother's words, jutted out his chin and blinked back the tears. He would be a man; he needed nobody. As darkness enveloped the little 'camp' he took out his blanket, folded it in half. He took off his shoes and put them into his satchel to keep them dry during the night. He rolled himself into his makeshift sleeping bag; using his mackintosh as a pillow, he fell asleep almost immediately. He missed completely the two flying bombs that fell some miles away, wreaking further havoc, havoc that would keep his father busy until well into the following afternoon.

He awoke to the chatter of a group of starlings; he had no way of knowing that the time was already well past seven o'clock as all church clocks, town hall clocks and so forth, had been silenced years ago. It took him a few minutes to realise just where he was; no bedroom curtains, no carpet underfoot, no Desmond getting the breakfast ready. Instead of feeling homesick he experienced a sense of freedom. He sat up and stretched in the clear air of the spring morning. This was the life! He celebrated with a whole 'doorstep' sandwich washed down with water from his bottle, realising that he would need further provisions to see him through the next day and night. Could he shoot home later to get more sandwiches and water, he wondered? If he was extremely careful, he knew that he could do it. So, putting on his shoes, leaving binoculars, blanket and mackintosh in the camp, he took the satchel with the empty bottles and greaseproof paper and set off down the long road. Instead of turning into his own road, he clambered through a hole in a fence and crept along it, past the back gardens of the houses until he had arrived at his 'tunnel'. He carefully negotiated the fence and used what cover he could find to sneak quietly into the kitchen. His mother and Robert were not yet awake. Silently, he washed his face and hands at the kitchen sink, made more sandwiches, filled water bottles. Finding some biscuits in a jar, he added these to his booty. He retraced his steps via the embankment fence and, an hour later, found himself back in his camp. To celebrate this minor triumph, he awarded himself two precious biscuits. Then, with binoculars on hand, he crept out of the camp to spend the day 'spotting' possible enemies. He was at peace with the world, in his natural element.

Mrs Bedford was the first to note his absence. There being no answer of 'Adsum' to his name at assembly, she merely noted that he was not there; nothing unusual about that as many boys were absent for a variety of reasons during war time. However, at lunch, by which time she would have expected a 'phone call, she decided to contact his grandparents; she knew full well that to contact his home was a waste of time. Elder brother would be at school, father would be busy with police work, mother would be either vague or indifferent. Alfred answered the call. At first, he was also not in the least concerned; Jamie was probably at home, press-ganged into 'helping' his mother. He remarked that he was 'just popping over the road' for a moment; he found Margaret reading to Robert. Asking if Jamie had left for school that morning he was told, 'Oh, I suppose so'. He went back home to telephone the school. Jamie had still not turned up. By now, he was starting to feel a little alarmed. He telephoned the local police station; they had no information and wanted to know if he was reporting a 'missing person'. Alfred thought that this was a little premature, but told the sergeant on duty that the boy was not yet six years old, was not at home, was not at school. The sergeant, two teenage boys of his own, thought it likely that the 'young rip' had simply taken a day off. Was he with his friends, he asked? No, replied Alfred; his two best friends were at school at this very moment, had been all morning. The sergeant asked if Alfred would let him know if Jamie had not turned up when school was finished; the man obviously thought that the boy would time his reappearance to coincide with this, to allay suspicion that he had simply taken a day off. Alfred promised to do so and put the earpiece of the candlestick telephone back in its hook.

He and his wife spent the afternoon wondering what could have happened; knowing their grandson, his growing independent streak, they thought it increasingly probable that Jamie had just wandered off for the day. However, when they had been over to Jamie's home and spent two hours there, Alfred again telephoned the police; Jamie was well overdue. He attempted to call to John, only to be told that the Chief Inspector was still out at the bomb sites, was not expected back for another hour or more. He asked that a message be relayed to his son-in-law, to have him call as soon as could. He made no mention of the missing boy, did not want to worry John until it was necessary.

Soon after that, a police car drew up at the gate; the local Inspector was admitted to the front room and started to make enquiries. "When did you first notice that Jamie was missing?" he started. Alfred replied that the school had called him at lunchtime to let him know. The Inspector looked at Margaret who was quietly reading a magazine article, apparently oblivious to the worry of the two old folk. Robert was playing with his spinning top.

"Are his outdoor clothes missing as well?" he continued. Alfred went out to the hall to look. "His school shoes are not there, nor is his mackintosh. But, knowing small boys, they really could be anywhere!" The Inspector nodded; indeed, they could!

The Inspector cleared his throat loudly to make sure that he had the mother's full attention. "Is Jamie in the habit of going off on his own like this, madam?"

Margaret gave him a puzzled look. "Sometimes, I suppose. I never know where he is from one minute to the next. After all, I'm not his keeper!"

'Yes, you bloody well are – or *should* be!' thought the Inspector. However, controlling his thoughts, he continued aloud. "Have you any idea where he might go? Any favourite haunts?"

"As I have already told you, he could be anywhere. I do *not* understand what the fuss is all about. He's well capable of looking after himself!"

Alfred and Gertrude were quite embarrassed by this public display of indifference. They were about to make excuses, somehow to cover up their daughter's remoteness, when Desmond arrived home from school. He was quickly told what had happened, was deeply worried about his little brother. The Inspector, who knew exactly whose son Jamie was, went into a huddle in the hall with Alfred, Gertrude and Desmond. Did they have any idea where on earth the little chap had got to? The grandparents were by now extremely worried, Desmond equally so but able to throw more light on the subject due to his closeness to Jamie.

"He's got a special tunnel up the embankment at the back – I wonder if he's hiding up there?" He hurried out of the house and managed to squeeze his way up to Janie's Advance Camp. He returned, brushing twigs and old leaves from his trousers. "No sign up there, I'm afraid", he reported. He cudgelled his brains thinking where else they could try. "What about the pond down the end of the road?" he mused. "Jamie loves to prowl round there looking for birds' nests. Also, I've just had a thought – would he have disappeared up to the beech woods; it's one of his favourite haunts!"

"Well done, lad", said the Inspector. He was just on the point of setting up the relevant searches when the constable driver poked his head round the front door. "Desk Sergeant on the blower for you, sir". The Inspector hurried out to grab the microphone. "What is it, Sergeant?" "Chief Inspector Small has just called in, sir. Wants to know what all the fuss is about – got a call from his father-in-law some time ago and can't raise the old folks at home; thought he'd try here; over". The Inspector thought for a moment. "Tell him that his son Jamie had gone walkabout – I'm at the house now. Tell him to get his arse down here as soon as he can; I need all the opinions I can get; over". "Wilco, sir; over and out". The Inspector hurried back into the hall. "Your Dad will be here soon, knows all about it now; take him about fifteen minutes at the most if I know these mad Met drivers! Now, any more thoughts, young man?"

Desmond had been mentally ticking off all the possible places that Jamie might have gone. "What about the brigadier's house?" he asked. Alfred, who knew all about this old gentleman, shook his head. "He *is* a particular friend of Jamie's; but that man is far too sensible to allow Jamie to stay without his parents' permission – and he *would* have checked!" The Inspector went out to the car and took up the microphone again.

"Sergeant", he thought aloud. "Call those two chaps off traffic for the time being. Tell them to take the spare car up to the beech woods – you know, just off the common. Tell them that this is a possibility. I'll take the elder brother with me down to the pond at the bottom of Buttermere Gardens. This is another possibility. That way, we can have two search parties talking to each other; over!" "Wilco, sir. Over to you. Come in traffic patrol, over". The Inspector was pleased to note the alacrity with which this was answered; obviously monitoring the radio! "Traffic patrol here, over". The message was relayed; the traffic car sped off to the common to start the search.

Returning again to the hallway, the Inspector was just about to tell the others what he had set in motion when Margaret called from the front room. "Desmond, you have not forgotten Robert's tea, have you? Get it now, please". The Inspector stood open mouthed. 'Get it yourself, you lazy cow!' he thought. Desmond shrugged and hurried into the kitchen. There came a screech of brakes from the road; John ran into the house, saw his colleague. "Hello, Willy; thanks for taking charge here. What's the story?"

"Seems like Jamie was not at school today. Your other son wasn't here last night, doesn't know when exactly he went missing. Sorry mate, but I can't get a single thing out of your missus. Seems she hadn't even noticed he was awol. Doesn't seem all that worried either!"

John went into the front room, faced Margaret. "Did you hear him go to bed last night?" he asked. "I cannot say that I really noticed", Margaret shrugged. "Well, what about this morning – did you see him before he set off?" Margaret by this time was getting heartily sick and tired of all these questions. "Look!" she spat. "I cannot be expected to keep tabs on that boy all the time; he comes and goes as he pleases. I have my hands full with Robert. Anyway, Jamie is well capable of looking after himself. I really cannot see what all the fuss is about; he will come back when he is good and ready".

John knew that it was useless to continue the questioning; she had washed her hands of the entire episode, would slam out of the room, take to her bed if he persisted. He went back out to the hall. The Brooke Hill Inspector had heard the conversation. 'If she was my wife I'd give her a good smack in the mouth", he thought. Why John put up with it was beyond him. Poor Alfred and Gertrude were still standing very uncomfortable at the foot of the stairs. John broke the silence. "OK, Willy; it's your manor, your chaps; I'll stay here and leave you to get on with it. Keep me in the loop, all right?"

"Soon as we hear anything, old man!" promised the Inspector. He called Desmond and the two went out to the car, shot off to search around the pond. John finished preparing Robert's tea and took it in for Margaret to help the little chap feed himself.

"Look, I didn't mean to go on about Jamie", John was trying to be soothing. "Just that we are all worried about him, that's all". Margaret looked balefully at him. "That boy is a complete mystery to me – always has been, always will be. He is noisy, dirty, cheeky; all the things that I simply cannot stand. You know how delicate I am, how I need peace and tranquillity. Nobody considers my feelings, least of all that boy! That brat of yours, Desmond, is always with his head in a book; you are never here. I have to manage all on my own *and* be expected to watch over a boy who seems to have no sense of responsibility, no discipline!"

John looked at the carpet. He was used to hearing all about Margaret's feelings, her requirements. After all, Jamie was no noisier, dirtier or cheekier than many a five-year-old. Desmond was studious, was working as hard as he could to secure a good future. He looked up at the beautiful face and sighed. But where the hell was Jamie?

The Inspector with Desmond's help had drawn a complete blank, covering all possible areas around the pond. He radioed the other car to see how they were getting on but got no reply; obviously searching, he thought. They climbed in and shot off up the hill to join in. By now it was getting quite dark. They and the driver took torches to join the others who they could see quite a distance away, calling Jamie's name and peering into the trees and bushes. They found the 'camp' after about a half hour of searching, found the blanket and the mackintosh. Desmond immediately identified the coat as belonging to his brother. The all stood around the hazel thicket calling for the little boy, flashing beams from their torches in all directions. They heard and saw nothing further. "Well, he *was* here", said the Inspector. "Any more ideas?" Desmond shook his head sadly. He could think of no other places to search. As they went back to the cars, they were observed by one very small boy; he was perched half-way up a sycamore tree, safe in the fork between a sturdy branch and the trunk. He scanned the scene through powerful binoculars, munching at the same time on a sandwich of bully beef which he had taken from a satchel that hung from another branch. He giggled to himself. He was a bit sorry for old Des but was having the time of his life. He noticed with a start of disappointment that the coat and blanket were clutched in his brother's arms. Oh dear, he thought. I'll get very cold tonight without my sleeping bag. He determined to try and find a replacement before the light went altogether. He climbed down and made his way through the wood to the eastern boundary where it abutted the back gardens of a row of small houses. He peered through hedges and fences until he saw what he had vaguely thought he might find – a shed and a greenhouse. He wriggled through the hedge, leaving his satchel and binoculars hidden; slowly and very carefully he made his way to the shed and found, to his relief, that the door was unlocked. Inside, he could barely stifle a whoop of victory; there, on top of an old wheelbarrow, was a dusty rug. He had hoped for some old curtains or a sheet, but this was a real bonus. He rolled up the rug, made his way back through the hedge to collect his other possessions. Unerringly in the darkness he made his way back to the hazel camp, wriggled into the centre and wrapped himself up in the rug. There, he thought; warm as toast. He snuggled down and was soon fast asleep.

The Inspector, plus his two traffic patrolmen, had long been back at Jamie's house. He conferred with John and Desmond. They all came to the same conclusion; Jamie had been at his camp; would, in all probability, go back there. They would give it another hour and go back, this time quietly to give no warning. Desmond made a large pot of tea for his Dad, his grandparents and the four policemen, none of whom could understand why this was not undertaken by the lady of the house. Desmond had prepared Robert for bed, had rocked the little chap to sleep. He was tired from all the excitement but was determined to go back out to search later. He sat next to his Dad as Margaret calmly announced that she was going to bed.

Alfred and Gertrude volunteered to stay until the search party returned, with Jamie, they hoped. Nobody remarked upon Margaret's behaviour; John and Desmond because they saw nothing unusual about it; Alfred and Gertrude because they were acutely embarrassed; the Brooke Hill policemen because they were too well mannered.

The two cars went slowly up the long road; near the top they extinguished all lights and clicked the doors shut as quietly as possible. With Desmond leading, they went in single file through the woods to the hazel thicket. John switched on his torch, hooded to a small ray through his fingers. There, asleep and seemingly without a care in the world, was a tousled ginger head poking out of a roll of old and very dusty rug. John crawled in and lifted the little bundle into his arms. Desmond gathered up the satchel and the binoculars. They went back to the cars as they had come. Just out of the woods, Jamie opened a sleepy eye and looked at his father. "Hello, Dad", he muttered before falling asleep again.

His grandparents were much relieved to see the little bundle being carried back into the house. John unrolled him and carried him up to his bed, kissed the unruly curls and crept downstairs. More tea was on the go and he sank down gratefully, a steaming cup in his hand.

"Plucky little chap!" said the Brooke Hill Inspector. "Wish I had one like that!" His own two sons wouldn't say boo to a goose, he thought. "How long do you think he was there?" Alfred asked.

"Knowing that little rascal, I'd say he was on his second night", replied John. He was feeling alternately cross at and proud of his son.

"But why on earth would he feel the need to disappear like that?" Alfred was puzzled.

The door opened and Jamie looked at them. "Sorry, Dad", he said "Woke up with all the talking!"

"Well, as you're here, you can answer a couple of questions", began John. "First of all, when did you disappear?"

"Oh, Tuesday afternoon, Dad", came the reply. John was not surprised; neither were Desmond or his grandparents. The visiting policemen, on the other hand, were astounded.

"Nobody noticed you were gone!" said the Inspector. Jamie grinned.

"Ok, then. Second question; why did you run away?" asked John, trying to divert attention from the lack of parental responsibility.

"Mummy told me that I should act like a man", replied Jamie. "So I thought that I would go and live all by myself and be grown up!"

"Why did Mummy tell you that?" asked a tearful Gertrude.

"Oh, that's easy Nana. I was getting all upset about the plane and the burning man so Mummy told me to snap out of it; I should be a man and not snivel so much!"

That elicited the need for John to tell the story of the downed bomber and Jamie's observance of its horrific end. The policemen listened in silence. No wonder the poor little chap was upset, they thought. It would have given any one of them nightmares as well! Yet apparently not one shred of comfort from the one person who might reasonable have been expected to give it; just an admonition to 'snap out of it'; to 'be a man'. 'Sodding hell!' thought the Inspector.

Gertrude took her little grandson on to her knee and cuddled him. He soon fell asleep and was again carried to bed. John thanked the Brooke Hill police for all their help and ushered them out. He walked his parents-in-law back to their bungalow. Not one of them spoke a word about Margaret's attitude; they were not in the least surprised that she had acted as she did; they would have been amazed had she done any differently.

Jamie had no regrets for his escapade; he thought that he had done exactly as he had been told, had acted like a man; that he had shown them all that he could be grown up.

Desmond was horrified at his little brother's actions; what might have happened to him had he not been found? Fortunately, he was much too sensible to voice his fears to Jamie; there was no sense in frightening him unnecessarily.

John was secretly proud of his little son, was somewhat in awe of the boy's pluck. It was, he thought ruefully, exactly what he had wanted to do as a young lad, to escape the awfulness of his own childhood. Luckily for him he had had his own brother to turn to, a brother not a great deal older than himself. He missed his brother terribly.

Margaret hardly ever thought about her son's adventure; she had far more pressing worries. Robert, now walking about and 'into everything', needed to be restrained, to be kept close to his adoring mother. He was starting to show a real liking for drawing; he would sit quite happily for an hour or more making strange pictures on scraps of paper. There was a difference between his 'drawings' and those of little children of a similar age – one could usually tell what his represented. Already, he was producing pictures of his beloved 'uff-uffs' with the correct number of wheels, the right configuration for each type. Where this would all lead was anyone's guess; Margaret felt that it should be encouraged. Already, she had produced a small scrap book of his efforts. In this, she showed unusual percipience. However, she was convinced that little Robert was as 'delicate' in health as she firmly believed herself to be. This conviction enabled her to keep her child close to her, to come to believe that he was, in some ways, 'special'. She had no such feelings for Desmond or Jamie; Desmond because he was not hers; Jamie because he was far too independent – an independence that had literally been forced upon him. Of Valerie and Peter, she never gave the slightest thought.

# A COUNCIL OF WAR

Three brothers sat around a table covered in crisp linen, silverware resplendent in the glow of overhead chandeliers, glassware sparkling with deep red Burgundy. The restaurant of a famous hotel in The Strand had functioned perfectly throughout the entire war; neither bombs nor rockets had dared interfere with its smooth operation; it was an oasis of calm and never-changing standards in a world turned to dust and sorrow. The restaurant manager, a tall and elegant Frenchman, had greeted the three elderly brothers as he had greeted every guest since he had been appointed some twenty-five years ago. He tugged down his already immaculately fitting white waistcoat, gave the merest of bows. "Good evening, gentlemen. Your table is ready if you would care to follow me". There was no need to enquire how he had known to address the tallest of the three as 'milord'; Jean-Luc knew everybody, even though Edward had not been to that particular restaurant for more than three years.

Edward Clements, first Viscount Caversley, had invited his brothers Alfred and Frederick to join him at dinner for two reasons. The first was one of filial devotion; he had not seen anywhere near enough of his brothers during this damned war; he missed the close relationship that they had always enjoyed as his duties in the House of Lords had taken far too much of his time. The second was due to his need to know a lot more about his great-nephew, the little boy who would one day inherit his title and duties. The little chap was coming up to his sixth birthday and it was his intention to hold a small gathering for the whole family to celebrate this occasion.

Despite the strictures of wartime rationing, the restaurant had managed to produce a menu that was as appetising as it was inventive. During the soup – vegetable with cheese croutons – the brothers discussed general matters; Both Alfred and Frederick were kept vastly amused by Edward's narration of the vicissitudes of the House – the rambling inconsistencies of some members, the ranting and raving of others. During the fish – actually coley disguised with a very ingenious mushroom sauce – he enquired about his sister-in-law, expressing his admiration for that dear lady; remembered with great fondness their departed sister Amelia. During the entrée – and God knows where chef had obtained the venison – he turned at last to the subject of little Jamie. He hardly ever saw the young boy, was eager to find out how he was progressing. Alfred and Frederick, who were geographically and emotionally much closer to Jamie, took it in turns to relate the boy's progress. Alfred told of the episode of the downed bomber, how it had affected Jamie so very deeply. Edward was shocked that one so young should have had such an experience, although he knew fully well that it was no more than thousands of little children had experienced in the East End, the docks, in Coventry, Liverpool, Bristol – in fact, a host of other locations throughout the length and breadth of the country. Frederick, who had eagerly lapped up the story, told of Jamie's 'break for freedom'. They all enjoyed a good laugh, imagining themselves running away from home and setting up camp in the woods. Not that any of them would have done so – their childhood had been happy and very secure.

Alfred, scrupulously honest with himself and with others, recounted his daughter's indifference to the welfare of her first-born. Edward, who had gently tried to persuade his brother of the inadvisability of his marriage to his cousin, was not in the least surprised. Her attitude fitted exactly with his image of the self-centred young woman, caring little or nothing for the welfare of anyone but herself. Frederick, who knew Margaret much better, was convinced of the basic instability of Margaret's character, her fantasies, her dream-world. He could find excuses for her but could never actually *like* her. She was remote, unreachable.

Edward then dropped a bombshell into the conversation. His wife, the irrepressible Constance, she of the vicious tongue, had suddenly and without any warning whatsoever, decided to make a life for herself with her one-time dancing tutor; this man, now in his forties (and twenty years her junior) had been in his younger days a bit-part actor, living precariously on the fringes of the West End theatre. He had taken to tutoring rich ladies in the art of ballroom dancing, had relished the role of gigolo that he had consciously fostered. Now, it appeared, Constance had somehow renewed the old acquaintance. Edward seemed remarkable calm whilst telling his brothers.

"Had the damnable cheek to tell me that she was 'in love' with the chap; that she wanted to be with him; that she was fed up to the back teeth – common expression, that – with my cronies whom she had the effrontery to refer to as 'boiled shirts'. So, off she has gone these two weeks past".

Alfred, who had never liked his sister-in-law, was quite happy to hear that his brother was now free of a person he had long regarded as nothing but an embarrassment and an encumbrance. Frederick, who been just a little enamoured of the vivacious Constance, was sorry to hear it – not for his brother who seemed relieved that years of turmoil were now over – but for himself. He stopped these thoughts with determination. This was no way for a loyal brother to behave, he remonstrated with his inner self.

"So, you see; now it is imperative that I concentrate on the family, make sure that all will be well for the future. I have altered my will as a consequence of my marital hiatus (Alfred thought this a superb understatement), have made over all my assets to you two, to be held in trust for the youngster until he reaches maturity".

Frederick saw a snag here. "Edward, dear chap; Jamie is not quite six years old. By the time he reaches twenty-one in fifteen years time, even I, the youngest of us all, will be seventy-nine. I for one am not confident that I will be alive and sufficiently compos mentis to carry out the burden of trusteeship at that advanced age!"

The three chuckled at the thought. Alfred added his thoughts that they needed an alternative plan of action. He made a suggestion.

"My solicitor Frank West, just round the corner from here incidentally, is relatively young – a mere forty or so. He is level-headed and I give you my assurance of his trustworthiness. He would be an excellent choice for trustee to replace the first of us to shake off the mortal coil".

This seemed to be quite acceptable to the others who had the highest regard for Alfred's solid common sense. Alfred then decided that the time was ripe to take them further into his confidence. "Gertrude and I have long known that we simply cannot allow Margaret to inherit our combined estate. This is a matter of great sadness to us both, as I am sure you can appreciate! We have decided that we, also, will leave the lot to Jamie and Robert in trust. We have drawn up wills to that effect, appointing each other as primary trustee, with young Frank West as the second; he to appoint another when the surviving partner dies. We realise that to leave Margaret any sort of fortune would be a recipe for disaster; she, poor soul, simply is not capable of managing affairs of that complexity. I fear that she would fritter the lot away in a very short space of time".

Frederick agreed wholeheartedly with this and said so. Edward, ever the diplomat, wondered if there was any sort of compromise possible. Alfred explained further.

"Margaret will have the income from the estate during her lifetime. I know that young John is exceeding all our expectations, but the salary he now earns still is not really sufficient to afford school fees and the like. I just hope that he does not feel slighted by all this. I have a real regard for the man; he is as honest as they come and is utterly loyal to my daughter".

Frederick kept his thoughts to himself. How, he had often wondered, could the man calmly abandon one set of children and be praised for his 'utter loyalty' to a second set? Was there not some fundamental weakness in his ability to 'change horses mid-stream'?

Edward had thought of one other pitfall. "What about young Desmond? Will he not feel bitterly disappointed to be completely left out?"

Alfred felt this too. However, he really had no choice in the matter. "That has weighed very heavily with us both", he admitted. "But, consider the implications, if you will. First, Desmond is *not* our blood relation. Of course, we both realise that he does not actually *know* this fact, is totally unaware of even the existence of his other brother and sister. However, if we make provision for him, Margaret will be outraged at what she will see as a betrayal. She would make sure that the boy felt included only for reasons of compassion. No, I'm afraid that this just cannot be, much as both Gertrude and I know it to be unfair".

Frederick felt that he just had to make a point. "Alfred, you know as well as anyone that Margaret has little or no feeling for young Jamie; she spends all her time and affection on Robert. What makes you so certain that she will act any differently to Jamie as she would undoubtedly act towards Desmond for whom, I may add, I have the deepest respect?"

Alfred spread his hands in a gesture of capitulation. "I have no confidence at all that she would treat them the same. After all, we know our Margaret! Once an idea has taken root wild horses cannot drag it from her. She is convinced that she has a real artistic prodigy in little Robert. Mind you, I cannot but agree that he is showing exceptional talent for one so very young. No, I cannot give you, or myself come to that, the assurance of even-handedness. In any case, we have decided not to let the provisions of the wills be known until after our deaths". He held up his hand to forestall the inevitable. "Yes; I am fully aware that this sounds like cowardice, cannot escape the charge. Both Gertrude and I have come to the conclusion that things are far better left as they are until the boys are much more advanced in age, which I sincerely hope they will be; neither of us has the desire to pass over quite yet! Apart from that, there is always some hope that Margaret will improve with the advancing years".

'Little or no hope in that direction', thought Frederick.

With an unspoken consent the three brothers decided that enough was enough where personal matters were concerned. They turned instead to the war and its consequences. Edward, being the closest of the three to the main sources of information, led the way.

"There is no way the Germans can hang on for much longer", he stated. "The Russians are deep into northern Germany, will soon be on the outskirts of Berlin itself. I fear that Poland has gone from us for ever; there is no way on this earth that the Russians will allow its independence now. They will want it as a buffer between themselves and what they see as their natural enemies. Stalin, despite all his bravado, is basically a peasant, with a peasant's mentality. I sincerely hope to be proved wrong, but I predict that Russia will surround itself with a massive buffer zone. Czechoslovakia, Hungary, Romania, even Austria may well be lost to civilisation for many years to come".

"That's a rather bleak outlook, surely?" queried Alfred.

"I'm afraid it way well prove to be quite optimistic!" replied Edward. "What the devil will happen to Bulgaria and the Baltic States is anyone's guess. As for Greece, there are already signs of a vicious communist uprising that we will do well to contain!"

"Given that the war will soon be won, surely there is some hope for a peaceful future for Europe?" pleaded Frederick.

"The best that we can hope for is a very uneasy peace! With the Americans so strong, perhaps there will be a peace brought about by stalemate. I think that our allies can be persuaded to remain as a shield against a Red expansion. At least, I hope so. But, with some elements in Washington, one can never be sure. Look how that criminal Kennedy behaved; it was a miracle that Roosevelt managed to win the argument back in 'forty. Otherwise, heaven alone knows what would have happened to us. Mind you, we will be paying for this war for fifty years at least!"

"Well, that *is* a cheerful thought!" laughed Alfred.

Dessert proved to be just as imaginative as the preceding courses; it consisted of an apple 'turnover' with custard. Nobody bothered to mention that the custard had had to be made with powdered milk. Very few palettes had survived the war to differentiate between it and the real thing! The brothers, having finished with a pot of indifferent coffee, went their separate ways. Edward took a cab to his Knightsbridge apartment; Alfred and Frederick walked to Charing Cross Station to catch their train southwards to Brooke Hill. The darkened train slowly made its way past the ravages of Canon Street, but was held up for some time just after Waterloo. They had to change at London Bridge, crossing to the large lower section for their train southwards. The wait was proving very tiring. The huge station concourse was darkened, with only the odd hand-held lamp being carried by the station staff. Eventually, amid much shouting, their train was announced. It was a fast train to Brighton, Brooke Hill being only the second stop that it would make. They climbed aboard and settled into the dusty seats of a first-class non-smoker. After much rattling over points, the train settled into a steady fifty miles an hour passing endless rows of blacked-out houses; silent streets of shops, bombed-out sections of warehouses, all presented a depressing picture of five and a half years of war. How long would it take, Alfred wondered, to put the country back together again?

Eventually, after passing Wandleford and its equally devastated areas, the train deposited them at a silent Brooke Hill station. They walked home in silence, the gloom settling on them like a mantle.

# WHY PARIS?

Jamie had undergone his last music lesson. Mrs Worthy had finally admitted defeat, had called on his grandparents and announced that the little lad really was making so little progress that they would indeed be throwing money away for him to continue. What she did not say was that, if Jamie were not removed, she feared for her own sanity! Gertrude was particularly upset by this; she had hoped that his obvious talent would flourish, that he would take to the discipline of proper lessons. She had failed to read her grandson as well as she might have. Jamie and discipline did not see eye to eye. However, he was astute enough to call on his Nana, to apologise for being a disappointment to her. He was very sorry to have 'let her down'. Of course, that kindly and loving old soul forgave the lad; did not go so far as to reward him with one of the beloved rockcakes but forgave him gladly. After all, she mused; the little chap had had a lot to contend with recently.

One afternoon, a week before his sixth birthday, he returned home from school to find that Desmond was in the front room with a visitor. His mother and Robert were up at Frederick's house for the day. Why Desmond was there at that time, Jamie hadn't the foggiest. However, he politely said 'good afternoon' to the visitor whom Desmond introduced as 'Father Simpson'. He was a small, fat man with black hair plastered down on his skull. He wore a rather grubby black suit over a black shirt and 'dog collar'. Jamie knew that he was not the local vicar, who he would have easily recognised. He scuttled out to the kitchen leaving his brother to talk to the visitor. He felt quite curious; visitors to this house were rare. His curiosity, getting the better of him, would be satisfied only by finding out a lot more. Therefore, taking off his shoes, he tiptoed back to the front room to listen at the door which he had left propitiously slightly ajar. A deep rumble came from the visitor, punctuated now and again by Desmond's rather lighter tones. The conversation seemed quite impenetrable to the young eavesdropper.

"On that last day", came the sonorous tones. "On that last day, when all shall be delivered up to the one Sovereign Lord Jesus Christ, all shall be revealed; every sin, every good work; every prayer, every omission; all shall be put into His balance, and we shall all await his judgement. If you are deemed to have been a good Catholic, have attended Holy Mass without fail on every day that you should, then all will be well. If you have taken the Holy Sacraments, you will be judged to have been truly faithful. There can be no lapses, no excuses!"

"But father", came Desmond's querying voice. "Can heaven be reserved only for good Catholics? What about good Anglicans? Are they to be excluded?"

"Of course!" came the stern rejoinder. "They will be put into a place specially made for those who need to repent their unfaithfulness".

Desmond, ever curious, came back with, "But what about those who have never heard of Jesus, those tribes in, say, South America who have never had the word brought to them!"

"Heaven has no place for the unbeliever, whatever the cause of that unbelief!"

Jamie, by now, was listening with only half an ear. It was far too deep for him. Still, he stayed where he was partly out of fear that he would betray his presence if he moved during a lull in the conversation. Therefore, what followed was only partially heard by the little boy.

"Now, when you are ready, we will discuss your Confirmation, Desmond. The bishop will be conducting the service later in September. I would like you to attend a few more classes first. But remember always the reward that, on your own last day, He will bear you up on angels' wings to be with Him forever in paradise!"

Jamie slid on socked feet back to the kitchen. He was extremely puzzled at what he had just part-heard. Why would Jesus want him to go to Paris? He understood just enough Geography to know that Paris was in France – was indeed the capital of that country. What was so special about Paris? Did

God have a special place there for the really good people? He would have to ask Desmond later.

Dismissing these higher topics from his mind, he went, with his binoculars, up to his Advance Camp. He was just comfortably settled in there when a massive goods train approached from the north. It comprised two large locomotives pulling a succession of flat wagons. On each wagon was a large tank; each tank bore the white star of the American forces. He well remembered the enormous Master Sergeant who had called him his 'little buddy', had given him chocolate. At the end of the train was attached the usual anti-aircraft gun wagon, manned by more Americans. He wondered if they had a supply of their 'candy bars'. They seemed to him such a happy lot, always telling jokes and giving food to everyone they met. He really liked Americans!

The train came to a halt just as the last wagon had passed him. He held his breath; would any of the men jump down as last time? His luck was out; the stop was just temporary as, with screeching axles, it started to roll slowly forward again. Jamie cursed his luck and waited patiently for the next train to pass.

Desmond, meanwhile, had bidden farewell to his visitor who was the local catholic priest. This worthy individual had been preparing Desmond for his entry to the church, had given instruction and supervised his study of the very detailed and complex catechism that he had to learn. He had much to ponder. Did he really want to enter this very strict religion? On the one hand, he relished being a part of such a disciplined movement, wherein everything was properly ordered. On the other hand, he was daunted by the knowledge that his enquiring mind would be hamstrung in the face of such unwavering certainty. He had a hard decision to make. So, putting it all aside for the moment, he started to prepare his and Jamie's tea.

Jamie came back just in time to see the final items put on the plates. He was, as usual, ravenous.

"Why aren't you at school, Des?" he enquired through a mouthful of sandwich.

"Had a free day to do some research", came the reply.

"Was that chap a vicar?" asked the ever inquisitive boy.

"No, he's a catholic priest. I'm thinking about joining their church", Desmond replied.

"Heard something as I was passing", said Jamie, dodging the truth of his deliberate eavesdropping. "He said that Jesus wants us all to go to Paris. Why do we have to go to Paris, Des?"

Desmond had to think long and hard. Eventually, the penny dropped. He laughed.

"Not Paris, you twerp – paradise! It's another name for heaven!"

"Oh, that's all right, then!" said Jamie, much relieved to have that cleared up. He had wondered why God would have chosen somewhere foreign. After all, there were lovely places to go in England, weren't there?

"Will Dad be home this evening", he asked. Desmond was not sure; his father had not said anything when he had departed for work that morning. Desmond cleared the things away and left Jamie to dry up the dishes and put them away. Out came the inevitable homework. Jamie, with a sigh, went up to his bedroom to read.

# DILEMMA

John, meanwhile, was sitting in the Chief Inspector's office; he was in something of a quandary. The Divisional Commander had visited the Wandleford station that morning and had passed very favourable comments about John's work and organisation whilst he had been 'acting up' as Chief Inspector. He was in the process of reorganising the entire Division that included Wandleside and two other large stations. What he wanted to achieve was a management team to run the Division that had, at its centre, a Chief Inspector of Operations who would co-ordinate the work of all three stations whenever the need arose to run tasks that were bigger than one station alone could handle. These, as the war had amply demonstrated, were becoming increasingly frequent, would in all probability continue to do so once the war had ended and crime once again became the attractive alternative. The coming of peace would be the ideal hunting ground for the criminally minded; the opportunities would be endless, or so was the current thinking among the Met hierarchy.

The Superintendent had asked John to come to his office early that afternoon. Sitting with him was the Commander, a squat Chief Superintendent who was sipping a cup of coffee by the window.

"Come in, John; sit down. Coffee?" John had declined the offer politely. He hated coffee. He sat down wondering why he had been called in, was aware of no sins of omission that could be laid at his door.

The Commander again praised his work since the bombing of the station. The Superintendent nodded his agreement. Then the Commander dropped his bombshell.

"John, I've been wondering about the new position of Chief Inspector, Ops. You would be the ideal choice for the post. Have you any thoughts on the matter?"

John was astounded. He had absolutely no thoughts at all on the matter; it had come like a bolt out of the blue.

"But sir; I've only recently been promoted to Inspector, hardly had time to get my feet under *that* desk yet. I know I've been doing the Chief's job for a bit here, but that was only to fill a very unfortunate gap, as it were."

"Yes, I know all that; you have filled it very well indeed. There is something in you that appeals to me. You seem to have a flair for organisation, putting down all possibilities on paper and coming up with the correct solution – a solution that actually works".

"Well, yes, sir; I do like to think my way through in a logical way. But surely what you need is more a man who can think on his feet – someone who can react to a changing demand – react quickly and decisively. In all honesty, that isn't me!"

"What I need most of all is a person who is steady, methodical and completely reliable. Anyway, you hop off and give it some thought. Give me a tinkle on Friday morning, let me know".

And so, John sat at his desk, the work of that day in temporary abeyance. It would be just about as far as he could reasonably expect to get in the police force. His lack of a formal education would, in all probability, bar him from progress to Superintendent. Why should he not grab this opportunity with both hands? It could well be his last real chance to join the ranks of the senior officers.

But what would be the effect of his appointment? Almost certainly, there would be social occasions, times when he would be expected to attend with wife on arm. The thought made him shudder with apprehension. All it would take was for Margaret to make one disparaging remark about him to his colleagues and he would be finished, a laughing stock. He turned away from such thoughts; they were unworthy of him. He worshipped the very ground that Margaret walked on, would put up with any torment that she chose to mete out. But he just could not contemplate the prospect of such public humiliation. He knew that, by now, he should have been used to it. But, up until now, he had been able to keep it all separate from his professional life. As far as any of his colleagues were concerned, Margaret was a semi-invalid, thus never seen on the very rare occasions that a Sergeant (or recently, an Inspector) would need to attend. That would almost certainly not be the case if he moved into Divisional Headquarters; he would be a very senior part of the team. Avoidance of social obligations was not an option. Therefore, he would accept the position and live with the inevitable humiliation, or he would decline the promotion and forget about his own advancement.

He sat with a cold cup of tea; he was not a happy man that afternoon. By rights, he should have been quite elated. Instead, he sat and moped.

The next day he was at his desk as usual and had to apologise to Mary for his short temper – a very rare occurrence for him. He resented the fact that he was in this position but was fair-minded enough to realise that it was a position of his own making. Perhaps, if he had taken a firmer line with Margaret from the outset, he would not now have this dilemma. But he had to be honest just that bit further; would he have *dared* to take a firmer line? Would that not have ruined his chances of spending the remainder of his life in the service of that beautiful woman, whose very glance could have him jumping through hoops? No; for better or worse, he was committed. But could he take the awful chance of her public criticism? No, he finally decided. He could not. He determined to call the Commander the following morning, thank him very politely for the offer, but decline on the grounds that he was not ready for such responsibility. Mind made up, he donned hat and gloves and strode purposefully from the station to the Council Offices where he was due to meet with the Town Clerk. The subject under discussion was to be the speedy removal of traffic diversions around bomb sites. Gripping stuff! After all, he consoled himself; he would soon be able to revert to being an ordinary Inspector, keeping his hand in, alongside the troops. Probably, he consoled himself, where he would be happiest in the long run.

# A MUSICAL INTERLUDE

Jamie, his birthday now imminent, was getting into quite a lather of expectation; would he at last get the bicycle that he had longed for? Would he, instead, have to settle for some far more prosaic gift, one that was deemed 'sensible' by his elders? He hoped not. A bicycle would free him from his immediate vicinity. So far, in his short life, his world had been proscribed to an area capable of being walked to and from in an hour or so. Even the wonderful go-kart imprisoned him within local confines. A Bicycle, on the other hand, would allow him go miles and miles! Yes, a bicycle would certainly fill the bill as far as he was concerned.

But reality brought the realisation that things wished for seldom came to pass; therefore, what alternatives could he reasonably hope for? A small box Brownie camera would be very nice, as would a wristwatch. A new suit would be absolute anathema, as would a new pair of shoes. He realised that it was by now probably far too late for him to start voicing preferences upon the matter; nevertheless, he determined to broach the subject with his Dad; try to sound him out to see if any firm conclusions had already been reached.

As John returned home that evening, mind still firmly made up, he was surprised to find young Jamie fluttering round him, offering to get slippers, to tidy up the table so that he could eat his tea. 'Hello', he thought. 'Birthday coming up. Easy to see just what he is after!'

Jamie, blissfully unaware of such transparency, happily brought in his father's plate and mug of tea. "Dad", he began. 'Oh, oh; here it comes' thought John. "Dad; have you and Mum picked my birthday present yet. I don't want to know what it is, of course! Just wondered if you had decided yet".

John played along with the game. "No", he replied with a straight face. "Why, had you something special in mind?"

"Well, I *did* wonder about a bike", Jamie said with some trepidation.

'I'll bet you did!' thought John. Aloud, he replied, "Well, we would have to think long and hard about that. After all, you are quite young to ride about on your own, you know".

This was definitely not what Jamie wanted to hear. In his mind he was well old enough to cycle to Scotland and back. However, diplomacy was the thing on these occasions. "I promise that I would never go too far, dad. I would be ever so careful!"

The thought of this impulsive young lad ever being in the remotest bit careful was enough to make a cat laugh, thought John. He said that they would 'take the matter under the most serious advisement'. Jamie, not having the slightest idea what that actually meant, had to accept it as final for the time being; at least, he thought, the strange sentence did not contain the word 'no'. He went off about his own business leaving his father chuckling to himself. Jamie was always good for a laugh, he thought.

Cecily Bedford had noticed that recently Jamie had not played with his special friends during the breaks; nor did he seek them out after school; the lad appeared to have retreated into his shell. Not that he seemed unhappy, she reflected. On the contrary, Jamie appeared to be his usual, cheerful self; he answered questions during the lessons, the inevitable joke never far from the surface; he whistled his way around the school grounds during the after-lunch break – but always on his own. She remarked on this to her assistant, Julia, who had noticed much the same. It was strange, they thought. He was the only boy in the school who seemed to be completely happy with his own company. Cecily took him aside the next afternoon.

"Jamie", she began. "Why don't you play with Matthew and Tommy anymore? You used to be such good friends!"

Jamie seemed not in the least put out by the question. "Oh, they aren't interested in my things anymore", he shrugged.

"What, birds and trees and so on?" prompted the headmistress.

"Yes; they want to talk about football and cricket and other things. I'm not interested in those at all!"

"I'm sure that there are other boys who could share your interests", Cecily said, hoping to draw him out a bit more.

"Well, p'raps!" replied Jamie. "But I'm happy to be on my own. My mum says that I should never rely on other people as they always let you down".

"I'm sure that she did not mean that you should never talk to your friends!" replied Cecily, wondering what would have prompted his mother to say such a thing to a little boy.

"Oh yes", said Jamie, nodding his head for emphasis. "She said that other people always get in the way; she said they are unrelatable!"

Cecily correctly interpreted this as 'unreliable'. "Surely Matthew and Tommy wouldn't let you down".

"Well, they said I was getting boring when I started telling them all about the trees in the woods, said they didn't want to know!"

"But there *must* be other things that you could talk about with them", insisted the headmistress.

"Yes, there prob'ly are", agreed Jamie. "But I don't want to talk about them, you see!"

Mrs Bedford left it at that, knowing that she was probably not going to win. She conferred with Julia. "Is there anything else that you know Jamie is interested in?"

"He's terribly keen on music", she said. "He has a rather uncanny ability to play any tune that he has heard; he seems to be able to recall it, in its correct key, and reproduce it almost as if the manuscript was in front of him. I understand that he has had a few music lessons, but his teacher gave up because he made mistakes all the time with his scales".

"You know, that doesn't surprise me in the slightest", chuckled the headmistress. "He doesn't strike me as the sort of boy who would take kindly to any form of structured learning. You seem to be implying that he has some sort of natural gift – can play anything by ear".

"Yes, that is exactly what I'm implying", said Julia, firmly. "If you agree, I'll hold him back after school today and demonstrate it to you. After all, his mother will hardly notice if he's a little late, will she?"

"No!" agreed Cecily. "I don't suppose for one moment that she will!"

Jamie was quite puzzled to be asked to remain after school; what had he done now, he wondered? He was even more perplexed when Julia asked him to sit at the grand piano and to play for her.

"What shall I play, Miss?" he asked. Julia had thought this through. "Do you know the hymn 'Abide with me'", she asked.

"Oh yes; that's easy!" said Jamie. He closed his eyes for a few moments and then started to tap out the melody. Cecily quietly came up behind him to observe for herself. She had the hymnal open at the correct page. Sure enough, Jamie was playing it in the correct key of G major. He came to the end and sat quietly, his hands in his lap.

"Why did you play it in that key?" she enquired.

"Well, I thought about it and hummed it through before I started. The top note seemed to be right as sopranos never seem to go above an E. Of course, the really good ones can, but hymns never take them any higher than that".

"Can you play any of the other parts – the altos, tenors or basses?" ventured Julia.

"Think so", said Jamie. He went into his silent humming mode again then started to play the bass part. Cecily followed her four-part score; he was uncannily accurate.

"I'd like to sing bass!" said Jamie. "When I've grown up, of course. They seem to have really *interesting* parts – not like the others – they seem boring".

"Can you hear all the four parts in your head – all at the same time?"

"Oh yes!" said Jamie. "But my hands are a bit little to reach them properly. Sometimes I have to fiddle about a bit".

"Where do you practise?" asked Julia, knowing that his music teacher would never have permitted such unstructured behaviour.

"I sometimes sneak into a little church in the next road and play their organ. I've never been caught yet!" he said proudly. Cecily correctly identified this as a small Baptist chapel that would have been within about a ten-minute walk of Jamie's home.

"Would you like me to ask the local vicar if you could practise on the big organ at the parish church?" Julia wondered. "I sometimes sing in the choir there; I'm sure that he would not mind!"

Jamie's face lit up in a huge grin. "That'd be smashing; I'd love to do that!" he almost shouted.

They sent him off home, skipping with barely suppressed excitement. He had seen the large organ console, the massive bank of pipes, had heard the wonderful tones emanating from the instrument.

"Well!" exclaimed Cecily to her assistant. "You were not overstating the case, were you? I've heard some small children play very well from manuscript, but I've never heard a boy so young with such an unerring ear. What a great pity that he cannot buckle down and learn properly!"

"You know, Mrs Bedford", replied Julia. "I honestly believe that Jamie thinks he *is* already playing properly. He obviously hears it all somehow in that unruly head of his, can reproduce it whenever he wants to. He obviously thinks he has no need to be taught to do something he knows he can already do!"

"I still think it's a great pity. He could be very successful if he just put his mind to it. There's always been something about that boy that disturbs me; he's one moment full of himself, shouting his little jokes; the next he's sunk back into his shell - or is far away, in a land of his own making".

"I just think that, at times, he's terribly lonely", mused Julia. "He seems to have the most peculiar home life. If it were not for his elder brother and his grandparents, I think he would be completely lost".

The two women parted for the day. Cecily went upstairs humming the tune she had heard played; Julia walked home wondering just how she was to keep her word to Jamie; would she really be able to convince the vicar to let him have a go?

# DECISION MADE

On the Friday, the day before Jamie's birthday, John made the 'phone call that he had promised the Area Commander. He had not altered his mind; he would not accept the post that had been offered, could not dare take the risk. He was honest enough with himself to realise that it was a real shame; he had worked long and hard for any improvement in his life, had weathered all the setbacks that had occurred. However, for his future life to have any peace, he needed to keep work and home entirely separate – and this he could manage in his present rank. It would only be a matter of time before a new Chief Inspector was appointed for the Wandleford station; he would then happily revert to his old job as one of three operational Inspectors. He would be able to slide back into anonymity, into his safe and private world. He picked up the receiver and asked the operator to connect him with Divisional Headquarters.

The Commander came on the line, brisk and cheerful as ever. "Hello, John", he boomed. "Right – come to a sensible decision, then?"

John faltered, indecision once more taking hold; was it the right decision, he asked himself. The Commander obviously wanted him, thought him capable of the post. He needed to be able to talk it through with someone, had needed that from the outset. But, how on earth could he say that he had been offered a really good job but was afraid that his own wife might ruin it for him? No; the idea was ridiculous; he would appear a complete weakling. He had to stick to his guns for his own sanity.

"I've come to a decision, sir that I am sure is sensible", he said. "I would like to thank you most sincerely for considering me for the post, but I cannot accept it".

"What?" came the booming voice. "Bloody madness! Why in God's name not?"

John had rehearsed this many times. "Sir", he said in as strong a voice as he could muster. "You and my own Super obviously think that I could do the job; however, I am convinced that I couldn't! I simply do not have enough confidence in myself. I have never made a secret that my education was very basic; I've had to teach myself, as it were, to be able to cope with the paperwork. Any way, I'm very happy at my present rank. I fit in; I can cope with this. I hope that you understand, sir".

There was a silence for a few minutes; John could almost hear the Commander's mental cogs going round. "Big mistake, if you want my opinion! Look; I wouldn't have asked you if I did not think you capable. You have a lot of things going for you – you're honest and straightforward; you learn fast; above all, the men actually respect you. Think again and give me a call after the weekend!"

John realised that he was going to have to bring this to an end once and for all; to delay yet again could well prove disastrous. "No – I'm sorry, sir. I'm going to have to turn the job down. I realise that I may well be shooting myself in the foot, but I am happy with what I'm doing. I would feel very uncomfortable as a senior officer – out of place. What is that new phrase the trick cyclists use – out of my comfort zone?"

There came yet another silence. "Well", came the eventual sigh. "I suppose that I'll have to respect your decision. I think you are making a very big mistake; but one thing I'll promise you right here and now. You have not shot yourself in the foot, as you call it. If and when another senior post comes up, you will be considered equally with any others. Now, I'm going to have to scour around to find someone else. Thank you for your thoughts, John".

John heard the click as the far receiver was put down. He had done it! If he had taken the trouble to analyse himself at that point, he would have found that, instead of rueing the loss of an opportunity, he felt nothing but a wave of relief. He would now be able to concentrate on his own job, to retreat back into his usual anonymity. He got up from his desk and went to his own Superintendent's office. He owed that man the courtesy of first-hand information.

"I've told the Commander, thanks but no thanks", he said, reluctantly accepting the formal cup of coffee.

"You, my son, are a bleeding idiot!" said that blunt individual. "If I'm honest, I am glad not to lose you; but that doesn't alter my opinion – you are a complete bloody idiot!"

"Thank you for that vote of confidence, sir". John knew his Super well enough to be able to talk to him this way. He felt, though, that he had to go a bit further. "My decision was not easy; it's for purely personal reasons". That, he knew, would put a full stop against any further interrogation.

"Must respect that, I suppose! Now, I have managed to get a replacement for Chiefy – chap coming down from North London somewhere. He'll be here next Monday; so, you and Paul need to be able to do a double hand-over. That OK?"

"Yes, sir, no problem. Have we got any new bobbies coming as well? We're very short staffed on the reliefs".

"Yes, three more coming next week and a promise of two more later. What do you feel about any of the senior bobbies who have been acting sergeant? Any of them good enough to keep permanently?"

John did not need to consider this question; he had already, with Paul's agreement, decided to seek approval for two of them to be promoted. He made his immediate recommendations and was relieved to note that the Super did not demur at either of them. They would be told later that afternoon.

With the muttered words, 'bloody idiot' following him out into the corridor, John returned for almost the last time to his temporary, superior, office. It was over at last, he thought. Now he would be able to concentrate on his job without the background nagging worries. He felt quite light-hearted as he set about producing his hand-over report. He wondered what the new chap, his new boss, would be like.

# THE WORST BIRTHDAY EVER

Jamie returned home that afternoon in quite a lather of excitement. Tomorrow would be his birthday and, for the first time in three years, had absolutely no idea at all what form his present would take. Would his Dad have taken notice of the plea for a bike, or would he have other ideas? He had yet to reach an age when he would have an understanding of the decision making process in his home. He hopped around his bedroom, unable to concentrate on any one thing for more than a few minutes. He was relieved to hear the early arrival of Desmond. His brother, knowing exactly the jumble of thoughts that were revolving in that little head, decided that the only course of action was resort to diversionary tactics. As he was preparing their tea he said that he thought it a good idea to go for a long walk that evening. He had something special to show his young brother. Jamie was intrigued; what could that be?

Desmond led the way down into the town of Brooke Hill, past the shops and into an area that Jamie hardly ever visited. To the west of the town was an area of very expensive houses, each set in its own extensive grounds. It was an area of manicured lawns, precisely clipped hedges, sparkling paintwork; Jamie wondered if he was going to be shown a new, huge house that they might move into. They passed gates in expensive wrought iron bearing nameplates such as 'Greenlands' and 'Avon House', passed the tennis courts barricaded with a notice 'Brooke Hill Tennis Club. Strictly Members Only!', came to yet another broad tree-lined avenue. The third large house was their destination, apparently. Where the house had stood was now just a vast crater.

"You remember the other week we heard that V2?" Desmond said quietly. "Well, here is where it landed. How it did not take out the two houses on either side is anyone's guess! Just look at the size of that hole!"

The area had until the previous day been cordoned off whilst the site was cleared of the remains of any possessions, of all the rubble of a previously magnificent house. Now all there was to see was a gaping crater surrounded by torn tree stumps, blackened grass. The two boys wandered to the lip of the crater and peered into its depths. The hole was roughly circular, some hundred feet in diameter. It descended like an inverted cone to a depth of twenty feet at least. Not one sign of brick or timber remained. It would never fill with water as the sub-soil around the town was of deep chalk. It would drain very quickly. Jamie and Desmond stared in awe at the size of the hole. There was an eerie silence about the place. Jamie, after a minute's contemplation, started thinking about the people who had lived there. He posed the question to his brother.

"The whole family was wiped out", Desmond said quietly. "Mother, father, three children, their nanny and two maids – all gone just like that!"

Jamie felt tears pricking at his eyelids. What would it like, he wondered, to be blown up, to be dead in an instant? Would they all go to heaven?

"Did they all go to heaven, Des?" he asked.

"If they had lived good lives, they most certainly did!" Desmond nodded, sure of his facts. "Two of the children were very little – I think they were twins, about Robbie's age. They would certainly have gone to heaven!"

Jamie felt an almost overwhelming relief. It would be horrible for the whole family to be kept apart.

"They are all together, then?" he wanted reassurance.

"Oh, yes; I'm sure they are", replied Desmond, knowing that his little brother would want to hear that. Apart from anything else, Desmond actually believed that this was nothing but the absolute truth. God would not punish this poor family after such a terrible ordeal, would He?

"What's it like to be dead, Des?"

"Haven't the foggiest", said Desmond. "Nobody ever knows until it happens to them, and they can't tell us because they are no longer here. It is all about believing that we go to a better place, somewhere we can be happy and at peace for ever and ever".

Jamie could envisage no better place than his beloved beech woods. Where, he wondered, could there be a place that was better than that? He was sublimely happy there with his birds, their nests, the variety of trees and foliage.

The two brothers left the site, each very quiet with his thoughts. They made their way home via the town centre. Instead of going under the railway bridge, they turned up to the front of the station itself, walked through the booking office and through the tunnel that ran under the tracks and platforms. They climbed the steps to the last platform and went out the back entrance into the station car park. No cars were parked there, had not been for years. They went past the coal yard where the next morning's household deliveries were being loaded in sacks on the backs of three horse-drawn carts. The men doing the loading all wore sacking hoods that flowed down their backs to protect them from the dust of the coal and coke. Their faces were blackened with the stuff, their hands grimed with years of accumulated coal dust. They spoke not one word to one another as they heaved the sacks upright onto the carts. Then, past the long cliffs that had now overgrown with stunted birch and hawthorn, into Buttermere Gardens and home. Cocoa was welcome after the long walk. Jamie had not thought about his birthday for at least three hours. Desmond looked at his little brother and grinned to himself. Job done, he thought.

The nature of his present returned to the little mind as he tried to get to sleep; he tried to think of other things – the poor family now all dead; no, that made his too sad. The possibility of playing the big church organ; no – that probably would not happen. The fact that he would, in just over a year's time, have to go to another school; no – that did not bear thinking about. Somewhere amidst all this jumble, he eventually fell asleep.

The next day, Saturday, dawned with grey skies and the threat of rain. It was a depressing day. The early news bulletin spoke of yet more setbacks to the advance into Germany; would it ever be over, wondered John? Then came news of ships sunk during the night, bombs and rockets that had devastated the port of London yet again, the prospect of a prolonged period of bad weather. Nothing but gloom and despondency. And, thought

John, the birthday would do little to alleviate the gloom! He dreaded the coming day.

Desmond and Jamie had joined their father for an early breakfast. Had Jamie been more alert, he would have wondered about the sameness of that meal; nothing special at all. Desmond *did* notice it but said nothing; perhaps, he thought, the ration books were not in a state to have afforded anything out of the ordinary. Nothing, of course, could happen until Margaret came downstairs. At least an hour before she made her appearance a now confident Robert came down the stairs in his new-found method. He would lie on the top stair with his head uppermost, slowly dangle his feet over the edge and commence to slither feet-first down the fourteen risers and treads. He was getting quite good at this. He rose to his feet at the bottom and waddled happily into the kitchen. John reached down and put the giggling child into the highchair, filled the little bowl with some cereal, poured on a small quantity of milk. Robert proceeded to tuck into this with his favourite spoon; little rivers of milk, with the odd cornflake attached, ran down his cotton bib.

Jamie jumped up to help his tiny brother get the last spoonful into his mouth. To do this required that the bowl be tipped; Robert had not yet mastered this art. As the washing up was completed, Jamie was starting to hop around the kitchen in an agony of anticipation. Desmond looked at him and smiled. John looked at him and dreaded what was to come. At long last Margaret's footsteps were heard descending the staircase. Jamie ran out to say his 'good morning, Mummy' and received a stony glance of dismissal. Jamie was perplexed. What had he done? Why no 'Happy Birthday'. Desmond had said this to him when he first woke that morning. His Dad had said the same. Why did his Mum not wish him a happy birthday too?

Margaret went to her usual armchair in the sitting room and waited for Desmond to bring her the usual glass of milk and three plain biscuits. Robert came in and patted his mother's knees. Jamie and Desmond also came in and sat expectantly on the sofa. John made his reluctant entrance and sat in the window seat with a cup of tea. Margaret took a sip of her milk and turned her deep brown eyes to her son. John took a deep breath.

"You may wonder why I did not wish you a happy birthday, Jamie", she began. Jamie looked at her, puzzled. "That is because I do *not* wish for you to have a happy birthday. I shall now tell you why".

Jamie looked at her, his eyes already misting over.

"All my life", Margaret continued, addressing the space above Jamie's head. "All my life I have striven for truth and loyalty. You, by running away, have demonstrated that you have absolutely no loyalty to me. You do not know the meaning of truth. By your own actions you have shown that you do not wish to be a part of my family. Therefore, I have decided that you shall not have a present; you simply do not deserve one!"

Jamie, by now was in floods of tears. What had he done? He had honestly thought that he was acting as his mother had wished, had faced up to life and acted like the 'man' that she had demanded.

Margaret had not finished. "I have instructed that your grandparents do not recognise your birthday either! You are a wicked boy. I have tried to set you an example of truth and honesty and this is the way that you repay me. You are a great disappointment to me! And now you have made me feel rather unwell. I need to rest!"

So saying, she got up and went back to the front bedroom. John just knew that this presaged a further two or three weeks of isolation in the darkened room. He was near to tears himself. He got up and went after her, to attend to her needs. Desmond went over to Jamie and put his arm round the little heaving shoulders. Jamie raised a tear-stained face.

"All I did was to try and act like a man", he cried. "She told me to! She did!"

Desmond, who had heard that earlier diatribe, knew that it was no more than the absolute truth. His mother *had* told Jamie to be more upright, to act like a grown-up. He knew exactly what she had meant by this; had not instructed Jamie to branch out on his own. He also understood why Jamie had acted as he did, why he thought that his actions would prove that he was listening to advice. Not for the first time he wondered what life would be like if people actually *talked* to one another, made sure that their meanings were clear, treated one another with kindness and understanding.

It never entered his head to question his mother's motives; she was perfect – beyond reproach. Jamie knew that he had done something terrible, had deeply offended that wonderful person – the person that all the family members obeyed without question. What could he do, he wondered, to make amends?

Out of sight of his parents, Desmond hugged his distraught brother, trying to bring just a little comfort to Jamie, who was obviously completely bewildered at the turn of events, not having the least ideas that his actions should have been so misinterpreted.

John stood by the curtained window, looking down on his wife who lay supine on the bed, her eyes firmly closed. She started to address him. "What nobody seems to realise is that I need absolute calm and peace. I pray for this every night, but I am never given what I so desperately require. I never once deviate from absolute truth – you know that don't you?"

John simply could not reply in words; he simply nodded. Deep down he knew that Margaret was probably the most untruthful person he had ever come across. In his life in the police he was more than used to villains telling all manner of lies in the interest of self-preservation; he expected them to act no other way. With Margaret it was entirely different; she seemed to exist on another plane altogether. Her lies were all a part of her fantasies, were not really her fault, were they? She uttered the most preposterous stories at times, all the proceeds of her imaginary life among the well-to-do and the beautiful. Her lies were necessary to keep up the pretence, weren't they? How far, he wondered, had she strayed from the real world? Was she ever a part of this mortal family at all? She had not finished yet.

"I have been cursed with an ungrateful child. I told him that I wanted him to act like a man; and what does he do? He acts like a spoiled brat – runs away, if you please!"

"Perhaps he thought that he *was* acting grown up as you wanted", ventured John.

"Don't you *dare* defend the boy after all he has done to upset me! His actions were absolutely beyond forgiveness. He has made me quite ill yet again. I named him for the most perfect gentleman that I have ever known; and this is all the thanks I get!"

'Oh dear God – not that bloody Marcus again!' thought John. Would she never speak of him, her husband, in the glowing terms she reserved for her imaginary 'friends'?

"I wash my hands of him! And, before you go behind my back, I absolutely forbid you to offer him the slightest crumb of comfort. Don't you *dare* give him a present or even a card. He is simply not worth it! Also, while you are at it, tell Desmond that he is under exactly the same orders. The boy is to be ignored. I cannot even bring myself to utter his name – a name that he has, to his utter shame, besmirched".

John wondered when her wrath would be turned on little Robert. Already he was seeing signs of her slight indifference to the little chap. Robert was now walking freely all over the house, did not need her constant care and attention. She would probably see this as a betrayal as well. He sat down beside her and took her hand. Impatiently, she shook him off. "I wish to be left alone", she said in parody of one of her favourite actresses. He looked at her face, which had now assumed the well-known 'noble suffering' pose, nostrils slightly flared, mouth turned down. He sighed and went downstairs to see what was happening, saw Desmond with his arms still clasping his brother.

"Your mother has said you are to leave Jamie alone", he said. Margaret, listening intently, nodded her satisfaction. John turned to Jamie.

"You know that you have upset your mother, don't you?" he said as sternly as he could. Jamie nodded, tears still flowing down his woebegone face. "Well, you must think long and hard about what you have done. She thinks you are beyond control!"

"But *you* don't think that, do you Dad?" sniffled Jamie. John, for a moment, did not know how to reply to this, whether he should even reply at all.

"You were a very naughty boy", he temporised. "You must expect some punishment, you know!"

Margaret sneered in the darkness. Weak as dishwater, she thought. The man had no backbone, was a weakling. She had to be the strong one all the time, had to pay for things as he had little money; had to be the one to write letters as he had little education. She despised him. If it were not for her the boy would run wild. Well, from now on, let him! She washed her hands of the boy. She contemplated changing his name as he had utterly ruined the one that she had given him.

Jamie squatted in the corner of the sitting room; he was terribly confused. His Dad had treated him with such love and care when he had been found alive and well in the woods. Why now was he saying that he needed to be punished? Desmond, the one safe haven in his life, had been told to leave him alone. Desmond, he knew, would never disobey his parents. He was all on his own. Robert was too young to be much help to him. He wiped his eyes on the sleeve of his pullover and crept out of the back door. Despite the dark clouds and the imminence of promised rain, he walked disconsolately to the only place where he felt happy; he went up to the beech woods and snuggled into his hazel clump. He had, some months ago, plaited some of the pliant shoots into a roof. Although the leaves were yet to appear, the camp would afford him some shelter if the rain did materialise. He sat in his camp and watched the life around him. Squirrels were busy making or repairing their drays; birds were collecting matter for their new nests. Beetles and other insects were crawling over the ground, burrowing under the last season's compost to find food and hiding places. He felt utterly at home in this place where there were no human voices; only the rustle and chirp of the wildlife. How different his day was turning out to be. Instead of the happy laughter and the wonderful present, he was now a virtual outcast, as he saw it – no present, no special tea, no cake – nothing. The tears started again as he curled himself up into a ball of misery.

The rain started to fall in small drops in the early afternoon. By four o'clock, it was settled into a steady drizzle. The camp offered him shelter from the very worst, the plaited canopy directing most of the water down the sides of the 'dome'. But the occasional drop landed on his head, further deepening his mood of despair. He had spent some time wondering how on earth he could make amends. Various ideas had come and had been just as quickly dismissed. What about doing all the shopping for a month, he wondered? No, he would not be trusted with the money or the precious ration books. How about doing all the dusting and cleaning? No – Nancy came in to do that. How about making a picture for his mother? No – only Robert was praised for his artwork. What if he simply walked and walked and never went home again? No – he just didn't know where to go. Why didn't he kill himself? He hadn't a gun so he could not shoot himself; did not know how to hang himself. Besides, God would be very cross with him and would not let him into heaven. He would be just as lost as he was in this life. It was all hopeless. His little brain gave up and he nodded off into a sleep disturbed by dreams of angels scolding him, mother turning away from him, father holding him tight, Desmond telling him stories to make him happy. He woke with a start at just before nine that evening. It was quite dark, and he had eaten nothing since breakfast. He was hungry, thirsty and utterly wretched. With a shrug of near desperation, he started to walk home.

He was very wet by the time he got to the back door. Desmond was, as usual, deep into his books. He looked at Jamie and gave him a broad grin of welcome, caught himself and returned to the problem of varying stresses in a horizontal metal beam. Jamie, slightly encouraged by that brief welcome, shrugged out of the sodden pullover, went upstairs to his bedroom. There, he dried himself and got into his pyjamas and went down again to get something to eat. He ate ravenously the sandwich that he cobbled together with the remains of a bowl of dripping and some fish paste. He drank some water and went up to bed. His parent's bedroom was in darkness, Robert obviously fast asleep in his cot. Soon, the little chap would need a bed and had been promised the small third bedroom over the hall. Of his father there was no sign whatsoever. He rolled himself into the blankets and fell asleep, wishing with all his heart that he never had another birthday as long as he lived.

John, meanwhile, was pouring his heart out to the two people he liked and admired most – his mother- and father-in-law. He had turned up after supper and had accepted a glass of wine. His own father had died very young from the effects of cancer and drink – the drink used as an anaesthetic against the awful pain. John had never forgotten the drunken arguments, had determined never to resort to alcohol. However, now and again, he could be persuaded to take the occasional glass. He sat, nursing the wineglass and related to them the happenings of the day.

Alfred and Gertrude listened with deep sadness to the story. Gertrude, unable to help herself, cried out, "Oh the poor little mite!" Alfred nodded quietly.

"Of course, I realise that I'm a great disappointment to her", he said, barely able to restrain a tear. "I am not properly educated, and she despises that in me".

Alfred looked at his son-in-law with great sadness. When, he wondered, would this man ever realise that his good points outweighed his bad? The never ending drip-drip of criticism had so undermined him that he now saw himself through her eyes – a worthless failure. Gertrude was far more concerned with her grandson. She, more than Alfred was able to, understood her daughter's problems. She was getting to the point of needing real help – someone who might, possibly, be able to drag her back into the real world, away from all those fantasies. She blamed herself for not taking action when Margaret had been much younger. Was it now too late, she wondered?

"Where is Jamie, now?" she asked. John shook his head. "I don't actually know", he replied. "Probably gone back to the beeches to mope, if I know him!"

"You know, John; this really will not do!" she said firmly. "That little boy is six years old. He is still a little child and needs proper care. For you to shrug your shoulders is just not good enough!"

"Margaret had forbidden me to offer him any comfort. And she's probably right".

"In this instance, she is most certainly wrong", came the stern admonition from a lady who normally spoke in the most genteel of tones. "That little boy needs all the love and understanding that you can give him. He is probably at this very moment totally confused, utterly wretched. The poor little mite needs you more than ever!"

"But I can't and won't go against Margaret's wishes", John said in such a defeated voice that Alfred looked up sharply.

"Are you going to abandon this son as well as the other two?" he asked.

John was crushed by this. It was exactly what he had just been thinking, and hating himself for. However, loyalty to Margaret was paramount at all times.

"I can only repeat that I cannot be disloyal to her. She is not very well again, and this is all down to Jamie and his stupidity".

Alfred and Gertrude exchanged looks. It was hopeless. They would have to make extra efforts to make sure that Jamie had somewhere that he felt special, felt wanted. They said that they would call for him the next morning so that he could spend the day with them, somehow make up for the hurt and loneliness.

John said goodnight to his in-laws and made his way with a heavy heart back to his home. He undressed quietly and slid under the blankets, feeling the resentment flowing from his wife's slumbering form next to him. He, also, fell into a troubled sleep.

The next morning, being Sunday, was the day that Julia had promised herself that she would try to get Jamie a try on the organ. She dressed for church with all her accustomed care and sat through the service, singing in a clear voice her alto part in the choir's rendition of the psalm, the various hymns, the Sanctus and so on. She loved choral music, delighted in the clear harmonies. She deliberately left it late in changing out of her royal blue cassock, donning once again her outdoor coat and gloves. The vicar returned to the vestry, having bade farewell to the last of the congregation to leave through the old porch door. He was immediately joined by George, son of the brigadier, who had been assisting at the sung Eucharist service.

"Vicar", she began, somewhat nervously. "I have a small favour to ask of you".

That kindly man turned a benevolent face in her direction. He was removing his stole and folding it properly into the long drawer. His face asked the question.

"Well, a boy in the school where I teach is showing a very particular talent for music. I have never come across anyone who can play as he does. I was wondering if you would be so kind as to let him have a go on the organ one day?"

"I don't see why not", replied the vicar, extricating himself from his vestments. "If he is showing such promise, I think we should do all in our power to encourage him. Who is this prodigy?"

"Oh, I think prodigy is going a trifle far", laughed Julia. "He's showing exceptional talent, is all I'm saying. His name is Jamie Small, by the way".

"Can't say I know him", said the vicar.

"Oh, but my father and I know him very well!" said George. "He's a very sprightly little chap. The old pater has taken quite a shine to him, tells him stories. Came one night to see the badgers, if I recall".

"Well, with such glowing endorsements, how could I possibly refuse", smiled the vicar.

Julia was delighted; she had not expected such rapid success. Thank heaven for the assistance of George, she thought. She regarded this young man with new eyes. He had been wounded, she knew; but was coping very well and never complained. And, moreover, was quite good looking!

"Bring him along any afternoon", said the vicar. "I'm always here between, say, three and four. Let's hear for ourselves the master at work!"

Having thanked the vicar for his kind help, Julia hurried home. She wondered if she could call at the Small household, tell Jamie the good news. Instead, she called first at the bungalow, was invited in and told Alfred and Gertrude her news. At first, Gertrude was a trifle put out; hadn't she wasted considerable funds already on futile music lessons for her grandson. But slowly, as Julia told them of her knowledge of Jamie's musical talent, she relented. It could just be what the little chap needed. By the time Julia left, both grandparents were quite taken with the idea. They determined to tell Jamie all about it when they collected him for lunch.

# HIGH 'TEMPITURES'

Jamie had spent quite a wretched morning; he had looked out dismally at the rain that pelted down past his bedroom window. The sky was a uniform deep grey with not the slightest hint of a break anywhere. He could see his tunnel leading up to the Advance Camp at the top of the railway embankment; no hope of getting up there in this weather. His thoughts turned again to his camp in the beech woods; no hope of getting there either. His soaking the previous day had left him feeling unwell; his head was aching and hot to his touch; his throat was a bit raw. He ate his breakfast in silence and went back up to his bedroom to rest on his bed. He felt quite ill, which was unusual for Jamie, normally the healthiest of boys. Desmond had gone for the day, his father long gone to work. Nancy O'Brien had collected Robert as Margaret was just starting another of her prolonged periods of isolation. Not a sound came from her bedroom as Jamie dozed off and on throughout the morning.

A soft knock at the front door woke him at about one o'clock. He slowly went down the stairs to find his grandfather, well covered up against the weather, standing on the doorstep.

"Ready for lunch, young man?" he asked. Jamie had completely forgotten that he was going to one of Nana's lovely lunches. He brightened a bit, put on his shoes and mackintosh and went off with his grandfather. Alfred noted that he did not call out a 'goodbye' as he shut the door after him. Hand in hand the old man and the young boy went across to the bungalow. Nana was waiting with open arms as he went into the hall, ran to her and gave her his customary squeeze. Gertrude fondled the ginger curls.

"My, you *are* hot!" she exclaimed. "I wonder if you are running a temperature".

Jamie said that he had got very wet the previous day and had felt quite unwell all that morning. Gertrude went into the bathroom and fetched her clinical thermometer. She sat Jamie down on the big sofa and put the bulb under his tongue, telling him to keep his mouth shut and not to bite. Jamie sat very still as two full minutes ticked by on the long-case clock that stood in the far corner of the lounge. Gertrude took the thermometer out and examined the scale.

"Good heavens", she said. "One hundred and three point five! That is far too high!"

She crossed to the telephone and dialled the number of the family doctor, was put through and explained why she was calling. Doctor Talbot, their GP of many years standing, agreed to come as soon as he had finished his lunch. Daisy bustled in and out of the dining room, bringing with her the roast meat and potatoes, the vegetables and the gravy. She announced that lunch was ready and stood by as Alfred, Gertrude and Jamie went in to take their places at the large table in the dining room across the hall. Frederick arrived just as they were sitting down. "Got immersed in the paper", he excused himself as he took his place. "We are nearly at the outskirts of Berlin – soon be over now!" Alfred grunted; it would be over when it was over, he thought.

Jamie managed but one mouthful of the meat and played with his potatoes and gravy. Usually, he would eat the greens first, then the meat and finish off by mashing up the potatoes with his fork to mix with the gravy which he would then arrange as a castle or a hill. He just was not very hungry. He was also very quiet. Frederick asked him what was the matter. "Don't feel very well, Nunky", came the subdued reply. Gertrude said that he was running quite a high temperature and that she had phoned the doctor.

Alfred told his brother all about the birthday fiasco; Frederick was horrified that his little great-nephew could have been treated that way, had spent his birthday all on his own getting soaked. His kindly heart went out to the little fellow; most of all he wanted to go over to see his niece and give her a piece of his mind. He had never agreed with the way in which the entire family had given way to that impossible woman. Even as a little girl she had repulsed him with her constant demands for attention. However, he knew that any remonstration would be unwelcome. He was not her father. He just had to keep his own counsel. Nevertheless, he was determined that he, at least, would make a fuss over the boy, would make sure that the birthday did not go unrecognised.

When the dessert of baked apples had been finished, there came a ring at the doorbell. Daisy ushered in the good doctor who went to Jamie, took his wrist in one hand and his gold hunter in the other. "Hmmm", he mused. He touched Jamie's forehead, not bothering to take the temperature. He then opened Jamie's shirt and sounded his chest, front and back.

"Some form of chest infection", he diagnosed. "Pulse quite fast, forehead hot and a trifle wheezy on the left side. Bed for you, young man. Drink lots of water and get as much sleep as you can!" Jamie nodded. That was all he felt like doing anyway.

Gertrude took him back to the lounge and lay him down on the sofa. Daisy had produced a soft pillow and a blanket. She tucked this around him, then went to fetch a big glass of water which she put on a small table by his head. She had a very soft spot for Jamie who had helped her on washing day when he was quite small. She had stood him on a stool so that he could turn the handle on the mangle. She delighted in his jokes, his infectious laugh. Gertrude and Alfred showed the doctor out and thanked him for his prompt attention. Now what, they thought? Jamie obviously could not go home; Desmond was away; John was at work and would be for most of the night. It was a dilemma for the old couple.

Frederick came into the lounge and drew up a chair to sit by Jamie. "Been in another spot of bother, I hear", he said. Jamie told him the whole story, how he had thought he was doing exactly what his mother wanted. Frederick could not help feeling so very sorry for the little chap. He obviously had got hold of the wrong end of the stick – not an unusual happening, he mused. However, there was absolutely no excuse for his being treated in that appalling manner.

"Look, old fellow", he said. "How about, when you are better, you come up to my house and we'll sort you out your own microscope. I've got at least three, possibly four if I could only remember where I put the dashed thing! Anyway, we can sort you one out and it can stay at my house for whenever you want to come and use it. I'll tell you what – we could go out for walks and find some things for you to examine. I'll mount the slides and we can start your own collection. Would you like that?"

Jamie's face split into his usual smile. "Thanks Nunky. I'd like that lots and lots", he broke off to start coughing. Fiddling in his trouser pocket he came up with a rather grubby handkerchief to wipe his mouth. Frederick was quite alarmed to see a trace of red blood. He patted Jamie on his head and went out to his brother. Gertrude was the first to react. She went into the lounge to find her grandson having another bout of coughing. The red staining was quite prominent. She crossed to the telephone to inform the doctor of these new developments. "Still sounds like a chest infection to me", he said. "If there is no improvement, or if the blood discharge gets any worse, do not hesitate. Call the ambulance and get him transferred to the hospital. In any case, I'll call again this evening to see what's what".

Frederick came and sat with Jamie for a time. Having found out that his little brother Robert was being cared for by the daily help – again, thought Frederick – he realised that, apart from Margaret, there would be nobody in the house to look after him. Why were children wasted on some people, he wondered; there were some couples who desperately wanted little ones and couldn't manage it whilst others, Margaret in particular, seemed not to care one jot whether her first-born was alive or dead. It all seemed monstrously unfair; but who, he mused, ever decided that life would be fair anyway?

To keep Jamie amused, he started telling him stories of when he was a boy. He had been, still was in fact, a quiet and sober chap, liking nothing more that walking in the fields to observe nature at work. In that, he and Jamie had a lot in common. Jamie was, admittedly, scatterbrained at times but his love of nature was there. Frederick was the youngest of the three Clements brothers. Edward, the oldest of the children, had been born two years before Alfred. Amelia had followed one year after and Frederick two years after that. He had been born in eighteen seventy-eight to moderately affluent parents. He had received, as had his brothers and sister, a private education. His childhood, when he looked back on it, had been spent in perpetual sunshine – or so it had seemed. There had been no financial worries, no turmoil in the placid family home; servants had catered for their needs, coachmen on hand to transport them wherever and whenever they required. It had been, in every sense, an idyllic childhood. Their parents loved and cared for them, loved and respected one another; harmony had reigned. His business life had been one smooth progression to top management; it had ended with his retirement on a very substantial annuity. There had been but one flaw in his life; when he had just turned twenty-three, the year that the old queen had died, he had met a very charming young lady from an impeccable family. They had slowly and properly got to know one another over the course of a couple of years; an engagement was confidently expected by both families. However, one awful day, the young woman had mysteriously disappeared from her home. Frantic searches were made by police and family; eventually, private detectives were employed; there had been no sign of her. One morning, almost a year later, Frederick had received a letter with an Australian post mark. In it was a long letter from the young woman. She pleaded his forgiveness, but had met another man, ten years her senior, who was emigrating to the other side of the world to commence sheep farming. She had been infatuated with him from the start and had agreed to accompany him on the journey out. They had married in haste just before the boat sailed and that was why the detectives could have found no trace of her as she travelled under her married name. Frederick kept the letter, showed it to his and her families. Her own mother and father had commiserated with Frederick, had disowned their daughter from that day onwards. Frederick had never married, the only one of the siblings to remain single. When he thought of Edward's disastrous union with the dreadful Constance, he was not sorry. Alfred's and Amelia's marriages had turned out very well indeed. But, from all four of them, only one child had issued. His niece had been a mystery to him during her childhood; he had watched her turn into one of the most beautiful young women he had ever seen, with the most impenetrable mind he had ever encountered. Sometimes quiet and withdrawn, at others loud and demanding; always concerned solely with her own interests – Frederick had no time at all for his niece, could not fathom why on earth a simple soul like John had ever contemplated marriage. He never did understand John's infatuation, his self-deprecating acceptance of his menial place in her order of things. To Frederick, it was all a disaster.

Jamie listened to his great-uncle relate a story of the day he had actually seen the prime minister of the day, Mr Gladstone, arrive at the local station to open the new town hall. The mayor, coming down the steps to greet the illustrious visitor, had tripped over the hem of his flowing robe, tumbled down the steps, had broken his nose. Jamie thought this hilarious and laughed loudly, causing another bout of coughing. Frederick noted that the bleeding was no worse. He had also been amused as a young lad to see the downfall of the mayor; this man, according to their father, was a pompous jack-in-office who had deserved all he got. He told the little boy of his expeditions into the countryside to find birds' nests, his experience of the first motor car to be seen locally, the furore it had created. Frederick had the same gift of narration that Alfred displayed with his ghost stories.

After a very late tea, the doctor called again to check Jamie's progress. "No worse, no better", he said, having sounded Jamie's chest again. "Just keep him warm with plenty of liquids. He'll be as right as nine-pence in a couple of days".

Daisy offered to keep an eye on 'the young maister' during the night. "I'm a light sleeper, mam – it'll be no bother to me!"

Jamie slept right through from nine that evening until seven the next morning. He awoke to find Daisy hovering over him. She gave his shoulder a squeeze, noted that his colour was nearer normal, his head nowhere near as hot as it had been the previous afternoon. She went out to the kitchen and returned with some buttered toast and a glass of water. Jamie wolfed down the toast, his appetite apparently miraculously returned. Daisy ran him a bath. Jamie always watched this operation in his grandparents' bathroom with great interest. Sitting above the bath, at the tap end, was a large gas geyser. Water filled it at the top and a ring of gas jets heated it from below, the water trickling out into the bath via a long, spouted pipe. It took a good twenty minutes to produce the maximum six-inch depth that war-time restrictions demanded.

As Jamie happily soaped and splashed, Daisy went quietly over the road with Gertrude's spare key. She went upstairs to collect a change of clothes for the boy. On her return, she reported to Gertrude. "Mistress be still a'sleepin, mam".

Jamie dressed in his fresh clothes, was feeling ever so much better. He wondered if he could push his luck and walk up to Nunky's house to pursue the promise of his own 'mickoscope' – he could still not master the pronunciation. However, he decided to let matters take their own course, as he did not want to land himself in any more trouble.

Jamie followed his granddad out to the old greenhouse, once the official breakfast had been eaten. This was yet another place that fascinated him. The main occupant of the greenhouse was a vine that arose from the ground in one far corner and spread to the pitched glass roof, along its length, with small branches going to left and right. The previous summer had been hot and had produced many bunches of small grapes. They were not sufficiently sweet to be eaten raw, so Alfred had bought some large glass demijohns, piping and gas traps. He had used a fine grade of sugar to mix with the crushed grapes, to start off the fermentation. He had opened the first bottle at the previous Christmas. It had been pronounced variously as ghastly, revolting and undrinkable. He, himself, had used the word revolting. It was an experiment that he had decided not to repeat.

On the shelves that ran along both sides of the greenhouse were his seedlings and cuttings. There were pots of geranium, pelargonium, lily, aster, a whole variety of bedding plants all in their very early stages. Jamie's job was to pick a new, small flowerpot, to fill it with a sand and compost mix from the heap under the shelf. He handed the pot to his granddad who pressed seeds into the top. They worked happily side by side until, from the house, came the sound of the gong for luncheon. Hands were washed in the scullery, places taken at table. Daisy had managed to produce a wonderfully smelling soup from bacon rinds (removed after cooking), potato and carrot. Jamie thought it superb and said so. Gertrude looked fondly across the table as the spoon went from bowl to mouth at a speed that she would have called 'unseemly' at any other time. The little chap was certainly on the mend. He also managed to eat three slices of crusty bread.

Frederick called in after luncheon was finished; Jamie's hopes soared.

"Are you feeling fit enough for a short walk?"

Jamie was in no doubt at all. "Oh yes, please Nunky!"

Hand in hand the old man and the little boy walked down the road and up the short hill to the house that Jamie had always thought of as a treasure trove, so many interesting artefacts did it contain.

Frederick, as good as his word, had managed to locate the old microscope. He had eventually found it in the attic beside an old kettle, a Russian sword in its scabbard, a Smith and Wesson .38 revolver, and a box of .45 ammunition. He wondered why on earth he would have kept this mismatched arsenal, could not even remember where either had come from. He decided, probably wisely, to leave the weaponry exactly where it was. What Jamie would have made of it, would even have done with it, was not something that he wished to contemplate.

The microscope was set on the dining table; Frederick had arranged a series of interesting slides in a cedarwood box. He had made the box himself many years before, had used cedar because it deterred insects with its deep resinous aroma. Jamie was thrilled and gave his Nunky a huge squeeze. Frederick looked fondly at the little chap as he started to feed slides one after another into the grooved platform. The boy was entranced. Frederick was ever so glad that he had had the idea. Perhaps, he thought, it would make up for his disappointment over that terrible birthday.

Eventually, Jamie had exhausted the collection of slides. The microscope was put safely away in a cupboard with a yellow duster covering it. "Right, old chap; that's yours whenever you want to come and use it. Now, don't forget; we must go on some field trips to collect more specimens for mounting". Jamie was thrilled with his present and at the prospect of putting together a huge collection. He had been able, all that afternoon. to forget all about his bitter disappointments.

He stayed for dinner with Frederick who, amongst other attributes, was quite an accomplished cook. Jamie watched as the old gentleman put together a pasty for which he made the pastry; the filling was produced from a variety of chopped vegetables and the remains of a piece of pork belly. Jamie pronounced it 'absolutely delicious' and the dessert of apple pie and custard as 'scrumptious'. He was almost back to his old self again, noted Frederick with pleasure. He sent the little boy on his way home just before dark, waving goodbye from his front steps until Jamie had disappeared from sigh at the bottom of the short hill.

Jamie went into the kitchen via the back door, his usual method of entry to his home, to find his mother pouring her evening glass of milk from the quart bottle on the larder's marble shelf. She looked across at him, scowling.

"Oh, so there you are!" she said crossly. Jamie said nothing, not knowing whether he ought to apologise once more.

"Nothing to say? Well, that's a novelty! You usually seem to have enough to say for yourself. I don't suppose for one minute that you are going to tell me where you have been today!"

"I stayed at Nana and Granddad's last night as I wasn't feeling well, Mummy"

"And what was supposed to be the matter with you?"

"I had a sore throat and a' tempiture'; the doctor came to see me", Jamie explained.

"Well, you seem all right to me! I suppose that your grandparents made a fuss of you, did they?"

Jamie was just about old enough to recognise the trap that was being laid for him to fall into. "Oh, not really, Mummy", he said quietly. "They just looked after me".

"And there's me thinking you were old enough to look after yourself", said Margaret bitterly. "After all, you ran away to care for yourself, didn't you?"

Jamie hung his head; he had not the faintest idea what he was expected to say. Margaret gave him another sidelong look at went upstairs to put herself to bed. Not one word of kindness, not a hug for her son; Jamie, feeling completely unwanted, also went up to bed. He was feeling tired again, the infection not yet having run its course.

Laying in bed, he thought again of the kindness of his Nana and Granddad, the love and attention of his Nunky. He knew that Desmond really loved him, always had. He started to say his prayers, whispering under the blankets.

"Dear God", he began. "Thank you for making me better; thank you for my mickoscope and for my Nunky. Thank you for my Nana and Granddad. Please look after Des and make sure he gets home all right. Please make me a better boy so that my Mummy will love me again. Thank you and amen".

Wondering what on earth he could do to get back into his mother's favour, he fell into an uneasy sleep.

# GUILT AND FAILURE

The end of April brought, with lowering skies, an abundance of rumour and speculation; was Hitler already dead? Had some of his generals at last managed to rid themselves of their tormentor? Were the Germans on the very point of capitulation? Berlin, besieged on all sides, was in flames, only the most desperate resistance being offered by a remnant force comprising the wounded, the old, and children of the Hitler Youth. It simply had to end soon, or so declaimed the pundits on the wireless, whose name now seemed legion. Some voices over the air trumpeted victorious platitudes; others spoke in tones of quiet confidence; yet more spoke of the looming menace of Russian dominance in a shattered Europe. All had opinions; none appeared saddened by the wasted years – at least, not yet.

Jamie Small lay in his little bed, staring at the ceiling; should he get up early to help with the breakfast? Should he stay where he was and think of any other way in which he could get back into his mother's good books? Some time had passed since he had fallen so drastically out of her favour, time in which he had gone from one extreme to the other. At times he felt that whatever he did would bring him no nearer to any sort of rapprochement with her – so, to hell with trying! At others, he felt near to desperation; he had lost the love of his mother; the help of his adored elder brother was denied him; his two school chums had deserted him; what *could* he do?

It sometimes seemed to him that the whole world was against him; the fact that his two friends had 'deserted' him due to his insistence on their always following his lead – well, that never occurred to him. He was too convinced of his own rightness to allow of any other course of action; he was, in some ways, arrogant to the point of rudeness. This had been forcibly pointed out to him by his mother only the previous day. Jamie had happened to mention that his erstwhile friends no longer spoke to him at school. Margaret had told him, in no uncertain terms, that this was his own fault; he had no time for the opinions of others; he was an arrogant little boy! Take the case of his music lessons, she added; his insistence that he did not need instruction was proof positive of his appalling arrogance; she had no time for such selfish conduct!

The irony of this statement was, of course, lost on the little six-year-old. It contained, however, more than a grain of truth; Jamie *was* an arrogant little boy. The fact that he meant no harm by it was neither here nor there; he alienated those who wanted to befriend him. He was, for the most part, a lively, eminently likeable child but had the unfortunate appearance of being complete within himself – beyond the need for others. Only his grandparents, old Nunky and Desmond, could see beyond this façade; they knew him to be vulnerable and, at times, desperately lonely. He could, they feared, grow up into a very lonely man, forced by his own believed invincibility into a life of solitude. None of them had any idea what to do about it.

Jamie remembered well the talk that he had had with his mother some weeks before; he could envision the silent, strong man whose name he bore; his mother had spoken of this man with such pride, such adoration. He had failed to provide her with a living reminder of this wonderful individual; he had let her down totally. The burden that Margaret had placed upon this little boy was unforgivable; not only had she demanded near perfection from a child; she had based this on the attributes of a person of her imaginings – a falsehood – a downright lie. Jamie was not to know this; only that he had not become the person that she had wanted. Therefore, to his mind, he was a complete failure.

A partial solution to his problem was nearer than he realised; Julia had told him that she had obtained permission for him to 'have a go' at playing the organ in the parish church. He rushed out of school as soon as he could possibly get away; it was May Day and the sun was shining. A brisk twenty-minute walk took him to the parish church; this was not a very old structure – had, in fact, been erected in Victorian Gothic style only some sixty years before. It consisted of the traditional main aisle running from west to east; had only one transept to the south that housed the vestry; the main doors were under a covered porch at the west end. Above the meeting of the south transept and the main aisle rose a small spire, in which was one bell that was rung mournfully by the old verger before services – silent these past war years.

Jamie dashed into the church in his usual manner, managed not to skid to a halt at the altar rails. Remembering to snatch off his school cap he looked at the large crucifix that hung from the pitched sanctuary roof. "Hello, Jesus; I've come to play for you", he said aloud. He went over to the vestry door and gave a polite knock. A deep and sonorous voice bade him 'enter!' He creaked open the heavy oaken door and peered into the gloom. There, on a hard chair placed before a row of hanging cassocks, sat the vicar; he was reading some large leather-bound volume that, to Jamie, looked mind-numbingly boring.

"Ah, hello, young fellow", greeted the vicar. "Come to play for me, have you?"

"Please, sir; yes, sir", Jamie managed. The vicar closed the tome, placed it on the sloping vestment table, rose to his feet and beckoned Jamie to follow him. Jamie trotted after the tall figure as it made its way back down the aisle towards the west doors. Half-way up the inside of the west wall was a large stone balcony, supported by carved stone figures. Above the balcony rose the ranks of organ pipes. Quite unusually, they ranged from shortest innermost to tallest outermost. Nestling before the shortest middle pipes was the organ console. The vicar turned left and opened a small door. He led the way up a tiny, circular stone staircase that emerged suddenly on the balcony. He pointed to the organ bench. "Right, young man; you get yourself seated on there and I'll show you how to get things going".

Jamie perched himself on the polished wooden bench; his toes dangled a good twelve inches above the pedal board. Suddenly, a small light came on above the two-manual console and a slight humming noise started up. The vicar pointed to a switch immediately to the left of the lower manual. "All you have to do is to switch that on and you're in business", he said. "Never forget to turn it off again when you have finished. Now, you see that large pedal down there?" He pointed to a spot above the pedal board, roughly in the middle. In a recess was a very large pedal. Jamie nodded. "Well", said the vicar. "That pedal must *always* be left fully open when you leave. It's the swell pedal – you'll find out what it does when you play the top manual". Jamie couldn't wait; he squirmed with impatience. He pointed to the left of the manuals where a series of pistons were arranged in two vertical ranks. Each had an ivory head with strange words written on them. "Now, the top lot of those control the 'voices' of the swell organ – that's the top manual. Under those are the stops, or 'voices' for the pedals." He pointed to a similar configuration on the right. "Those are for the 'voices' of the great organ – the lower manual". Jamie thought that he had understood, was itching to get going. "Right, then, over to you. Just have a go and try to find your way around it all. I'll be in the vestry". He went back down the stairs, leaving a very excited little boy to experiment.

He reached over to his left and pulled out a stop labelled 'Flute 4''; he pressed a key on the upper manual; a sweet note, reedy and soft, came from the appropriate pipe. He was thrilled. He tried another stop, adding a 2' flute; depressing the same key he heard the original note topped by a twin one octave higher. The 8' flute added another one octave lower; it was magical. He left all three stops out and played the single note melody of the Evening Hymn. Greatly daring, he added his left hand and played the bass part as well. In the distant vestry, the vicar listened, a smile on his lips. This little lad was really quite gifted, he thought.

Remembering the purpose of the swell pedal, Jamie managed to slide forward a little and reach it with the tip of his right toes. He closed the pedal and the sound diminished; he opened it and the sound 'swelled'. Then, using the right stops, he had a go at the lower, 'great', organ. It was quite loud. He found a trumpet stop and started to play the famous melody by Jeremiah Clark. He was happy, but only up to a point. The magnificent sounds of an organ were just not coming. He pulled out a left-side stop labelled Bourdon 16' and reached down off the bench with his left foot to press the lowest of the pedals. A magnificent low C boomed around the church. He realised with a rather sick feeling that, until he was much taller, the full sound that he longed to produce would be completely beyond him. He could have wept with frustration.

He switched off the power, remembered to open the swell pedal and went down the stairs to the vestry. The sad little freckled face peered round the door. "I'm too little!" he said. He turned round and went out of the church. He would just have to find a piano somewhere until he had grown a lot taller. He sidled round the back door and was about to slip up to his bedroom when his mother called to him. "Where have you been to now?" she asked in her imperious tones. Jamie explained. "I'm too little – I can't play it properly", he sobbed. Margaret was quite astonished to hear her son admit that there was something that he could not do; normally, Jamie was full of his own abilities, often precocious and boastful. It would do him the power of good, she thought. At the same time, she was quite dismayed at the extent to which his failure had affected him; she sometimes surprised herself with her, normally suppressed, maternal feelings for her first-born. She found herself consoling him. "Never mind, Jamie – you will just have to hurry up and grow, won't you?" Jamie nodded and went upstairs to read. In future, he vowed, he would eat all his vegetables as all the grown-ups said that they made you grow and caused your hair to curl. The latter, he had no need of!

# A CHANGE OF HEART

Later that afternoon, Desmond having stayed at school for an evening lesson, Jamie came downstairs to make little Robert his tea. He made a sandwich of bread, margarine and Marmite, cut off the crusts and chopped it into little bite-sized pieces which he then put into Robert's little bowl. He took it in to the front room where Margaret and his little brother were playing. Margaret automatically reached for the bowl to feed her son with one piece after another. Robert grabbed the piece in his tiny hand. "No! Me do dat – me do dat!" he shouted. It was the first time that Margaret had experienced anything in the way of a show of independence from the little son that she fondly imagined relied upon her for all his needs. She conveniently forgot the many occasions when these duties had been handed over to Desmond, Jamie, her parents, to Nancy. She sat back on the sofa, tears pricking at her eyes; she felt rejected for the first time in her life. Robert munched his way through all the pieces and turned to his brother. "Dwink, Jamie!"

Jamie went out to the kitchen and got the 'sipper' beaker, took off the top and poured a small quantity of the precious Ministry of Food Orange juice into the bottom. He topped the beaker with water, replaced the top and shook the beaker. Robert snatched it and drank. Jamie, took it away from him. "Say thank you, Robbie!" he admonished.

"No – dwink!" shouted Robert.

"Say thank you, or I'll take it away!" repeated Jamie holding the beaker behind his back. Robert, knowing that he was on a losing streak, muttered an almost inaudible 'tank you', took the beaker, and waddled over to a corner to finish the drink.

Margaret , instead of putting the whole episode into perspective, sat and brooded at her dismissal. She thought herself badly wronged – yet again! Unable to come to grips with the fact that her son was actually growing up and needed some measure of independence, she concentrated on the hurt that she had felt. Now, she had literally no-one, she thought. Her deepening self-pity gathered momentum, spiralled downwards, dragging her into another of her deep depressions. Jamie looked at her as she sat there, the picture of misery. He had seen it many times before, knew exactly what it foretold. "Mummy not feeling well?" he asked. Like Desmond, he believed absolutely that his mother was extremely delicate, needed constant attention; she was 'special'. Margaret nodded, got up and went upstairs. Jamie just knew that she would soon be in bed, probably would stay there for many days. Poor Mummy, he thought!

After about a half hour, he went up the stairs and poked his head round the bedroom door. Margaret, under the eiderdown, was staring at the ceiling, the curtains firmly closed. "Is it time for your milk, Mummy?" he enquired. Margaret nodded silently, too overcome with her self-pity to speak. Jamie scampered down the stairs to get the glass of fresh milk. He added two plain biscuits on a saucer and took them up. He set them down on the bedside table. "There, that'll make you better!" he said confidently.

There was something in Margaret's mental make-up that obscured any rational perspective. If something went wrong, if she felt the slightest discomposed, it would take on increasingly magnified proportions until the feeling of utter wretchedness literally overwhelmed her. Sometimes, unfortunately nowhere near as often, something would happen to make her happy; it would become magnified out of all recognition, sending her into a mood of ecstatic joy. It was at times of these deep pits and impossible heights that her fantasies would take control; somehow, the appropriate 'acquaintance' would appear to her, would embody the mood that she had either sunk into, or had soared up to. Laying there, her mind filled with the self-composed image of the wonderful Jamie Marcus, she wondered if her own son could ever attain the perfection of that impossible man. He was being very helpful at the moment, but could just as easily slip into noisy, uncontrolled mischief. He was, she thought, an enigma. However, she reached out a hand to fondle his curls. "Thank you, Jamie – you're really a good boy, aren't you?" she murmured. Jamie, happy to be in her good books once more, replied that, yes, he was!

Until John came back later that evening, Jamie ran the household. He washed and changed Robert – who screamed throughout the entire proceedings, 'Me do dat!' Jamie took no notice and presented his mother with a clean, if somewhat disgruntled, little son. Margaret planted a sad kiss on the little forehead before Jamie took his brother into the small boxroom that was now Robert's own little bedroom. He tucked him in and told him a very silly story about a pig and a sparrow that he made up as he went along. Robert found it all very funny and fell asleep, tantrums forgotten.

Then Jamie had to set about his own supper. He carved himself a small wedge of pork pie from the covered plate in the larder. This pie had been obtained by John the previous day, a special 'treat' from a butcher whose shop was near the police station. It was such a rare delicacy that the entire family had vowed it would last them at least three days. He prepared yet another glass of milk for his mother and started to get her own miniscule supper ready. After persistent cajoling from Dr Talbot, she had at long last agreed that a little steamed fish would not harm her. Jamie had watched Desmond and his father prepare the sliver on more than one occasion. He took a shallow pan and put a small quantity of milk in it. He watched it carefully as it came to the boil, turned down the gas to a low simmer and placed the half-fillet of plaice in the pan. After a few minutes he poked the point of a small knife into the thickest part of the flesh, twisted it a little to see when the flesh was a uniform white throughout. He was satisfied and scooped the fillet out with a fish-slice on to a plate. He put two dry biscuits by the side and took the plate, glass of milk, knife and fork carefully up the stairs. Margaret raised herself on the pillows, started to eat the fish in very small bites as Jamie thundered down again to get his pie and drink. He sat on the bed and ate, watching his mother delicately pick her way through her meal.

Margaret put down the knife and fork, placed the plate on the bedside table. "That was nice, Jamie", she said quietly. "There, you can be a really good boy when you want to, can't you?" Jamie nodded. "Yes, Mummy", he agreed. The plain fact was that Jamie, with his small brother to look after and an 'invalid' mother in bed, had no choice in the matter; he knew that, if he did not get on with things, the house would have ground to a standstill. "I hope that now you can see why I was so strict with you over your birthday", she added. Jamie thought it best to agree, although he did not for the life of him understand why she had been so intransigent. "Well, you are certainly making up for it now!" said Margaret. "I'm trying my best, Mummy", muttered Jamie through the last tiny bite of his delicious pie. "Well, I'm tired now, darling. Thank you for my supper. You really *could* be like your namesake, you know!". Jamie planted a somewhat sticky kiss on his mother's proffered cheek, took plates and glass downstairs to wash them all up. By now, the milk in the pan was cold, so he was able to drain it all off and wash the pan as well. He sat down at the kitchen table, still bitterly disappointed at his inability to make dream music on the organ. However, he was back in his mother's good books; so, he considered, not too bad a day, really! If he tried really hard, he might some day come to emulate the man whom his mother idolised – oh, he thought, how wonderful to be such a perfect person!

John came back home quite late and was surprised to find Jamie still up. "Had a good day, old chap?" he enquired. Jamie told of his disappointment, his mother's latest relapse into 'illness', his making of the supper and putting Robert to bed. 'What on earth would I do without Desmond and Jamie', John wondered. Jamie said 'nighty-night' and went up to bed.

John sat at the table, deep in thought. Still no response from Valerie! He had almost got to the point of giving up writing letter after letter. He had not expected to hear from Peter. Now, with Margaret yet again taken to her bed, he felt a wave of despair sweep over him. Why could he not, just for once in his life, be decisive? Why could he not take the initiative? Back came the usual, depressing answer. Because you dare not jeopardise you place by Margaret's side! No, he argued with himself; *not* depressing at all! He was privileged to be the husband of such a unique person; she had allowed him into her life, had showed him many of the finer points of existence, had borne him two sons – he should be utterly content!

In reality, Jamie and Robert had been conceived by John in a state of complete devotion and by Margaret in a performance of duty. There had been no mutual passion whatsoever, never had been; probably never would be. On the one side, there had been passive adoration; on the other, disdainful acquiescence. Gone, long ago was the mutual love he had shared with Dorothy; it had been replaced by a puppy-like devotion that was slowly rotting away all his self-respect. He was still sitting at the kitchen table when Desmond came in, laden with books. The lad looked exhausted, thought John. They both went up to bed a little later. Desmond collapsed into a deep sleep. John lay awake beside the quietly sleeping Margaret. All was a normal in that strange household.

# A STRANGE PEACE

The first five days of May were alive with barely suppressed excitement; the war was as good as over. Daily bulletins came over the wireless from the multitude of BBC correspondents. Berlin was smashed beyond recognition, hardly one brick left standing on another. Hitler had committed suicide – hadn't he? He and Eva Braun had taken poison, had been shot, had been cremated – speculation abounded from every quarter. The Allies were preparing to accept an unconditional surrender, some reported; the German High Command was insisting on a fight to the finish, declaimed others. For every pundit interviewed came forth yet another differing opinion. Winston Churchill proclaimed a total victory. Others, knowing what was about to be unleashed, said that phase one in the struggle for Eastern Europe was over; phase two would start immediately 'peace' was declared.

At long last came the official announcement; the seventh of May would be Victory in Europe Day. The final act of surrender had been drawn up and awaited only signatures. Throughout the Wandleford Police Station, joy knew no bounds. Hardened coppers went dancing and whistling down corridors; The Superintendent attended morning parade wearing full dress uniform and one of his wife's most flowery hats; he blew kisses at the assembled constabulary and was cheered to the rafters. The crop of drunks, rounded up the previous evening, were feted with a breakfast of bacon and eggs – sent on their unsteady way with claps on the back. John felt an enormous weight lifted from his shoulders; at last, he would be able to be a simple Police Inspector – not a combination of copper, fireman, burrowing rescuer, air raid warden and a multiplicity of other roles. He had never for one moment regretted his decision to decline the promotion to Chief Inspector at Divisional Headquarters; he was a bobby at heart, was contented at his present rank – would be happy to retire as such in nine year's time.

Margaret, still deep into her current 'episode', knew little or nothing of the state of the world – cared even less. She mentally 'switched off' whenever the subject was raised, showed no inclination to join in the festive mood. Desmond was caught up in the whole euphoria – staying very late at school to join in celebrations. Jamie was extremely puzzled by it all.

Why, he wondered, was everybody dancing in the streets; why were the lights on? Didn't they know there was a war on? On the evening of the seventh he walked down the street to see light blazing from nearly every window. The bell in the parish church was ringing; from afar came the peal of bells of yet another church. It was all terribly confusing to the little lad. He eventually found his way to great-uncle Frederick's house, to be greeted with a massive bear-hug from that old gentleman.

"Isn't it wonderful, Jamie?" he beamed. "Why is it all wonderful, Nunky?" demanded a puzzled face. Frederick realised that he had a deal of explaining to do; indeed, had all the time in the world to do so. Sitting the little chap down by his side, he started to explain.

"Well, we have not *always* been fighting the war, you know. When you were born, we were not fighting anybody at all. That only started when you were six months old – although you won't remember that, will you?"

"Oh no, Nunky", agreed Jamie. "I'd have been too young then!"

"Right then! We started fighting the Germans when you were just a little baby and, now that we have beaten them, we can go back to being at peace. Therefore, there is no need to black-out the windows anymore; the streetlights will come on again; weather forecasts will start up once more. Nobody else needs to die. Now do you see why it is all so wonderful?"

"But my Dad says he was fighting the Germans when he was young", Jamie pointed out.

"Yes, but that was a different war", replied Frederick, knowing instinctively that this would in no way suffice.

"How was it different, Nunky?"

'There', thought Frederick. 'Told you so!' Aloud, he tried to go into things in a little more detail. "Well, that war was called the First World War and it began thirty-one years ago. We joined with the French, the Belgians and some others because the Germans marched into Belgium. That war lasted just over four years and it ended when the Germans gave up. This one started when you were a baby. It is called the Second World War."

"Why, did the Germans march into Belgium again?" asked Jamie.

"No; this time they marched into Poland", said Frederick, opening the floodgates.

"Why are the Germans always marching into somewhere? Don't they like Germany?"

"I suppose they just want to make war on someone", replied Frederick, knowing that this was a gross maligning of a whole race of people. He had spent hours discussing the causes of the wars with his brother Edward – who had as good an insight into the matter as anyone. They both agreed that the first war was caused by trade, the second by bitterness and misunderstandings. However, this was far beyond the grasp of a six-year-old.

"Well, we won, didn't we!" Jamie marched up and down in excitement.

"Yes, old chap – we did indeed – but, with a lot of help from America".

Jamie remembered his first encounter with Americans, particularly the massive master-sergeant. He also remembered the doughnuts, the generosity of the Marines who had spent time with him on the railway embankment. To Jamie, they had seemed wonderful chaps. The British soldiers he had met had not given him doughnuts; they always drank tea rather than 'cawfy'; Jamie *still* did not know what that was.

He danced a little jig of celebration with his Nunky and sped off down the hill to call on his grandparents. Granddad, as he shot into the lounge, was on the telephone to his brother Edward; he was as excited as Jamie could ever remember; even Nana, that most staid of ladies, was almost dancing about the room. Alfred, seeing his grandson cavorting with his wife, called him over.

"Your great-uncle wishes to have a word with you, Jamie". He handed the heavy earpiece to the little boy. Jamie jammed it to his ear and spoke into the mouthpiece atop the 'candlestick'. "Hello, Uncle Edward!" he shouted.

"Hey – not so loud, young man! I'm not deaf, you know!"

"Sorry!" whispered Jamie, toning things down. Edward paused. Nobody had ever breathed a word to the little boy of what the brothers called his 'Great Expectations' – and nobody would until he was far older than he was now. "Great news, is it not, Jamie?"

"Oh yes, Uncle Edward. I've just been with Nunky and he explained all about the two wars and how the Germans are always marching into somewhere else!"

As a brief summation of the century so far, that, thought Edward, was not at all bad!

"Well, you must all have a big party". Jamie liked the thought of that. "When it is arranged, you must tell me, and I will come down to see you all".

Jamie turned away to address his grandmother. "Nana, Uncle Edward says we have got to have a party and he's coming too!" Back into the mouthpiece he queried further. "Why do the Germans always march into everywhere? Why can't they walk like everybody else?"

Edward thought that his little great-nephew seldom walked anywhere either. However, he was spared the necessity of explanation as Alfred commandeered the telephone, leaving Jamie to ponder the mystery of a race of people that always marched. What a great pity it was, thought Gertrude, that Jamie had never met Hans, husband of dear Amelia. He was definitely Germanic, but a more peace-loving, gentle individual it would have been hard to meet. Perhaps Jamie would have had someone with whom to compare a race of people vilified by the whole British nation for so many years. Hans had never been a Nazi, had indeed fled his birthplace when he had realised what was about to happen. Gertrude sighed; what a sad and wicked waste it had all been.

Jamie, buoyed up with the thought of a big party, shot off once again to let his family know. Margaret heard the news of the party with mixed thoughts; she would not be able to participate in the gorgeous food as she was too 'delicate'; the noise and conversation would all be too much for her nervous constitution. Desmond received the news with a huge grin; he was all in favour. Little Robert, three years and a bit old, looked up from his latest drawing and gave a yell of 'YIPPPPEEEEE!' 'Oh no!' thought Margaret. 'Not another excitable boy!' She need not have worried; Robert buried his head back into the drawing, all other thoughts expunged as he concentrated on the perspective of the train that he was trying to reproduce on paper.

The following weekend saw the party in full swing; it was held in the large lounge of the bungalow. Somehow or other, Gertrude had managed, with help from Daisy, to conjure up an impressive buffet which was arrayed on salvers or the best china platters. Much baking had been undertaken, resulting in a wide variety of cakes; much to Jamie's delight, rock cakes were piled in an inviting pyramid; where the dried fruit had come from was Gertrude's secret.

Edward had arrived that morning; Frederick was amusing Robert with a piece of string that he made into a huge, complicated knot that, with a flick of his fingers, completely disappeared leaving one length of string again. Cecily Bedford, an old friend of Gertrude's, was talking with her host and hostess; Doctor Talbot and his wife had arrived some minutes before and had also been welcomed as old friends. With Jamie's family, eleven people were present, easily accommodated in that large room. Alfred attended to the gramophone, playing favourites from the pre-war musical shows. John never felt quite at ease in the company of his wife's family; keenly aware of his educational shortcomings, he found himself unable to converse properly with any of them. Edward, the most accomplished of them all and a peer of the realm to boot, instilled in the stolid policeman a sense of distinct inferiority; this would have dismayed the Viscount had he been aware of it for he was the most polite and diplomatic of men, always striving to put people at their ease. John, therefore, stood on the periphery of the assembled company uttering only subdued 'Yes' or 'No' whenever he felt called upon to make any sound at all. Desmond, naturally quiet most of the time, stood with his father; there was no way in which this teenager could compete in company with his six-year-old brother – nor would he have wanted to as he had an inborn dread of being the centre of attention at any time. Margaret sat in a large easy chair; as usual, she expected the world to revolve around her, to be the centre of everyone's admiration and attention. Today, she was to be disappointed. Robert, upset that Nunky would not show him how the trick was done, was now sitting at the table, busy with the inevitable pencil and paper. Jamie, in his usual brash way, cavorted round the room to show off to anyone who would grant him a moment's attention. He was, to put it mildly, being a bit of a pest. Gertrude, noting that neither her daughter nor her son-in-law was prepared to do anything about it, spoke to the lad; she told him quite firmly that 'I think we have all seen enough of that, thank you!' Jamie, subdued for a good half hour, retired to the floor and disappeared under the table with a plate of food. His period of favour with his mother had not lasted long; Margaret, in one of her typical 'about-faces' had returned little Robert back to favour, recognising in the child a budding artist; this was something for her to get her teeth into, to push his interests for all she was worth. Jamie, by comparison, seemed hardly worthy of her attention. In any case, thought that strange woman, Jamie hardly needed her attention anyway!

Alfred, Edward and Frederick held a quiet conversation about the eventual heir to the Viscountcy.

"That lad will need to have some discipline installed in him sooner or later", declared Edward. "Are his parents unaware or unwilling?"

Alfred saw it as his duty to defend his daughter. "Margaret is, as you know, of a very delicate disposition; she dislikes making a scene in public".

"In that case", Frederick broke in. "She would be well advised to instil that dislike into her child".

"How is Margaret these days?" Edward asked, more out of politeness than real interest; he had, for some years, shared Frederick's thinly veiled dislike of his niece.

"She has good days and bad days", admitted Alfred. "Her imagination, I must admit, sometimes has Gertrude and me quite worried!"

'With good reason', thought Frederick. Aloud, he said, "Perhaps, Alfred, you could prevail upon John to take a slightly firmer line with young Jamie".

"John will", replied Alfred, "as I am sure you both realise, follow any lead that Margaret chooses to give. She told me the other day that she has washed her hands of that young lad; she believes him to be beyond control!"

"Poppycock!" retorted Frederick. "He is no more beyond control than any of us were at his age. Ask Cecily over there – she and that young assistant of hers manage to control him easily enough. All right, he is very high spirited and races off at the most alarming tangents at times, but – and it is a big but – he has little malice in him and can be directed into the most interesting pursuits; Why, look at the way that he absorbs himself in wildlife; you cannot tell me that he is, as Margaret says, out of control".

"Must agree with that", nodded Edward. "After all, where would we have been these last few years without that arch example of the unruly at the helm? I just thank the Good Lord that Winston had calming influences at his elbow during the struggle".

Jamie, blissfully unaware of his dissection at the hands of his seniors, finished the last sandwich and emerged to seek more delicious things that he might devour. His eye lighted upon a large bowl of trifle.

Cecily had almost given up her attempt to cajole some social pleasantry from Jamie's mother. Margaret was getting to a point of near desperation; what might she announce to the assembled company that would arrest everyone's attention, turn herself into the centre of attraction. Her normal ploy was to display signs of physical distress, knowing that all would flutter around her; would pay her fawning obeisance; say how brave she was to put up with such a life of discomfort. This was denied her by the astute headmistress. Cecily, who well knew how that woman's mind worked, saw the tell-tale signs, reached out her hand and grasped Margaret's none too gently. "Don't you dare!" she hissed into Margaret's ear. "Your parents deserve better that that, you know". Hence, Margaret's feverish attempt to find some arresting remark about her imagined acquaintances. She remained sitting quietly with that give-away look of noble suffering on her exquisite face. Cecily slid away to talk to the good Doctor and his wife.

Edward beckoned to Jamie to come and sit by him on the long sofa. Jamie hopped up by his side. The Viscount felt that the time was long overdue for him to get to know his eventual heir far better than he had up to now.

"Well, young man; your Nunky tells me that you know a lot about birds and their nests and so on. So, tell me; which is your favourite?"

He could tell by the immediate way Jamie's face became serious that he had broached a subject that was of great importance to the boy. Jamie gave the matter some thought before answering.

"I've always loved blackbirds – they are cheeky and have a nice song. But thrushes make better music; starlings are funny – the way they walk and how they swoop all over the sky in the evening. Did you know that they come here for the winter?"

Edward looked over at Frederick. He raised an eyebrow a fraction. Frederick returned this with a face that said, 'told you so!'

"Yes, I know they come down from the far north for the winter", he said. "What about sparrows and robins?"

"Oh, they're funny", replied Jamie, "they row and argue all the time. Sparrows are called 'spadgers' by some people! I've made a tunnel up to the railway and there's a robin's nest at the top. He takes bits of bread from my hand sometimes. I've seen an old buzzard up there as well; he doesn't seem to fly – just sort of glides round looking for mice and voles on the ground. Must have very good eyes!"

"I have a cottage down in Devon". An idea had come to Edward. "Go there now and again when I can get away from London. It is just by Dartmoor. Perhaps you would like to come down there for a week or so and we could go out on the moor to look for wildlife. Would you like that?"

Jamie's face lit up at the suggestion. "I'd love that!" he said. "My friend round the corner – he's a brigadier, by the way – showed me his badgers. He gave me a pair of binocklers".

"They will come in very useful down in Devon. There is a lot to see round the cottage – animals and birds that you will never see here. I'll have a word with your mother and father – see if you could come down in the summer holidays. Shall I do that?"

"Oh, yes please, sir!" stuttered Jamie. A thought struck him. "Mummy'l prob'ly say no, though; she called me a hooglian and says I'll come to a sticky end!"

"Oh, we'll see about that", laughed Edward. He patted Jamie on his head and went over to the imperious Margaret for a word. Jamie watched his mother's face as his great-uncle spoke to her. Margaret, in the presence of someone she both admired and feared, was deferential. She nodded. Jamie's hopes soared. Edward then spoke to his father. Daddy, Jamie noted, almost gave a small bow before answering. Edward, having spoken to Desmond, drifted back to the sofa.

"There, told you so!" he laughed. "All fixed up. You, your Nunky and I will go down in August, I mentioned that your brother Desmond might like to accompany us, but he apparently has secured a couple of weeks of work with a local engineering firm". Jamie wriggled with excitement. "Thank you!" he said ever so quietly.

Jamie, who longed to romp about the floor again, knew that he really *had* to be on his best behaviour for the rest of the party. The consequences of falling into his great-uncle's bad books were too dreadful to contemplate. Instead, he borrowed a piece of paper and one of Robert's pencils and sat at the table, trying desperately to draw a thrush perched on the branch of a tree. Even to him, the result resembled more a misshapen tea-cosy atop a roll of barbed wire. He looked across at Robert's effort to see the definite outline of a steam engine coming towards him on rails that widened as they neared the bottom of the page. Jamie did not know what the word perspective meant; neither did Robert.Jamie did not begin to understand how to make a picture in two dimensions appear in three; Robert, by some inner miracle, did. Jamie sighed in frustration; would he ever be any good at anything, he wondered? Robert could draw and Desmond could make things with a deep understanding of their function and purpose. His Dad was a successful police officer, his Mum (he *never* used that word aloud) knew all sorts of very important people. His Granddad had been an architect, Nunky a very successful banker; great-uncle Edward had a title that he could not, at that moment, remember. He was just a naughty boy, constantly getting into 'hot water'. He really tried to do the right thing but his idea of what was 'right' often was in direct contradistinction from what everyone else thought as 'practicable' or appropriate. He tore up his effort, sunk into gloom. His period of grace with his mother had not lasted long. Margaret, now totally convinced that little Robert was 'delicate' kept the little chap close to her. Jamie was useful on the odd occasion, but a damned nuisance for most of the time. Desmond, useful all of the time, was quiet and reserved, deep into his studies; apart from any other consideration, he was the despised Doris's child. John was absent for most of his waking life. Margaret had come to the conclusion she wanted nothing more than a peaceful, quiet time to live her dreams, punctuated with periods of attention to her 'poor, delicate Robbie', when, of course, her own 'poor health' allowed such activity.

Desmond had actually given some thought to the proposition that he accompany the others to Devon; he had, somewhat reluctantly, come to the conclusion that his studies really had to come first. He had thanked Edward politely but firmly; Edward, thinking it a pity, could not but admire such dedication. Desmond had noticed recently that his mother, when referring to him to his father, called him 'your son'; he realised with a jolt that she had nearly always referred to him in that way. It puzzled him. Of course, when Jamie had been naughty, *he* was referred to as 'your son' by one parent to the other; this, Desmond knew, was the normal way of 'passing the buck' for the offspring's misbehaviour. In his case, he felt that there was some other, underlying reason for it. It made him feel slightly uneasy. However, he cheered himself with the thought, he would be leaving his school in a few weeks time, would attend the 'placement' during the holidays and then start at the Wandleside Technical College to complete his education. He desperately wanted to do well so that he might go on to take an engineering degree. He knew that his Nana and Granddad would fund this, had already assured him that he could make his plans. Bless them both, and Nunky as well, he thought; the three had never done anything but encourage him.

John stood quietly by his wife, mulling over the long years of the war. He was still deeply saddened by the loss and enmity of his son Peter; he had hopes that some sort of private reconciliation could be reached with Valerie. Desmond, he thought, did not need him in the slightest. He was a self-reliant lad who had mapped out his own future without his assistance. Jamie, he knew, would go his own way whatever was said to him – or threatened. Robert had Margaret's love and care. Margaret herself treated him with disdain most of the time, was scathing about him in her remarks to others; but she needed his devotion and care. Without it she would be hard pressed to live a life of self-indulgent ease. All he felt it incumbent on him to do was to work hard and to bring in as much money as he possibly could. If he did his duty, all would be well. He had signally failed to realise that, since his marriage to Margaret, what his children needed was his time; Margaret, apart from her devotion to Robert, had failed to give either Desmond or Jamie any of hers. The resulting lack of cohesion, of understanding, in that family was nearly total.

John, not for the first time, recalled a conversation he had had with Frederick some years previously. That kindly man had never been able to find much real liking for his niece Margaret but was fair-minded enough to see well below the surface of her character. "You know, of course, that my brother Alfred and my sister-in-law Gertrude are first cousins. That can lead to the most odd outcome where any children of such a marriage are concerned. What the world sees of Margaret is what she has made up for herself. And she cannot in all conscience be blamed for what she has become. Geneticists are always telling us of the dangers of a too pure bloodstream. That is why, for hundreds of years, farmers know instinctively to bring in an outsider to father the next generation of animals. Somehow or other that produces a stronger generation than would be the case if it were kept 'in the family', as it were. So, although I cannot ever pretend to like what you wife has become, I can fully understand why it has happened. Somehow or other, you have to go along with her self-delusions. I shudder to think what might happen were you to challenge them! But - and I urge this most sincerely, do not lose touch with your children – and by that I mean all five of them. They are just as much deserving of your love and care as does your wife. How you manage that, I have no idea – but you simply have to try!"

John had never forgotten that advice. He freely admitted to himself that he succeeded in the first part – never challenging Margaret, supporting her throughout the most difficult of times. He also admitted almost total failure where his children were concerned. Glancing at his fourth child, a mass of ginger curls just visible beneath the table, he could have wept at that failure.

Jamie, sensing a growing despair at his isolation from his parents, felt more and more drawn towards his older brother, his grandparents and uncles. They, at least, did not shun his company; he felt encouraged by them. His first six and a bit years had been bizarre, lived as they had been in war and strife. The strife would, in all probability, continue. But, as for the international conflict, Jamie's war was over.